THE *Sum* OF OUR *Sorrows*

Lisette Brodey

SABERLEE  BOOKS

Published by:

SABERLEE BOOKS
Los Angeles, CA
United States of America

Copyright @2020, Lisette Brodey
Published, November 2020

Copy editing: Chryse Wymer, D.L. Savvides
Cover illustration: Charles M. Roth

ISBN-13: 978-1-7340894-2-4 (paperback)
ISBN-13: 978-1-7340894-1-7 (e-book)

For Michael

With much love, always ...

"I love you in a place where there's no space or time
I love you for in my life, you are a friend of mine."

— *Leon Russell (A Song for You)*

"Sorrow is a fruit. God does not make it grow on limbs too weak to bear it."

—*Victor Hugo*

ACKNOWLEDGMENTS

To Charles Roth, for his devotion in creating the cover illustration;

To Chryse Wymer, for being such a supportive editor and friend and always being in tune with my vision;

To D.L. Savvides, for her friendship, for allowing me to bug her endlessly, and for *everything* she did to help me with this book;

To Lisa Wentworth, for being such an amazing friend over the past ten years, and doing so much to support the writing and production of this novel … and for helping maintain the dwindling sanity of the author;

With great appreciation to all of the following people who lent a hand with my research: Ward Foley, Sue Janson, Sarah Loveless, Tina-Marie Miller, Cynthia and Mike Pecoraro, Richard Ray, Rachel Rostad, Terry Tyler, and Sue-Ellen Wellfonder;

Special thanks to Deborah Nam-Krane for being an invaluable beta reader;

To Talatha Allen, Shykia Bell, Kenneth Brodey, Dody Cox, PattiAnn Cutter, Robert Helle, and Sheri A. Wilkinson for their ongoing support and kindness;

And to Kathleen Harryman, for creating such a beautiful animated graphic for me.

There are so many people who have supported me in so many ways. I wish it were possible to thank each and every one of you. I hope you all know who you are. And last, but not least, thank you to my fellow authors for your support, advice, inspiration, and friendship. You all mean so much to me.

PART I

Altrusia, California

CHAPTER ONE

Lily Sheppard twisted her torso as she sat in her mother's floral armchair, her back now facing the assemblage of darkly dressed people in the living room. The furniture had been rearranged to accommodate the guests … and absolutely nothing was as she knew it.

She fixed her stare on a large raindrop that slid down the side window, following it with her eyes until it had ceased to exist. The drop, she contended, had the mere lifespan of a few seconds. Now, it was indistinguishable from the pool of water it merged with on the base of the sill.

"Lills?"

Her trance broken, Lily turned to look at the blonde woman in the black dress not too dissimilar from her own. "Sorry, Hannah. I was off in my own world."

"I don't blame you one bit," Hannah told her. "I'm not feeling as well as I could be, so Mom and I are going to cut out a bit early. But there's no way I was going anywhere without saying good-bye. I love you, Lills, and I'm so sorry."

"I know. Thank you." Lily sniffled. "Hope you feel better soon. I'm grateful you were here … and at the service. You've been such an amazing friend." She looked up at the woman standing next to Hannah. "And thank you, Mrs. Alistair. It means a lot to me that you were here too."

"I don't have the words, sweet Lily. Not for you, not for Charlotte and Willow, nor for your father. Your mother's death is a terrible tragedy that we are all grappling to understand. Abigail Quincy Sheppard was truly one of the finest women I've ever known. Such a horrible—"

"She knows, Mom," Hannah said, her face contorting in discomfort.

"Of course she does." Deferring to her daughter's wisdom, Grace stepped back with an uncomfortable smile as Hannah bent down, preparing to hug Lily.

"Lily. Please stand and say a proper good-bye to our guests." Dalton Sheppard, his salt-and-pepper hair neatly brushed to one side, his distinctive round tortoiseshell frames a bit low on his nose, stood stoically next to his oldest daughter. "Set an example for your sisters. Be the young woman your mother taught you to be."

Choking on the response she knew was better left unsaid, Lily stood, hugged Grace, then Hannah as she took care to avoid her father's unforgiving eyes.

"I guess you'll be taking time off from the diner," Hannah said. "But don't worry; everyone is prepared to cover your shifts until you feel ready to come back. And there's no hurry. We've already discussed it."

"Lily will not be returning to work," Dalton said. "Not a week from now, not ever."

"But ...." Lily, stunned for the second time in a minute, yet fully grasping the consequences of articulating her dissent, hung her head ... but not before she and Hannah exchanged sad looks.

"Let's go, honey," Grace said to her daughter.

Lily noticed an angry flash in Grace's eyes land on her father as the Alastair women turned to leave, but she knew her friend's mother would never openly broadcast her disapproval under such solemn circumstances. Nonetheless, Lily was heartened to know Grace disagreed with the stop-work edict her father had just sprung on her. And his edict was far more inappropriate than her being settled into an armchair, weak from standing, weak from mingling, depleted from crying, and utterly incapacitated by having existed an entire eight days on Earth missing her beloved mother who had been taken from her in less time than a raindrop lives.

Ellis Quincy, dapper even in mourning clothes, tall with a thick head of brown hair, a closely trimmed beard, smelling faintly of expensive woodsy cologne, took his eldest niece by the arm and walked her to an empty space in the Sheppard dining room.

"Lily Alexandra ..."

"Oh, please tell me you're not leaving, Uncle Ellis." She cast her eyes downward. "But I know you are."

"Sorry, love. It's the last thing I want to do. Being a business owner, I've already been away too long, especially with things in such a frenzied state." His face tensed. "Bloody hell, I don't mean to sound as if my sister was killed at an unsuitable time. Unfortunately, my company is in the middle of expanding our manufacturing sector with the acquisition of a major client in Manchester and ... well, if I'm not there, my efforts over the past several years will crumble like a freshly baked scone." He looked at Lily's blank face. "Your mum loved scones."

"I know. She made them often so we could love them too. I knew what you meant. I just feel so empty."

"How could you not?" Ellis frowned. "My flight from Sacramento to Los Angeles leaves in two hours. Then I've got to hang around LAX and wait for my flight to Heathrow. Going to be a long night." He let out an exhausted sigh. "I wish I could stay here; I long to spend more time with all of you. I don't know how any of us are going to function properly in this world without Abby." He let out a breath. "I've already said good-bye to your sisters and your father, but you're the hardest one to leave." He reached over and stroked Lily's long chestnut-brown hair, then lifted her chin. "I never saw a brighter light in your mum's eyes than I did when she held you for the first time." He smiled. "I could see straight away that you'd grow up to look like her."

Lily looked at him in amazement.

"Even though I was only four when Abby was born, I remember exactly how she looked." He chuckled. "Photos may have helped retain my extraordinary memory ... a wee bit." He took her hands in his. "So, when you came into this world, the moment I saw your face, it felt like Abby being born again. There was overwhelming joy in our family." He let go of her hands and bit his lip as tears pooled in his eyes. "And now, there's so much sorrow. More than any of us know what to do with."

Lily glanced toward the living room to make sure nobody was within earshot. "I wish we didn't live so far from one another. I don't know how I'm going to manage." She hesitated. "This will sound awful, because what could be worse than Mum dying, but I have a bad feeling about Dad."

"How's that, love?"

"For starters, he announced, right in front of my best girlfriend and her mother, that I'm not allowed to go back to work." She huffed. "I'd be stupid if I didn't think there was more to come. I know I've always been a sensitive person, but that doesn't make me wrong."

Her uncle's furrowed brow registered his concern. "No. In fact, more times than not, it makes you right because you examine things more thoroughly. I know what your job means to you. And I haven't forgotten that you're graduating high school next month and starting fashion school in late August, right? I know you're keen to make as much money as you can."

"For sure. And as much as I don't like thinking about life going on without Mum, I know she'd want me to. I also know she'd want me to be with my friends at the diner. I've worked with most of them going on four years. They're like a second family to me."

Ellis put his arms around Lily and pulled her close. "I hear you, love. Let's hope it's Dalt's grief talking. Right now, it's hard for any of us to imagine life without Abby."

"Next to friggin' impossible."

"Listen, sweetheart. I need you to know that I'll be in touch soon, as you and I have some business to discuss. Important business. But that's for another day."

"Can you give me a hint?"

"Wouldn't be proper on the day you've buried your mum. Just know I'll be here to help you through everything. And by the way, because it bears repeating: your aunt and cousins were all gutted that they couldn't be here with all of you. I was told at least seventeen times to make certain I conveyed that."

"You have. Is everyone okay?"

"Well, your cousin Caroline's dating a bloke who I think is a bit of a tosser, but your aunt says he's okay … no more than a bit daft at times. But we'll see." He sighed. "My mobile is vibrating in my pocket. I think that means my car is here. My bags are tucked away on your lovely covered porch. Hope this bloody rain doesn't impede travel. I think it followed me here from England."

"I'm going to miss you so much, Uncle Ellis."

"Cheerio, love." He fought back tears as he hugged her one last time. "We'll talk soon."

⟨⟨⟨

Willow Sheppard sat on the couch and twirled the ends of her long light-brown hair around her finger. As the last guest left, she turned to her father. "May I be excused?"

Dalton removed his suit jacket and draped it over the arm of his recliner. "You may."

Fidgeting with the fringe of a throw pillow on the couch, Charlotte Sheppard barely made eye contact with him. "I'm gonna go to my room too."

Dalton took a deliberate stride toward the couch as Willow hurried up the stairs. His piercing eyes fixed on his middle child, but he spoke with unusual calm. "If your twelve-year-old sister can show some manners, surely, at the ripe old age of fifteen, you can as well." He paused to collect his thoughts. "You've been through torture, Charlotte; I won't dismiss that, and I recognize all that you've suffered. But as a testament to your mother, it's more important than ever that we don't allow our manners to run amok. Is that understood?"

"Yeah. Sorry. Whatever. May I be excused?"

"Upstairs then," Dalton said with a hand gesture that appeared to brush her off the couch like a speck of dust.

As Charlotte followed Willow, Lily stood in the empty space where her mother's chair normally sat, still looking into the foyer at the front door that allowed her beloved uncle to leave. She turned to her father as she prepared to echo Willow's polite request to be excused.

"Sit down, Lily." Dalton eyeballed the spot Charlotte had vacated.

"I'm so tired, Dad. I don't think I can talk anymore. I'm drained. This isn't a good time. I feel like an old car that's been out of gas for so long it's forgotten how to run."

He pointed to the couch. "Then park yourself and turn off the ignition. I'm going to do the talking. For now, I only need you to listen."

Exasperated, she sat. "I could listen much better tomorrow. Please."

Dalton fused his lips together as he struggled to preserve his presence of mind. After a long moment, he looked at Lily before turning his thoughts into words. "I hope you understand that you're not the only one who is mourning the loss of your mother … that you're not the only one in pain. Because I'm here to tell you: you've got lots of company." His eyes searched the living room as if something would give him the words he needed. "I appreciate that you are worn out, as are we all … but right now, there are no convenient times for anything. Not for listening, not for death." He sighed. "Your mother's death certainly wasn't 'convenient' for me. Not for any of us. It's hell." He collapsed into his recliner and stared out the bay window behind her. "And now … life as we knew it has irrevocably changed for the worse. But … we've got to adjust … even if we are grieving." He spoke softly as he made eye contact again. "And that adjustment begins here and now with you and me."

Lily felt an odd fuzz travel from head to toe, numbing her body as if she were leaving it. She gulped, then looked at her father, her eyes saying the words she knew she was forbidden to utter.

She wished, only this once, he would have sat next to her on the couch … maybe taken her hand or put an arm around her. But she knew why he didn't: sitting at the couch, facing her at eye level, touching her, would be too intimate. No, her father needed to sit atop his 'throne' to exert his authority.

With his thumb and his middle finger, Dalton pushed his glasses back into place, then focused his attention on Lily. "Your mother's death is the worst thing that could have happened to us. We have to be grateful that Charlotte wasn't killed in the accident too. She easily could have been. But God spared her." He stopped speaking and closed his eyes, his face distorting as if an image before him was too painful to see.

Lily said nothing, studying her father's face until his eyes reopened.

"Clearly, Lily, all of our lives are going to change. We have to adjust in the best way we can." He glanced at a framed wedding photo on a nearby shelf. "We can't wait for the pieces of our lives to fall into place. Because they won't."

"I know."

"So … as we plan for anything else, we have to plan to go on … without your mother … my extraordinary wife."

Lily looked down and spoke above a whisper: "I don't see how we do that."

"I don't quite see it either." He took a moment to swallow his vulnerability. "You're the oldest. In two months, you'll be graduating high school, and in fourteen months, your teenage years will be behind you. Someone has to take over the running of this household. It can't be me; I go to work every day, and, as you well know, I often work overtime. Someone has to be here. More importantly, someone has to be a mother to Charlotte and Willow, to cook and clean, to arrange schedules, and to do much of what your mother did. And that someone is you. Your sisters can certainly help with chores, but you are, in every way you can be, the lady of the house. And with that title comes responsibilities."

"No way, Dad. I can't do all that. I—"

"I'm sorry, Lily. I am. But for the foreseeable future, the lion's share of the burden will be yours." He sighed. "This brings me no pleasure."

"I'm not saying it does, Dad, but I can't—"

"Charlotte is quite shaken from being in the car and seeing your mother slammed into unconsciousness. Good God, even though Mum held on for three days, for all intents and purposes, your sister watched her die instantaneously. That's why I have forgiven her earlier impudence." With despair etched into his face, he looked down. "I can't imagine what that was like for her." He took several moments before speaking again. "Frankly, I'd rather not, but I recognize that trauma may prey on Charlotte forever." He gulped. "I'm not made of stone, you know." After another brief respite from his speech, his voice grew more intense, his tone steadier. "You have to acknowledge that Charlotte is suffering in ways we have been spared. The doctor at the hospital cautioned me to look out for signs of post-traumatic stress disorder. I'm cautioning you to do the same. As for Willow, she isn't yet a teenager. She'll need more love and guidance than ever. She only turned twelve last month."

"But …."

Dalton pressed on as a light sweat formed on his brow. "And so, Lily, I hope you'll accept your new responsibilities like a woman. You're no longer the carefree eighteen-year-old who used to work at McCauley's Diner with her friends."

Lily straightened on the couch, as if a more adult posture would change her father's perspective. "I may work … have worked … with my friends, but it's not an easy job. Because we like each other doesn't mean we don't … didn't … bust our butts every single time we put on our uniforms."

Dalton nodded. "I'm glad you understand the concept of butt busting. Because that's precisely what you'll be doing here. Only for a far more significant reason."

"Dad, I need time to work on my entrance project before

school starts. I found the perfect material for the dress I'm going to make. I'm so eager to bring it to life, even though I miss Mum's input more than I can say. You've seen my sketches; you know which design I chose. I've been working so hard on all of it. And as for my job, I'm going to need that money for college expenses. I'm leaving in late August for Los Angeles. There's not that much time for me to get ready."

"No, Lily. Fashion school isn't going to happen. Not now anyway. I'm not sure you understood what I said … about taking on your mother's responsibilities. I wasn't talking about the next four months." He sighed. "I'm sorry. If you want to pursue further education, I'll allow you to take some classes at the community college once we get settled into a new routine here. That's as far down the road as I can see right now. I don't want to make promises to you that I can't keep. As for money, I'm going to allot you a weekly allowance … for yourself, your sisters, and for the household. You'll have to learn how to budget for food and bills. And you'll do the shopping, of course. Your mother handled everything with ease. It's not rocket science."

Lily stood and looked down on her father. "Mum would *so* not want this!"

Dalton's face reddened as he leaned forward in his chair. "Your mum would not have wanted to be dead at forty-three; that's what your mum wouldn't have wanted. She didn't teach you to be a lady so you could act like an irresponsible teenager."

"I've never been an irresponsible teenager. Never."

"No." Dalton lowered his voice. "I'll give you that. You haven't. In fact, everyone has always said you're wise beyond your years. And that's exactly why you won't exhibit any sort of irresponsibility now as your teenage years draw to a close." He got up and walked over to the makeshift bar he'd set up by the fireplace at the end of the living room. Steadying himself, he fixed a shot of bourbon. Lily could only watch as he poured the gold liquid down his throat before walking back in her direction.

Tears now streaming down her face ... in synchronicity with the rain on the bay window, she could not look at him, but she could feel his eyes on her.

"I'm sorry, honey. Cry all you like ... tonight ... but tomorrow begins a new life for all of us." He took a moment to exhale. "I trust that you will officially terminate your employment and also withdraw from school in Los Angeles. I'll continue to do everything I can to provide for this family. Now go upstairs and leave me with my memories. And hold onto your own. Cherish them, sweetheart. Our memories are all we have left of your mother. They're all very beautiful ... full of love and life ... as she was."

Lily made no further eye contact with him, most especially because she knew he would hate for her to see him cry. She could hear his voice beginning to falter and knew tears would be forthcoming. As her peripheral vision caught him heading off to fix another drink, she rushed upstairs, her mind racing with every possible scenario of what lay ahead in the hell that had swallowed her young life whole.

CHAPTER TWO

"I'm so happy to see you, Lily. But you didn't have to come here. I would have gladly swung by your house."

Lily threw her arms around Kady Harrigan, the elegant fifty-something-year-old-woman whose trademark long blonde-and-gray hair was swept up on her head, a jeweled clip holding it stylishly in place.

Kady hugged her back, holding Lily close before pulling away to study her face. "How are you managing, honey? I wish we'd been able to talk yesterday. There were so many people and so much grief to process. Quite honestly, the entire day was a blur."

"For me too. Having to talk to everyone when I just wanted to lock myself in my room and cry. But the end of the day … with Dad … well … not so much a blur."

Lily, seeing the discomfiture in Kady's eyes, recognized it as a reaction to the fear in her own and made a mental note to deaden the disquiet that haunted her, fully aware of her inability to do so.

Taking Lily's hand, Kady led her over to the plush burgundy sofa. "Sit down, honey. We'll talk. First, what can I get you to drink? Are you hungry?"

"I'm thirsty. Crying tends to dehydrate a person."

"It certainly does. I made a pitcher of lemonade. More precisely, I made the lemonade, not the pitcher. How about I do some magic and turn that into two glasses?" Kady winked. "I'll be back ... as your mum would say ... in two shakes of a lamb's tail." She pulled two red marble coasters out of a holder on the coffee table, placing them down as welcome mats for the lemonade, then hurried off to the kitchen.

In no time at all, Kady was back. She placed two frosty glasses down before sitting next to Lily.

"Thank you." Lily took several big sips out of her glass. "This is what I needed." She put the glass on the coaster and sighed.

"I want to ask you what's wrong, and while that sounds like the most unnecessary question to put to you at such a time, I'm quite certain there's something else beyond what grieves us all." She paused to study Lily's reaction. "Am I right?"

"Yes. You are." Lily reached into her pocket and pulled out her phone, glancing only at the home screen before putting it back.

"Is the time a concern?"

"Kind of ... yeah," Lily answered with a nervous edge in her voice. "Dad is probably timing my errands. I'm afraid he'll call and ask where I am."

"It's Monday. Didn't Dalt return to work today?"

"Yeah. But he's already called me twice. Before school and right after —the minute the 'effin bell rang. Creepy. Like he was watching."

"Watching for what, sweetie? Tell me."

"I don't even know where to start." Lily fought back tears. "I guess with Dad telling me I'm the new 'lady of the house.' He made me quit my job and withdraw from fashion school in the fall. Now, it's my job to take care of my sisters, shop for all of the food, manage the household budget, pay the bills, keep track of everyone's activities, cook all of the meals, and, oh yeah, clean the house."

"Heavens no! Is this what your father told you? Are you sure you understood him correctly?"

"Very sure. And yes, he told me all of this last night. As soon as everyone left and Willow and Char had gone upstairs. He said that I have to run the house because Char is traumatized by the accident, Willow recently turned twelve, and I guess because I'm the oldest."

"And why did he call you twice today?"

"To make sure I was 'clear' on everything." She fumed. "Like I could forget something like this."

"I can understand your resentment; I do. And I don't want to disparage your father in any way, but this is wrong."

"Dad said it's what Mum would want."

Kady, who had been holding her glass, put it down with a light thud. "As your mother's best friend for the past eighteen-plus years, I can tell you, without a shred of doubt, this is the last thing she would want. She gave up her own aspirations for fashion school when she moved here to northern California to be your father's wife and start a family. She told me, many times, that while she willingly let go of her dreams, having her daughters fulfilled her in a way nothing else could have. Of course, her talent didn't go to waste. As you know, she often made clothing for all of you, for herself, and sometimes for friends. But I think she got the most joy out of teaching you how to love the art of design and sewing. Needless to say, it meant the world to her that you were chasing the career she had laid aside. If she told me that once, she told me a hundred times."

Lily noticed that Kady looked as if she wanted to say more, but stopped herself in time. She pushed the thought away. "That's why I came here, Kady. I needed to hear you say that. I know Mum confided in you the way she didn't in anyone else." She let the tears fall. "Please tell me why Dad is doing this!"

"I wish I understood, Lily. I know what a traditionalist your father is, and I was concerned he'd be unable to handle the lack of structure in what has always been a well-run house. Losing your mother is already too much for any of us. That's why I had a talk with him a couple of days ago. Sabrina and Oliver are grown and living their own lives. It's only Patrick and me. I told Dalt I could manage a fair number of Abby's activities, and in time, help all three of you to do your share … but only in ways that wouldn't upend your young lives." She sighed. "He put the kibosh on my offer in no time flat."

Lily stared at the satin paisley-fringed scarf that was looped around Kady's neck. "You have the most beautiful taste." Her eyes swept the living room as she admired the art and the décor in the Harrigan living room. She hesitated before looking directly at Kady. "Because mine is the only life Dad wants to mess with. He also made it quite clear that he wants me to be a mother to Willow and Char. Like I could even do that!"

"Oh hell no," Kady blurted out. Her jaw tightened, and Lily could see her take pains to calm herself. "Just no." She took a deep breath. "I'm trying hard not to use any expletives."

The corners of Lily's mouth turned up ever so slightly. "Well, you could always use Mum's expletives."

They both laughed.

"Ah, yes." Kady smiled as she remembered. "The first one I ever heard was 'go to Helsinki.' She even used 'Oh, helicopter' occasionally. Then there was 'Hoover dam it.'"

"My favorite was 'shiitake mushrooms,'" Lily said. "I loved that one."

"Indeed. Her most daring of the bunch."

Within a moment, both of their smiles turned upside down in tandem.

Kady placed a firm hand on Lily's knee. "Honey, would you let me talk to your father?"

"You already did. And we both know how that turned out. If

anyone could have changed his mind, it would have been you, Kady. For now, I don't want him to know that I clued you in on all of this … or that I was even here. He might think I was plotting against him or something … or that I was trying to make him look bad under tragic circumstances. And I'm not … I'm only trying to survive this nightmare." Lily took a moment to replay her words. "Thank you for the offer, but no, he definitely wouldn't understand. Maybe it would be more accurate to say that it isn't convenient for him to understand. I don't know. Only that it wouldn't end well if you tried. Especially after he already turned you down."

"Now that I have another think, you're right, honey. I won't say anything. Promise. He's a proud man." Kady removed her hand and picked up her lemonade. "But his stubborn pride can be maddening. It drove your mother crazy at times."

"Yeah, I know."

"But she loved him deeply, Lily. Make no mistake there."

"He wasn't the one who sat with her in the hospital for three days until she died. That was you."

Kady took a sip of her lemonade. "He needed to be with the three of you. Especially that first night when Charlotte was hospitalized for tests. After that, all of you came to visit, what, twice a day?"

"Yes. I wanted to stay longer … with you, but he wouldn't let me. He said he didn't want me to burn that image of Mum into my brain forever." Lily lowered her eyes. "It only took two minutes for that to happen, so what could it have mattered if I stayed all day?" She wiped a few tears away. "I hope I don't remember her that way forever."

"You won't. But I understand your fear. I do. When my mother died, I watched her grow weaker every day. I cried as I saw her mind move on to another reality and leave us all with ours. One day, I told my uncle Ivan that I was so afraid I'd never remember my mother as she was, but only as she had become. And he promised me that my memories would revert back to the mother I'd known all my life, not to the sick woman who had not only forgotten my name, but her own. And he was right."

Lily put her hand on Kady's. "Thank you for that. And I do visualize Mum's smiling face when I think about her. But I want that other image to go away." She pulled her phone out of her pocket and checked the time again. "I should go, but I need to ask you one more question."

"Anything."

"When we were at the hospital, the second day after the accident, you know, after Char had been released, I heard the doctor tell Dad that Mum had woken up briefly when you were there. I thought for sure he'd share that with us, but he didn't. I need to know: Did Mum say anything? Did she recognize you?"

"Oh, my." Kady took a moment. "Yes, Abby did open her eyes, and she did speak to me ever so briefly. She asked me to look after you all and to never let any of us forget how much she loved us. There might have been a bit more; that's all I can remember. Her awakening was so unexpected, and a part of me feels as if I only imagined it. But it happened." Kady closed her eyes as the tears ran down her cheeks. "I said good-bye and told her I loved her."

"And you didn't tell Dad."

"I told him she had awakened briefly to say she loved us all." Kady pulled a tissue out of her pants pocket to dab her tears.

"Oh, I wonder why he didn't share that with us."

"I don't know, Lily. Maybe he wasn't ready. Maybe he thought it would give you false hope. You know, that she would wake up again for good. It's impossible for me to know his reasoning, but another part of me thinks that he may have felt as if she died all over again. I can only speculate, but even doing that feels wrong."

"I wish I'd had those extra few minutes with her. At least I could have said good-bye too. For me, she died the moment that

pickup truck hit her car. Just like that, no more Mum. No good-bye."
Lily didn't bother to wipe away the tears that fell.

"Oh, honey …."

Lily jumped as her mother's favorite song, "Across the Universe," played on her phone. Pulling it quickly from her pocket, she answered.

"Hello?"

"Where are you, Lily?"

"I stopped to get some lemonade. I was so thirsty that I couldn't wait until I got home."

"Why didn't you have something when you went to the diner to terminate your employment?" He cleared his throat. "You did quit your job, I hope."

"Yes. But I forgot to grab all of my makeup work from school, and so I had to go back. When I was at my locker, a few teachers stopped to offer their sympathy, and by the time I got back in the car to come home, I was thirsty, and so I stopped at the convenience store."

"And that's where you are now?"

"I'm drinking my lemonade. I wasn't going to drink it while I was driving."

"I see. Well, I hope you enjoy it. Unfortunately, these are the kind of luxuries you'll have to learn to forgo. You should head home as soon as you can. No doubt your sisters need you. We've got plenty of homemade frozen food that our friends left, but a dish needs to be chosen, thawed, cooked, and served. Table set and all that."

"O-okay."

"But you know, Lily, on second thought, since you're already out and about, please get some fresh salad for dinner. Also, I have a prescription at the pharmacy that needs to be picked up and a suit at the dry cleaners on Bella Vista. I'll reimburse you. Oh, and don't worry if I'm not home on time. Being out for a week, like you, I'm behind on my work. Make sure your sisters eat on time."

"I'll get everything. See you when you get home, Dad."

Lily glanced at the phone to make sure she had properly ended the call before speaking. "Oh, Kady, I've lost Mum, and now I've lost my life."

"What is this?" Willow asked, poking her fork at the dish in front of her.

"Lasagna," Lily said. "Mrs. Fanucci made it."

"How come it's green?"

"They're homemade spinach noodles," Lily explained.

Charlotte looked at her younger sister. "They're actually tongues of the Jolly Green Giant and his family. Cut out of their mouths while they were sleeping. You should see when they wake up and try to say, 'where the eff is my tongue?'" Charlotte uttered several strange sounds to go with the unusual mouth gestures she was making.

"Gross," Willow said. "And if I was five, I wouldn't have believed you."

"Then what's gross about it?"

"The thought of it makes me not wanna eat it. And those sounds you made were disgusting."

"Ask me if I care," Charlotte said, her eyes bulging maniacally at her younger sister. "Because I don't."

"C'mon, Char," Lily said. "Let's all be cool. This lasagna is actually good. None of us are happy, but we still have to eat."

"I miss Mum's cooking," Charlotte said.

"There's still some of her English Garden Soup in the freezer. I couldn't bear to thaw it out yet. I don't know. There's something comforting in knowing we'll be able to taste her cooking again."

"It won't be long before all of the frozen stuff runs out …

including Mum's soup," Charlotte said. "Then we'll have to eat *your* cooking. Can't wait for that ... not!"

"I won't mind your cooking," Willow offered.

Charlotte twisted her face in disgust. "Like you've ever tasted Lily's cooking. What would you know, Willow Tree? Except how to weep."

Willow burst into tears and put her fork down. "Why are you being so mean, Char? We all lost Mum."

"I'm not being mean."

"You tried to gross me out so I wouldn't eat my dinner, then you insult me."

"Seriously? I grossed you out with a joke about the Jolly Green Giant? Like that even sounded remotely true."

Willow leaned toward her with conviction. "I told you that I knew it wasn't true. But you made it sound and look gross so I wouldn't want to eat my dinner. I already don't feel like eating because Mum is dead. But you had to make it worse."

"I was making a joke. You're a delicate flower," Charlotte said. "Who knew? And I thought lilies were the delicate flowers."

"Stop!" Lily said. "Please, Char. Enough! We're all hurting. You don't have to turn our dinner table into a battlefield. What do you think Mum would think of this?"

"Whatever .... And making a dumb joke isn't turning anything into a battlefield. Maybe I was trying to lighten the mood, and you're trying to make something out of nothing."

"No she's not," Willow said. "You started it, Char. And you weren't trying to lighten anything. I know you. You were trying to darken something."

"Quiet," Charlotte said.

"Mum would *hate* this," Lily said to Charlotte. "And you know it."

"Wow! Didn't take you long at all!"

Lily laid her fork on her plate in disgust. "What are you even talking about? It didn't take me long to do what?"

"To try and be Mum. Except right now you totally sound like Dad. 'What do you think Mum would think of this?'" Charlotte said, mocking her. "Totally a Dad question."

"I'm trying to have a nice dinner with my sisters under the worst circumstances ever."

"You got that right," Charlotte mumbled. "Worst circumstances ever."

Willow looked at Lily. "I'm not hungry anymore."

Her right elbow on the table, Lily let her head drop into the palm of her hand. She closed her eyes and let her mind run away, but when she saw herself running up a hill, only to be carried away by a powerful gust of wind, she opened her eyes with a start.

"You okay?" Willow asked. "You sure don't look it. You're kind of shaky and stuff."

"Good observation." She glanced at Willow's plate. "How about if you eat your salad? I picked up the ingredients, and I made it fresh. Can you at least do that?"

"Oh my God," Charlotte said. "Dad tells you to step into Mum's shoes, and you're like this parental monster in no time flat. 'Can you at least do that, Willow?' Ugh. Well, let me tell you, Lily. There's no way you're going to boss *me* around. And you'd better not even think of lecturing me, yelling at me, or anything even close, because I'm living with nightmares, daymares, and memories you will never have. And you trying to be Mum will push me over the effing edge. So stop it."

Lily put her palms over her eyes to brush away the tears. She took a long breath, then, with the greatest calm she could muster, looked at her sister. "What did Dad tell you, Char? Please, I need to know."

Charlotte shrugged.

"I'll tell you," Willow said. "Before you came home, Dad went outside of his office building and video-called us. He said that he sent you on some errands so he'd have time to talk to us and that he wanted to do it in person but had to work late."

"And?"

Willow ignored the dirty look Charlotte was giving her and continued. "He said that with Mum gone, you would be taking over all of her responsibilities. And that you were now the lady of the house and you would be like a mum to us. And then he went on and on, repeating it in different ways and saying we can't let the family fall apart."

"Did you hear that part about how you would be Mum to us?" Charlotte asked, her brown eyes flickering with anger.

Lily leaned back in her chair and put the palms of her hands up. "Whoa, hold it right there, Char! First, I could never be Mum. Willow said it correctly: be *like* a mum. And even that's nothing I want. Do you think I wanted Mum to die? Do you think I wanted to quit my job, to drop out of fashion school before I even got started, to be a mother to my sisters? Do you *really* think there's any freakin' thrill in that for me? Do you think I want to do all of the shopping, cooking, cleaning, and everything else? Do you?"

"You're traumatizing me," Charlotte yelled. "Do *you* think I want to see Mum's head getting smacked by the force of an oncoming pickup truck for the rest of my life? Do you? Her life was over in a nanosecond. I never saw her conscious again."

"I know that! I'm not talking about the accident," Lily protested. "You are!"

"Stop it!" Willow cried. "Please stop! Both of you." She got up from the table and ran away. "Come back, Mum! Wherever you are, come back!"

Lily glanced at the empty space where Willow had been. "This is great." She looked at Charlotte. "Of course I don't want you to be traumatized for the rest of your life. How did I do anything to cause that? All I did was fix dinner like Dad ordered me to do."

"Oh, totally. You did. And what a great meal it's been." Charlotte snickered at the lasagna, then at her sister.

"Would you like to be in my position? Would you, Char?"

"Actually. No. Because when Dad hears what a disaster your first meal was, he's gonna be *so* unhappy with you, Lills."

The fight gone from her, Lily looked at her sister. "Why are you so angry at me? I'm every bit as wrecked as you are. My heart is shattered into a million pieces. Just like yours."

"See ya." Charlotte pushed away from the table. "I need some metal to clear my head from this bullshit."

"And I need to wake up from this nightmare," Lily said to herself. She looked upward. "What Willow said, Mum. Wherever you are, please come back!"

CHAPTER THREE

Lily's stomach flipped the moment she saw her name on the small white envelope lying on the kitchen table. Saying a silent prayer she hoped her mother could hear, she picked up the envelope, opened it, and read the short note inside.

> *I know these are dark times for all of us, Lily. But the last thing I expected from you was to engage your sister in an argument the first night the three of you had dinner alone. You can do better. The sooner you accept your new role in this family, the happier we'll all be. I believe in you. You've got this.*
>
> *Love, Dad*

She shoved the note into her pocket, then crumpled up the envelope and put it in the garbage. Reaching into a cupboard to grab a box of cereal, she saw Charlotte approaching the kitchen. Lily turned and looked at her. *What did you say to Dad last night?*

Charlotte said nothing as she walked in, barely acknowledging her sister's presence.

"Good morning." Lily hoped the thoughts she was forbidden to articulate would somehow travel to Charlotte's brain. "Did Willow leave already?"

"She always leaves for school twenty minutes before we do. You know that. But hey, it's a 'mum' thing to say. You're getting the hang of it. Oh, wait. You already have."

Not playing your bullshit game, Char. Ignoring the remark, Lily grabbed a bowl out of the dish drainer and put it on the counter. She poured a smaller portion of cereal than usual. Feeling Charlotte's eyes on her back made routine tasks more difficult. Trying not to appear rattled, she took a banana out of the fruit bowl, quickly peeled it, cut it into slices, and tossed the peels into the garbage. Angry words lodged in her throat, but she swallowed them and persisted with her routine. Cupping the banana slices in her hand, she felt an urge to throw them, but instead, with feigned calm, dropped them on top of her cereal. As she put her bowl on the table, her peripheral vision caught a glance of Charlotte, staring at her, intent to break her. As nonchalantly as she could, Lily returned to the counter and cleaned the cutting board. That done, she put the cereal back into the cupboard and turned to Charlotte with counterfeit composure. "Did you want to have this for breakfast? There's plenty left."

Charlotte sat at the table. "I can never eat that again. The morning of the accident, Mum told me that she bought extra boxes of the oats because they were my favorite. Three hours later, she was dead and I could have been too. And yeah, I know she hung on for three more days, but for me, she died in that second. The cereal is the last thing she ever bought for me, and I never want to eat it again. It would traumatize me even more. So I'll have some eggs and toast. And a small glass of orange juice."

Halfway into a sitting position, Lily's jaw dropped as Charlotte's not-so-subtle breakfast order jarred her. She silently counted to three as she sat. After a few more seconds, she turned to her sister. "I have to leave soon. Can't you scramble up a couple of eggs?"

"I get dizzy when I stand too long. Then the memories come back to me, and I feel faint. And sometimes frightened."

Lily stood. Relegating her resentment to a compartment in her brain, she prepared the eggs and toast. Her expression blank, she put the plate in front of her sister. "Here you go."

"Thanks. How about the orange juice?"

Lily was sure the veins in her neck must've been popping, but she gently took a small glass with painted orange slices out of the cupboard, filled it with juice, and placed it on the table next to the eggs and toast.

"Thank you," Charlotte mumbled.

For two minutes, they ate in silence. Finally, Lily looked up at her sister. "Do you want to ride to school with me?"

"Are you serious?"

"Um ... yeah. Why wouldn't I be?"

"I can't get into your car right now. It's Mum's first car ... too many memories. Francesca's mother, Kia, is going to pick me up. Dad only took me yesterday because it was my first day back. So I won't be riding to school with you anymore."

"I guess that makes sense. You're both in the ninth grade, and you have the same classes. Besides, you usually go home with Francesca anyway ... both of you getting out at the same time and all."

Charlotte finished her eggs and looked at Lily. "I remember at Thanksgiving, when someone asked what grade I was in now. I told them I was a freshman, and Mum said, 'No you're not, Charlotte. You're a fresh woman.'" She broke a piece of toast in half. "That was so funny because Mum never meant it to come out that way. To her, it was ..."

"Almost like cursing," Lily finished. "I remember that. Mum turned bright red."

"Yeah, she did. She was so embarrassed, but she was laughing too." Charlotte choked up. "And now she's dead."

"Oh, Char …." Lily reached for her hand.

Charlotte took hold of her glass as if Lily's hand were invisible. Chugging down most of the juice, she grabbed a piece of toast and got up from the table. "Frannie's here. She just texted me."

Before Lily could say good-bye, Charlotte had lifted her backpack off a chair in the dining room as she headed toward the front door.

Lily stood and walked through the kitchen to the knotty pine, glass-paned door that led to the patio and backyard. As she spied three squirrels scampering up a nearby oak tree, her reflection in the window demanded attention. She watched as a lone tear drizzled down her face. Lily pointed to it. "I know you. You must be a cousin of that raindrop I met the other day. And in a few seconds, you'll be leaving me too."

"So, Ray, that's pretty much it," Lily said. Sitting on the grass under the blue oak at Altrusia High, Lily reached into her purse and handed her friend a note. "This is what awaited me this morning."

Raymond Bostwick, the shy senior, pushed away a stray lock of hair covering one eye as he took the note from Lily and read the unsettling communication. His eyes, weighed down with sadness, stared at the words before handing the piece of paper back to Lily. "I feel like the worst friend in the world. Everything you've been through—everything you're *going* through, well, it's tragic." He looked at her awkwardly. "Okay if I hug you?"

"Of course." Lily threw her arms around him and buried her head in his chest. "You're the best friend I have at this school. And you and Hannah are the best friends I have *anywhere*. Full stop."

"Full stop?"

"Oh, you know … period. Full stop is one of those British things I got from my mum."

"Duh. I knew that," Raymond said, tentatively stroking her hair.

Lily, fully understanding his untried relationship with intimacy, sat up and met his eyes. "You know, after the funeral, when everyone came over to our house, after you had left, Hannah and her mother walked over to the chair I was sitting in to say good-bye. For a split second, my grief cracked open, and I thought how having both of you as my best friends … plus my 'second family' at the diner … would help me get through this, and I would be as all right as I could ever be without Mum."

"And then your father lowered the boom on you."

"Oh, yeah. I should have seen that coming, but I didn't. In fact, I thought, if anything, Dad would push me toward my friends, talk up fashion school, and do things like that to get my blood pumping again. The last thing I ever expected was for him to drain it. And then there's Char … I can't even go there now. It's impossible—"

"What can I do to help? I don't want to tell you how inadequate I feel, because this is all about making *you* feel better, not me." Raymond plucked a few blades of grass and studied them. After a contemplative moment, he let them flutter away in the soft breeze.

"Be here for me. Like you are right now."

Lily watched as Raymond bit his lip so hard, she thought it would bleed. "What's wrong? Are you seeing someone or something? You looked freaked when I said that."

Making a fist, Raymond ground it into the earth in frustration. "No, not seeing anyone, beautiful girl. But I have news. Got it last week … the same day as the accident. I haven't had the heart to share it."

"Is it bad?"

"No, not at all. It's incredible news, but not so much at the moment."

"Tell me then. I need to hear good news."

Raymond locked his fingers together and squeezed them. Finally, he let go of his own grip to push the same stubborn lock of hair out of his eyes. "This is pissing me off."

"Maybe a haircut … or a different hairstyle might solve the problem." Lily's brown eyes gazed tenderly at him as she tried to remedy his habitual uneasiness. "Tell me your news."

"I got into Princeton," he blurted out. "To the School of Applied Science and Engineering. I'll be leaving in the middle of August. That only gives us four more months together."

"Oh, Ray. That's the *best* news. That was your number-one choice, right? You're so brilliant. Super brill. Remember, I used to call you that in the tenth grade."

"I do. My first and only superhero name. You've always been so amazing to me, and all I want now is to be the same to you. Except I'm moving three thousand miles away."

"I know. But I'm happy for you. I am."

"I honestly didn't think they'd accept me."

"You sound like you're apologizing or something. Stop. And I'm not the least bit surprised they accepted you." She reached over and hugged him, giving him a kiss on the cheek. "Why wouldn't they?"

"I don't have as many extracurricular activities as most kids do. I haven't been involved in student government, sports, band, debate … or any of that. I only have the internship I did last year and again this fall, science club, and my volunteer work with the homeless. I don't think of my job at Paulie's Pizza Palace as a wow factor, either, except to show responsibility."

"How about winning a prestigious national science competition? Um … hello? That was insanely impressive. And then there were those summer programs you attended with the smartest of the smart. How about membership in the honor society? Or maybe those straight As and perfect SAT scores. Hmm. Want me to go on?"

"No thanks." He laughed. "And yeah, those things might have helped. But as social activities go, the most social thing I've done was take you to the junior prom, which, if I may say, was one of the best nights of my life." He smiled crookedly. "Anyway, my point is that I'm not the most outgoing person."

"You're super brill; don't forget that."

Raymond frowned. "Book smart maybe. But if I were as 'brill' as you think I am, then how come I don't know what to do to help you?"

"I don't think anyone can. But it helps to be able to talk to a few people I trust. You, Hannah, and Kady. You've met her ... Mum's best friend."

"I know Kady." He pulled out a couple more blades of grass. "Do you think maybe your dad is in shock? And that maybe he'll see what he's doing to you and change his mind?"

"I wish. When he told me, it was clear that he'd carefully thought out every part of his miserable plan. Well, not *every* part. He thought about what was best for him, Willow, and Char and forgot all about me."

"That's what I'm saying." Raymond touched her with his grass-free hand. "He did forget about you. I don't think he'll be that way forever. There's a good chance he'll come around. And if ... *when* he does, then that will make dealing with Char's stuff a whole lot easier."

"I don't think so. I don't see it. Kady called him a 'traditionalist.' Yeah, I know, there's nothing 'traditional' about forcing your oldest daughter to be a mother to your younger ones, right? Or to snatch her life out from under her to play 'lady of the house.' But I don't think Dad wants to think about alternative solutions. No, he's good there in his box. He's not exactly the kind of guy who colors outside of the lines, you know? So eff fashion school and eff my job and my friends, you know? Oh, but there's a bright side. I'll be allowed to go to freakin' community college when things 'settle down' or whatever words he used. As for Char ...."

"I know ... you can't even ... I get that." Raymond brushed the same lock of hair out of his face for the third time and laughed at himself. "I *will* be getting a haircut." He looked down at his hands. "I'm also going to stop playing with grass." He laughed awkwardly as he rubbed his hands together to free the captive blades. "But what I most want you to know, besides the fate of my unruly hair, is that physical distance won't stop me from being there for you. Besides, I'll be home for the Christmas holiday. And, I know it's only April now, but my cool aunt and uncle, who live in Sonoma, are having a huge party at their house. They're musicians, and they invite other musicians, actors, and artists from all over. It's a blast. So, will you be my date on Friday, December nineteenth?"

"Absolutely. Knowing I'll see you then and have something special to look forward to makes your leaving a little easier." She paused. "And don't take that to mean I'm not thrilled for you, because I am."

"I know." He choked up. "You know I'll always love you, right? Living in New Jersey won't change that." He smiled.

Lily smiled back. "Good to know." She looked away, wishing she could have held her smile longer.

Lily, Charlotte, and Willow sat on the couch and faced their father, who sat across from them in his leather recliner, a glass of whiskey on the rocks in his left hand and a legal document lying on the small table to his right.

"Well, that's it," he said. "Judging by your blank faces, I'm glad I waited until after dinner to read your mother's will." He looked at Lily. "Thank you for preparing dinner and setting such a nice table. Mum would have been proud."

Lily tried to force a smile, but her mouth barely moved.

"Do any of you have any questions?"

"I do," Willow asked. "Why did Mum have to die? I don't want the money. I want her."

"We all want your mother, honey. If the four of us agree on anything, that would be it."

"So, I have a question," Charlotte said. "How come Lily gets all of that property in England, plus twenty-five-thousand dollars, and Willow and I only get trust funds? That property has got to be worth way more."

Dalton gritted his teeth. "*Only* trust funds? A six-figure trust fund is nothing to sneeze at, and, in capable hands, it should grow quite a bit in value by the time you need to access it."

"But we can only access half of it when we're twenty-one and the rest when we're twenty-five?"

"That's correct. But it can certainly be used sooner than that for school and expenses. Believe me, Charlotte, you'll be glad to have set something away for later in life. I can't admonish you strongly enough to use it wisely."

"So I can use some of the money to go to professional makeup school in LA?"

"Absolutely. And with your talent, I see you earning a good living in no time."

Willow looked at Charlotte. "Will you learn how to turn people into monsters?" She smirked. "Like Jolly Green Giants with their tongues cut out?"

Charlotte ignored the dig. "Yup. Special effects, prosthetic makeup, beauty makeup, and a whole bunch of other stuff."

"Won't you be nervous if you have to work on movie stars?"

"I doubt it. Nobody works on famous people right out of school. Probably, if I'm lucky, I'll work with background actors or day players. Actually, I don't have a clue. I just hope that one day, down the line, I'll be good enough to do the cool stuff … like transform actors into monsters, aliens, or whatever. That's really my dream."

"So you don't really want to make people look pretty," Willow said. "You want to make them look ugly and unrecognizable."

"Yeah, Tree, if you put it like that."

"Your mum would be thrilled to know she'll have a hand in helping make that dream come true." Dalton grabbed the will and put it in his inside jacket pocket. "I'm going upstairs. It's been a long day. And there are two more days before the weekend comes around again." He stood. "Good night, girls. I love you all."

The three of them watched as their father took his drink and climbed the stairs. Once the sound of his bedroom door being shut was heard, Charlotte turned to Lily.

"You still got way more money with that property in the Cotswolds. What, you now own a four-bedroom, two-and-a-half-bathroom cottage with a big-ass garden and a row of four terraced two-bedroom cottages? And twenty-five grand. Plus, you get all of the rent money starting now? Math isn't my best subject, but I know that's gotta be worth a truckload of money. And you don't even have to wait until you're twenty-one."

Willow slunk in her seat as she usually did when she felt dread at something to come. Lily stood and walked over to her father's armchair and sat in it so she could more comfortably face Charlotte. She thought for a long minute before she spoke.

"First of all, Char, yeah, I'll earn money on rentals … leasing or letting, as they say in England, and that means that I also have to pay a management company. Didn't you hear Dad explain that when he read the will? There are taxes, repairs, upkeep, gardening, and insurance … to name a few. And I'll have to stay on top of all of that. Like Mum did when she owned it. It's not all profit."

"Whatevs," Charlotte said.

"Second, maybe you forgot about how Dad made me drop out of fashion school. I'm graduating high school next month, and he said that all he'll promise now is that I can take some courses at community college … down the road … so I can be here to handle everything Mum used to do. Does that sound like fun? Do you think I'm happy about any of this? Dad threw all of my plans into the fireplace and lit a match. When *you're* eighteen, you can go to LA, learn how to be a movie makeup artist, and live the life you've always dreamed. *You* don't have to put your plans on hold."

"You could sell that real estate for millions, I'll bet," Charlotte said.

"I would *never* sell Quincy family property. And it's right across the street from Uncle Ellis, Aunt Millie, Caroline, Andrew, and Edward." Lily inclined forward as if to give her words more heart. "I fell in love with the Quincy properties and the area when I was a child. Mum, Uncle Ellis, Granny, and Grandpa used to tell me stories about our ancestors. You know, great-grandparents, uncles, aunts, and cousins who used to live in the same homes as they did. All of them have been in our family since they were built … hundreds of years ago. I loved writing stories about them and imagining what went on inside. You know, all of the things people said and did, right down to their secrets. I loved learning about the history of the area, the monarchy, and everything about England. It fascinated me; it still does. It's just money to you. Don't you think there's a good reason Mum willed it to me? She knew I would cherish the property as she did … and I wouldn't sell it."

"She should have split her estate evenly; then at least Willow and me would get an equal share."

"Willow and I," Lily said, wishing she hadn't.

"Well look at you, correcting my grammar like Mum used to do so I'll know how to be all proper and stuff." Charlotte crinkled her nose in disgust. "Maybe I said it that way on purpose. Maybe I wanted to see how far you'd take this Mum act."

"I'm happy with the trust fund Mum left for me," Willow squeaked out. "I'll be able to go to any college I want, and I'll have six or seven years for the money to grow. I have to get good grades, of course, so they'll let me in." She frowned. "Mum couldn't leave me good grades."

"No," Charlotte said. "But she left Lily to make sure you work hard and be a good girl."

"Stop! Mum knew exactly what she was doing. We should be lucky that at least we have our dreams when we don't have our mum. And Lily has always loved those cottages … maybe it's because she looks the most like Mum that the cottages love her back. I guess that's silly. I don't know. But I don't want to fight. And I don't want to hear anyone else fight, okay?"

"So what does Dad get?" Charlotte asked.

"He gets his share of this house, all of the stuff in it, and all of the money that Mum didn't leave to the two of you. He told us that."

"Oh, right," Charlotte said. "My head hurts. I'm going upstairs to listen to some metal."

"Your head hurts, and you're going to listen to metal? Really?" Willow asked.

"It's my nirvana," Charlotte said. "Do you know that word?"

"No, but I will soon. I look up every word I don't know. Mum told me that if I do that, I'll have a superior vocabulary someday."

"Well, since you're thinking of being a teacher or whatever, I guess that will come in handy," Charlotte said. She stood. "Laters."

As Charlotte ran up the stairs, Willow turned to Lily. "Mum totally hated 'laters.'"

"I know. Char said it intentionally … hoping I would correct her so she could have another go at me. But I don't care. She can talk any way she wants. I need to remember not to bite when she sets traps for me. Like before. So stupid of me to react."

Willow twisted her mouth. "Don't say that. You're not stupid. But I think she might be doing that a lot. You know, setting traps. I don't like saying that, Lills, but, well, you ...."

"I know."

"Do you want me to stay down here with you?"

"No, but I appreciate the sweet offer. I need to sit here and think. And I've got to video chat with Uncle Ellis in a bit so he can give me my first lesson in being a property owner, but it's still too early in England."

"Oh, yeah. Guess there's a whole lot you need to know."

"There is. Thanks again for wanting to hang out with me. It means more to me than you know. And don't forget, Wills, I'm always here if you need me."

"Thanks."

"Always for life. Wills and Lills."

Willow jumped up, hurried over to the recliner, and threw her arms around Lily. "I love you so much. You're the absolute best sister." She pulled away to look at Lily. "Mum knew what she was doing, leaving her part of England to you. I'm so glad she did. I don't know why Char isn't more grateful for what we got."

As Willow squeezed onto the leather seat cushion, Lily slid over so they could sit side by side. "I don't know. Char has always been a rebel. You know that. And she was in the car when Mum got hit. And that's about as traumatic as it gets. I think the anger is her way of grieving and fighting back because she was helpless to stop it then, and she's helpless now. I know that; the trick is to remember it. Even more so, to deal with it."

"You're such a good person, Lily."

"We're all good people." Lily twirled a lock of her little sister's long hair around her finger, and then let it fall loose. "But we're *different* people."

Willow stood. "I'm going to go write in my journal about how much I love you. Tell Uncle Ellis I said hello, okay?"

With the back of her hand, Lily brushed away the tears. "I'm going to write the same thing about you in mine. Good night, Wills."

CHAPTER FOUR

"Oh, look. The Queen of England swapped out her banana for some strawberries," Charlotte said as she entered the kitchen to find Lily and Willow eating cereal at the table.

Lily didn't respond, but Willow put her spoon down and challenged her sister. "C'mon, Char. Can't you give Lily a break? She didn't do anything to you."

"What are you still doing here, Weeping Willow? You should have been on your merry way twenty minutes ago."

"There's a teachers' meeting today, so we're going in later."

"Oh." Charlotte turned her attention to Lily. "Aren't you going to make my eggs?"

Lily looked up. "No, I don't think so. But I bought three different kinds of cereal so you can pick something new. And you know how to scramble eggs."

"Me and Willow aren't used to cooking breakfast."

Willow shot an I-told-you-so glance at Lily.

"And I'm not used to cooking breakfast either, much less yours when you're totally able to do it yourself."

Charlotte sat, her elbows on the table, her chin resting in both palms, and stared at Lily. "I get dizzy when I stand. And I guess you're too busy, or maybe too snobby, now that you own half of England because you look the most like Mum."

"I don't own half of England. And you know it." Lily raised a spoonful of oats only to let it drop back into the bowl. "I own all of it."

"Wow, so you are totally bragging now! Shoving it in my face."

"No," Lily said, pushing away her cereal. "That was a ridiculous thing you said, and I was being ridiculous back. You don't have exclusive rights on ridiculosity."

Charlotte turned to Willow. "Don't bother to look that one up in your dictionary. It's not even a word."

"You think I don't know that, Char? Sometimes words don't have to be real ones to know what a person means. And sometimes even when a person uses real words, you don't know what they mean at all."

Charlotte sat back in her chair, her arms folded defensively. "If only I looked like Mum … I'd be a property-owning multi-millionaire."

Lily responded with a blank stare.

"That's not all you'd be, Char," Willow said.

Charlotte turned to her younger sister. "What would I be then?"

"You might have to give up everything in your life to step into Mum's. Good-bye, makeup school. Good-bye, life on TV and movie sets. You think you'd like that? Huh? Do ya?"

Charlotte blanched, then stood. "I'm going to wait for Francesca and Kia outside." She looked at Lily. "I've got an energy bar in my backpack. Oh, and yeah, I'm gonna be late coming home from school. So there's that. Don't do any kind of Mum-like freak-out over it." She turned her back on her sisters and hurried away.

"I don't know why she acts that way. But I hate it," Willow said.

Lily stood, walked over to the sink, and poured the uneaten cereal and fruit down the garbage disposal. She turned to Willow. "If she's going to resent me, I'm not sure what I can do about it. Mum left me that property because I'm the oldest, and she knew I would always take care of it and keep it in the family. She tried to be fair by leaving a whole lot more money to both of you. Her inheritance from Granny and Grandpa was sacred to her. She told me that. And I'm sure she thought about everything carefully before finalizing her will. If she hadn't died, she might have changed things down the road. But she could only do what she thought was best at the time she wrote it. You know, Wills?"

"Totally. I think Mum got it right. Char has always been rebellious, and she's totally into her own zone. Especially with her music, her clothes … and her makeup." She pushed her half-eaten bowl of cereal away. "I don't know what she would do if she owned some of that property, but it wouldn't have been what Mum wanted and it would make you crazy. Me too."

Lily picked up Willow's cereal bowl. "Have you lost your appetite too?"

"Yeah, I guess. Sorry. Mum hated when we wasted food."

"She probably hates being dead even more." Lily dumped Willow's uneaten food into the disposal as well.

Willow stood and ran to her sister, throwing her arms around her. After a long moment, she disengaged. "I hope Char comes around. But I'll never be like her. I promise. Is it okay if I come home late after school too? Issy texted me last night to see if we could hang and watch a movie. I'd be home before dinner."

"Being with your best friend is good for you." Lily kissed her sister on the forehead without even realizing her mother used to do exactly the same thing. "I'll see you at dinner."

"Bye, Lills." Willow smiled at her sister and left the kitchen.

Lily flipped on the disposal switch and listened to the ugly sound of the grinding chamber below as it chopped all of her angry, unspoken words into tiny particles, then washed them down the drain.

"I was so relieved when Char and Willow both said they'd be home late," Lily told Kady as they sat on the burgundy sofa. "I wanted to come see you so much and didn't know if I could manage without Dad getting angry."

"Oh, honey." Kady poured Lily a cup of tea. "You shouldn't have to endure this. Your father is mad with grief."

"Why can't he see that we all are?"

"I don't think he knows how to handle any of this." Her voice trailed off. "Not that any of us do...." With a tentative smile, Kady filled her own cup. "You know what a strict upbringing he had, especially because his parents were in their early forties when he was born. Believe me, his mother was much more lax as a grandmother than as a mother, which is often the case with people. When your father graduated from college, he got his first taste of true freedom. His parents gave him the trip to Europe as a gift, which is how your mum and dad met and how your lovely self came to exist. You know that. But it took his parents forever to let go of the reins. Even when he was at college, they kept close tabs on him."

Lily lifted her teacup from the saucer. "I knew he was raised with strict parents. He told us that a lot. You know, like an if-he-could-do-it-so-could-we kind of thing."

"He was far less strict on you than his parents were on him. Because your mum knew the difference between bringing up children well and inflicting unnecessary rules on them. Her family was a bit uptight at times but fun-loving as well."

"I'm surprised Mum fell for Dad. She was such a bright light in every way."

"That's why he fell in love the moment he saw her. She had all of the charms that had eluded him, most especially joy and laughter. And he was a good-looking man with a college degree, only four years older than Abby, but she felt like her knight in shining armor had arrived. She said your father was full of life and eager to live it after such a sheltered upbringing. Your mum wasn't interested in any of the boys from the other well-to-do English families. She told me she was 'over them' by the age of twelve. Your father was someone new and exciting to her. They spent a glorious week together. Reluctantly, Dalt continued on his trip as planned, but when he got to Paris, he missed your mum so much that he went back to England and spent all of his remaining time abroad with her. You know the story. She gave up her dreams to be a fashion designer, and six months later, she came to California to be his wife."

"Yeah, you mentioned that part the other day, but I'd forgotten about the rest." She looked curiously at the teapot and the cups. "Did Mum give this tea set to you? I kind of remember it. We have something similar."

"She did." Kady picked up her cup. "It's Wedgwood. Your mum bought it for me on your first trip to England when you were five, and Charlotte was a baby. I cherish it, as I did her."

Lily tried to smile, but the result was meager.

"Oh, sweetheart. Do you want to talk some more about what you're feeling?" Kady took a sip of tea before placing the cup back on the saucer. "It's upsetting that Charlotte reacted so poorly to the will. I don't know if she realizes what a tidy sum of money she and Willow got in place of the property. And she doesn't have any of the responsibility of being a property owner."

"I don't know, Kady. It's like everything and anything makes Char angry. I made the huge mistake of correcting her grammar last night, which was only a stupid reflex action, and now she's purposely using bad English and slang to get me to do it again. So she can rail on me for sounding like Mum when I correct her. Only, as I told Willow,

I don't care. She can speak any way she wants."

"Your mum had quite the proper English education. It's not surprising she passed it on to her girls. But she never needed nor wanted anyone to speak with perfection. She only wanted her daughters to be properly educated. Actually, her love for grammar is what bonded us the third time we met."

"I don't think I knew that."

"Well," Kady said, smiling at the memory, "you were a baby, and my kids were in the sixth and ninth grades. Being a high school English teacher, I was part of a city community club that focused not only on education, but also on activities for both children and adults. The first time I saw Abby, I was surprised to see this lovely young woman with an infant. I figured she must have had older kids in school, but she said she didn't. When I introduced myself, she told me education was so important to her, she wanted to get a head start and learn all she could about the Altrusia schools and community. I met her only briefly that time, and her darling baby, you, but I knew I liked her immensely. I had so many people to speak with that day and didn't have the opportunity to get to know her better.

"The next time I saw her was at a meeting in November, but I had to leave early to attend an event for Patrick's firm, and I couldn't linger."

"So what happened the third time you met? When you became friends."

"Flash forward one month to late December. Your mum had volunteered to work at a community Christmas event held at the high school. Well, two of the volunteers, both independent—or should I say *stubborn* women—each had their own idea of who should be hired to play Santa Claus. For some reason, after all of their quibbling, they each thought the other had conceded the hiring process, but, as it turned out, they had both hired their own choices to play Santa. Multiple elves and reindeer are one thing. Two Santas … not so much.

And the Santas happened to be brothers who weren't speaking to one another!"

"Oh no!"

"Here's the funny part. We had two brothers dressed like Santa, arguing about who'd been offered the job first. Standing nearby, also arguing, were the two agitated and obnoxious women who'd hired them. Their shrieking, contentious voices all blended into one hideous racket. In the midst of this public squabble, your mum ran over to a table where some poster boards sat. She grabbed a black marker and drew a giant semicolon on one of the boards. Then, with a big smile, she walked over and stood between the two Santas holding her sign.

"Huh? You've totally lost me."

"I was completely befuddled as well. Then, before I could even ask her, it came to me and I blurted out, 'I get it! A semicolon between two related independent clauses.' And, gleefully, Abby broke out into the most beautiful laughter and said 'yes!'"

Lily's smile turned into a laugh. "Oh! That's so funny!"

"What cracked us up even more was all of the confused stares we got, even from a few of my fellow teachers. Abby was thrilled to find a fellow grammar enthusiast. From that moment on, it seemed like we had been best friends forever. Ten minutes later, we discovered that her Irish great-grandfather was from the same place Patrick was born: Glengarriff in County Cork. Such a beautiful town on the Beara Peninsula."

"I didn't know any of this."

"Probably because there was always so much going on in our everyday lives to talk about it. But I'll tell you this, Lily: more than any of the things we had in common, our spirits simply connected."

"You lost your best friend. And here I am being so selfish talking about myself."

"Oh, no! Not at all, sweetie." Kady moved over on the couch

and gave her a hug. "Having you in my life is like keeping a piece of Abby while gaining a new friend."

"Because I look so much like her?"

"Not at all. Despite your physical resemblance, you are a unique human being, and I've never seen you any differently."

"That's good. Do you cry about her?" Lily frowned. "I cry myself to sleep most nights."

"Oh my goodness, yes. There were a couple nights I slept in the guest room so as not to disturb Patrick … much to his dismay. Usually, he will comfort me until I fall asleep. He doesn't want me to be alone." She sighed. "I've never been so distraught in my life. Abby was the sister I never had, my confidant, my partner in crime … the dearest friend one could ever have. I feel as if when people look at me now, they're only seeing half a person … or a ghostly image. That's how much I miss your mum."

"I'm so grateful for you, Kady. You understand things I can't talk about with anyone else. I hope you know I'm here for you too, okay?"

Kady smiled as a tear fell. "You're a special soul, Lily Sheppard. I hope we can prop each other up and develop our own friendship, if that's good for you."

"That's wonderful for me." She paused. "I think I better go. I don't want to, but I have to buy things for the house because that's what I do now. I hope Char hasn't complained to Dad that I didn't scramble her eggs. I don't want another note, or worse … a lecture."

Kady touched Lily's cheek. "I wish I could say, 'this too shall pass,' but I have neither a say nor control in any of this. Between you and me, this is wrong, Lily."

"Remember that mood board I made for fashion school? It's something all students do. We post inspirational images and things like that."

"Oh, tell me about it. I'd love to know more."

"I can't. There's no point. And last night, before I went to bed, I destroyed it. I ripped the fabric samples, and then I tore the paint swatches and all of the photos I'd been collecting for years. I only kept three things: Mum's engagement photo, pressed wildflowers from Uncle Ellis and Aunt Millie's garden in Bibury, and antique buttons from Granny's wedding dress. Then, I went outside and stomped on the board until I broke it. I threw the entire thing into the trashcan, under rotting garbage, so it would be every bit as nonexistent as my future plans. And you know what? I felt even worse. Because after I did all that, memories of Mum inspiring me to create the board started drifting back to me. I thought about how heartbroken she would be. And then I hated myself for doing it. I hated myself so much. But at least I kept her photo, the flowers, and the buttons. I cherish those." Lily frowned. "I wanted to blame Dad for pushing me to do that, but I have to own this one."

Kady dropped her head in sadness.

Lily felt as if she could see the angry words festering inside Kady's head, screaming to be spoken, demanding to be heard by her father. Through the tears that streaked her face, she reached over and hugged her mother's best friend as tight as she could. Then, barely choking out a good-bye, she left.

CHAPTER FIVE

Willow stood under the archway in the dining room and watched Lily as she robotically set the dinner table.

Placing the last napkin under a fork, Lily noticed her youngest sister gazing at her. "Hey, there."

"Hi, Lills. Didn't mean to freak you out by staring."

Lily walked over and gave her a hug. "You could never freak me out. Did you have a nice time with Isabelle?"

"Well, sort of. We were sitting on her bed streaming this movie, a love story, but then one of the characters got into this horrible car accident. I burst out crying, and Issy felt so bad because she didn't know that was going to happen. All she wanted to do was spend some happy time with me. When her mother heard me crying, she came in, and they both tried to make me feel better."

"Did that help?"

"A little. But it helped me the most when Issy's cat Brucie came over to me … he's such a sweet boy. He's a brown-and-white tabby, and his paws look like he's wearing three brown socks and one white one. He must have known I was upset because he started rubbing up against me, and then he settled in my lap. He didn't want to leave. I could have sat there with him forever."

Lily put her hands on Willow's shoulders. "What if I ask Dad if we can get a cat for you? Do you think that would help?"

Willow brightened. "Do you think he would agree? I would love that more than anything! You know I've always wanted one so much."

"I do." Lily went back to setting the table. "The only reason you couldn't have one before is because Mum was so allergic."

"I hope Dad will say yes. That would be so awesome." Willow looked through the dining room and fixed her gaze on the bay window in the living room. "Oh, no!"

"What? What are you looking at?" Lily glanced out the window but saw nothing that wasn't usually there.

Willow twisted her mouth. "You'll see."

Seconds later, the front door opened, and Charlotte hurried in and dropped her backpack by the stairs with a thud. Seeing her sisters in the dining room, she hurried through the living room and walked over to them, a sly smile on her face.

Charlotte stood sideways and touched her hair. "I know, I look totally 'gorge' and you guys can't stand it."

"What color is that?" Willow asked, staring at her.

"Vampire Blood, Wild Cherry, and Angry Red."

"Cute cut," Lily said, refusing to give Charlotte the distressed response she was anticipating. "Who did the layers?"

"Francesca's sister, Camille, did it. And her boyfriend did the piercing." Charlotte turned to face them, showing off the silver nose ring on her left nostril.

"I like it." Lily smiled. "Camille is way talented."

"Dad is *so* not going to like that ring in your nose," Willow said.

Lily shrugged. "I guess we'll have to let him know how cool it is."

Charlotte fumed, her disappointment over Lily's agreeable

reaction all too visible.

"I'm guessing you did your makeup and nails," Lily said. "Nice."

"Black as Death nail polish. And the makeup is totally my creation."

"You have a talent for it." Lily studied her face. "You've learned a lot from all of the videos you watch. You get better all the time."

"Where did you get that black skull shirt?" Willow asked. "You are so goth."

"I'm self-expressing. Not trying to fit into any labels. This is me. I'm tired of only wearing my personality on the inside. And now I'm going upstairs."

"Don't forget to do your homework," Willow said.

Charlotte snarled at her and hurried out of the room.

Willow turned to Lily. "I said that so you wouldn't have to."

"Aww. That was so sweet. But don't worry. I'll be okay." *Maybe in another lifetime.*

A doubtful look on her face, Willow turned to go. "Guess I better do my homework too." She paused. "Hope Dad doesn't do a total freak when he sees Char."

"I'll handle him."

"That's what Mum always said."

As Willow walked away, Lily let several expletives fly in the privacy of her thoughts before heading into the kitchen to finish making dinner.

"I'm impressed by the table you set," Dalton told Lily as he took his seat at the dining room table.

Willow, in her chair, looked up at Lily, who was standing by the table. "I know you worked hard to make everything pretty."

"Thank you," Lily said to both of them, unable to provide a smile to accompany her words.

Dalton peered at Charlotte's empty seat. "Is my middle daughter looking particularly invisible tonight, or do I need to change the prescription for my glasses?" He grinned ever so slightly.

"Um, no, she's more visible than ever," Willow said.

"I see. Well, actually, no I don't. Where is she?"

"I guess still in her room." Willow pulled her phone out of her pocket. "I can call her and tell her to come down."

"This house is quite a comfortable size. But not so large that we need to call one another."

"Here she comes now," Lily said. "I'll go get dinner."

As Lily passed under the archway to the kitchen, Charlotte sauntered in and took her seat. She looked around nonchalantly as if nothing had changed.

Willow glanced at Charlotte, then at her father, where her gaze remained.

Dalton, who had picked up the glass of water at his place, put it down, his eyes landing on and sticking to Charlotte. After examining her for a good thirty seconds, he spoke: "When your mum was growing up in England, the family often dressed for their evening meal. Dressing for dinner and 'playing dress-up' for dinner, however, are two entirely different and distinct things."

"Who's playing dress-up?" Charlotte looked at her father, then at Willow, her gaze continuing through the archway until it reached Lily, standing by the kitchen table and tossing a salad in the large wooden bowl that sat atop it. "Oh, you mean that apron Lily is wearing."

Willow gulped and shot a glance at Charlotte, then looked at her father.

"I have a sense of humor, Charlotte. In fact, it was your

mother who taught me that laughing often lessens the fear and the drear of daily life. But let's not be silly … especially when a total metamorphosis appears before my eyes."

Charlotte looked at Willow. "Be sure to look that long M-word up. Drear too. I think it's from the dark ages or something. Or maybe just England."

Willow cast her eyes downward, as if doing so would absolve her of any association with her next-eldest sibling.

As Lily walked into the dining room and placed the large salad bowl at the head of the table, close to her father, Charlotte spoke to her. "Dad thinks you look completely different in that apron."

Willow put the palm of her hand over her mouth in dread, then looked at each family member.

Lily gave Charlotte a hard stare as she took her seat. "Yeah. Big change for sure. It's so … apron-y."

Dalton fixed his gaze on Charlotte. "I'm not sure what element of the human artwork before me I should comment on first." He picked up the salad tongs and filled his bowl, then passed it to Lily, who sat closest to him on the side of the table to his right. As Lily quietly filled her bowl with salad, Dalton continued to speak. "I don't suppose that's a wig you're wearing."

Charlotte tugged at her hair as hard as she could. "Nope. All mine."

"Help yourself to salad," he said to her, nodding toward Lily, who was holding the bowl for her to take.

Charlotte scooped out a small amount, then put the bowl in the middle of the table where Willow could reach it.

"I suppose that shocking representation of the color burgundy washes out," Dalton said. "Or grows out."

"It's not a temporary color, and I don't want to let it grow out."

"I must be clairvoyant. I had a feeling you would say that." He took a bite of his salad. "Excellent dressing, Lily. Like your mother made it."

Lily nodded in response but said nothing.

After a few more bites of salad, Dalton returned his attention to Charlotte. "I'm concerned about the mutilation to the cartilage on your honker."

Charlotte burst out laughing. "My honker? Ha ha ha!"

"Only trying to infuse a bit of lightness where I'm disinclined to see any. Please tell me that ring is merely an accessory that clips rather than pierces."

"Nope. I'm afraid it pierces right through my honker." Charlotte laughed while her family looked at her.

"I can't imagine piercings are legal under the age of eighteen in California," Dalton said. "Except with parental permission, which you clearly did not have."

Charlotte gulped. "Um ...."

"Did you forge my name? Or God forbid your mother's? Truth, Charlotte."

"No, um, Camille's boyfriend did the piercing in Francesca's room."

"Wasn't that thoughtful of him. Does this piercer have a name?"

"Um ...."

"Um what? Um Smith, Um Jones?"

"Alex. I don't know his last name, and they're only piercings, Dad. His equipment was totally sterile."

Dalton sat in silence for a moment as his daughters watched the contemplative look they knew so well.

"I'm not going to press this any further, Charlotte. But no more piercings, especially while you're underage. Understood?" He studied her face, paying particular attention to one side of it. "And I see that you've added several holes to your left earlobe. Looks like you have five earrings where one used to be."

"Six, actually. I was gonna go for seven, but then I thought ...

nah. I don't like attracting too much attention to myself."

Dalton exhaled to indicate his diminishing patience.

"You said that humor helps to get rid of fear and whatever that word was ... drear?" Charlotte challenged him.

"I'll admit it; the word is a bit archaic, but it's the way your mother said it to me. And I cherish the memory as I cherished her. And yes, she did believe humor was the best way to diffuse unpleasantness."

"What's unpleasant about me?" Charlotte tightened her jaw.

"Nothing is unpleasant, but I do find that black lipstick rather alarming. Silly me. I also prefer my daughter not to look like someone who has been punched in both eyes by Rocky Balboa."

"Going into the kitchen to get dinner," Lily announced as she stood.

"So," Charlotte said, leaning back in her chair, "you're not happy with ... let's see: my hair, my nose, my ear, my eyes, or my mouth. Did I miss anything?"

"Perhaps that large skull on your shirt is a bit morbid, considering the grief and trauma this family is going through ... that *you* are going through and have been through."

"This shirt has nothing to do with what happened to Mum. It's self-expression. My whole world is different now, and I am too. It's how I'm dealing, okay? Besides, after you read the will, you said you thought I'd make a nice living as a makeup artist. Do you think that people with zero imagination get noticed ... or go anywhere in the business? Because they don't. Creativity is the key to my future, and it's not something I only turn on when I go to school. I need to think it, wear it, and *be* it ... *now*. It's how I roll and how I deal."

"Emphatically and well stated," Dalton said as Lily placed a plate of linguine with marinara sauce in front of him. "I'm less than thrilled, but we all have our individual needs."

"I have an individual need!" Willow exclaimed.

Dalton smiled and looked at his youngest daughter. "Oh, what's that, honey?"

Willow looked helplessly at Lily, who was still serving the pasta.

"Oh," Lily said, realizing her sister was prompting her to speak. "Willow is wondering if she can get a cat. Her friend Isabelle's cat, Brucie, was quite a comfort to her today, and she was hoping she could have one of her own. It's something that's been on her wish list for a long time."

Surprised, Dalton looked at Charlotte and then at Willow. "Well, I don't see any reason why not. Sadly, your mother's allergy is no longer an issue, and we all need our ways to cope with this grief. I need to be assured that you'll be fully responsible for the animal's care."

"I totally will, Dad. Thank you so much." She turned to Lily, who had sat down again. "Can we go to the pound this weekend? Like Saturday."

"Sure, Wills. I'm having lunch with Hannah before she goes to work, so I can come home and pick you up after that. Sound good?"

"Perfect. Thank you so much."

"Cats can live to be twenty," Charlotte said to her father. "Willow might be off to college while the cat's still young. Then what?"

Dalton finished chewing his food. "Perhaps, if Willow rents an apartment, she can take the cat with her. If not, Lily is likely to be here. We'll work something out. The cat will be cared for, and that's a good six years or more from now."

Lily turned ashen and felt as if her chair was sinking lower by the second.

Noticing her pale face, Charlotte smirked, and Willow frowned.

"Um ... then maybe I shouldn't—"

"No!" Lily said. "You should totally get a cat. We'll go Saturday afternoon. That's a promise."

"You sure?" Willow asked with an apprehensive smile.

"Absolutely."

"Well, good," Dalton said. "That's settled. Make sure you get a scratching post and the cat knows how to use it. You'll have to keep the cat in your room until we're confident it won't shred any furniture and knows how to use a litter box properly."

"They all learn the first time they use the box," Willow said. "As I've heard."

Charlotte turned to address Lily. "So, did you have a nice time with Kady Harrigan today?"

"How did you know I was visiting with Kady?"

"When we were out in the car with Camille, we passed by the Harrigans' house, and I saw your car there. I'm smart that way."

Dalton took a few more mouthfuls of pasta before speaking. Finally, he looked up, his focus going straight to Lily. "Why were you with Kady Harrigan today?"

Lily could feel the tears forming in her eyes but managed to keep them at bay. "She was Mum's best friend. Talking to her was helpful. For both of us."

"I see." He took another mouthful of pasta before continuing. "Kady is a lovely woman. But I prefer you socialize with your peers."

"I do. But they didn't know Mum the way Kady did."

Charlotte grinned. "Isn't a katydid like a large insect or something? I think it's some kind of grasshopper, and it sings its name. 'Katydid, katydid, katydid ....'" She turned to Lily. "And you thought I didn't pay attention in science class."

"That was amusing, Charlotte," Dalton said pleasantly before addressing Lily again. "I understand Kady's special connection to your mum. But I'd prefer you spend time with your own friends. Not your Mum's."

"But Kady is my friend too."

"Thank you for understanding and respecting my wishes. No more on this topic."

Why don't you put a muzzle on me, Dad? You can take it off and on when I'm allowed to speak. Maybe like if you pre-approve what I'm going to say. She snarled, not caring how obvious her discontent was. *How much more do you want to steal from me before I lose my mind? First my life, now my friend ... I'm seriously beginning not to like you.* She stared at her food.

Willow looked sorrowfully at her oldest sister while they all ate in silence for several minutes.

Finally, Dalton spoke again. "On a different subject, Lily, I have a custom-made Oxford shirt that needs ironing. It's blue with Italian collars." He laughed. "Well, I don't need to describe it because it's lying on your bed. You can't miss it. I need it ironed for tomorrow. I have an important meeting with the board and need to look my best."

Willow contemplated the last of the linguine on her plate.

Lily could barely meet his eyes. "Uh ...."

"Please don't tell me you don't know how to iron. Your mother taught you all about design, sewing, and yes, even ironing. So, it shouldn't be any trouble for you. And I will be most appreciative."

Do it yourself! "Okay, then, what if I go do it now?"

"Before you've finished dinner, cleared the table, and done the dishes? No, absolutely not." He took the last bites of the pasta from his plate. "This was divine. Which one of our friends cooked it?"

"Actually, I did. I made it fresh."

Dalton beamed. "That's wonderful. Have I told you how proud I am of you, honey? Dinner was delicious. The table looked beautiful, and I couldn't be happier with how well you're adjusting. Now, I'm going to retreat to my den to polish my speech for tomorrow. Going to make a nightcap and get to it. Please don't disturb me unless it's important." He looked at each one of his daughters. "I love you all dearly. Please don't ever forget that."

The girls all muttered good night, but no one spoke until Dalton had fixed a drink and headed off to the sanctity of his den on the opposite side of the house.

"I'll help you clear and do the dishes, Lills," Willow said.

"Thanks. That would be a big help. Being in your company always makes me feel better."

"Oh, sorry I can't help," Charlotte said. "Still having vertigo from the accident." She looked at Willow. "That means dizziness."

"I know what it means. And you are lucky that Dad let you get away with all the stuff you've done to yourself. I can't believe you let Alex drill all of those holes into you."

Charlotte laughed. "He did more than that. Wanna see the skull and crossbones on my ass?"

"Ugh. I don't think so. Are you even for real?"

"What Willow said," Lily added. "And it's totally illegal to get a tattoo if you're under eighteen. I remember when Hannah tried to get one when she was sixteen. The guy told her to leave the shop and come back when she was legal. Tell me you're kidding."

"I'm not kidding. And I didn't break any laws. About a year ago, Alex bought this professional tattoo kit for not even two hundred buckaroos. He's a good artist, and he knows how to use the guns. He's done tats on several people already."

"I still hope you're playing," Lily said.

"I'll be more than happy to moon you both right here." Charlotte got up from the table. She put both hands on the top button of her distressed black jeans. "Say the word, and I'll 'drop 'em.'" She looked at her sisters' stunned faces, shrugged, then started to walk away. "Okay then. My ass going once, going twice ...." She stopped and turned back to face the table. "By the way, don't you guys think about telling Dad about my butt modification. I mean, I can't stop you, but it's probably not the best idea. If he goes after my friend's sister's boyfriend, it won't be good for anyone."

"Is that a threat?" Lily asked.

"Nah. Just a wisecrack." Charlotte laughed to herself.

Lily rolled her eyes, wishing she hadn't before she even finished doing so. "What you do to your ass is your business … after you turn eighteen. So no more tats. Good night, Char."

As Charlotte walked away, Willow looked across the table at Lily. "Do you think she did all of that to get to you?"

"Yes and no. What she did definitely suits her personality, but yeah, doing it now, doing *all* of that now … yeah, I think she's testing me. And I don't care how many tats she gets, but I know Dad would blame me somehow."

"Did you notice how she keeps saying 'you guys' because Mum hated that?"

"Yup. Hard to miss. But that's fine. I'm not her mother, and she can do what she wants with her life."

Willow looked mournfully at her sister. "I wish you could too."

CHAPTER SIX

"It's Lily. Can you hear me?"

"Yes, honey, I can. But you've got me worried. What's wrong? Where are you?"

"I'm embarrassed to tell you." She sighed. "I'm in my bedroom closet. With the door almost closed."

"Are you serious? Why on earth …?"

"Oh, Kady. Char saw my car at your house this afternoon, blabbed it at dinner, and Dad pretty much told me not to see you anymore. He said you're a lovely woman, but he prefers I only socialize with my peers. When I tried to explain, he cut me off with some kind of thank-you-for-respecting-my-wishes BS. I'm seriously going to lose it."

"This isn't good. I was afraid this might happen."

"You were? How come? I know I told you that I didn't think he'd like the two of us communicating. But I said that because I knew he would hate the idea of you knowing how he's rearranged my life. I never expected to be forbidden to see you, though. He didn't use that word, but that's what he meant."

"Your first instinct wasn't wrong, Lily. No doubt you recall that I asked your father if he would allow me to step in and help assume some of your mother's responsibilities?"

"That would be hard to forget."

"As you know, he gave me the speediest 'no thank you' I've ever received. I think he's far more concerned with what I might tell *you* than with what you might tell me."

"Like what?"

"Nothing specific I can state now, but I was your mum's best friend for nearly nineteen years. We couldn't have been closer. Dalt didn't like it, but he knew Abby confided in me and that he had no power to change that. He doesn't have any idea what she shared and what she kept private. What he does know, however, is that your mother would not approve of the way he's handling things ... and that as her best friend, I know that, and I don't approve either. So, whereas your peers can only surmise that your mum wouldn't agree, I can say so with certitude."

Lily moved to the back wall and slid down with a clunk. "Now I'm sitting on the floor of my closet. Sweet, huh? I think I rearranged my glutes on landing. Ow! That hurt. Oh, and you know those embroidered jeans that Mum decorated for me? They just slapped me in the face. Then, there's an old sneaker under my left thigh, and I can't even move an inch without getting a high heel up my butt. Sorry to be crude, but I'm so angry, Kady. I'm so effing angry. I'm almost nineteen, and I'm taking cover in my closet like it's a foxhole in a war zone ... all because I want to talk to a wonderful and caring friend. This is insanity."

"Good grief, Lily ...."

"Oh, and after I set the table, made, and served dinner earlier, I was informed that there was a shirt waiting for me on my bed ... Dad's blue Oxford ... and that it needed ironing for tomorrow. I wanted to tell him to iron his own effing shirt so bad, but I didn't." She fumed. "And I won't go into it now, but during dinner ... wait for it ... he implied he thinks I'll still be here in six years ... running the house. After Wills and Char are gone! I can't even … I was so blown away; I didn't say anything. I couldn't. If I had, I might still be screaming at him."

"That's outrageous! If it means anything at all, you're doing a more-than-admirable job of keeping your cool."

"For now, Kady. Because eventually, I think this is gonna drive me over the edge. I'll be a raving lunatic because I'm totally headed in that direction." Lily swatted the hem of a dress that brushed her eyelids. "It's not right to bother you with all of this. I shouldn't have called."

"No, I'm so grateful that you did. You never need to ever apologize for your healthy reaction to an insane and grievous situation. I'll always be here for you. And know this: my loyalty now is to you and to your mother, not to your father. I respect Dalt, and I take his suffering into account, but it ends there. And don't worry; we'll find a way to get together. You can always call me. Change my name in your phone to that of a phantom school friend. Do whatever you need to. I'm not going anywhere."

"Thank you, Kady. I needed to hear you say all that. I'd better go before he finds me in the closet. What's your middle name?"

"Samantha. Why?"

"That's the name I'm going to put in my phone. Does Dad know it?"

"I would highly doubt it. And if we're speaking on the phone and he's nearby, call me any name at all. I'll understand. One more thing."

"What's that?"

"Try not to look too far ahead. For now, let's deal with this situation in the smallest increments possible. Please, call or text me anytime. Know that I'll meet you anywhere you'd like. Allow me to be your lifeline. You are so loved, Lily. Please know that."

"Thank you so much, Kady." She paused. "I can't believe it!"

"What?"

"I swear, I'm not crazy—not yet anyway—but I heard Mum speak to me. Like a few seconds ago. She said I should have faith that everything will be okay." Lily's breathing became labored as she listened for a response. "Kady, are you there?"

"I am."

"Is something wrong?"

"I wasn't going to say anything because when I heard your mum thank me, I thought my grief and my imagination had joined forces to play tricks on me. But then you said what you did … and now, I believe Abby *was* here. I have goose bumps!"

Tears rushed down Lily's face as if they were in a race to reach the base of her neck. "Me too. But it's so comforting to believe Mum is looking out for me, for all of us. I don't think I'm going to tell anyone, though. I feel like telling Willow, but in a way, it might make her pain ever greater. And other people might not believe me. But I know Mum is here, and so do you."

"It's our beautiful secret. If you ever want to share, that will be up to you. But I won't say a word."

"And that's the lowdown since I saw you and your mom last Sunday," Lily said quietly, looking around the restaurant for the fourth time to make sure nobody was in earshot.

"Mom hasn't stopped asking about you," Hannah said. "She would never want to badmouth your dad, but she practically went off the rails hearing him tell you to quit the diner."

"I know. I saw her give him a dirty look."

"I hope he didn't see that." Hannah picked up a quarter of her club sandwich.

"No, your mom is cool. She knew he wasn't looking her way."

"She's gonna be blown away when I tell her this."

Lily poked a square of feta cheese in her Greek salad with a fork. "Actually, I'd appreciate it if you don't tell her anything, okay? Not now."

"Why not?"

"Because every part of me hopes that my dad will realize what he's doing and change. Yeah, it'll be too late for me to go to fashion school because I already axed all of my plans ...." Lily choked on her words. "But I still hope he'll come around. Not to mention that I don't want all of Altrusia knowing our business. Sorry. I'm super paranoid right now."

Hannah picked up a piece of bacon that had fallen out of her sandwich. "Yeah ... I can see that. You keep scanning the room. See, you're doing it now ... again. What are you even looking for?"

"I don't know." Lily made a gallant attempt to stab a Kalamata olive with her fork, but failed. "I told him I was having lunch with you. Maybe I'm worried someone who knows him might overhear ...."

"You know what I think?" Hannah lowered her voice. "You're almost nineteen. You're a legal adult. I think you ought to hightail it outta Dodge before things get worse. Come to Boston with me and Rob."

"What? Seriously. I thought I heard you say—"

"Oh, shit!" Hannah smacked her forehead. "That came out in a bad way."

Lily waited for a server to pass the table before answering. "You think? Are you moving to Boston?"

"I was going to tell you, but then, when you told me about Ray going to Princeton, I thought maybe I should wait, or at least be a bit more delicate about sharing my news."

"When are you leaving?"

"In a month or two. Not sure yet. I wanted to leave Altrusia last year, when I graduated from high school, but Rob was still finishing his undergrad degree at Berkeley, for one. As you know, he was crazy busy with school, so there was no point in us moving in together then. I didn't want to start college until we knew for sure where he'd go to med school. I told you all this, Lills. Also how I decided to keep working so I'd have even more money when the time came. I just didn't expect to be going so far and under these circumstances. Um ...."

Lily finished chewing a mouthful of salad and laid her fork down. "I'm shocked because we've been such close friends, and you never told me you had plans to go anywhere. Ever. What's up with that, Han?"

"What's up is that I thought we'd probably never go farther than Marin County."

"So what changed?"

Hannah finished the third quarter of her sandwich and wiped her mouth with the napkin. "You mean what didn't change. Rob got into Harvard Medical for one."

"Wow. Tell him I send my congratulations. It's pretty phenomenal that Rob and Ray were both accepted by their dream schools."

"And you withdrew from yours. That sucks."

"I'm happy for them. I'm not the kind of person who wants to see other people unhappy because I am. You should know that. I'm just in shock."

"We are too. Rob thought he'd be going to UCSF School of Medicine. But this will work out well because his parents are in Lowell, and his mother doesn't work and mine has a full-time job."

"I'm lost. Why would that matter?"

Hannah sighed. "Um ... because I'll need someone to help me with the baby."

Lily's eyes widened as her jaw dropped. "You're pregnant?"

"Yeah. Passed my first trimester three days ago. Remember last Sunday at your house when I said I wasn't feeling well … that's why. And then there were a couple of times at the diner when I felt sick out of nowhere."

"Gee, I should be a detective. Not."

"I kept it well hidden. We didn't want to tell anyone until I got to the fourth month."

"I can understand that. Will you bring the baby home at Christmas?"

"Oh, shit." Hannah blew out a puff of air. "No, Lills. I won't, because my parents are moving to Massachusetts in early July, and Rob and I are getting married two weeks later."

"I don't know what to say."

"It's a lot to take in. Even for me. It feels surreal telling you."

"So your parents are okay leaving the Sacramento area after all of these years? Your brother's still in San Francisco, right?"

"He is. But he flies to the East Coast on business at least three times a year. As for my parents, they'll miss a lot of people, and so will I, but my dad is cool about it. He's from Rhode Island, so he's got mega fam there. As you know, he works from home when he's not traveling, so moving isn't an issue. As for Mom, she doesn't want to be three thousand miles from her first grandchild, so she's good to go. Her company is massive, and she's getting a transfer to their Boston office. Rob's mom is going to help me with babysitting, and eventually I'll go to college part-time."

Lily played with the locket around her neck that her mother had given to her on her eighteenth birthday. "You've got your life worked out. I'm happy you'll all be together. I'm going to miss you … like I'll miss Ray, but that's how life is: people move on. Besides, you're almost twenty-one. I didn't exactly expect you to work at McCauley's Diner forever."

Hannah reached across the table and grabbed Lily's hand.

"What I was trying to say before I spilled all of this without softening the blow … is that you're an adult too, Lills. You'll be nineteen in June. You don't have to stay here and play house. Your sisters aren't babies. Leave already! Your dad can't stop you. His hands are tied. And you've got your inheritance now. *Adios*, Altrusia. C'mon, Lills. Say it."

Lily pouted. "I can't. I hate the mess my life is right now, but I love my family. And Willow needs me desperately. Leaving her after our mum has died? I don't think she'd recover. And I know I wouldn't because I would hate myself forever and miss the heck out of her. And Char drives me up the wall, but she needs me too. Even if right now I'm only someone to direct her anger at." She paused. "The only problem is that it's hard not to direct it back. As for my dad, I think he could do things differently."

"And you're okay with that? Having your dad turn your life into something unrecognizable, dictate what to do with practically every minute of it, and stomp on your dreams like they're cockroaches? What the hell is wrong with you, Lily? You can't be okay with any of this!"

Lily blinked and stared at Hannah. She opened her mouth, but only silence fell out.

"Oh shit again." Hannah dropped her head. "That came out all wrong. I meant to say that … uh …."

Lily folded her arms. "Don't bother. You can't even come up with something. You know why? Because you said exactly what you think, and you know it."

Hannah took a slow and deliberate breath. "I meant that you shouldn't let your father trap you into a life you don't want … and that you know you have the right to leave."

"My mum is dead. At forty-three. And my family is in shock. I have to do what I can. And I have to believe that when some time has passed, my father will wake the eff up … even if I have to scream in his ear to get him to do it. Then, when my sisters are a bit older and they've had time to adjust, I'll be able to leave with a clear conscience."

"Your dad is taking you for a pushover, Lills. Someone has to tell you that, and I guess that someone is me."

"He's not making me do this because I'm weak, Hannah. But because I'm strong."

"Oh, Lily ... puh-leeze, girlfriend. Do you have Stockholm syndrome now? You're deluding yourself, and you're changing everything around to justify putting up with this nonsense. Why are you even going into this family loyalty bullshit when you'd be leaving for LA in four months if your father hadn't pulled the plug on school? From here, that's a six-hour drive on the boring I-5 route if you're lucky. LA isn't exactly around the corner. Don't you see that you're contradicting yourself?"

"No. Because if I were going to LA, I'd still have four months with my family, and I wouldn't be so far away that I couldn't see them at least once a month. But now that school is off, I don't see the point of leaving just because I'm a legal adult. I'd much rather leave with my father's blessing than have him hate me right after my mum has died."

"He should worry about you hating *him*." Hannah face turned red with anger. "I don't know why you axed your school plans either. You could have gone anyway."

"No, I couldn't. For one, I didn't have the money my parents were going to give me for tuition and housing. So there's that. Kind of a major thing, you know?"

"You've got money now. Use it."

"Mostly in property. And no way I'm messing with that. I have to stay and help ... for the time being."

"You keep telling yourself these things, Lills, and see how life works out for you. Time has a way of putting sneakers on its feet and running right past you. Even though I'm still young, I see people wasting their lives because they thought they had time."

"You're making my life sound so hopeless."

Hannah pressed on. "I want you to wake up and think about your future. You're so beautiful, Lily, but you're going to end up being an old maid. I get that you've never liked Ray as more than a good friend, and I know you might have stayed with Brian if he hadn't moved away … though maybe not … because he was kind of a douche. But that relationship was in your sophomore year … an eternity ago, and I haven't seen you making eyes at anyone since."

"Actually, there was a guy at this party in Roseville who blew me away. I think I could have fallen in love with him. But Brian pulled me away … knowing he was moving to Virginia in a few days. I guess that's what macho pricks do."

"You never told me about some other guy. How did you even meet anyone else if you were with Brian?"

"Because he was outside flirting with someone else's girlfriend. That's how."

"And how long did you talk to the other guy?"

"About a half hour. Maybe a bit more."

Hannah made a face. "So you talked to some dude for a whole half hour, like years ago, and you could have fallen in love with him, not knowing fuck all about him, but since then, you haven't found anyone else who remotely interests you? Is that what you're saying? Sounds pretty fantasyland to me, if you wanna keep it real."

"Is that a bad thing … that I haven't met another guy who interests me that way? Well, it's not bad, and I'm not in any fantasyland. You sound like you're dissing me, Han."

"I'm only pointing out that you haven't looked for anyone, and you know it."

"Maybe because I feel like if the right person comes along, I'll see him. Like that guy at the party I never got to know."

Hannah distorted her face in disgust. "If you end up being an old maid, don't say I didn't warn you."

"That's extreme, Han. Like way out there."

"How about Joe? He's had a thing for you going on three years now."

"So what? I never liked Joe that way. He's sweet … and funny … in a goofball kind of way, but I'm not attracted to him. Besides, I wouldn't date a coworker." She thought for a moment. "I guess I might have if there was real chemistry."

"Do you even *want* a man? Ever?"

"Of course. Maybe not right now, with the hell that my life is, but absolutely. I just don't want a guy so I can say I 'have someone.' I'm more of a loner in that sense. You know that. When I find the right man, I'll know it. And I'll be happier than ever."

"Yeah, okay. Keep that lame script going, Lills. I hope you won't be a lifetime loner. Trapped at home playing mommy and 'lady of the house' while the people you know have all moved on."

"Wow, Hannah. Thanks for that post-apocalyptic picture you painted of my family life. It's kind of obvious that you've lost all respect for me. And probably everyone at the diner has too because nobody has returned any of my texts. Not one person has contacted me in any way since my mum's funeral. Not even Joe … who supposedly 'likes me so much.'"

"Probably because it's tough to know what to say to someone in your … uh … situation."

Lily felt her body go limp from Hannah's revelation. "Are you serious? My friends have dumped me because of my 'situation?' So nobody respects me anymore because I'm taking care of my family?"

"It's not that, Lills. I think people don't know what to say. Plus, you're not exactly available to hang out, and probably nobody wants to make you feel bad with all of the plans they're making when you're not doing anything. You know?"

"*Not doing anything?* I don't even know what to say. But clearly I was right. You guys don't respect me anymore."

"I can't speak for other people, but I totally respect you, Lily.

If I didn't, I would go and let you flounder in this nightmare your father has created for you. It's *because* I care about you that I have to do so with tough love. Subtle isn't going to make you budge."

"Get a clue. Neither is anything you're saying." Not even trying to stop the tears, Lily let them roll down her face. "I'm happy about your baby, I'm happy about your move, and I'm happy about Harvard and your upcoming wedding. It's great when the pieces all come together, isn't it? That's clearly not happening for me right now, but you don't have to make me feel like it's my fault for loving my family. And you explained why you stayed at the diner for over a year after your high school graduation. I haven't even had mine yet. So don't be a hypocrite."

Hannah handed her empty iced tea glass to the server who had come by to see if they needed refills. She softened. "I know this. When you give in, even for the best of reasons, people will expect you to give forever. They'll accuse you of abandoning them when you stop to live your own life. I saw it happen with my aunt Delia. And you know where she is now … God rest her soul. I'm telling you, Lily, despite this tragedy, you'd better look out for yourself because nobody else will. Leave town soon, or you'll regret it. Oh, to be clear, when I stayed here for a year after graduation, I wasn't giving into anyone's demands. I made that decision myself. So there's the difference, and I'm not a hypocrite."

Lily reached into her purse, pulled a twenty-dollar bill out of her wallet, and laid it on the table. She stood and looked at Hannah. "You're lucky you haven't lost a parent so tragically and can't relate. Unlike your mother, mine won't ever see her grandchildren." She picked up her napkin and wiped a stray tear away. "I don't know what else to say. I'll never forgive myself if I don't try to do the right thing, as much as it's hurting me. I'm sorry you don't get it. And maybe I'm the one who doesn't understand, but I guess I'll figure that out in time. In the meantime, I've got a lot of things to 'not do.' I wish you a happy life. Good-bye, Hannah."

"We're in luck, Wills," Lily said as she pulled into the last parking space in the crowded lot. "Must be a good sign."

Willow, sitting in the passenger seat, turned to her sister with a worried frown. "Are you sure you wanna do this? I want a kitten more than anything in the world, but if it's gonna mess up your life …."

Lily switched off the ignition, unbuckled her seat belt, then shifted to face Willow. "Don't be silly. I'm excited about getting a kitten too." She tugged at Willow's seat belt. "Are you going to take this off? Unless you want to walk into the Altrusia Humane Society with a car attached to you, it might be good to unbuckle. You might start a new fashion trend if you don't, and that's cool too, but you probably won't fit through the doors."

Willow giggled. "You're so sweet to make me laugh when you're so down. I thought you were upset about me getting a kitten because you barely said anything after you came home to pick me up."

"Sorry. I had lunch with Hannah, and things went way differently from what I expected. I guess I zoned out on you there … replaying it all in my head. I shouldn't have let that happen. But none of this has anything to do with you or adopting a kitten." Lily unbuckled Willow's seat belt and smiled. "From now on, my attention is all yours, okay?"

"Thanks!" Willow grabbed the door handle. "I'm so excited."

Five minutes later, surrounded by the sweet sound of meows and human chatter, Lily and Willow walked through the rows of cages, stopping to study each cat.

"Oh, check out these kittens," Willow exclaimed. "There are

four of them in this cage, and they're all so adorable." She stuck a finger through the metal rails, immediately prompting a black-and-white kitten to lick her finger. "It likes me. And look at that one, Lills. It could be Brucie's twin."

"They're all precious. Do you care if it's a boy or girl?"

"I want the one that likes me the best. Look at the black one with the white tail and paws. Totally cool markings. It's almost like it has a little mustache on its face too. Gee, I hope it's a boy."

"Yeah." Lily smiled. "Wouldn't want it to get teased in school."

Willow laughed as she turned to a pet-adoption counselor who was approaching. "Is this black cat with the white tail a boy or a girl?"

"It's boy," the woman told her. "And so is the brown tabby. The other two are girls. Are you looking to adopt?"

"For sure. It's so hard to know which one to pick."

"Have you ever had a cat before?"

"No," Willow said. "But I'm close with my best friend's cat, Brucie. I even know how to clip his nails and brush him. We're BFFs."

"Sounds great. So you know, if you decide to adopt a cat here, we'll have to go through the adoption requirements with you. We'll explain what basic care is required, as well as talk to you about food, exercise, interactive play, and other things."

"Cool."

"Are you looking for an indoor cat or an outdoor one?"

"Only indoors. I would never want a cat roaming around outside."

"Absolutely indoors," Lily confirmed.

The woman smiled. "Good. That's what we like to hear. So, when you find a cat you might be interested in, let me know. I'll take you into one of our little rooms, and you can spend some alone time with it to see if it's there's a love connection." She laughed. "I should also tell you that the adoption fee is one hundred and twenty-five dollars. That includes chipping, shots, and, of course, neutering or spaying. Oh, and the fee includes a first visit with the veterinarian of your choice. And if all that isn't enough, you'll be given some toys to start your cat off to a happy life."

"That sounds great," Lily said.

The counselor turned to Willow: "Be sure to see as many of our furry friends as you can before you decide." She looked at Lily. "Do you rent or own?"

"We live with our … family. Why?"

"In a house that your family owns?"

"Yes."

"Then you should be all set. We're careful not to allow adoptions if the intended home isn't pet friendly. It's heartbreaking to see animals returned." She looked at Willow. "My name is Darlene. Just flag me down when you're ready."

"Thanks. I'm Willow and this is my sister Lily."

"Nice to meet you both. If you'll excuse me, ladies, I see that a prospective parent is trying to get my attention. Hope we'll connect in a bit." Darlene hurried off.

"So, Wills, do you have any idea which kitten you want to meet?"

"Maybe, but like Darlene said, I want to make sure to check out all of the cages. Then I'll decide."

"Let's keep going then." They turned the corner and walked down a new row. "Hey, Wills, you were right. Here are some more kittens."

"Cuuute!" Willow cooed. "Are they adorable or what? This little white one has one green eye and one blue one. And a patch of black on its head." She stuck her finger through the bars. "Cool. I got my first little love bite."

Lily watched as a black-and-white tabby came over to meet her. Immersed in watching the kittens play, she didn't notice that Willow was now staring into a cage a few yards away, the expression on her face completely different from what it had been.

"You okay, Wills? If I didn't know better, I'd think you were sad."

"Because of this cat. See how sad it looks … like it's gonna cry. So now I'm sad too. It's lonely; I can tell."

Willow stuck two fingers into cage and the all-gray cat rubbed up against them. "I think it likes me."

"Would you like to know more about this cat?" Darlene asked, reappearing by the cage.

"Yes, please," Willow said. "It looks so sad."

"You're quite astute." Darlene turned to face the cage. "First, this cat is about a year old, and he's a boy. He came in two days ago because his owner died suddenly. And she was his only caregiver. So, I'd guess he's quite sad and confused."

"I want to go in the little room with him. Can I do that?"

Darlene glanced over at the glass-enclosed spaces. "There appears to be a room free right now." She opened the cage, carefully picked up the cat, and led Lily and Willow to a private area. "I'll leave you ladies here," she said, handing the cat to Willow. "Take all the time you need. We want everyone to be happy … humans and animals alike. Let me know what you decide."

Darlene closed the door behind her as Lily sat down on the wooden bench and let Willow bond with the cat. Immediately, he nuzzled up against her several times, looked up at her, then nuzzled some more.

"Lills, he's purring! I made him purr!"

"He's taken a liking to you. 'A loving' is probably more accurate."

Willow scratched the cat's neck as he continued to purr. "You're such a sweet boy. I came in here to get a baby, but you know what? So many people want kittens, and I know they'll all get homes. You, little gray boy, are so special. I could tell the moment I saw your precious face. You and me both lost our mummy when we were young. It's horrible, isn't it? I mean, there's no warning at all, and then suddenly life is so different. It's only been two weeks since my mum died. I cry every day. Only they didn't put me in a cage like they did to you, and I know what happened to my mummy, even though a part of me will never understand. You'll probably always miss your first human mummy, but I want to be your new mummy, even though I'm twelve. I promise I will love you forever. I'm totally responsible too." She picked up the cat and turned him to face Lily. "This is my oldest sister, Lily. I call her Lills most of the time, and she calls me Wills. But you can call me Mummy, Meow Mummy, or whatever you want. We're so lucky to have Lills to take care of us too." Willow put the cat back on her lap and continued to pet him as he purred. "Lills is like the best sister in the world, and she's the reason I haven't lost my mind."

The cat nuzzled up to her some more, putting his right paw on Willow's hand.

"Oh … this means you want to come home with us, right?"

The cat continued to purr as Willow bent down to kiss him. "I love you so much already."

Lily, tears streaming down her face, looked at Willow. "What are you going to name him? Do you know?"

"Yup." Willow looked into the cat's eyes. "Would it be okay if I called you Quincy? That was my mum's surname before she got married. And you'll be Quincy Sheppard, like she was."

"That's the perfect name. If Mum were watching us, and maybe she is, she'd be so happy." Lily stood and waved at Darlene, who happened to be glancing in their direction.

"Mum would be totally jazzed." Willow laughed. "Only she wouldn't say 'jazzed.' She'd say something like, 'he's absolutely delightful, Willow. I'm chuffed you found such a perfect pet.'"

"Exactly."

Darlene carefully opened the door and closed it behind her. "Looks like some serious bonding has happened here. Is this the cat you want?"

"Totally like a thousand percent," Willow said. "Do we have to wait to take him home?"

"No, you don't. If this were a kitten, then yes, as we would have to spay or neuter it. And if the cat had been found, then we'd have to wait in case an owner turned up. But in this boy's case, he's been surrendered to us, is neutered, and is almost good to go. For some reason, he was never chipped, so we'll have to do that before he leaves. It's all for the best because you'll be able to put his new name and your information on the chip. That information will then be put in a pet recovery database."

"Does the chipping take long?"

"Only a few seconds. We'll insert one between his shoulder blades. Do you know his name?"

"Quincy. Quincy Sheppard."

"Great," Darlene said. "I'll need you to do all of the paperwork. Lily will have to sign because only legal adults can adopt animals. Once all is in order, then Quincy will be chipped, and the three of you will be good to go. And if you're interested, we have our own pet store down the hall to your right. You can get whatever Quincy might need. We do provide a cardboard carrier, but you might want to buy something nicer and more comfortable. Our staff can help you with any questions you may have."

"Thank you," Lily said.

"Yes, thank you," Willow added. "I'll be the best cat mum ever in the world."

Darlene lifted Quincy out of Willow's arms. "I'm going to take him to the clinic. I'll meet you both at the front desk in about five minutes or so."

Willow turned to Lily as Darlene walked away with the cat. "I don't know how to thank you for this … for everything, Lills. I know you're hurting too, but you still work so hard to make my life better."

Swallowing the lump in her throat, Lily smiled and wrapped her arms around Willow with all the tenderness she had to give.

CHAPTER SEVEN

Willow beamed as she looked down at the purring cat on her lap.

"I think you and this little feline fella were meant to be," Dalton said, petting Quincy. "The moment you brought him home, he sniffed out every inch of your room along with the three of us. But it didn't take long for him to hurry back to you."

"He knows I'm his new mummy," Willow said, her eyes shining with pride. "Oh, by the way, Dad, when we were going through the adoption papers, the person who surrendered him to the shelter said that he never scratched any furniture … only the scratching post. So when we got him a new post, we bought some catnip spray for it too."

"That's music to my ears. But we'll still confine Quincy to your room until we're sure that's the situation here. Okay?" Dalton looked through Willow's room into her bathroom. "I see you've got a litter box with a hood. You're going to keep that clean, right?"

"For sure. I'll clean it out every day. And I'm cool if he only stays in my room for a while. This is a big house and I don't want him to get scared by seeing too much of it at once. Besides, I could cuddle in here with him forever."

"It was love at first sight for both of them," Lily said, smiling.

"They'll be great comfort for one another."

"Lucky you, Weeping Willow," Charlotte said. "Something to love you unconditionally."

Dalton turned to Charlotte. "As we all love you, honey."

Charlotte shrugged.

"You know, I'm kind of getting used to that burgundy hair," Dalton told her. "It's going to take me a while on the piercings, though. At forty-seven, I'm a bit set in my ways. Working on that. But I must say, you do have your own sense of style."

Charlotte shrugged again. "I'm going to my room now, okay?" She looked at the cat. "Nice to meet you, Quincy. You're actually super cute."

"Thanks, Char," Willow said.

"Guess she didn't hear you," Lily said, looking across the hall at Charlotte, who was hurrying into her room.

"Lily," Dalton said. "Now that Quincy is settling in nicely, would you mind coming downstairs to my den for a chat?"

"Oh, okay, Dad. Sure." She looked at Willow. "See you two later."

"Ready then?" Dalton asked, nodding toward the door.

"Lead the way."

As soon as they entered the den, Dalton shut the door. "Have a seat on the sofa." He pointed to a small brown corduroy sofa across from a matching armchair, both beneath an impressive wall of books that spanned the length of the room.

Lily sat down and waited for her father to settle. She said nothing as his creased brow cautioned her not to relax.

"I'm concerned about Charlotte," Dalton said. "She's withdrawn, easily angered and irritated. I don't know if you know this, but those are some of the many signs of PTSD. I've been reading up on this." He paused. "You two share a bathroom between your bedrooms. Do you ever hear anything concerning through her bedroom door?"

"Not too much. But I don't exactly eavesdrop."

"What does 'not too much' mean?"

"Well, when I went into the bathroom last night, around three a.m., I heard her moving around. So I guess maybe she's having trouble sleeping. Or maybe she woke up for some reason."

"Disturbed sleep is also another sign of PTSD."

"Yes, but I'm having trouble sleeping too. Mum just died. Doesn't that ever keep you up at night?"

He nodded. "Yes. Sadly, that's all true. But I'm concerned nonetheless."

"Most of the time she has her headphones on, so I don't hear her make much noise."

"I just hope she keeps the volume for that head-splitting music at a safe level. I need you to look into that."

Lily squirmed in her seat. "Dad, telling Char her music is too loud won't go over well. In fact, I can pretty much guarantee she'll turn up the volume to spite me if I do."

"I know your mum was concerned about the dangers of listening to loud music. She warned Charlotte many times that it can lead to hearing loss."

"Yeah, I remember hearing Mum talk to her a few times." Lily fumbled with her locket. "So Char definitely knows she needs to be careful. But Mum warning her about loud music was a totally different thing than if I say anything."

"She knows you're in charge now."

"And she absolutely *hates* it." A pleading look in her eyes begged him to understand. "Besides, I don't think of myself as being 'in charge.' As for Char, I'm trying to be as chill with her as I can, you know?"

"No, I don't know, actually." Dalton sealed his lips as he went into thinking mode. After a minute, he spoke: "Lily, you can't always tell what a person is thinking or feeling from their exterior. Charlotte is likely in a lot of pain and would welcome your comfort and wisdom, whether she shows it or not. I know she can be cocky, obstinate, and incorrigible at times. But that's the pain talking. When we leave a person alone with their suffering for too long, it will often deepen and possibly become utterly incurable."

You think? How about my pain, Dad? You've forbidden me to see the person who has been helping me the most. What about me? What about—

"You had a lovely lunch with a friend today, Lily. Then you had the joy of taking Willow to find a cat. Charlotte was alone in her room the entire time. I'd like you to go back upstairs now and offer her some nurturing."

"I don't think she wants me to, Dad. I need to—"

"She's proud. But she needs and wants her older sister."

"Actually, I distinctly get the impression that she doesn't. She wants Mum."

"Don't we all, Lily. Don't we all." Dalton frowned. "Right now, I'm only trying to manage the things within our control. Which brings me to another matter. Charlotte needs psychological counseling. She's had some in-depth appointments with her GP, but that's not enough. Her doctor suggested that if signs of trauma persist after a month, she should see someone. I know it hasn't been a month yet, but I'd like you to talk to her about the possibility of therapy and how it might expedite her recovery. It's what your mum would have done."

"I'm not Mum! And I'm not in any position to explain the benefits of psychological counseling to her. You know what I am in a position to know? That she'll go ballistic if I even mention it. Way worse than if I speak to her about listening to loud music. I agree counseling could help, but if you want her to go, then you need to tell her. If I say anything, she'll never, ever go. I can pretty much promise you that."

"You may have a point. I just thought …."

You thought how Mum would have done it, and you want me to be her. Only I'm not, and I never will be. "Maybe before school ends, one of the counselors there might be able to talk to Char and refer her to someone."

"That's not a bad idea." He smiled as best he could. "I am so proud of you, Lily. Your mum would be too. And I almost forgot to say: you ironed my blue Oxford shirt like a pro. I'm im*pressed*."

Lily stared blankly at him.

"Bad attempt at a pun, I'm afraid." He grinned. "Next time, I'll say thank you; well done! How's that, honey?"

Lily felt blind rage as she walked up the stairs to fulfill the latest request from her father. When she got to Charlotte's door, she slowed her breathing and tried to calm herself. Char will pick up my anger in a heartbeat. She'll think it's directed at her. I have to be cool.

"What?" Charlotte cried out, hearing the loud knocking.

"It's Lily. Okay if I come in?"

Charlotte opened the door and stood, blocking her sister. "What do you want?"

Ask me what Dad wants; I'll have a better answer. "I want to chat. Spend a little time with you. I had some nice moments with Wills, so I thought maybe you and I could have some alone time."

"You didn't have to knock so loud. It scared me. Like when that pickup truck hit us and took Mum away. Such a loud and horrible sound out of nowhere."

"I didn't mean to be so thoughtless. Sorry, Char. I guess I'm used to having to do that when you're listening to music and have your headphones on."

"Well I wasn't, and I didn't. I was surfing social media to see what random bullshit people are talking about."

"Being a lurker today?" Lily attempted a lighthearted laugh. "May I please come in?"

"Whatevs." Charlotte moved out of the way so Lily could enter.

"Mind if I sit on your bed?" Lily looked at the heavy-metal music posters taped to the walls before noticing the distressed lumps of linen on the mattress.

"As long as you don't dis my new art or give me a Mum-like lecture on how I didn't make the bed today." Charlotte sat on her swivel desk chair and watched as Lily moved some sheets and pillows to clear a seat.

"I barely made mine either," Lily said.

"Yeah you did."

"Well, I changed the sheets and didn't do hospital corners … so there's that."

"Wanna bet you did?" Charlotte challenged her. "Let's go look."

"Okay, Char. So maybe I did. I don't know. But I didn't come in here to dis you for not making your bed or anything else. I thought maybe while Wills was bonding with Quincy, you and I might go to a movie or something."

"Nope."

Lily's face went blank.

"Oh, sorry: nope thank you. Is that better?"

"Are you angry with me? What did I do?"

"It's not about what you did. But you don't understand how I feel. And your head isn't so messed up that you keep replaying Mum getting hit by that pickup truck and dying three days later." Charlotte fumed. "No, you get visions of that property in England, how you own it and are worth millions now."

You're thinking way more about the property than I am. "I hate that you have that horrible memory. It's the worst. I know you don't believe me, but I would take it from you if I could."

"Well you can't. But you can let me take that property from you."

"No, Char. Sorry, that's not going to happen. What would you do with it anyway?"

"Have Uncle Ellis sell it for me; that's what."

"No way he would ever do that. The property is in my name for a reason. Mum wanted it to stay in the family."

"She could have left it to all of us then, with some kind of stipulation or whatever that it can't be sold."

"Then what good would it do you, Char? Listen, I didn't write Mum's will. I had zero to do with that. You need to respect her wishes. Maybe you should talk to a financial person who can explain to you that you actually have quite a large chunk of money, and it can grow into a whole lot more."

"Will it grow if I sit and stare at it? Huh?"

It probably will, but I'm not an effin' financial advisor. "Do you want to go shopping?" Lily smiled brightly, trying to mask her exasperation. "Maybe get some more clothing to go with your new look?"

"You hate the way I look."

"No, I don't. I think it's pretty rad. It would be weird on me, but it totally suits you. What do you say, Char? My treat."

"I'm gonna stream a movie … by myself."

Sorrow in her eyes, Lily met Charlotte's defiant stare. "Okay, then. I'll leave you alone. But there's a rain check with both of those offers: the movie and the shopping trip. Oh, and if you ever want to talk to me about all of the things you're suffering as a result of the accident, I'm here to listen for as long as you like. Even if you need to wake me up in the middle of the night. I'm here for you. And I mean it."

"Can you close the door on your way out?"

"Sure," Lily said, defeat overwhelming her. "I'm real good at closing doors. I'll be in my room if you need me."

"Why would I need you?"

"I don't know, Char." Lily fought back the tears. "I don't know."

CHAPTER EIGHT

"Congratulations, Lills," Willow said, holding out her arms. "I'm so proud of you."

Donned in a maroon graduation cap and gown, holding a diploma in one hand and flowers in the other, Lily smiled as her youngest sister embraced her.

"Mum is looking down at you from heaven with tears of joy," Dalton said, moving in for a hug and giving Lily a kiss on the cheek. "The time has flown by, and now here you are, at such an important time in your life."

Why is it an important time? I have nothing to look forward to. I'm probably the only person in my class with absolutely no plans except what to make for dinner tomorrow. And I couldn't care less about that.

Charlotte gave Lily an awkward smile. "Congrats to you."

Lily looked into her eyes, seeing more sorrow than anger. "Can I have a hug to go with those congrats?"

"Sure," Charlotte said, giving her a much weaker hug than the others had.

"Photos!" Dalton said. "We need photos."

"I can take them for you," Raymond said as he approached the family in his own cap and gown. "I just finished taking a couple hundred with *my* family."

"That's all, Ray?" Dalton laughed as he tried to mimic the mood of the elated families swarming the graduates on the football field.

"You're right, Mr. Sheppard. More like four thousand."

"Thanks, Ray." Lily handed him her phone. "Make sure you and I get some together too." She looked at her family. "Come on. Let's do this."

Willow and Dalton immediately put their arms around Lily, who noticed that Charlotte's eyes were filling with pain.

"I've got a better idea," Lily said. "Char, why don't you switch places with Wills, and Wills, you can stand in front of me."

"No way! That would block your gown," Willow said. She paused. "I've got a better idea." Giving Lily a knowing look, Willow filled the empty space on the other side of their father, leaving Charlotte no choice but to nuzzle up to the graduate's side.

Lily gave Charlotte an extra squeeze and whispered to her. "I'm so happy you're here, Char." She looked at Raymond. "Okay, go for it."

"Everyone ready?" He smiled.

"Wait … one thing before you take any photos," Lily said. "Does this gown make me look fat?"

Raymond laughed. "I think every female in our class has asked that question."

"I know," Lily said, struggling to keep up the happy facade. "I didn't want to be the oddball."

"You look beautiful. You always do." Raymond took several photos, glanced at the phone to see how they looked, then changed his position to take more. "I've got about twenty. The sun's perfect and they came out great."

"Take some for me, please!" Willow said, handing Raymond

her phone as he handed Lily's back to her.

Raymond obliged as he added another ten photos to Willow's camera roll. "Well, now's the time, if you're anything like my family, you'll all want individual shots with the graduate."

"Me first," Willow said.

Lily smiled, then opened her eyes in stunned surprise as she saw Kady, wearing a red-and-green cherry sundress, walking toward her with a floral gift bag, adorned with ribbons and faux wildflowers. "We'll do that in a few minutes, Wills. Promise."

Lily hurried away and threw her arms around Kady as they met. "I didn't expect to see you. I'm so glad you came."

Kady tenderly brushed a lock of Lily's long hair out of her face. "Wild horses couldn't keep me away … or your father," she said softly. "There was no way I wasn't going to see you graduate." She handed Lily the bag. "This is for you, honey. Open it later."

"Thank you so much, Kady. I love you."

"I love you too, dear girl. And we'll talk soon. I don't want to—"

"Hello, Kady," Dalton said. "How thoughtful of you to attend Lily's graduation."

"I wouldn't have missed it for the world."

Dalton responded with a chilly stare.

"I'm going to go take some photos with Wills," Lily said, unnerved by the tension but wanting to give her mother's best friend a fighting chance of getting through to her father. She acknowledged Kady. "And I want to get a few with you too."

"Absolutely."

Dalton waited for Lily to walk far enough away that he couldn't be overheard. "It's nice to see you, Kady. I know you think I don't appreciate you, but I do. When Abby moved here from England, I worried that she wouldn't ever feel at home. Altrusia is a far cry from the picturesque Cotswolds. But when she met you, her heart fully opened. She had a friend and finally felt she belonged. I'll always be grateful for the role you played in her life."

"Um hmm. I see. You're grateful, but it ends there, yes? You've forbidden Lily to see me. And I'm sure you don't want me seeing Charlotte or Willow either. But Lily needs me."

"Lily's interests are better suited with friends her own age."

"Oh, hell, Dalt. That's nonsense, and you know it. First, no doubt you are aware that her two best friends are moving to the East Coast. She no longer has her job, so she can't see her friends at the diner. She needs to be home to take care of the house, you, and her sisters, so she doesn't have much of an opportunity to make new friends. But you don't want her to see someone who's known and loved her since she was an infant. Someone who shares her grief and who can help her manage her new and unexpected life."

"I know you don't approve of how I'm handling things."

"That's an understatement if I ever heard one. But more importantly, do you think Abby would approve? Of anything you're doing? Do you? Lily turns nineteen in a week and a half. I know your grief is unbearable, but please, let her live her young life. I told you, Dalt. I'll do the shopping; I'll pay the bills; organize whatever needs organizing. I'm at your service. Sabrina and Oliver are off living their adult lives. Please, let me help *your* children."

"We're managing as best as we can without Abby. And I'm not comfortable with you and Lily being friends. Isn't that enough explanation?"

"No, it's not." Kady's eyes glistened with anger. "Lily is an adult. Surely, that decision is hers." She took a breath and let her emotion cool. "Dalt, if you think I'm going to share Abby's secrets with Lily, you're wrong. She may bear a strong resemblance to your wife and my best friend, but it stops there. I want to know Lily in her own right. She's an incredible young woman. And I need her friendship as she needs mine. Please, don't stand in our way." She glanced over his shoulders. "Now if you'll excuse me, Lily is waving at me to come take some photos. And I'm going to do exactly that."

His eyes grew dark. "If you respect my wife, you'll respect me. It's what Abby would want you to do."

Kady, who had started to walk away, turned sharply and stood firm. "No, Dalt. She wouldn't. She'd think you were being a horse's ass … arse, to be precise … and she'd be angry as hell that Lily is being guilt-tripped into assuming a role that is not meant to be hers. I know your pain is crippling, but please, don't cripple Lily while you deal with it."

"I'm not crippling her!"

"Aren't you? Let me get this straight: she's lost her mother, and your idea of doing the right thing is to strip her of everything else she holds dear? Am I correct?"

Dalton said nothing.

"You can't be serious. Please tell me it's the grief."

"I've tried to be civil and to show my appreciation to you for your friendship over these many years. But after you take those photos, you stay away. Far away."

Dalton smiled as he held the front door open for his three daughters. "Before we all go our separate ways, I'd like to talk about dinner. I would love the four of us to go out and celebrate Lily's special day. Anywhere the graduate chooses."

"Great," Lily said. "As long as we can make it on the early side. Ray asked me to go to a graduation party with him later. How about that Italian restaurant on Rushton?"

"That sounds nice. Raymond Bostwick is an impressive young man."

"He sure doesn't do jack for me," Charlotte said. "He's kind of boring."

"And your music is torture to my ears," Lily told her. "There's a reason we were all born to make our own choices." *At least some of the time.*

"I'm going upstairs to un-torture myself from this conversation," Charlotte said.

"Be ready to go out at six-thirty," Dalton told her.

"Whatever." Charlotte rushed upstairs.

Dalton smiled awkwardly. "I hear 'whatever' is the new slang for 'sure, Dad.'"

"Yeah. In 'Charspeak,' I think it is. Anyway, I'm going upstairs to take this gown off."

Willow, who had already started to climb the stairs, stopped and turned to Lily. "Not until you pose with Quincy boy. He's part of this family now too. We'll wait for you in my room. Now I've got to go see if my son is all right."

"Sure, Wills. I'll be there in a minute."

Content, Willow continued upstairs.

Lily noticed a brief flicker of pain in her father's eyes, but it was too fleeting for her to divine any meaning. "See you at six-thirty, Dad."

He nodded as Lily rushed up the stairs.

Waiting in front of Lily's room, Quincy in her arms, Willow smiled and opened the door. "Quincy said he wants to see what your place is like, so I thought we'd take photos in here instead … if that's okay. My boy has been a member of our family for about six weeks now, and he's only seen my room."

"Then it's long past time that we expand his territory."

"You'd better take photos with him right away. Before I put him down. In case he freaks and goes hiding under your bed or something."

Laying the flowers, diploma, graduation cap, and gift bag on top of her dresser, Lily smiled. "Maybe you should hand him over now."

"You have to wear your cap." Willow grabbed it off the dresser and put it on Lily's head. "Perfect."

Taking the cat from her arms, Lily spoke to him. "Mind if your Aunt Lily holds you for a bit, Quincy?"

The cat nuzzled her chin.

"He loves you, Lills. Just like I do. Poor thing thought he would be stuck in that cage forever. He was so scared. But he'll be happy here for always and forever."

"I'm so glad we brought him home. Now, where do you want me to stand?"

"Um...." Willow pulled her phone out of her pocket. "How about by the dresser near the framed photo of Mum. So she can be in the picture too."

"Best idea." Lily walked to the designated spot. As her eyes soaked in her mother's image, she felt a surge of adrenaline go through her. Not wanting to alarm Willow, she stood there, blank-faced, until she noticed that Willow was wearing an expression similar to hers.

Willow studied Lily's face in wonderment. "You heard what I heard, didn't you, Lills? Please tell me. I can handle it."

"I'm not sure of anything, but it sounded like Mum saying she was proud of us."

"That's what I heard!" Willow rushed to gently embrace Lily without frightening the cat. "Mum is with us. I know she is!"

"Let's take the photos while she's still here," Lily said, fearful that her sister's vulnerable awe might escalate to a place neither could handle.

"Okay. For sure." Willow took several shots, moving closer and then moving farther back. She checked the photos on her phone. "You can put the boy down now." She put the phone back in her pocket. "Oh, Lills, do you think Mum is here?"

Lily gently let the cat jump onto the floor. "I do. Actually, this wasn't the first time I heard her."

"When was the other time?" Willow watched as Quincy sniffed his brand-new territory. Returning her attention to Lily, she sat on the bed. "Sit down, Lills. Tell me about the other time! Please."

Lily sat. "It happened when I was on the phone with Kady, back in April after Mum died. And not only that, Kady heard her too. But it wasn't like now when we both heard the same thing. Kady and I believe she said different things to each of us. There's no way to prove any of this, you know."

"I hear you, but I still believe. How come you didn't say anything then? Were you afraid I'd freak?"

"A little." Lily offered a sheepish smile. "Forgive me?"

"Of course I do. And maybe I *would* have freaked. It's fine that you didn't say anything before. I'm not upset. You always know when the time is right."

"You give me too much credit there, Wills. But in this situation, today, since you heard Mum too, I thought it would comfort you to know it's happened before."

"So you think she'll always be here watching over us?"

"I hope so ... maybe not as close by as we believe she is now, but yes. I don't think anyone can know for sure. But I have heard that when people die suddenly, they're more likely to stick around if they have an abrupt passing and don't get to finish things. You know ... like saying good-bye."

"Then why don't we hear her more?"

Lily put a comforting hand on Willow's knee. "A mystery of the universe we may never know."

"We miss you so much, Mum." Willow looked up. "I hope you can hear us."

On the floor, Quincy suddenly arched his back ... looking at something only he could see. After holding his pose for several seconds, he relaxed.

Lily and Willow exchanged a startled look.

"Could be," Lily said, without needing to hear her sister's question aloud. "Could be."

"Wow." Willow exhaled. "Major wow. I'm not going to tell Dad or Char, though."

"Oh, no. I don't think we should. Do you want to stay here while I see what Kady brought for me?"

"For sure!"

Lily got off the bed and grabbed the gift bag before sitting down again. She held the faux wildflowers and ribbons attached to it in her hand. "Kady is so elegant. She has such good taste. One of the many things she and Mum had in common. Mum loved putting little extra touches on things ... like these flowers."

"Look inside," Willow urged.

Lily reached in, pulled out a card, then a beautifully wrapped box that had a bit of weight to it. "If you don't mind, Wills, I'll save the card for later. Let's see what's in the box."

"Sure. I know she wrote something special to you, and I don't need to know. But you better open that box!"

Carefully, Lily unsealed the wildflower wrapping, taking care not to tear even a bit of it. She pulled out a gold box, lifted the lid, then pulled out a miniature English cottage, complete with dormer windows on the roof and open windows on the front, back, and right sides.

"This is absolutely exquisite. Look, Wills, it's the Quincy family cottage that Mum left to me." She touched it with care. "This is so beautiful. The detail on the thatched roof is mind-blowingly realistic. And look, there's ivy growing on the walls, flower boxes in the windows, an adorable dog sleeping under the front window, and a hinged door."

Delicately, Willow pulled the miniature door toward her. "It actually opens. Like it's welcoming us inside."

"I can't imagine where Kady would have gotten this from. I need to read her card now." Lily reached to her side and picked up the gold envelope with her name written in a beautiful script:

Dear Lily,

I do hope this little cottage will bring joy into your heart. Believe it or not, I have been working on this for a year now, learning all sorts of new skills as I put it together. It was to be a gift for your mum on her next birthday. With only a few photos to offer as reference, I was searching online for an artisan to construct it for me. But somewhere along the road, I switched gears and decided I was up for the challenge. After a good bit of research, my solo endeavor began, and I made this little cottage myself ... with hard work and lots of love. Don't look too closely, or you'll see the flaws.

On second thought, it's perfectly fine if you do. We are all flawed human beings looking to find our place and fill our hearts with love. And the real cottage, sitting in Bibury, has certainly earned its dings, scratches, creaky floorboards, and many other signs of lives well lived over the years.

May this cottage always bring you comfort and fond memories of your mum. Please know that I am always here for you. I am here for your sisters as well, if the situation ever permits us to engage. I treasure you as I treasured your mum.

With all my love,
Kady

P.S. It will be a bittersweet honor to see you graduate. I'm so glad I can be there.

"What a special person Kady is. I'm so glad to know Mum always had her as a friend. I'm going to put the cottage right next to Mum's photo." Lily stood and gently placed the miniature home on the bureau. "I'm going to get some tea lights to place inside … so when I look at the cottage, it will always be like someone is home."

"Oh, that will look so pretty." Willow let her eyes soak in the beauty of the tiny home. "I forgot to say that I'm glad you're going out with Ray tonight. I'm sorry that Char said he was boring. He's not. And I like him a lot. Who's giving the party?"

"Jimmy Norwich. He's the president of our senior class. He's going to Cal Tech. He's a genius. Like Ray. Anyway, if you think we have a big house, his family has a monster house: seven bedrooms with a giant deck outside. Should be fun. I'm not a big party person, but I have so few chances to do anything with Dad's blessing, so I jumped on Ray's invitation. I was invited, of course, but I wouldn't have gone alone."

"I'm glad Ray asked and that you said yes."

"Me too." Lily glanced at the clock on her nightstand. "It's six o'clock. We've got to leave for dinner in a half hour. So we better get ready."

Willow bent down and picked up Quincy. "Come on, boy." She kissed the top of his head. "Sure wish you could tell me what you saw."

CHAPTER NINE

"There are so many cars here," Lily said to Raymond as they walked up the twisty path to the large house on the hill. "I'm not a party animal, but I'm glad you asked me to come with you. Otherwise, I'd be home crying into my pillow."

Raymond put a comforting arm around her. "I wish I could teleport to Princeton so I could still be here for you."

Lily put her arm around his waist. "You're so brill. If anyone can invent a teleportation machine, it would be you."

He laughed. "Don't give me any ideas. By the way, Lills, before we go in, I want to tell you—"

"Move it, slowpokes," said a voice behind them. "We're starving. Jimmy texted me a photo of the spread Mrs. Norwich put out. It'll all be gone by the time you two turtles crawl at a snail's pace to the front door."

Raymond and Lily disengaged and turned around. Jake Lassiter, six-foot-three captain of the Altrusia High football team, good-naturedly nodded for them to hurry along as his girlfriend laughed.

"Um, turtles walk at turtle paces," Raymond said, laughing. "And snails crawl at snail paces. Your metaphors are seriously fucked up."

"He's confused, and I'm afraid it shows," his girlfriend said with a smile. "Jake hasn't had dinner yet, so his brain is like total mush. Be careful, you guys. He's so hungry he might eat the tables. Or you! Better get out of his way."

The four of them laughed and walked to the front door.

Lily gulped when she saw all the people inside. Despite knowing most of them, she had never seen them all with drinks in their hands, nor was she comfortable with the cacophony of voices made even louder by the high ceilings and bad acoustics.

"Yo!" a lanky male redhead yelled out to someone in the crowd. "The food is outside. And check it out, Jimmy's got the biggest deck …."

A blonde in a tight black dress laughed. "Did you say he's got the biggest *deck*? I'm sure I heard the word slightly differently this afternoon. And here I got all dolled up in my LBD … for a deck!"

Boisterous laughter broke out as Jimmy Norwich swooped in and put his arms around the blonde. "Both are true, baby," he assured her.

"He's big as fuck," an unknown female said quietly to Lily. "We fooled around a couple of times in the eleventh grade. I should know …."

Lily blanched. "And maybe I shouldn't. Not exactly on my stuff-to-find-out list."

"She won't be disappointed," the young woman continued. "I've moved on to greener pastures, so I'm cool. But I hope she can handle—"

"What can I get you to drink?" Raymond asked Lily, seeing the look of discomfort on her face. "I know how thirsty you are."

"*So* thirsty," Lily said, turning away from the blabbermouth who had already moved on to a more willing set of ears. "I'll start with a flavored water if they have any: lime, lemon, black cherry. It doesn't matter. Maybe later I'll have a glass of wine. And thanks for rescuing me. Some people are way TMI."

"So I heard. Always glad to be of service. Maybe next Christmas she should ask Santa for a filter. You know, a practical gift … something she doesn't have."

Lily laughed as best she could.

"Hey, are you okay without me while I go fetch us some drinks?"

"I'm fine. See you when you get back."

Raymond nodded as he took off through the celebratory crowd.

"Lily!" a familiar voice said.

Turning around, Lily was stunned. "Hannah. I didn't expect to see you here. Or anywhere. I thought you'd left town."

"I'm leaving tomorrow, and I've got a million last-minute things to do. I'm only here to see you. I spoke to Raymond at graduation, and he told me you were coming to Jimmy's party with him. I know Jimmy from the diner. He used to come in with his team after the games sometimes. What am I talking about? You know that. Duh! You were there."

"I was. So is Jimmy the reason you came to our graduation?"

Hannah pulled her by the elbow to a corner of the room that was relatively empty. "Definitely not. You're the reason. A friend of Jimmy's had an extra ticket. I was on my way over to you and your family when I noticed that Kady and your dad were talking … and neither one of them looked happy. I was chomping at the bit to see you, but it felt like seriously awkward timing. All of the alarm bells in my head were ringing and red lights were flashing stay-away warnings. I wasn't going to risk doing something that might make the situation even worse. Especially after what happened between us six weeks ago. Anyway, Ray saw me from a distance and made a point to catch up with me after you and your family went home. I told him I needed to apologize to you and that I was planning to be here tonight. He said he would tell you, but I guess he forgot." She thought for a moment. "Or maybe he was afraid you wouldn't come if you knew."

"I think that's what he was starting to tell me as we were on our way to the front door … but we got interrupted."

"So maybe he was afraid to tell you earlier." Hannah put both hands on Lily's shoulders. "Let me have it straight: do you hate me, girlfriend?"

Pain filled Lily's eyes. "Of course not. I could never hate you, Han. I think we're going in different directions, though, and we don't see as many things the same way … not like we used to anyhow. I left the restaurant that day because our convo was getting too intense, and I didn't want any ugly words to be the last words between us."

"I know that." Hannah dropped her arms to her sides. "I didn't like it, but I understood. I came down on you hard." She sighed. "I still have the same opinions as I did that day, only when I went home, I mulled over what *you* said about having a parent die suddenly. And then I started adding up *all* that my mom has done and is doing to help make my life happy. I thought about how much she means to me, and for a painful moment, I tried to picture her gone. It was fucking brutal. I burst into tears … at the mere *thought* of it. And then it occurred to me how if I was grieving like you are, I might make different decisions too … because my world would be turned upside down. Sorry I was so out of line."

Lily listened as tears welled in her eyes.

"I still hope you'll get outta Dodge." Hannah's bottom lip protruded in a pout. "I'm not gonna lie about that now. But it's got to be on your timetable. Who cares about mine? It's your life."

"Thank you for saying that. I'm happy you came here tonight … and to graduation today. Just wondering why you waited until the final day. We could have had more time to talk."

"Truth?" Hannah shifted uneasily. "I wasn't sure you'd want

to see me. And then I didn't trust myself not to say some more dumb shit. I thought it would be better to keep it brief for now. Then, down the line, we can talk. Plus, I've been so scattered lately, not to mention crazy busy getting ready for the move … and the little one growing inside of me."

Lily smiled and looked at her friend's stomach. "That baby bump looks good on you, Han."

Hannah rubbed her stomach. "You think? I kind of like it too. Makes everything real, which is more than a bit scary, but it's also wonderful."

"Thank you for going to all this trouble to see me before you left. I feel so much better. And I'm going to miss you. I *have* been missing you."

Hannah reached over and gave her a hug. "I've been missing you too. I'll send you all of my new information when I get to Boston. I'm keeping my 916 number, so you've got that." She paused. "Um … unless you deleted it."

"Of course I didn't," Lily said with a smirk.

"Good. And now I've got to run. Ten a.m. flight tomorrow. At least it's nonstop. Maybe I'll be able to make up for the sleep I'll probably miss tonight."

Lily reached over for another hug. "Love you, Han. Safe travels."

A wistful look in her eyes, Lily watched as her friend disappeared into the crowd.

"Raspberry and pomegranate water," Raymond said, handing Lily a large red cup. "It sounded more exotic than lemon."

"Well, you made a great choice. I'm the epitome of exoticness. Or maybe exoticity. Are either of them actual words?"

"I'm pretty sure the first one is."

"Then I like the second one better. Shows off my creative side."

"Were you happy to see Hannah? I hope I didn't make a

mistake by—"

"No. I'm so glad you told her where to find me tonight."

"You look so sad. I thought maybe I did the wrong thing."

"No, not at all." Lily took a few sips of her drink. "This has a great flavor."

"What am I missing then? You've got this faraway look in your eyes."

Lily attempted to smile. "You do know how to read me." She paused for a moment before responding. "I'm grateful we had a nice good-bye. But somehow, I don't think I'll ever see her again."

"I'm glad we came outside," Lily said. "Too stuffy and loud in there." She glanced up at the stars as she and Raymond sat on two chairs, side by side, in the corner of the large deck, away from the crowd. "This is a beautiful night."

"It is."

"It would be more beautiful if Mum were still in this world."

Raymond reached over and squeezed her hand. "Forget the teleportation machine. I wish I could bring her back."

"You would if you could."

"Hey, you didn't say anything about my haircut. I graduated without pushing hair out of my eyes even once."

"I actually did notice. But then everyone was kind of crowding me, and I didn't get to mention it." Lily smiled. "Now that your hair is shorter, though, I think I'm missing that sweeping motion you did with your hand. It was kind of adorable."

"You think so? Well, you're in luck. I think I have phantom locks or something. The urge to push my hair out of my eyes is still there. I've been fighting it knowing how ridiculous I'd look. That's why I'm going to let it grow back."

Lily touched his hand. "I know there's someone here you wanted to spend time with. Why don't you go do that? Don't worry about leaving me alone. I'm fine right here, and I'd feel terrible if you didn't get to see your friend. For real."

"Okay. If you're for real for sure."

"Totally."

He stood. "I'll be over there by the gate. If you need me for any reason, come find me. Or text."

"I know what to do. I'm good." Lily turned her eyes back to the stars.

"I thought he'd never leave," the male voice said.

She turned to see a six-foot man, about twenty, with a long dark blond ponytail, wearing distressed jeans with a white tee shirt ... smiling at her.

"Hi." She noticed he also had a silver feather earring in one ear.

"Mind if I park my weary butt in this chair?"

"Sure."

"I'm Trevor Kent," he said, extending his hand.

"Lily Sheppard," she said, shaking it.

He put his beer down on the deck as he sat next to her. "I kept asking myself why the most gorgeous girl at this party was over in a corner with a dude who doesn't seem to be her boyfriend."

"He's my best friend. We've known one another since grade school."

"And he left you here? Or did he go to get another drink?"

"No, he's off to chat with a friend. I told him to go. Besides, I'm not the best company these days."

"That's hard to believe."

"My mother died in April. Car accident. Life has been horrible without her. I'm not a party person, especially now, but I came because I thought it would be good for me."

"Oh, man! You lost your mom. That blows. Sorry to hear that."

"We called her 'Mum.' She was English."

"Do you want to talk to a stranger about your mum? A stranger who hopes he won't be strange for too long?" He reached for his beer and took a few sips. "That didn't come out right." He laughed and put the beer down again, spilling a bit on his fingers, then wiping his hand on his jeans.

"Thank you, but no. Unless you can bring her back, there's nothing I want to say."

"I couldn't help but notice you keep looking up at the stars. Were you talking to her?"

Lily sighed. "You're so nice. But honest, I *really* don't want to talk about my mum at all, or I'll start crying. Not having her at my graduation today was so hard. It tripled the pain … which is already too much to bear." She picked up her drink and took several sips of the water. "Tell me about you, Trevor. You don't look like a recent grad."

"Two years ago. I've been working and traveling. Jimmy is my cousin … our moms are sisters. I thought I'd come say good-bye before I head out of town soon. But yeah, other than me, Jimmy's pretty good at keeping the party crashers away." He laughed.

"What do you do?"

"Photographer, art gallery manager, wanderer, deep thinker, explorer, painter, horseback rider, odd-job doer, and ripper-upper of detailed and long-range plans."

"Whoa," Lily teased him. "You're the fourth guy to say that to me tonight."

He laughed and pointed playfully at her. "You almost had me going there for a second. I'd better not be number four. And if I were, I'd never say anything like that again. I never want to be like all the sheeple. You know, the masses of humanity that make plans and blueprints for the rest of their lives. Society molds us when we're little kids. 'What do *you* want to be when you grow up?' Ever notice how kids are asked that same question all the time? And if they don't have an answer, the pathetic, one-trick-pony adults start hurling careers at you. 'How about a doctor? Or a fireman? Bet you'd make a great pilot.' Such bullshit. I've heard all three. I actually asked some friend of my mother's why she thought I'd make a good pilot. She gawked at me with her mouth open. I wanted to make a paper airplane and show her how good I could be at landing it between her lips. But I didn't."

Lily smiled. "I wasn't there, but it sounds like you made a wise decision."

"Maybe, but I wish I'd tried." He glanced at a large group of graduates laughing. "People can be obnoxious with that question. Bet you never heard any kid say he or she wanted to be a bean counter or a tax accountant. Or an addict in and out of rehab who can't hold a job for obvious reasons."

"You've got a point there. And yeah, now that you mention it, people did ask me that when I was a kid."

"What did you say?"

"Long story." Lily choked on her words. "Not for tonight. How about you, Trevor?"

"I used to make shit up to watch adults go full freak. I'd say things like I wanted to clean gutters, dig graves, wash skyscraper windows, build snowmen, and sell hotdogs and beer at Oracle Park. Literally, I came up with hundreds of things, and I got more creative as time went on. I never wanted to be boring … like my father."

"Oh. How's that?"

"By the time he was in the sixth grade, he was already getting As in math. Okay, that's cool. But what sixth grader already knows he wants to be an accountant? My dad, that's who. You'd think with those mad crazy math skills he's got, he'd have turned up the dial on his dream-o-meter. You know, like aiming for a job with NASA or doing something … anything to make a difference in the world. Nah. Not my dad. He couldn't wait to graduate, get his degree in accounting, and put on a boring-ass suit and tie. Every day, he goes to this lame silver high-rise in Sacramento where he fills out forms, adds and subtracts numbers, and attends weekly staff meetings. *Every* day of his working life until he retires. He's got a small office with dull-white walls and two paintings hanging on them that he bought at a yard sale. And no, they're not hidden treasures. They're junk. But at least he has something to look at between columns of numbers. I think I'd rather watch paint dry. At least, when the light hits it in a certain way, you can see shapes and patterns and maybe dream of another world. But not my dad; he just looks up at cheap art. And I'm being generous calling it that. I could never do what he does for a living. It pays well, but damn!"

"I guess if nobody wanted to do that job, we'd be in trouble."

Trevor nodded. "You've got a point there. But he never does anything exciting when he's not at work. On alternate Friday nights he bowls with his buddies, and on Saturdays, he takes my mom to dinner. Sometimes, if he wants to whoop it up, he'll take her to a movie. And on Sundays, he sits in his chair and reads the entire paper while my mom reads romance novels or crochets stuff." He flicked his feather earring with his thumb. "That's why I got this. To remind myself we all have wings, even if they're symbolic, and if we don't use 'em, we ground ourselves ... and not in a good way. My parents didn't teach me how to fly, so I taught myself."

"Do they ever go on vacation? Get a change of scenery?"

"Oh, yeah. They go to Big Sur, Carmel, and some other towns along the coast. And don't get me wrong. Those are beautiful places. I love them myself. Carmel's got about eighty art galleries, so that's pretty wicked. But who takes the same vacation twenty-something years in a row? After a while, they need a change of scenery from what used to be a 'change of scenery.'" He picked up his beer again, taking care not to spill it. "My parents are so incurious; it's maddening. I want to scream: travel the country; see more of the world. Go overseas." He paused and put his cup down. "Have you ever been abroad?"

"Don't I look like one?"

His face went blank for a second. He laughed and pointed at her. "You got me again. I guess because you said that with such a straight face. Okay, I'll rephrase. Have you ever been overseas?"

"I have." Lily grinned. "I've been to England four times, and also to Scotland, Wales, and Ireland. One summer, when I was twelve, we went to Paris and the south of France as well ... so exciting. I hope to see much more of the world someday. Oh, yeah, we did cross the border into Spain, but that was only for three days. My mum had a friend in Pamplona who we visited. We didn't have time to see any more of the country. But I loved it there. One of my favorite family photos is the five of us at the cathedral. It's such a beautiful place." She smiled as a memory drifted past her mind's eye. "I've seen some of this country, but not as much as I'd like. Oh, and when I was sixteen, we drove north to Alberta to Banff National Park. How incredible that was. Mum called it a little bit of heaven right there in Canada."

"I can see the adventuress in you. Your eyes are that of a worldly woman." He glanced over toward the mingling crowds. "I had four chicks hit on me tonight. Honestly, not saying that to brag, but not one of them said anything to me I haven't heard in some context before. 'I love your ponytail. Where's the pony? I'd love to ride it.' And then she winked at me like that was supposed to turn me on. Then there was the old standby: 'How come I haven't seen you around here before?' I almost wanted to say, 'because I knew you'd be here,' but I didn't. So trite. You catch my drift? Anyway, I kept looking over here, hoping your friend would leave ... and finally, he did."

Lily smiled awkwardly. "So where do you live now?"

"I've been working at my friend's art gallery for the past few months and crashing in the studio upstairs. On Monday, I'm headed to Santa Fe. I have another friend who owns a craft gallery, and I'm going to manage that while he goes back to spend six months in Italy with his family. While I'm there, I'll be doing my photography, including taking short trips into Mexico to photograph the people."

"That all sounds so stimulating and rewarding."

"It is." His tone softened. "People make the world go 'round. Even the boring ones, I guess. Many of the people I photograph live sad lives. There's a great deal of poverty. By capturing them with my camera, I hope in some way I can help. Not sure what that is yet, but I think about it a lot. I don't want to just see the world, Lily. I want to make it better."

"So you're coming back this way in six months?"

"Not even then. After I leave New Mexico, I'll be flying to New York and spending a few weeks rockin' the Big Apple. Then, I'm hopping on a giant silver bird from JFK and flying to Peru. Not sure where I'll venture after that. Like I said earlier, I'm a ripper-upper of detailed and long-range plans. What I told you is about as far ahead as I think about anything. I'll be back in this neck of the woods eventually because I'm going to have a showing of my photography at the gallery I've been working at. It'll be fly; I know that much. But that could be a year or so from now. Not sure and don't want to be."

"You keep the world interesting." Lily laid down the cup she'd been holding. "That's for sure."

"Listen, I know this sounds crazy, but I'd like to look you up when I come back."

Lily hesitated. "Uh, sure. But I don't even know what my life will be tomorrow, much less a year or so into the future."

"We never know. That's why we have to live in the now. You're an adventuress, and you can't ever forget that. Can I have your email address? I'd love to keep in touch. Send you photos of my travels here and there."

"That would be nice. I'm good with that."

He licked his lips. "You're stunningly beautiful. You have to know that, right? And I know the light in your eyes has dimmed with so much sadness, but I can see your light. Even in the darkness, it shines bright."

CHAPTER TEN

"Happy Birthday, Lily!"

"Thanks, Dad," Lily said into her phone.

"Where are you?"

"I'm still in my room. I was flipping through some family photos." She closed the album and laid it next to her on the bed. "Just needed a reminder of happier times."

"They'll come again. Mum will always be in our hearts." He sighed. "It hurts, I know." The call went quiet for a moment before the forced cheerfulness came forth. "This is your second special occasion in ten days. Your graduation and now your nineteenth birthday."

Yeah, real special, Dad. I'm probably the only person in my graduating class with absolutely zero plans for her life. And now I'm nineteen, all grown up with no effing place to go. And Mum is dead. Happy times for sure. Love these special days. "I suppose."

"I've left a gift for you on the kitchen table. Sorry I had to go to work today, but my workload is full on. I'd like us all to go to dinner tonight. Sound good?"

"It does, Dad, but actually, Ray is taking me out. He's only going to be here for another two months before he leaves for Princeton."

"Does Ray remember that you have a family?"

Does my father remember that I have a best friend?

"Yes, Dad. And he remembers he's my best friend. Can't we do it another night?" Lily glanced at her phone and saw the name "Samantha" on the screen. "I'm sorry. I've got a call coming in."

"From whom?"

Do you even remember that the purpose of this call was to remind me that I'm nineteen? "Sam ... someone I know from school. Thanks for calling, Dad. I'll talk to you later. Bye!"

Lily ended the call and swiped the screen to answer the incoming one, looking up to make sure her bedroom door was shut before doing so. "Kady?"

"Hi, sweetheart. Indeed it's me. Kady Samantha. Happy birthday."

"Thanks. I wish it were."

"I know, honey. Last night I was looking at the globe in Patrick's office. And I envisioned it with a slice missing ... because that's how the world seems to me without Abby. Listen, I was wondering if you'd like to meet me for lunch. Any place you'd like. You probably have plans but—"

"Actually, I'd love to meet you. I'm having dinner with Ray, but it would be great to go somewhere and have a salad."

"Terrific! And I know the perfect little place for that. It's called The California Cuisinery, and it's tucked away in Burke's Alley, that little shopping mall off Altrusia Avenue. There's a parking garage right next door."

"I know Burke's Alley."

"Oh, good. I'd suggest you come here and we'd go together, but you probably don't want to worry about your car being seen at my house."

"It's totally stupid, isn't it? But for now, I'm too stressed to deal with any more, so I'll meet you there."

"The restaurant is new, and it's right past the florist to your left. Is twelve thirty good for you?"

"Perfect. You've made my day better already. See you then, Kady."

Lily smiled sadly as she ended the call, putting the phone in one of her back pockets. Picking up the photo album, she walked to her bookcase and tucked it back in its place. Finding nothing else to keep her sequestered in her room, she opened the door and headed downstairs.

"Quincy!" she said, laughing, seeing the cat in the foyer. "You've escaped!"

Willow rushed to the bottom of the stairs from the living room. "Dad told me last night that Quincy can be loose in the house, except for his den, when I'm awake. I have to bring him into my room at night." She beamed. "Happy birthday, Lills!"

At that moment, the doorbell rang, spooking Quincy, who darted out of sight.

"Hope you can find him by bedtime," Lily joked. "Guess he still has a lot of territory to explore."

Willow opened the door as Lily descended the stairs. "Flowers for Lily Sheppard," the deliveryman said. "Tip already taken care of." He handed Lily the green vase, a large paper wrap carefully holding the mixed bouquet in place.

"Thank you," Lily said as Willow shut the door.

"Ooh, flowers," Charlotte remarked as she walked into the room, wearing a black shirt with a sobbing angel silkscreened onto it. "From your new boyfriend? The one you met at the graduation party."

"Trevor is so *not* my boyfriend. Besides, I never gave him our home address. We just met. And how do you know anything about him anyway?"

Charlotte smirked, running her fingers through her burgundy hair that now had black lowlights. "I heard you telling the weeping willow."

"You were eavesdropping?" Willow said.

"Not like Lily's gonna tell *me* eff all, you know?"

"W-well …," Willow stammered. "If you were nicer to her, maybe she would."

Lily smiled uncomfortably. "I can't stand here holding these flowers. I'll turn into a human plant stand. Let's go into the kitchen."

"Good," Willow said. "Because Char and I have a present for you, and Dad left a big box on the table."

"It's massive," Charlotte added.

As the three of them entered the kitchen, Lily eyed the large box with dread. "I can't even imagine."

"You won't have to imagine after you open it," Charlotte told her. "And neither will me or the weeping tree. Me and Willow are curious."

Lily started to speak but stopped herself, fully aware that Charlotte was baiting her with sentence constructions their mother had painstakingly taught them to never use. Putting the bouquet on the counter, Lily plucked the card from the arrangement and read it. She smiled and tucked it into her pocket.

"That is *so* from your new boyfriend," Charlotte said. "Did you guys have sex at the party? In his car? Under the deck? In one of the empty bedrooms? Where? Or did you give him—"

"Quiet!" Willow told her. "You're gross and not nice."

Keeping her cool, Lily addressed Charlotte. "He's not my boyfriend, and since you have such a desire to know my business, know this: I had zero physical contact with him. And that's the truth."

"Bullshit! I heard you describe him, and he sounded way hot. Stop being so prudish and spill your dirty beans." She laughed. "Or air your dirty laundry. However you wanna say it."

"Stop harassing Lily," Willow said. "And why is the angel on your shirt crying?"

Charlotte turned her back to shoo away the emotion that had materialized without warning. After giving herself a few seconds to recover, she looked at Willow again. "Because when Mum entered heaven, the angel knew she was way too early. So she cried for all of us, and she's still crying. Is that good enough for you?"

Willow sat at the kitchen table and glared at Charlotte. "You don't have to be so mean. We all miss Mum so much."

"Lily had the most time with her," Charlotte said, walking toward her older sister.

"I was born first. So yeah, I did."

Startled, Charlotte glanced out the kitchen window into the backyard. "Who the hell is that guy with the blond ponytail that's spying on us?"

As Lily's head made a sharp turn toward the window, Charlotte grabbed the little pink envelope out of her pocket, making a beeline to the corner of the kitchen, by the back door, to examine it.

"That was so wrong, Char! Give Lily back her card and don't you dare read it."

Ignoring Willow, Charlotte took the card out of the envelope and scanned the short note. After a few seconds, she uttered a sigh of disgust, walked toward them, and threw the card on the kitchen table. "Ugh. It's from Mr. Boring."

"He's not boring." Lily grabbed her card. "And gee, Char, if you're going to steal something that's not yours, make it worth your while next time." She sighed. "Can we be cool now? It's my birthday."

Willow stood and picked up the small package from the counter. She walked over and handed it to Lily. "Happy birthday, Lills. Please. Sit down and open this," she said as she returned to her seat. "It's from Char and me."

"Yeah. Me and Willow got it for you."

Willow and Lily shared a knowing glance, while Charlotte quietly stewed as her second attempt to bait Lily with bad grammar was ignored.

Lily took a seat at the table. "Oh, here's Quincy," she said as the gray cat sauntered into the kitchen toward Willow. "Sorry about that doorbell, boy. But don't worry, we don't get too many visitors."

"Hey, Quincy Wincy." Willow picked up the cat the moment he was within reach and put him on her lap while she watched with expectant eyes as Lily unwrapped the gift.

"I love this black-and-white polka dot wrapping. Cute." As Lily opened the flat white box and pushed aside the tissue paper, a smile landed her lips. "Oh, what a thoughtful gift ... this wonderful photo of all of us at my eighteenth birthday party ... in a frame with all of our names painted on it. This is so special. Thank you both. I'll treasure this forever." She stood and gave Charlotte a hug, then leaned down to give Willow a light squeeze so as not to disturb the cat.

Charlotte nodded toward the big box. "Come on! Open it. Start with Dad's card. Maybe it will be more exciting than that snoozer Ray sent. He's not exactly a tough act to follow."

"You totally need to stop," Willow said. "Ray is Lily's best friend, and he's nice. Which is more than I can say for you at the moment."

Charlotte turned to Willow and mouthed the word "boring" so that Lily couldn't see her. Willow flashed her a dirty look while Lily stared at the large wrapped box.

After a long minute, she snatched the blue envelope from the top, carefully opening it to reveal a floral card with cursive, embossed script that read: Happy Birthday, Daughter. She opened the card.

Dearest Lily,

Today, on your nineteenth birthday, I want to take this opportunity to tell you how proud of you I am. You have come through for this family like a champ. I know it hasn't been easy, but you are the one who has sacrificed so much to keep us all together in the way that is the closest to how we've always been. I don't know where we would be without your love and dedication. Mum would be every bit as proud as I am.

And so, I wanted to get you something that would truly show my gratitude and appreciation, but most of all, to choose a gift that I hope will make your life much easier.

I look forward to having dinner with my girls tonight.

Happy Birthday, Lily.

All my love, Dad

Lily stared at the card as if it had fallen from outer space, crashed through the kitchen window, and landed in her hands.

Charlotte and Willow could only look at one another. The birthday card, too big for her side pocket, fit into the one empty back pocket of Lily's jeans. With great trepidation, she slowly opened the wrapping, six eyes watching her.

As Lily tore the paper from the box, Quincy, still on Willow's lap, pawed at it with glee. Ripping away a larger piece, Lily crumpled it into a ball and threw it. "Go get it, boy."

The cat jumped onto the black-and-white checked linoleum floor, happily bounding over to greet the balled-up wrapping paper and playfully bat it around.

Charlotte twisted her lips. "Why do I think Quincy's gonna be a whole lot happier with that ball than you will be with … oh no!"

With one big tear of the paper, Lily revealed her father's birthday gift to her: a box with a photograph of a seafoam green stainless steel microwave oven on it. Lily gulped as she read the big black words on the box that described the product inside. Expressionless, she looked at her sisters.

"So ….," Charlotte said, "It's no longer just for reheating. You can cook a meal in it. And it's got inverter technology, whatever the hell that is."

Willow looked at Lily with despair. "So sorry, Lills."

Lily bit her lip to stop the pooling tears from cascading down her face. "Don't either of you tell me he meant well." She picked up the box with the frame inside. "I love this. Thank you both." She walked over to the counter and grabbed the vase of flowers. "Now I've got to go upstairs."

Lily was gone in a flash as Charlotte and Willow could only trade sad looks.

"That totally sucks," Charlotte said. "I couldn't even make a bad joke because the gift is a bad joke."

"You're not kidding … for real. Too bad nobody's laughing, huh?"

"Nice microwave, pretty color, but damn." Charlotte looked down at her shirt. "The angel is crying all over again. She wouldn't want a stupid microwave either." She nodded in the direction Lily had gone. "You gonna follow her upstairs?"

Willow watched Quincy as he continued to discover the joy of crumpled paper. "Not now. I think Lills needs to be alone. I know she's crying her eyes out, but that's what she needs to do."

Kady reached across the table and put her hand on top of Lily's. "It means so much to me that you are here with me on your birthday."

"Honestly, I can't think of anyone I'd rather be with now."

"Except your mum." Kady gave her hand a squeeze and then

took it away. "I'm so glad to see you, honey. Tell me how you're holding up."

Lily smiled as a male server placed a small cutting board on the table with a mini-loaf of sourdough bread on it, a small knife, a paper cup of whipped butter, and two butter knives.

"Oh, no. Temptation has arrived." Kady winked. "And it's hot … fresh from the oven. You know what that means, don't you?"

"You're going to have a piece."

"Indeed I am." She took the knife and cut a slice. "How about you, Lily?"

"Sure. It's better than birthday cake."

Kady transferred the slice to a small bread plate and handed it to Lily before cutting a second one. Taking a moment, she looked fondly at Lily. "How are you holding up? What are your days like? Are you surviving? Any changes?"

Lily put a small dab of butter on the slice of bread and tasted it. "This is so good." She looked at Kady. "I'm trying to take my life in small doses and not think too far ahead. Because when I think about the future, a part of me shuts down. Most days, I feel like I'm a robot Dad pre-programmed to carry on for Mum. My grief is sometimes the only thing to remind me I'm human. The pain of Mum being gone is hard enough, but Dad is great at giving me new things to cry about." She reached into her back pocket and pulled out the birthday card from her father. She handed it to Kady. "Like this."

Opening the card, Kady quickly read the words. She looked up at Lily. "Please don't tell me there was a light greenish-blue stainless steel microwave in the box."

"Exactly right! How did you know?"

Kady dropped her head and shook it back and forth several times. Finally, she looked at Lily. "Your mum was planning to buy that microwave. She loved the fact that it worked like a regular oven … and she was partial to the color." Kady leaned forward. "But when I say that she intended to buy it, it was a simple matter of making life a bit easier and getting rid of an old relic that had stopped being reliable. No more to it than that. The new oven would have offered her no more personal happiness than it would to you. It's an appliance, for Pete's sake. That's all. Abby would not have wanted a household item as a birthday gift and would be utterly appalled that Dalt gave it to you as one."

Lily looked up as the server put two frosted glasses of fresh lemonade in front of them. "Even Char looked horrified, and she doesn't seem to miss many opportunities to stick it to me."

"I find this so dispiriting, Lily. My heart aches for you."

"What's wrong with Dad? Seriously, does he not understand that Mum is gone, and I'm his nineteen-year-old daughter who thought she'd be starting a new life about now? What is he going to do next, Kady? I swear, I don't know how much I can take. I think I have a permanent dent in my tongue from biting it so much. She paused to breathe. "Why does he do these things?"

"I ask myself the same question all the time. His actions seem so obtuse, but he's not an unintelligent man. I think he's dealing with insurmountable pain and has allowed denial to comfort him … at your expense."

"Yeah, what you said about denial. At my expense." Her bottom lip bulged as she frowned. "Did you read the part at the end where he said he was looking forward to the four of us having dinner tonight? He assumed I didn't have any plans when he wrote the card. When I told him on the phone I was having dinner with Ray, I could tell he was pissed."

"I read it. He never should have assumed you were free, and he should have been happy to learn you had plans."

"I don't get to see Ray much because he works and has so much to do before moving to Princeton. I'm not giving up tonight with him. Time with friends is so rare. It's only the sixteenth of June, and I'm already looking forward to Ray coming home at Christmas and taking me to this phenomenal party. Because yeah ... my life is that empty."

"This is not forever; I promise. But you look depleted ... and so downcast. It pains me." She touched her heart with her palm.

"I'm both. You know what I did last week? I packed a getaway bag and shoved it in the corner of my closet. Because I feel like someday he's going to do something horrible, and I'll need to run away. I probably would never leave California ... but I'd leave Altrusia. And maybe I already would have if not for Wills and Char ... and even because of Dad. I want him to be strong enough to handle things." She stopped to fight back the tears. "I can't see myself going anywhere, though. I only know what I think about doing ... all the time. So I can effing breathe for a moment."

Kady handed the birthday card back to Lily and watched as she stuffed it back into her pocket. "About running away ... I hope it never comes to that, but if it should ... you call me. I'll help you." She took the round lemon slice off the side of her glass, placed it on top of the drink, and watched it float. "That said, honey, when the day comes that you do leave Altrusia, I'd like to believe it will be a planned and celebrated occasion ... certainly not anything remotely resembling an escape or a departure under duress." She sighed. "However, as unpleasant as it is to think about, I need you to know I can help."

"May I ask how?"

"I have a friend in Malibu, Cynthia, who has a gorgeous studio apartment guesthouse. It's right on the beach, attached to her home. She doesn't need to rent it, so she keeps it for visitors. But I know that if you ever needed a place to stay, or to live, she'd work something out with you."

"Oh, I love Malibu. But how do you know she'd be okay with me living there?"

Kady smiled and thanked the server as he placed a grilled Caesar salad in front of her before doing the same with Lily.

"Mm. Looks good. Well ...." Kady cut one of the grilled hearts of romaine lettuce. "I may have spoken to her about you a couple of times. She's been a good friend for years. She grew up in Fair Oaks, and we went through school together. Your mum actually met her many years ago when she came home for a visit. They liked one another a great deal. Anyway, when I told Cynthia about what was going on, she suggested I mention the studio to you."

"Wow." Lily tried to balance an unruly crouton on her fork. "That's so nice."

"Your father would be furious if he knew I was relaying this information to you, but you need to know that if you ever need somewhere safe to go, Cynthia's place is yours."

"Does he know who she is?"

"No. He was out of town the one time your mum met her, and Cynthia left Altrusia at least ten years before I met Abby. I doubt your father is even aware of her existence." Kady cut another piece of her romaine. "Understand, honey, I say this as a break-glass-in-case-of-emergency type of thing. I am in no way suggesting that you take off, but I know if it were me, I would rest easier knowing there was somewhere to go if that dreaded day ever came."

Lily cut another piece of lettuce and laid her fork down. "I can't see myself running away ... it's not me. But I'm shocked at how often I fantasize about it. Maybe it's because my thoughts are the one thing that belong only to me, and I have complete freedom within them."

"Indeed. And in your situation, I'd take solace in having an escape plan, even if I never intended to use it." She cut another piece of her salad. "By the way, Lily, I'm sorry that my chat with your father at graduation only made things worse. Against my better judgment, once more, I tried to appeal to him and to offer my services."

"I wasn't going to ask you what happened. But it didn't look pretty."

"It wasn't, but we'll leave it there. I don't want to put down your father. He's a good man. I only want him to come to his senses."

"I'm glad you tried again. It helps me to know that his first response wasn't a one-off thing. Don't ask me why I feel that way; I think it's because I need to know exactly what I'm dealing with, as difficult as that is. I don't want to stick my head in the sand."

"Good for you. I felt bad that it may have soured your graduation."

"Absolutely not. Mum's death and Dad's annihilation of my plans for school did that."

"Please tell me that at the very least you went to that graduation party with Ray."

"I did. I forgot to tell you the last time we spoke on the phone. Hannah came to say good-bye and to sort of apologize for jumping all over me that day at lunch. After she left, Ray and I spent some time together, and later this guy named Trevor introduced himself to me. He graduated a couple of years ago, but his cousin Jimmy was hosting the party. Trevor was on his way out of town in two days. I think he stopped by the party to see his family before he left. Then he kind of saw me."

"Oh!" Kady said after taking a few sips of lemonade. "I see. So you met someone?" She put her glass on the table. "Anything you want to share?"

"Well, he's quite good-looking. He's tall, kind of edgy, and has a long dark blond ponytail. Let me get that part out of the way." She smiled self-consciously. "He's different. He's a photographer, among other things, and he spends his time traveling, working here and there, and not making concrete long-range plans. I certainly don't have any of those, but I'm also not replacing my lack of plans with the cool kind of stuff he has going on." She sighed. "Right now, he's in New Mexico managing a craft gallery for the owner, Mario, who's home in Italy for six months. A couple of days ago, Trevor emailed me some photos of the art they sell along with some shots he took around Santa Fe. Did you know it's the oldest state capitol in the country? It was founded in 1610, I think." She took a long sip of her lemonade. "I love the Pueblo-style architecture there. And the reddish-brown clay of the buildings against the deep-blue sky is gorgeous. Looking at it takes me to another world in my mind."

Kady looked at her with interest. "Are you and Trevor able to talk about things, or are you keeping it light?"

Lily rocked her open hand back and forth. "Somewhat. But I think it takes a while for people to know one another. So far, it's been interesting. I might be a little bit attracted to him, but it's nothing major." She smiled uneasily. "What do you like best about Patrick?"

"Oh!" Kady grinned. "What a question. So much. But if I had to narrow it down, I'd say this about my wonderful husband: he's a hard worker, an ethical man, and he's laser-focused at work. When he comes home, however, he's laser-focused on me, and the same was true with Oliver and Sabrina when they lived at home. Of course, he still has a close relationship with both of his children. As for yours truly, he always makes sure to let me know I'm loved and cherished. He told me on our wedding day that the words 'love' and 'cherish' were not merely words to be said in a vow, but emotions that he would always feel and convey. He's stayed true to those words in ways I never dreamed. And he has the most endearing way about him. He plans wonderful surprises, he's interested in what I do and feel … and most importantly, he makes me laugh and comforts me when I cry. I'm a lucky woman."

Lily offered a sad smile. "I hope I find that kind of true love someday. Even though Ray and I are only friends, he cherishes me. And Trevor is still a stranger, but I'm enjoying our communication." She paused before speaking with emphasis. "I don't want to live vicariously through him, though. I want to have my own adventures."

"Of course you do, honey."

"I wanted to tell you again how much I love my graduation gift.

That cottage is the most special gift I've ever received … even more so that you made it."

Kady reached into her bag, which was hanging on the chair, and pulled out a small wrapped box. "I have something for you that I think you'll find even more special."

Lily noticed a few tears welling in Kady's eyes. "Oh, you didn't need to get me another thing."

"I didn't." Kady handed Lily the box. "This is from your mum."

Instantly, Lily's eyes welled with matching tears. "For real?" Taking the gift, she unwrapped it and put the paper on the table. Finding a small gold box, she glanced at Kady before lifting the lid.

"Your mum had this specially made for you, honey. It's in my possession because I have a friend who excels at gold craftsmanship. Your mum asked me to handle the arrangements so that you wouldn't overhear her discussing it on the phone or accidentally find the gift had it been delivered to her."

Laying the lid on the table, Lily picked up the rose-gold cuff bracelet and held it in her hand. "This is so beautiful. It says 'Lily Alexandra' and there are calla lilies on either side."

"Indeed. But look at what's engraved on the inside."

In awe, Lily held the bracelet up into the light. "I will always be here for you. Love, Mum." She looked at Kady. "This looks like Mum's handwriting. And this little heart looks like the ones she used to draw any time she'd write our names or sign her own."

"It is," Kady said through her tears. "Abby was so insistent that the message be in her own hand, and she wanted the engraving to be perfect. That's why she wanted my friend to do the work." She hesitated uncomfortably. "She chose to give you this on your nineteenth birthday so you would never forget she was here for you after you moved to Los Angeles for school."

Lily said nothing as she put the bracelet on her wrist and admired it. "But now this has even deeper significance."

"I had that same thought." Kady dabbed her eyes with the back of her hand. "So you see, honey, I don't mind my cottage taking a back seat in the gift department."

"Never a back seat," Lily said, unable to take her eyes off the bracelet. "This is so like Mum. To give me something so exquisite and meaningful that it makes that stupid microwave look like nothing more than a grain of sand on the beach. This beautiful treasure is the beach. Kind of reminds me of a Rumi quote she loved."

"Which one is that?"

"Something about the ocean. I can't quite remember now. My brain is so distracted by this gift." Lily looked at the bracelet and rubbed her index and middle fingers over the engraving. "Thank you, Mum." She looked up at Kady. "I can't thank you enough."

"Happy birthday, Lily. And I know it's not the same, but I'm always here for you too."

CHAPTER ELEVEN

"I'll get it!" Lily yelled as the doorbell rang. She hurried in from the kitchen to see who was at the front door.

"Ray! What are you doing here? I was making a shopping list so I could go to the supermarket after our brunch. I guess we're no longer meeting at the restaurant in an hour and a half." Her eyes took in his slightly disheveled appearance. "Come in. Please!"

He brushed a lock of hair out of his eyes as he walked into the foyer. "I tried to call you, but you didn't answer."

"Oh, sorry. I must have left my cell on my bed. You look so stressed. What's going on?"

"The airlines canceled the late afternoon flight I was booked on, and I had to take a seat on the earlier one or wait until tomorrow. And I couldn't do that, or I'd miss the Saturday afternoon orientation. So, *au revoir* to our good-bye brunch."

"Oh, no, Ray!"

"Yeah, you're not kidding."

Lily gestured toward the living room. "Can you stay at all?"

"I've got fifteen minutes tops. My dad is out in the car. He's fine waiting … has a bunch of business calls to make." Raymond followed Lily and took a seat on the couch. "I'm so bummed about this.

We've had to cancel our final get-together three times … and now this last-minute insanity happens."

Lily squeezed his hand. "Let's try to make these the best fifteen minutes ever, okay?" She looked into his hazel eyes. "I'm going to miss you so much."

"Tell me how you are. I've only seen you once since your birthday dinner … when we went to that movie in July, and our phone calls since have been way rushed. I thought we'd have more time together. I'm less organized than I've given myself credit for." He looked around to see if anyone was listening. "Are things getting any better at all?"

"They're exactly the same. Except that I feel worse every day because I see my life slipping away from me. Like water that goes down the drain or the tread that wears off tires. It's gone, and there's no way to get it back."

Lily could see the pain prick his eyes as he listened.

"I remember back in April, your father said he might be okay with you taking community college classes. Are you going to think about that?"

"No." Lily spoke emphatically. "Because if I do, then Dad will feel even more chill about what he's doing to me. You know, like, 'Lily's fine. She's in school, moving forward … I'm not holding her back.' I despise the kind of twisted logic he uses. I have to believe a part of him knows how unfair and horrible all of this is, but I'm not going to do anything to make him feel better, even if it's at my own expense. Who knows, he might not even *want* me to take classes now. And then I'd have to argue with him again. I'm too stressed to even go there. Not now anyway."

"I don't want to sound like Ollie the Optimist …."

Lily looked at him strangely.

"Oh, he's a Christmas collectible that my grandmother puts out on display. But beyond that, it's kind of a thing we say in my family when we think someone is being too cheerful or—"

"I remember now. I've heard you mention Ollie before. Go on."

"I was saying, Lills, that I know how strong you are. And the same strength that keeps you here taking care of your family is the same strength that will help you to move on." He put his hand on her knee. "Does that sound totally contradictory?"

Lily glanced down, closed her eyes, slowly opening them as she looked up. "See, this is why I'm going to miss you so freaking much. You know me, and you understand me in ways few people ever have." She kissed him on the cheek. "And thanks for that. I swear, I miss you already."

"This is the twenty-first century. For all of its good and bad, it's the age of technology, and we can easily keep in touch. And I don't mean the way Hannah has … or hasn't. Have you heard from her?"

"Only once when she sent a group email to her diner friends to say that she and Rob made it to Massachusetts and were moving into their place in Stoneham. I picked up this adorable 3-D welcome-to-your-new-home pop-up card. I mailed it to her along with a short letter inside. Never heard a thing. A few weeks later, I emailed her, and after that I texted twice to see how things were going. The only response I ever got was to my last text … and all she did was send hearts and smiley-face emojis blowing kisses … then TTYS with two x's and two o's. So, yeah … I'm not going to contact her anymore. I'll probably get a birth announcement when her baby is born next month … and maybe I'll send a gift. Or not. I don't know. But I think that's a wrap for my best girlfriend. It's not like I didn't see it coming. But it still hurts." Lily lowered her voice. "I'm so blessed to have Kady to talk to. Without her, I'd have lost it by now."

"She's one beautiful and classy lady."

"Oh, are you talking about me again?" Charlotte said, playfully sauntering into the room. "You totally can say that to my face."

"If I do, will you still roll your eyes at me when you think I'm not looking?" Raymond asked.

Lily laughed as Charlotte blanched.

Charlotte planted herself in front of Lily. "Not funny! What did you tell him, Lily? You suck. I know you said something. I can't believe you would do that." The chains on her black leather boot rattled as she stomped her foot.

"Lily didn't tell me anything." Raymond offered a warm smile. "I've got kick-ass peripheral vision. But I think you confirmed that I'm right. Yes?"

"Well, I … um … just … I didn't …."

"It's okay. I'm cool with it, Char. I get that you think I'm a geek. And I know a guy like me would bore you to death. For starters, you like metal; I like classical."

"I *hate* classical music," Charlotte screamed, her face reddening. "I hate it more than anything. It's boring and stupid, and I wish they never invented it. I hope every last note ever played vaporizes into space and is forever forgotten. It's like the worst thing ever!" She gave Raymond a dirty look and hurried out of the living room, cursing as she ran up the stairs.

Lily's mouth dropped open as she looked at Raymond. "So, um … I have zero idea what that was about. I know she isn't a fan of classical music, but that response was off-the-wall bonkers …

even for Char. Sorry, Ray. No clue why she went all mental on you like that."

"Don't be sorry. Clearly something is going on."

"For sure. I'll try to find out later. But right now, we don't have much more time. Tell me about Princeton. Did you get the housing thing squared away?"

"I did. Found an off-campus studio apartment … exactly what I wanted. The idea of a roommate chilled me to the bone. I don't mind going to a potluck dinner, but the idea of a 'potluck roommate' is absolutely terrifying. Or worse yet, room*mates!*"

"It's kind of hard to live with people you love sometimes, much less strangers."

"I know a lot of students try to connect before they move in together, but you can't know a person until you actually live together. I'm more of a lone wolf anyway; you know that."

Lily reached over and hugged him. "I am too. I guess that's why we've been best friends so many years."

Raymond held her, reluctant to let go. "I worry about you being too much of a loner. And it will be even lonelier for you next week when your sisters go back to school. How about that guy you met at Jimmy's graduation party? Trevor, right? Are you two still in touch?"

"Yeah. He sends me a lot of photos, but once in a while we have a quick video chat. I kind of like him, I guess ... but I wonder why he likes me. When he was telling me all about Machu Picchu and the Andes Mountains in Peru, I'm thinking, well, let's see, I could tell him what the weather's like in Altrusia. Or what I made my family for dinner. Because that's about all I've got, you know?"

Raymond took his finger and wiped away the solitary tear that fell onto her cheek. "You're an intensely sensitive and beautiful human being, Lily. Being in Machu Picchu, Bangladesh, Paris, or an island in Fiji has nothing to do with your identity. And this isn't going to be forever. Trevor may be learning a lot in his travels, but you're learning life lessons that will make all of the difference someday. There are many ways to look at your life, except thinking less of yourself for helping your family during a tragic time." He paused for a minute. "Bet Trevor wouldn't do that, would he?"

Lily mulled over the question. "No, actually. From what I know about him, he wouldn't. But I still like him. He's different and interesting."

"I'm glad you met someone who's become a friend to you. That's all I'll say. Except that—"

"You've got to go," Lily finished for him.

"I do." He hugged her. "But we'll talk often. And before you know it, I'll be back for Christmas, and we'll go to that party together."

"It gives me something to look forward to. More than you know." Lily took his hand as they got up and walked to the door. She laughed and brushed some hair out of his eyes. "You're so adorable. Maybe you should live the rest of your life with your hair flopping in front of your eyes. If you ever give up science and decide to be a detective, you can call yourself 'Sherlocks.'"

He laughed, and his eyes sparkled as he looked at her. "I'll let you know when I get to my place in Princeton. No matter how late it is there. And that's funny." He glanced up the stairs. "Maybe you should find out what's going on with Char. That whole thing was upsetting. Will you text and let me know?"

Lily opened the front door and saw Raymond's father making a beckoning gesture to him, which morphed into a wave as he saw Lily. "I will. Promise. Bye, Ray. Love you." She waved back to his father.

"Love you too, Lills."

Unable to endure the sight of her best friend being driven away, Lily closed the door and hurried up the stairs.

She stood in front of Charlotte's door. As she was about to knock, she heard sobbing. Lily put her ear to the door. The anguish of Charlotte's cries too much to bear, Lily knocked with an urgency she knew was ill advised.

"Go away!"

"Char, may I please come in?

"Go away! And don't try coming in through the bathroom because I've locked the door. Get the hell away from me."

Across the hall, hearing the voices, Willow opened her door and stood with Quincy in her arms.

Lily saw the distress on her face and motioned for her to go back into her room, which Willow did. "Char, please let me talk to you! I'm begging you, okay? Open the door."

Charlotte pulled the door open so hard that Lily nearly fell into the room. Her dark makeup streaking down her face, Charlotte glared at her. "What the hell do you want?"

"Can we sit and talk?"

"'Can we sit and talk,'" Charlotte repeated, mocking her. "Such a motherly thing to say? Well, no. We can't."

"Fine. We'll stand here. Thanks for letting me in."

"Well, I don't appreciate you being here, so say what you want and get the hell out."

"Char, please! What are you so upset about? Why are you so angry with me? And why did you rage against classical music like that? And why are you even all dressed up in the morning?"

"Because I'm going out with Francesca, Miss Nosy. That's why."

"Okay." Lily struggled to tamp down her angst. "Can you tell me why you're so upset?"

"Because you've been telling Ray that I said he's boring. I can't believe you would do that and embarrass me! I like to mess around; you know that, but no, you have to go all blabbermouth on steroids."

"No, no, no! You're wrong on this, Char. I didn't say a word to him. Do you think I'd want to tell my best friend that my sister likes to joke around about how boring he is? How can you seriously think I'd do that? Give me a break!"

Charlotte put her right hand on her hip. "Because I seriously heard what he said. That he knows I think he's a geek and probably boring or whatever. I can't even remember his exact words now, but you told him. You know you did."

As Lily put a calming hand on her sister's shoulder, Charlotte swiftly raised her arms and took a defiant step to her left. "Don't touch me! I'm not playing with you!"

Lily flinched. "Okay! I won't touch you and we won't sit. Let me explain about Ray." She saw Charlotte shoot her a look of disgust but continued on. "See, one of the things I've always liked about him, even from when we were kids, is that even though he is on the quiet side, he's an observant person. He's sensitive, aware of his environment, and he easily picks up on things a lot of other people miss. All. The. Time. So I guess he's seen you roll your eyes at him. He told you he has 'kick-ass peripheral vision.' Didn't you hear him? You can only blame yourself for the embarrassment, Char. You know, if you're going to make fun of someone, be real sure they don't hear or see you. But don't scream at me because you got caught. I had nothing to do with that. And Ray had a smile on his face the whole time he was talking to you. He wasn't angry. And you shouldn't be either."

"Liar! You told him! You are such a bitch, Lily!"

"Who's the bitch, Char? Because there are only two of us in the room, and it's not me. So I guess that leaves you! Why are you always treating me like dirt under your chain-wrapped boots? I've done every effin' thing I can for you. In case you forgot, I'm supposed to be in LA at fashion school now. But no, that dream is swimming in sewage, flushed away by Dad, so I can be here taking care of all of you. And all you do is attack me. Do you think this is the life I wanted at nineteen? To clean the house, shop for food, pay bills, make dinner, do the laundry, and take in and pick up Dad's dry cleaning? And that hardly covers it." She took a much-needed breath. "Well, Char, do you? Because I didn't fucking sign up for this! And definitely not the part where you abuse me so you can have relief from your pain."

"That's not what I'm doing!" Charlotte scrunched her nose and narrowed her eyes. "I already know your sob story, Lily. You're lucky you didn't have to watch that pickup truck take Mum's life away, and you don't have to deal with flashbacks and nightmares."

"I hate that you suffer with that." Lily softened as her rage ran for cover.

"Yeah, you feel real bad. That's why you had to make things worse for me by telling Ray some bullshit."

"I didn't, Char! I swear on Mum that I never said a word. Can you seriously stop with that already?"

"Whatever." Charlotte looked away from her.

Lily drew a calming breath and let a few moments of silence settle between them. "Listen, Char, there's no way you're crying over what happened with Ray. For some reason, you freaked out when he mentioned classical music, though. That's what set you off. Please tell me."

"I don't want to talk about it." Charlotte walked over to grab a tissue from a box on her nightstand and cleaned the black makeup off her cheeks. "Now I have to re-do my face."

"You don't need makeup to look pretty." Lily wished she could swallow her words the moment she spoke them.

"It's my look. I dig it. I'm a freakin' makeup artist. I wear makeup. It's what I do. I love it. If makeup was a person, the sun would shine out its ass. Okay? And for the record, you don't even sound like a mum. You sound like someone's grandmother. Hi, Granny!"

Lily turned and put her hands over her face and held them there for several seconds. Defeated, she took them away and looked at Charlotte again. "Okay. That was a stupid thing to say. Sorry. Excuse me for being human. I wanted to let you know I think you're pretty. I wish you would tell me what made you freak out like that. And like *this*, actually!"

Charlotte walked toward her. "Because I hate stupid music without lyrics. Makes me think of organ music and that reminds me of Mum's funeral. Because that's what Dad played at home when all of the people came over afterward. I hate the sound of all of those violins crying. It's old people's dead music."

"Then why the fascination with skulls? Why the tattoo on your—"

"My ass? Because I relate to the souls who have come and gone. I was probably one of them in another life. That doesn't mean I want to hear boring and depressing classical music. Besides, I think skulls are sexy. And ass tattoos are way sexy."

"Oh, my God. Are you having sex?"

"Wouldn't you like to know?"

"I hope you're not, Char. You're only fifteen."

"And I'll be sixteen in two months. Then you can say, 'I hope not, Char. You're only sixteen.'"

"Are you seeing Francesca's brother? What's his name … Nico?"

"Not exactly. But he's seen my ass. He watched me get the tat. He said it turned him on." She smiled to herself. "Later, when Alex and Camille left, he showed me the tat on *his* ass. It's a raven. But it wasn't about the tat. I know he just wanted me to see his ass."

"Holy … how old is he? Nineteen? Twenty? I hope that's all he showed you. If he touches you, it's statutory rape. I hope you know that. I hope *he* knows that."

"I'm not a statue. So we're safe." She paused. "And before you go all condescending and explain-y and adult-y on me, I know what statutory rape is. And he's almost twenty."

"Char, come on! If you're doing anything, and I pray that you're not, please be careful. Please use protection. Have him use a condom. But now is not the time. Please abstain. Trust me. You have your entire life ahead of you to—"

"Like Mum had her entire life ahead of her?"

"Please tell me you're not using Mum's death as an excuse to have—"

"Go, Lily. I answered all your stupid questions that I'm going to answer."

Lily swallowed the lump in her throat as despair consumed her. "Okay, but I'm here for you no matter what. I'll even take you to the doctor if you want to go on the pill. Don't ever be afraid to ask."

"Oh, puh-leeze! Stop with the Mum stuff. You'll never be her.

In fact, that sound you hear coming out of your mouth is you sucking at it!"

"I don't want to be Mum!" Lily screamed. She waited a minute, then spoke with calm. "I'm only trying to be a sister, but you clearly don't like me. No matter how hard I try, no matter what I say and do, you hate me."

"Girl, bye," Charlotte said with a dismissive hand gesture.

Tears falling down her face, Lily rushed into her room and shut the door. Picking up the phone where she had left it on her bed, she sat down and texted Ray:

Tell U about Char when we talk. 2 much 2 text. But what I can tell u is that I won't be able to leave here for a long time. It's how it is. My life is doomed but my fam needs me more than I thought. Sux I know. So I have to stay. Love u. xo"

As Lily lay down on the bed, muffling her sobs into a pillow, she heard her door creak open. Just as she was going to request time alone, she saw Willow delicately drop Quincy onto her bedroom floor and quietly shut the door.

Within seconds, the cat jumped up on the bed and nuzzled her face. As Lily stopped crying, Quincy nestled close to her and fell fast asleep. Minutes later, she was right behind him.

CHAPTER TWELVE

Lily sat at the kitchen table and stared at her half-eaten oatmeal. Transfixed by the stale existence that now defined her, she noticed that the blueberries in her bowl resembled dark little eyes, staring at her, asking what they'd ever done for her to want to eat them out of existence. The more she pondered the surreal scenario her mind had created, the less imaginary it became. "Sorry." She pushed the bowl away. "So sorry."

"Lily. Why are you apologizing to a bowl of oatmeal?"

Stunned, she sat upright in the chair and turned her head. "Dad. You scared me. Why aren't you at work? In fact, I remember hearing you start your engine at the usual time this morning."

"Well …." He pulled out a kitchen chair and sat. "Two reasons. I needed to take my car to the shop today, so I drove it there, and a young mechanic gave me a ride home. I could have asked him to drop me off at the train station and gone into work from there, but I've wanted to talk to you privately for quite a while now. I thought taking a few hours off from work, while your sisters are at school, would provide the optimal environment for a conversation."

Lily gulped. "What did you want to talk about?"

"A bit of this and that. I took my car in for a three-thousand-mile checkup; think of this conversation as *our* three-thousand-mile checkup."

Expressionless, Lily stared at him.

"How about something like, 'what's on your mind, Dad?' That would be preferable to a blank stare."

"Give me a script then. This is all I've got at the moment."

Dalton's face tensed as he thought. Finally, he spoke. "Today marks eight months since we lost your precious mum. Hearing you speak that way to me, it seems like your manners are dwindling as the expanse of time between Mum's life and death grows wider."

"I haven't lost my manners, Dad ... only my dreams and my plans. And sorry, but hearing your car analogy didn't exactly warm me to whatever conversation you want to have. I'm doing my best ... for all of you, but Willow is the only one who appreciates me."

"*I* appreciate you, Lily." He thought. "But if that's what you think, let's unpack this, shall we?"

"Unpack this? When did you start using that word for anything other than emptying suitcases?"

"Your old man isn't as out of things as you think."

"Okay, sure. Unpack away then." She watched his face redden as she spoke.

"You know, Lily, I would be a lot more comfortable in my recliner, and no doubt the soft cushions of the couch would be more cozy for you." He rose and made a sweeping hand motion toward the living room. "Shall we relocate?"

Lily got up, stoically walked through the dining room, and took a seat on the couch in the living room.

Visibly more at ease, Dalton sat back in his recliner and put his feet up. "Where to begin. I don't suppose you'd like to start us off, Lily?"

"Uh ... not really, since I have no idea what this is about. You called for this meeting. So why don't you say whatever is on your mind?"

"I'm not appreciating this defiance that seems to tinge your words. More and more, you're wearing your resentment on your sleeve."

Lily picked up a throw pillow and put it on her lap. "Dad, I'm doing everything you've asked me to do. But if acting thrilled to be living this life is part of what you want, well, sorry, I can only deliver so much, you know?"

As his eyes blinked rapidly and his fingers drummed the armrests, Lily watched her father's unease manifest into the same nervous actions she had come to know well over the years. Suddenly calm, as if by the magic of a kind wizard, Dalton pulled a pen out of the inside of his jacket pocket and examined it as if he'd never seen it before. "This pen has a sonic titanium metallic fusion resin barrel." His anxious expression turned sad. "When Mum gave me this for my forty-seventh birthday, that's exactly what she said as she read the description from that little piece of folded paper inside the box. Then, she dared me to memorize it. Took me a week, but I finally was able to say it flawlessly: sonic titanium metallic fusion resin barrel. Oh boy, we had some good laughs about it. I guess it doesn't sound too funny in the retelling, does it?" He looked down." I miss saying it, that's all. I miss my wife."

"I know you do. Me too. I don't know what else to say."

"Speaking of special gifts, I bought you a beautiful microwave for your birthday … and I can't say I was impressed by the thank you I received. For you, Lily, it was rather cold and impersonal."

"Sort of like the gift itself."

Dalton put the pen back in his pocket and sat upright. For two minutes, he said nothing. Just as she thought he would get up and leave, he spoke: "Lily, I … I'm sorry. I guess you're right. It's not a gift I'd normally have picked out for you, but under the circumstances, now that you're the lady of the house, I thought you'd like it."

I fucking hate being called that! "Please don't call me the 'lady of the house.' That's got to be from another time in history or something. I don't want that title, Dad, and it's not how I see myself. To be even more accurate, I despise being called that. And the microwave is nice … for the family … but not for me as a birthday gift."

"I'm sorry. Your mum loved it, so I thought buying it for you would …."

"Would *what?* Be like she was still alive and you were buying it for her?"

Dalton nodded. "S'pose so."

"Would you have given it to *her* as a birthday gift?"

"Oh, no!" He looked down in shame as he realized the impact of his response.

"Well, I guess it's good we got that out of the way. What else did you need to tell me?"

"I haven't mentioned this before, but since your birthday back in June, I noticed you're wearing the bracelet that your mum ordered for you. I also know that Kady was handling it for her. Something about her friend being a jewelry artisan or something or other … I don't know."

"Uh-huh."

"So how did you get it?"

Where do you think I got it? "When I had lunch with Kady on my birthday."

"Oh, that's great." He screwed up his face as his eyes seared with anger. "I asked you not to see her. I *told* her not to see you, but then you both defy me and get together anyway. Oh, yeah. I'm sure you told her all about my thoughtless birthday gift. What a perfect opening you provided for her to whip out Mum's gift to show me up. Did I get the sequence of events right? And how often do you speak to her or see her?"

"You want to 'unpack' things, Dad? Because you just handed

me a suitcase that's stuffed so full I can't close it. Let's start here." Lily straightened her posture. "I'm a legal adult. Isn't it enough that I'm here, taking over for Mum? I know a lot of people in this town, but they're acquaintances and casual friends. Kady is the only real friend I have in Altrusia, and I'm not cutting her out of my life because you don't like it. Not doing it. And no, she didn't 'whip out Mum's gift' to show you up. She gave me the bracelet to fulfill her best friend's wishes and give me the special gift that Mum wanted me to have." She paused, feeling the blood pulsate through her veins. "I have a question for you, Dad. Since you were so aware that Kady was handling Mum's gift to me, what would you have done if Kady hadn't had the chance to give it to me? Left it to rot so you could avoid having to talk to her and deprive me of the most special gift I'll probably ever get in my life?"

Dalton said nothing.

"Unreal. You can't even answer me because that's exactly what you would have done. Wow. Nice to know … not." *I swear, some days I can't stand to even look at you or hear your voice.*

"This conversation certainly isn't going the way I expected it would. But I suppose I deserved that. I can't say what I would have done because I noticed the bracelet on your wrist almost immediately and therefore never had to consider my options. I'm sorry. I'm not proud to say that, but it's true nonetheless."

Lily sighed. "I'm not trying to be mean, Dad. I'm *really* unhappy, and all of this gets harder for me all the time … not easier, as maybe you may have talked yourself into believing it would. Sorry if I haven't settled into the domestic routine you envisioned for me. That was Mum's life, and she loved it. But this is my reality, and I don't even like it. In fact, I hate it. I'm here because I love my family … very much … and I want to help."

Dalton sank into silence for another few moments.

"You've become more introspective and aware of yourself, Lily."

Yeah, because I have more time to think since you took an axe to my life. "And do you see that as a good thing or a bad thing?"

Flustered, Dalton took his pen out of his pocket and began nervously twisting it from the middle. "It's always good to be self-aware, honey. I guess I had only hoped you'd become more aware of what family means to you."

"Are you serious?" Lily's voice got louder. "Did you even *hear* what I said? Why do you think I'm still here? Char's angry with me more times than not. And you just said there's a 'tinge of defiance' that coats my words. Well guess what … there's always this taint of disappointment when *you* speak to me. Like bitter herbs on a sweet dessert."

"Oh, Lily, that's a bit much."

"No, it's not. Even when you compliment me on something, it always feels like a buffer for the hammer you're about to drop. You know?"

"Sweetheart, if I felt there was any other way for us to get through this nightmare, I wouldn't have stopped you from going to school in Los Angeles or from working at the diner. But your sisters and I need you. I know Charlotte is difficult a good deal of the time, but you have to understand how precarious her mindset is … even when she seems in control. It's worrisome. I can't work and watch over her at the same time. And yes, I'm disappointed you wouldn't ask her to get therapy, but as thick as I am, I get it. You probably know that I suggested it to her myself, implored her, rather, and she vehemently refused."

My mindset is precarious too, not that you ever give that *any thought.* "No, I didn't know that, Dad. Char doesn't exactly confide in me, and that's probably the last subject she'd want to discuss. You know?"

"And Willow," he continued, "she's always been such a sweet girl, but she's hurting, and I know that if you left, she'd fall into despair.

I worry about her too, which is precisely why I was happy to let her have a cat."

"I was pleasantly surprised … thrilled, actually, when you said yes so quickly."

"I'm not a monster," Dalton said quietly, almost to himself.

"And what about you, Dad? Couldn't you have found another way, rather than put me in Mum's shoes and take my life away from me? Kady offered …."

"I knew that woman would make me look bad. And that's precisely why—"

"Stop there, Dad. And don't call Mum's best friend 'that woman.' She thinks you're a good man who's trying to cope with his grief. She hasn't made you look bad. And she's been a lifesaver for me. You should be grateful for her. And if you're not, then please keep it to yourself. I can't stand to hear you hating on her. She's one of the best people I've ever known, and I'm sure you know how wonderful her heart is. I'm not cutting her out of the picture. I'm here, doing what you've asked. I've put my life on indefinite hold. How much more do you want to take from me?"

Dalton dropped his head in shame. "Nothing. In fact, I wanted to say that you gave Charlotte a wonderful sixteenth birthday back in October, and the Thanksgiving meal you prepared was divine. I know I said something on each occasion, but it bears repeating."

"Willow helped me a lot with Char's dinner and also with Thanksgiving. But it would've been so much nicer if we could've gone to the Harrigans' like we used to. But no."

"I won't try to stop you from seeing that wom … Kady. But I'm not going to pretend I like it, nor will I spend holidays with her family anymore."

"I get that, Dad. I feel the same way about my life here. I'm not going to pretend I like it. You've always gotten along so well with Kady. I have no idea why you've turned against her now."

As if he were flicking her words out of his airspace, Dalton made a nervous waving gesture with his hands, ignoring the unwelcome response. "I see you still maintain a healthy friendship with Hannah, despite her move to Massachusetts."

"Actually, I have no real friendship with Hannah at all anymore."

Dalton cast a suspicious glance at her. "Hmm. No friendship, but yet I saw a package addressed to her last month. Do you always send gifts to people you're no longer friendly with?"

"Why do you even care about Hannah and me, Dad? So you can rest easier knowing my life isn't as empty as I've said it is?"

Dalton looked down, confirming to Lily that she'd guessed correctly. "If you must know, Dad, Hannah had her baby, and I sent her a gift. Actually, I wasn't going to, but then I remembered something and changed my mind."

"What would that be?"

"Hannah had a son and named him Kenneth Robert. Her grandfather is named Kenneth, and the baby's middle name is after her husband, Rob. I remembered that Mum told me once that she was hoping to have a boy after Willow was born, and had that happened, she would have named him Kenneth Ellis or Kenneth Robert. Remembering that touched me, so I broke down and bought a gift ... sort of for Mum in an odd way. Besides, I'd rather have Hannah be the one to cut the ties that bind, not me. I hope—"

Dalton abruptly cut her off. "I'd like to talk about Christmas."

"Why did you interrupt me like that? You're the one who asked about Hannah." *I guess you didn't like the answer. Didn't fit into your playbook.*

"I did. But I didn't ask to be reminded of something that pained your mother ... and me. See the difference, Lily? Can we talk about Christmas, please?"

"What is there to talk about?" Lily sighed in frustration. "What more do you want me to do?"

"I thought maybe you'd shop for gifts that your sisters might like."

Buy your own effing gifts! "I'll buy Willow and Char the gifts that I want to give them … from *me*. But I'm not shopping for them like Mum used to do and putting your name on the tags. I know you don't want to hear that, Dad, but I'm actually doing you a favor on this one. It would only cause resentment all around. They'd think you didn't care enough to be bothered."

"That's ironic, seeing the reaction I got after selecting your birthday present. But all right. I hear you. We'll keep it simple. I'll find a way to handle the gifts." He looked at Lily and laughed nervously. "For starters, no household appliances."

She tried to smile, but her mouth wasn't interested.

He spoke with unnatural cheerfulness. "We'll have a family dinner on Christmas Eve and a breakfast in the morning before we open gifts."

Lily nodded. "That's about what I had in mind."

He forced a smile. "Well, hallelujah, we agree on something."

"I need to ask you a question." Lily hugged the throw pillow to her chest.

"Go on then," he said, the cheer fading from his tone.

"If Char was my age and I was her age, would you have asked her to do what you're asking me to do?"

He answered without a moment's thought. "Of course not. Charlotte isn't cut out for this. She'd have run away on day one. Day two, if we were lucky." Hearing his own words, he looked at Lily and frowned. "I know how that sounded. You must think you're being punished for being the wonderful person you are, Lily, but …."

"If you tell me that virtue is its own reward, I'll scream so loud the neighbors will hear me."

Dalton reeled back. "I was just …."

"Yeah, I thought so. Now I'm going to toss the oatmeal I left on the kitchen table down the garbage disposal and go for a walk in the park. So unless there's anything else you have to say, I'd like to leave now."

Too choked up to respond, his eyes watery and pained, he put up a palm as if to give permission, got up from his recliner, rushed into his den, and closed the door behind him.

"Have a great day, Dad." Lily stood in the empty space that had accommodated him as bitterness wrapped its arms around her. "Always good to have such a warm conversation with my father. Nothing like it."

CHAPTER THIRTEEN

"Whatcha doin', Lills?" Willow asked, walking into Lily's bedroom.

Lily, sitting cross-legged on her bed, turned her open laptop to display the family photos she'd been looking at. "I'm missing Mum." She patted the empty space next to her on the bed. "Sit with me."

Willow settled into the space. "I talk to her every night when I go to bed … and sometimes during the whole day. I hate how bad it hurts. I keep hoping we'll hear her again."

"Me too." Lily put her arms around her youngest sister and held her close. "Look how beautiful Mum looked in this photo by the lake. This was at Big Bear in Southern California. You were about seven. We rented a cabin for the week. It was so peaceful. Remember?"

"Yup. I kept asking Dad where the big bears were." Willow gazed lovingly at the photo. "Look how happy Mum looks in the canoe, wearing her sunglasses and crazy straw hat. And Dad. I forgot he could even smile this big. He hardly ever smiles anymore, and when he does, it's because he's forcing himself for our sakes." She sniffled. "If I didn't have you and Quincy, I wouldn't smile at all."

"Mum would be so happy you have your boy," Lily said as Quincy strolled into her room and jumped onto Willow's lap. "She adored cats, but her allergy was severe."

"There aren't any allergies in heaven. That's good, right? Maybe Mummy has a cat now too." She scratched Quincy's neck. "Maybe a hundred ... and one of every breed of dog that ever lived. Or maybe just corgis like the Queen." Willow smiled as best as she could. "And maybe even dinosaurs too!"

"You're so cute, Wills. I hope she does." Lily looked at the time on her computer. "It's later than I thought. Is Char home from school yet?"

"I haven't seen her. Are you worried?"

"I'm concerned. Not quite worried, but I will be if she doesn't come home soon ... or at least text me."

Willow looked at Lily's laptop. "Are you planning to video chat with your friend Trevor?"

"I am. He's in Paris now. I think it's about midnight there, so he'll probably call any moment. I was looking at the photos of Mum while I waited for him."

Willow stood and held Quincy in her arms. "Then I'm going to leave so you can talk in private. I love you, Lills. And just because you're the oldest, it doesn't mean you can't come cry with me when you miss Mum so much you can't stand the pain, okay?"

"Oh, Wills ..."

"See you later." Willow took two steps before Quincy leaped onto the floor. "Sometimes he likes me to hold him, but other times, he likes to do his own thing."

"He's a cat. They're independent creatures." Lily turned to her laptop as she heard the incoming call.

Willow gently closed the door after Quincy had scooted out into the hallway.

"Hey, Lily. Can you see me okay?"

"I don't recognize the background. You're not in your room."

"Yeah, I gave that up." Trevor stood in front of a large window and removed a large dark gray knitted scarf from his neck. "Met a friend of a friend who needed someone to house-sit for about two weeks and take care of his dog. Not to mention he's got a virtual rainforest of plants inside and a bunch of flowers outside … in this wrought-iron thingy below the window. So yay, two weeks that won't cost me a dime, and I'll make some pretty euros while I'm at it."

"From what I can see," Lily said, adjusting the screen, "the place looks nice. Upscale."

"Bling, bling for sure. It's on the Champs Elysées. What you can see are the lights from the buildings on the other side of the street. If you could look out the window to my left, you'd be going toward the Arc de Triomphe. The other way is the Place de Concorde. Super ritzy area and it's even prettier this time of the year. Only thing I don't like is that the little shops where I buy my food are a bit of a walk. But hey, that's cool, have legs will travel. You know? And now Monet, my new four-legged friend, will come with me. He's a Barbet … fluffy guy with white paws and some white on his chest. Smart as a whip."

"What does that actually mean?" Lily hinted at a smile.

"It means he's intelligent."

"No, I was making a joke … sort of. Like why are whips smart? I never did understand that expression."

"What's that? There was a lot of honking outside, and I didn't hear you. The French are impatient drivers … easily pissed off. They never met a horn they didn't like to use." He grinned. "They're real horny!"

Refusing to acknowledge him, Lily just stared.

Disappointed, he went on. "Sorry, Lily. What were you saying?"

"Nothing worth repeating. Never mind, Trevor."

"How are you doing, beautiful?"

"About the same. You know. It's getting harder, with Christmas being here in two weeks. Can't imagine it without my mum. Trying to make the best out of an impossible situation. The routine only gets old and never any better."

"I'm walking you over to the couch," Trevor said as the background behind him changed. "I need to sit my tired ass down. Speaking of old, I got some killer shots of these elderly Frenchmen at the Marché aux Puces today. That means flea market in French."

"I know. I was actually there. We have a painting in our living room that our parents found in one of the shops. The man who sold it to them was—"

"Oh. I forgot you'd ever been out of the country."

Lily's heart sank. "Yeah, remember I told you at the party when you asked if I'd been abroad? And I made a joke and said—"

"Your mother was from England or somewhere, right?" Trevor asked, talking over her. "Oh, here's Monet." He turned his head. "C'mere, *garçon.*"

Lily watched as the dog climbed up onto the couch with Trevor. "Oh, he's absolutely precious."

"He's an old breed. Jean-Paul, the guy who owns him, said he's a water-retrieving dog."

"Does he actually retrieve water, or only things in it?" Lily offered a slight smile.

"Huh? He doesn't go near water."

"Just making a joke," Lily said, openly wearing her frustration.

"Oh, guess I didn't get it. I went to the coolest place today. The catacombs. It's an underground ossuary and—"

"I know what it is. My parents were afraid it might freak us out, so we didn't get to see them when we were in Paris. But I think my sister Char would love to go there."

"Where's that?" Charlotte said, opening the bathroom door into Lily's room.

"Glad to see you," Lily said, wide-eyed at Charlotte's suspicious entrance. "I'm talking to my friend Trevor. He's in Paris. Do you want to meet him?"

Charlotte walked to the bed and nodded for Lily to move over.

"Hi, I'm Char!" She sat and waved to Trevor.

"Whoa, not the little sister I expected. I'm Trevor. Looking at you, I can tell you'd totally dig the catacombs."

"What are they?"

"They're like part of a tunnel network under the city of Paris. At one time, the French were kind of running out of places for dead people … and the city was starting to smell bad. So, in like 1786 or thereabouts, they started stashing their dead under the city. Now there's like six million people under there. Walls and walls lined with their skulls and bones."

"Are you serious? I would love to see that. I have a skull tat on my—"

Lily slapped Charlotte's upper arm with the back of her hand as she resumed the original conversation. "It would be fascinating to know the history of those people. Who were they? Were they from the lower classes? Did they have families?"

"Personally, I would love to see photos," Charlotte said.

"Oh, there are tons of them on the Internet," Lily said to Charlotte. She looked at Trevor. "Aren't there like fourteen catacombs in Rome?"

"I don't know," Trevor said, slightly irritated. "How would you know that?"

"Probably history class or something. Maybe someone in my family told me. Not sure how I know it."

"So do the skulls ever pop out of the walls and bite people on the ass?" Charlotte asked.

"Man, I was thinking something along those lines," Trevor said as his face lit up with enthusiasm. "Wouldn't that make a great horror film?"

"It could be like a combination porn and horror movie," Charlotte said. "Every guy who goes down in the …"

"Catacombs," Trevor said.

"Yeah … every guy who goes down … well I didn't mean it that way but same thing … you know. Every guy who goes down there gets a boner."

Trevor burst out laughing. "Man, you are funny! You're fuckin' hilarious."

Disgusted, Lily did her best not to let it show but shot a look at Charlotte.

"So how come people are allowed to go underground and look at bones?" Charlotte asked, pretending not to notice Lily.

"Because part of it is a museum now. I think there are like two hundred miles, so yeah, there's a whole lot that's not open to the public. But that hasn't stopped people from sneaking into those areas … and getting lost. I'm a thrill seeker and I dig a life of adventure, but I don't think I'd want to be trapped underground with the ghosts of Paris past. People have died doing that."

"So then they end up being part of what they were sneaking in to see, right?"

"In theory. But I'm sure they take the dead looky loos somewhere else, though it kind of would be a suitable resting place. Some guy at the museum was saying that once it took them three days to find some kids. They had bad hypothermia when they were rescued. It gets cold as fuck down there. If you get lost in that network, you could freeze to death."

"That's creepy."

"It is. Here's something else: the catacombs have lots of secret entrances."

"Wow, fascinating. I wonder why they needed them." Charlotte looked at Lily, then Trevor. "Sorry, but I gotta go. I'm being dirty-looked out of the room. Nice to meet you, Trevor. Thanks for telling me all of that. Way cool."

"Hey, you too, Char. Hope I get to talk to you again."

Trevor frowned as Charlotte got off Lily's bed and left the

room. "I like your sister a whole lot."

"I noticed. Would you rather talk to her?"

"No, beautiful. I called to talk to you. Hey, hope you're not jelly or anything."

"Um … no. For what reason would I be?"

"I don't know." He rubbed Monet's neck as he spoke. "Once I took this chick to a party, and when another chick started hitting on me, my date knocked the drink out of her hand, and the other chick punched her in the face for it. Man, talk about a catfight. Me-freakin-ow, you know?" He made a claw gesture with his hands.

"That sounds pretty horrible."

"Actually, I kinda dug … um, yeah, what an ugly scene."

"So what will you do after you house-sit?" Lily asked, eager to change the subject.

"Think I'll head south. Down to Arles. That's where that famous café is that Van Gogh painted."

"I know. I had lunch there. My entire family did. When we were in the South of France."

"Oh." Trevor slumped as disappointment took hold of him. "Well, I'll be going to other towns too. Lots of them."

Acting as if she hadn't noticed, Lily continued talking. "It's cool to look at Van Gogh's masterpiece even now and remember how we were all there once, having a meal. It's like we were magically transported into a famous painting and came out again. Eating there was my mum's idea. She always wanted us to experience as much of life as we could."

"Wish my parents thought like that. I called them the other day. It's like nothing ever changes in their world … except they got new wallpaper and carpet in their bedroom … so that was pretty exciting." His face contorted in disgust. "Oh, and they're going to San Francisco for a three-day weekend. My mother even booked tickets for Alcatraz. For them, that's like going to the moon."

"I think you might be exaggerating a little."

"You haven't met my parents. So, um, any plans for Christmas?"

"My friend Ray is coming home for the holidays, and that means the world to me. He's taking me to this special party in Sonoma. His aunt and uncle know a lot of musicians and artists of all kinds. They all come to the party and perform … even the actors. They read from books like *A Christmas Carol* and *A Child's Christmas in Wales*. Sounds amazing, doesn't it?"

"Oh, yeah," Trevor said, looking down as he pet the dog.

"Other than that, I'll be trying to help my family get through our first Christmas without Mum. Not sure how that will go."

"Sorry, Lily. I remember how sad you were when I met you. I know it's hard for you."

"Thanks." She smiled. "Looks like you'll still be in Paris."

"Yeah, I will. This house-sitting gig is actually until the second or third of January. Maybe I'll find some other people with nothing to do on Christmas. If not, I can hang with the misfits who don't give a damn what day it is as long as they've got a bottle of red plonk and a pack of Gauloises nearby. Lots of people like that. I help them in any way I can. Like maybe I'll bring some baguettes and cheese with me. Spend time listening to their stories. It always makes people feel good when you listen, Lily."

"Oh, I didn't realize you were so fluent."

He took a moment to rage internally, though nonetheless visibly. "Okay, so my French isn't that great. I have to pretend to understand more than I do … but they don't care. Just being there helps them. Ya dig? And I like to make the world a better place. Not sure what else there is to do on Christmas."

"Sounds like you'd like to be with your family."

Trevor shooed the thought away with the shake of his head. "Ah … I'm fine. Same old same old back home, you know?"

"Sometimes 'same old' is the most wonderful thing in the world. I'd give anything for a same-old Christmas here."

"Oh, yeah. I guess you would. Sorry. I didn't mean anything by that. I hope it's good for you. I'd better go. I think I trekked about fifteen miles today. You don't see much in Paris standing still. Kind of ready to hit the sack, but wanted to see your pretty face first. You're absolutely gorgeous, Lily. The first second I saw you, I knew I was looking at a beauty queen."

"Thanks, Trevor."

"I'll be in touch before Christmas, okay? And tell your sister I dug meeting her."

I think you made that quite obvious. "I will. Bye, Trevor."

Lily stared despondently at the screen as the call ended.

"So, were you gonna deliver the message?"

Lily jumped. "Char, why are you sneaking up on me? And were you eavesdropping before and now? Those were two extremely timely entrances."

"I wasn't exactly eavesdropping." Charlotte leaned against the wall. "But when I came home, Wills said you were worried about me. So after I put my stuff in my room, I came through the bathroom and heard you talking to that guy."

"And naturally you couldn't help but listen."

"Maybe for a minute. Until I heard you say my name. Right now I was fixing my hair in the mirror. So you see … no big whoop, Lills. But hello, Trevor is super hot. Do you like him? You know, *like him*?"

"He's just a friend. Sometimes it seems like he's more interested in impressing me than he is in getting to know me."

"Maybe he's on a high about all of the cool stuff he's seeing. A hot guy like that can find lots of girls. He wouldn't call you and stay in touch if he didn't like you."

"I guess you're right. Anyway, I'm glad you're home. I haven't started dinner yet, so is there anything special you want?"

"Do we still have Mum's frozen soup?"

"We do. Want me to thaw it out? Get some nice bread to go with it?"

Charlotte thought. "No, maybe not yet. Not quite ready to eat the last meal from Mum. It would be one more ending. I don't even know why I asked."

"I hear you."

Without saying another word, Charlotte turned and walked back through the bathroom, dolefully, to her lonely space on the other side.

Lily got up and closed the door. She glanced at the cottage on her bureau as she walked to the one window in her room. Looking outside, she saw the bare limbs of the trees and the dry patches of grass that oddly mixed with the green ones. Her mind wandered to the stream near her cottage in the Cotswolds. Lined with the ferns, plants, and flowers that grew untamed … the radiant flora represented every dream and ambition gone astray … so pretty and patient as they waited for her return. Rain had visited the village again. She loved how the lush greenery contrasted against the deep gray sky … a perfect light in an imperfect world.

How fortuitous … that her mind could travel as far away as she needed it to go ….

CHAPTER FOURTEEN

"Come in," Lily said as she sat on her bed looking at her phone.

"Good morning," Dalton said. "Are you busy?"

"I'm reading an email from Hannah."

"Ah! So you *did* hear from her?"

Lily read the email aloud: "Dear Lily, Thank you for the gorgeous, embroidered baby blanket for our Kenny boy. He's so snuggly in it, as you can see from the attached photos. It's hectic and crazy being a mom, but I love it. I could use a bit more sleep, but no complaints … except that it gets cold in Massachusetts. Hope you are well. Thanks for the lovely gift. Love, Hannah and Rob."

"I'm glad she wrote to you," Dalton said awkwardly.

"As you heard, she didn't ask me a thing about my life, despite what I'm going through, because she doesn't want me to write back. She has a new life now, and I'm not even the smallest part of it. That message was about as generic and impersonal as it gets."

Dalton shrugged off his unease. "What's this, Lily?" As he looked in the direction of her bureau, he walked over to examine the miniature cottage next to the framed photo. "This is your mum's cottage. Well, it's actually *your* cottage now. I never saw this, but then again, I haven't been in this room for a long time. This is extraordinary.

It looks like someone literally shrunk the actual family cottage. I'm guessing this was a birthday gift from Ellis and Millie."

"It's special to me ... as are they. That's why I put it next to Mum's photo."

"The perfect spot." He cleared his throat. "Lily, I have a delicate matter or two to discuss. I need you to come down to my bedroom. Can you do that?"

"You can't ask me here?"

"I can't. Do you mind following me?"

Lily put her phone in her pocket, got off the bed, and walked behind her father down the hallway and around the corner to his bedroom. She felt a slight chill as she went inside. "I expect Mum to come walking in any moment. I can feel her presence in here. It's so strong."

"Yes. I feel her too. It's a blessing and a curse." He let out a painful sigh. "What I'm about to say isn't easy for me; in fact, I've been in extreme denial about this moment, but I think it's time to part with most of your mum's personal belongings. For a long time, they comforted me, seeing her clothing hang in the closet. It felt as if she would be back to get them, wear them again, only that's not going to happen."

"No. It's not. And I think you're doing the right thing." She walked to her mother's dresser and fondly caressed a heart-shaped red velour jewelry box, trimmed in cubic zirconia. "She loved this ... the last gift from Granny she ever got."

Wearily, Dalton sat on the bed while Lily continued to take in the memories. "I'd like you to go through her closet and decide what you'd like to keep and what we might donate to charity ... or perhaps to a women's shelter. As for her jewelry, you can decide what you want to hold on to, and of course, what you'd like Charlotte and Willow to have. Aside from the clothing and the jewelry, there are shoes, scarves, and belts ... not to mention other items of a more intimate nature."

"I'll take care of it. And Char and Willow can help me."

"Oh, no. I don't want them to have any part of the process. I've said it before, Lily; they are each, in their own way, too fragile for such an undertaking."

"I'm not exactly a rock. So don't take me for granite."

"Not the time for jokes," Dalton scolded.

"I'm not joking." *You have no idea how much I'm not joking!* "As for Char and Wills, it's important that they both have memories from Mum that they'll cherish … that are meaningful to them. It's not my place to make those choices. They need to do that on their own. Do you honestly think Char would be okay with me selecting which pieces of Mum's jewelry she should keep? And Wills wouldn't complain, but I know she'd like to make her own selections as well. She's already asked me if she could have Mum's sea globe. You know, that gorgeous handblown glass sphere with sand and shells inside that she bought in San Francisco."

"Of course I know it. But that doesn't mean Willow is able—"

"Dad, if Wills and Char don't want any part of going through Mum's things, then I'll do it, but I'm sure that won't be the case. I think they can handle it. Besides, it will help us all to work through our grief."

"I suppose that makes sense." Dalton rose from the bed and opened the large walk-in closet. Stepping out of sight for a moment, he went inside, emerging only moments later holding a hanger with a beaded burgundy cocktail dress, covered in plastic, suspended from it. "Your mother bought this but never got to wear it. I know you're both the same size, so I thought it would fit you beautifully."

"Thank you." Carefully, Lily took the dress out of his hands. "It's stunning, and I have the perfect occasion coming up to wear it."

"So do I. Lily, have a seat on the bed, please."

Feeling a familiar sickness in her stomach, Lily obliged, folding the dress carefully on her lap as she sat. "What is it, Dad?"

Dalton took a seat next to her. "As I'm sure you know, Lily, your mum and I always attended the annual holiday gala at my company. It's a fine affair, and it's the only event of the year when I have the opportunity to mingle with the spouses and partners of my colleagues and to thank everyone for the jobs they do the year 'round. I'm not comfortable going alone, however. I'd like you to wear this dress that your mother chose for the occasion and to accompany me. I recognize that it's nothing you would want to do, but I need you to attend with me … *for* me."

Lily's lips parted, but no words came out.

"I would appreciate a response."

"I'm sorry, Dad. I don't want to go to your holiday function."

"Did you not hear me acknowledge that I understand it's not something you would *want* to do? It's something I *need* you to do."

"Are you ordering me to go to a party with you?"

Dalton stood and looked at her. "That is such a crude way to put it, Lily. This isn't an order. I'm humbling myself to ask you for a favor. I've never been at a function without your mother, and having my beautiful oldest daughter by my side will help me transition into this unbearable life as a widower."

"Okay, Dad. I hear you. I don't have any interest in going, but I'll do this for you … just this once. When is it? I'll put it on my calendar."

"Thank you." He sat down on the bed. "I'm most grateful. It's the nineteenth of December. The Saturday before Christmas."

Lily dropped her forehead into the palm of her hand.

"What is it? You look quite distressed."

"I'm sorry, Dad. I know I said I would go, but I didn't know the date when I agreed. The nineteenth is the one day I absolutely cannot make it."

"What could be more important?"

"I'm going to a party in Sonoma with Ray. I've been looking forward to it for a long time."

"Oh, honey. I feel terrible you'll have to miss the Sonoma party, but I'm sure Ray understands family loyalty and obligation come first. He'll be home for a good two weeks, yes? So it's not as if that's the only chance to see him."

Lily stood. "I'm not missing this party or the time with Ray. I'm *not*. There's no more to say, except that I'm genuinely sorry I can't go with you. I'm sure that Saturday night is a popular date for a whole lot of parties this time of year."

"You gave me your word!" His voice grew loud as he stood next to her. "And we don't go back on our word in this family."

"Come on, Dad, I didn't swear an oath in blood. I said yes before I knew the date, and I let you know, all within the space of thirty seconds, that I wouldn't be able to make it. That's hardly going back on my word."

"I don't care if you retracted your promise within a minute, an hour, or a month. This is an important event, and it's not like I'm trying to haul you off to an insufferable board meeting."

She walked to the door. "I sincerely apologize. But I'm not going, Dad. I don't care how nice the event will be, and I'm not doing this to be hurtful or to defy you. But for nearly a year, I've had other plans … with my best friend."

"Family comes first in the Sheppard home!" he bellowed, following behind her.

Lily headed down the hall. "That's a convenient phrase when it works in your favor, isn't it?" She turned to look at him. "How about understanding that your daughter, who has given up her effin' life to be here for this family has plans that mean the world to her, and maybe the least you can do is be gracious and not try to ruin such a special evening for her. How about *that,* Dad?"

As if synchronized, Willow and Charlotte, hearing their angry voices, both opened their bedroom doors and stood in stunned silence.

"You don't speak to me like that, Lily Alexandra. And now

you're disrespecting me in front of your sisters."

"No! You're disrespecting *me* in front of your daughters, and I'm outta here." She rushed into her room, dropped the dress on her bed, grabbed her purse and car keys, then came out of the room and continued walking down the hall.

"Where do you think you're going?"

"I don't know. Wherever the wheels on my car take me."

"Get back here!"

Standing at the top of the stairs, Lily, her face burning with rage, turned to face him. "No!"

"Don't get in the car when you're angry! Do you hear me? Don't you dare! Get back here, Abby!"

Charlotte and Willow looked at each other in astonishment.

Startled, Lily looked at her father. "Did you just call me—"

"Don't drive when you're upset," Willow pleaded, running after her. "Please, Lills, I don't want you to die too."

"She's right," Charlotte said, her voice shaking. "Don't get into the car. I'm begging you!"

As Dalton stormed down the hall after her, Lily, in her haste to get away from him, slid halfway down the carpeted steps and landed feet first on the marble floor of the foyer.

"My God! Lily!" Dalton screamed as he descended the stairs to help her.

Still on the floor, Lily put her hand up in the air. "Get away from me! I'm not kidding."

"Lills!" Willow screamed. "Are you okay? That must have hurt, even with the carpet. I know. I fell like that once. Please don't drive. You're too upset, and now you're hurt."

Writhing on the floor for only a moment, Lily put her hands on the bannister to steady herself. "Okay, I won't drive."

"Don't even walk. You might be hurt, Lills!"

Lily softened only briefly as she pulled herself up. "It's okay,

Wills. I'll check myself out when I get into the car."

"No! You said you weren't driving!"

"Oh, yeah, right. I won't drive. Promise. But I'm leaving." Limping from the impact of the fall, Lily grabbed her fleece jacket and scarf from a wall hook as she walked to the front door.

"Lily, get the hell back into this house," Dalton commanded as he descended the rest of the stairs and stood at eye level with her.

"You don't tell me what to fucking do!" Lily said in a scathing tone that surprised even her. Angrily, she pulled the front door open.

Dalton grabbed her by the wrist. "Your mother would be horrified to hear you speak like that. She never uttered a foul word in her life and taught you never to do the same. She would be ashamed of you!"

"I'm betting she'd be ashamed of *you!*" Lily yanked her arm away. "But we'll never be able to prove that, will we?" She pushed open the storm door and let it fly shut behind her. As expeditiously as her aching body allowed, she rushed down the brick path to the sidewalk.

"I'm going after her," Willow said to her father, hurrying down the stairs with Charlotte behind her. "I can't let her—"

"You will not, Willow! I want both of you to go back upstairs. I won't have Lily's egregious behavior escalate into any more tragedy for this family."

"Make sure she doesn't drive," Charlotte said. "She can't drive being so upset. She'll die. Like Mum did and like *I* almost did."

"Her car is still in the driveway." Dalton pointed through the glass of the storm door. "But you see that disobedient brown dot heading toward the end of the street. That's your sister running away." He looked at his daughters, trying to control himself. "I don't want to have to ask again. Go upstairs." Without another word, he rushed into the living room on his way to the dining room.

Charlotte looked at Willow. "We'd better go upstairs before he sees us and freaks his shit again. He's going to his boozery. He'll probably pour himself a triple. Then he's going to slam his den door … like that can keep out the monsters or something."

Willow picked up Quincy, who had cautiously ventured down the stairs. Without any fuss, he allowed her to hold him close. The girls walked back up the stairs, stopping at the top. After a long minute had passed, the sound of Dalton's den door being closed with force echoed up the stairs.

"Only you can't keep monsters out with a slammed door and a drink," Charlotte said to Willow. "You just can't."

ᏒᏒᏒ

"Lily!" the handsome man with the salt-and-pepper hair said. "You look like you've been hit by a car. Are you okay?" He opened the door to his house and held out his hand to escort her inside.

"Not by a car." Lily took his hand. "Only by the wrath of my father." She sighed. "I hate to intrude on your Saturday, Patrick. I didn't have anywhere else to go. Sorry."

"You're family. If you need to come here in the middle of the night, don't hesitate to do so. Not even for a second."

"Lily," Kady said, running to the door. "I thought I heard your voice. Oh, honey. What in the world happened?"

"I had the worst fight with my father ever. And I missed a step and slid halfway down the stairs. Even with the carpet, it was a bumpy ride, and it hurt. Especially when my coccyx hit the marble."

"Ouch!" Kady put her arm around Lily. "My goodness, let's go sit down." She led Lily to the burgundy sofa. "Hopefully there's only bruising, but I think you'll be black and blue in places by tomorrow."

"Do you want us to take you to the doctor?" Patrick asked. "Maybe you should be looked at."

"No. Only if it gets worse, but I don't think I broke anything. I would have never been able to walk three miles to get here."

"You didn't drive?" Kady said.

"No, I couldn't. I was too upset. I needed to get away from Dad."

Gently, Kady helped Lily onto the sofa. "What can I get you, honey?"

Patrick smiled at his wife. "You sit with our guest, sweetheart." He looked at Lily. "What would make you feel better? Tea, coffee, some hot chocolate? Cognac?"

Lily tried to smile. "The cognac sounds good, but I think tea is probably a better choice."

"Earl Grey, chamomile, ginger …"

"Either of the last two."

"For me as well," Kady told him. "And bring some—"

He winked at his wife. "I know what to do. Sit down, sweetie. I'll take care of everything."

"What a shame things have escalated this far." Kady put her hand on the teapot. "Would you like a second cup? I'm going to have one."

"Yes, please. Tea reminds me of Mum. It's so comforting."

Kady smiled and refilled Lily's cup. "I thought perhaps your father was coming to terms with things a bit better. I thought he was learning to respect your wisdom and even defer to it now and then. That doesn't seem to be the case."

"Well, it sure wasn't the case today. He's better in little pockets. His reaction totally depends on his mood … and on how a situation is going to affect him personally. He *really* doesn't want to go to his company party alone."

"And that's understandable. But taking his daughter, and

asking her to wear the dress his wife was going to wear, isn't going to make anything better. Honestly, if anything, I think it would create more problems than it would solve."

Lily looked at her.

"Whispers," Kady clarified. "Ugly whispers."

"That's what I thought you meant. And Dad would never do anything like that."

"No, Lily. He wouldn't. Beneath his grief is a man of decency and honor. And dare I say it: common sense."

Lily took a biscuit from the assortment that Patrick had brought out with their tea. "He must know I came here. I keep expecting him to pound on your front door."

"He won't do that. I guarantee it. But I'm surprised he hasn't called you."

"I turned my phone off while I was walking over here. That's why I didn't even call you first."

"It's fine that you didn't."

Lily looked uncomfortable. "How come you're so sure he won't show up? And why doesn't he want you in our lives anymore?"

"As I've explained before, honey, he doesn't know what I know and what I don't know. Heck, even I don't know that." She paused. "I can only surmise that I make him uncomfortable. He won't show up here because he is likely afraid I may know and will blurt out something he may want buried forever. But he should know that's not something I would do."

"Do you know any of Mum's secrets you're not telling me?"

Kady took a sip of tea and placed the cup on the plate. "I do, Lily. The last thing I want to do is lie to you. But unless there's a good reason to share them, I have to respect the confidence in which they were told to me. That's what best friends do, honey, as I'm sure you know."

"I get it. Mum trusted you. And that's one of the reasons I trust you too." She gulped. "Kady, today when I was on my way here, I thought a lot about leaving Altrusia. Not today or anything, but maybe after New Year's. I know how much my family needs me, and I probably shouldn't do it, but after this horrible fight with Dad, well, I got scared and started wondering how much worse it could get. And if it *is* going to get worse, is it worth staying? How will that help Willow and Char? It may traumatize them even more. I'm so confused."

"I know you are. But I'm glad you're examining all sides of this." Kady put a gentle hand on her leg. "I support you no matter what you decide. Of course, if you told me you were headed out of town tonight, I would do my best to talk you out of it. I don't think that would solve anything."

"No." Lily picked up her tea and took several sips, letting silence replace her words.

Kady, following her lead, did the same.

"I think I might have to go," Lily finally said. "Does that shock you?"

"No. Not at all."

"Here's something that might. I can't believe it, but I screamed the eff word at my father today. And I've never even *said* it in front of him before. I rarely even use it. But I did today, and I actually cursed at him ... right to his face." She looked down. "He told me Mum would be ashamed."

A faint smile crossed Kady's lips. "Your mum would understand. While she wasn't comfortable using expletives, it doesn't mean she didn't think them at times. Once, she got unusually angry with your father when he'd had too much to drink and was being quite difficult about something. An 'arse,' she said. And you know even that was bold for Abby. The next day she told me that she'd given him 'the gesture' behind his back."

"The finger?"

"Of course."

"Then how come she couldn't say she gave him the finger? It's not like that's a curse word."

"Ah, but to your mum, because 'the finger' is used to mean something crudely, she sanitized it for her own purposes."

"Yeah, that sounds like Mum." She thought for a moment and frowned. "I love her so much. I don't know why people always use the word 'love' in the past tense after someone has gone. I mean, you still love them as much as when they were here, right?"

"That's a good point, Lily. I think it's a habit of language." She broke a biscuit in half. "Are you still in touch with Trevor?"

"I am."

"Do I sense a lack of enthusiasm?"

"I've enjoyed his emails and the video chats we have now and then. But the other night, well, he seemed distracted and uninterested in me. Instead of being happy that I'd been to some of the places in France he was talking about, he seemed angry that I had … like that kept him from bragging about being there or something. Who knows? Maybe I'm wrong. He sure liked meeting Char, though. The thing is, after I thought about our conversation, I think he's missing his family and wishes he could be home for Christmas, but he can't admit it. This feels kind of strange to say, me being at home with no life and him traveling the world … but I almost feel sorry for him."

"Interesting. Tell me why."

"Because I think that even if he finds the perfect place to live, he'll keep moving so he can assure himself that he's not settling for the boring life he thinks his parents have. Only I think his parents have a happy life. But their life bores *him*, so he travels the world."

"A lot of people overcompensate. Often out of fear. You're quite perceptive. So, you're going to keep up the friendship?"

"Probably. I think maybe I can help him more than he can help me. We're two lost souls, I guess, but in different ways. And I don't think I'll ever hear from Hannah again." She frowned.

"I'm sorry to hear that. I thought after she came to find you at your graduation party, things might resume between the two of you … at least to some extent."

"I think she wanted closure. Like she didn't want to leave the person who had been her best girlfriend on a bad note, but at the same time, she didn't think I deserved a place in her life anymore. I felt that even as she walked away." Lily paused. "Real truth? I'm pretty sure Han thinks she's better than me now. Like she's evolved and I'm pathetic man-less Lily who's rotting away in Altrusia. She's lost all interest in knowing me."

"If that's what she thinks, she's wrong. You've always been intuitive. I don't think I ever told you this, but your mum noticed that about you when you were only five."

"Did I overthink things then?" Lily asked with a lopsided smile.

Katy laughed. "Maybe a little. But your mum loved her little 'over-thinker.' She always wanted you to learn to trust your gut before anything else."

"That's so good to know." Lily slipped away for a moment before reality pulled her back to the conversation. "So yeah, with Hannah gone, it's nice to have Trevor for a friend." Delicately lifting her teacup again, Lily looked into Kady's eyes. "I think I need to leave Altrusia, though. I really do."

CHAPTER FIFTEEN

"It's eleven fifteen. I was beginning to wonder if you'd ever come home."

That makes two of us.

Standing in the foyer, Lily removed her jacket and scarf and hung them on the wall hook. "Hello, Dad."

"Well, I'm sure the Harrigans are now well versed in the unfortunate events that transpired here earlier today, though whether or not they know all of the facts is quite another thing."

"Is that what you're worried about, Dad? What the Harrigans know or don't know?"

"I suppose not. Just trying to find a way to ease into an uncomfortable conversation. But thank you for confirming that you were with them. You turned your phone off, and I was worried sick. Not that you care how I feel."

"I'm sorry about that. I did what I needed to do … and I never wanted to worry anyone." Lily took a few steps toward the stairs. "I don't know about you, but I'm wrecked. Can we have this conversation tomorrow?"

"I've been in my den all day … waiting for you. And now you want me to wait until tomorrow. Is that correct?"

"Dad, I say that only because it's been a difficult and emotional day for both of us. And it's late. I think with a good night's sleep, we'll both be better equipped to talk. Don't you think?"

"You sound like you're trying to parent your own father; that's what I think." He took a few steps in her direction.

Lily recoiled as the smell of bourbon greeted her. "I'm not trying to do anything of the kind. I want what's best for both of us. And I apologize for cursing at you. That much I can say tonight." Her eyes begged him to understand. "I'm sorry, Dad. I'm drained, and I'm going to soak in the tub for a bit and then get some sleep." A weary sigh followed. "Okay? So we'll talk tomorrow?"

Mumbling words that were indecipherable to Lily, he turned and walked back toward his den.

Lily couldn't remember the last time she'd opted for a bath instead of a shower. But the lavender-infused bath salts she'd forgotten she had were a welcome elixir to soothe her bruised body and her tortured mind. After forty minutes of being immersed in the fragrant water, visualizing nothing but happy places, most especially her Cotswolds cottage, she climbed out of the tub, a sense of calm renewing her.

After another ten minutes, dressed in the cloud-motif pajama pants and sky-blue ribbed top that her mother had bought her two Christmases ago, she walked into her bedroom, pulled her rose comforter down, and slipped into bed. Still visualizing what made her happy and pushing away the unpleasant events of the morning, Lily was crossing over from the alpha state to the theta state when Charlotte's screams shocked her awake. Sitting up in her bed, it took her a minute to get her bearings and put the assault to her senses into perspective.

"No, Mum!" Charlotte screamed. "Mum!"

Now fully cognizant of her environment, Lily got up and hurried through the bathroom into Charlotte's bedroom.

Thrashing in her bed, Charlotte's anguished cries continued. "Mum … don't die, Mum!"

Lily rushed over, sat on her bed, and softly called her name. "Char. It's Lily. Wake up. You're having a bad dream." She paused for a moment until the cries stopped, then put a gentle hand on her. "It's okay. You were dreaming."

Charlotte opened her eyes, her tear-streaked face and look of absolute terror hitting Lily in a way she hadn't allowed herself to fully grasp before. In that moment, Lily was there in the car during the tragic moment that changed her family's lives forever. She saw her mother's light go out in as little time as it took to scream her name. She understood why her father was far more acquiescent to Charlotte's behavior than he once would have been. Her sister's anger, fear, piercings, tattoo, and resentment stood tall and vindicated while simultaneously making Lily wonder what else that tragic moment in time would justify bringing into their lives.

Charlotte's voice was weak. "I had the dream again."

Lily squeezed her sister's hand. "I've never heard you cry out like this before. Not ever."

Still dazed and traumatized, Charlotte took a moment to respond. "I don't know what I do. But I've had this same dream a whole bunch of times. But this was the worst ever. Mum only lost control for a second when that pickup truck plowed into her."

"Is that how it actually happened?" Lily asked, caution edging her words.

"Yes, but I don't ever want to talk about it. Ever. I told you that the day it happened!" Charlotte pulled her hand away.

"Okay, I'm sorry, Char. I only asked because—"

"Whatever! I want to stop living this nightmare over and over again."

Her back toward the bedroom door, Lily did not see her father quietly open it to assess what was going on. "Just like Abby would do," he mumbled as he saw Lily comforting his middle daughter. Taking another look, feeling assured Lily had the situation under control, he closed the door and walked down the hall to his bedroom.

"Do you know why tonight's dream was the worst yet?"

"I don't know …," Charlotte said, trying to shake off the remaining terror. "Probably because of this morning. And maybe because I'm scared what will happen if you leave. I wouldn't know how to do all the things you do or even how to survive. And because I miss Mum more than ever."

"I'm sorry you had such a terrible dream."

"More like a flashback. Dreams aren't real."

"Yes. That's true." Lily frowned. "Oh, Char. I hate to see you in such pain. I want to help you so much."

Fully awake, Charlotte eyed her suspiciously. "I hope you're not gonna tell me to go to therapy like Dad did. Because that doesn't bring Mum back … and you know it. What's the point of telling a stranger what happened and how I'm feeling? So they can make money off my pain?"

"Do you want me to answer that?"

"You can, but I'm not gonna go."

"Well, for starters, when a person can talk through what is bothering them, rather than pushing it aside, the subconscious doesn't have to take on the burden, and therefore the nightmares are more likely to go away."

"Are you a psychologist now?"

"No. I studied it in school, and I find it fascinating. Only said what I did because you asked … so there's that."

"Why don't you, Dad, and the willow tree go into therapy? None of you had to be in the car to have bad thoughts. How come?"

"That's a good question, Char. And I don't have an answer."

"I don't want some creep analyzing me."

"And nobody wants you to see a creep. You could go for one session, to meet a person and see if you think you might like them. Finding the right person is as important, if not more important, than the therapy itself. At least that's what I think."

"Whatever. Besides, even if the dreams go away, the memory never will. And Mum will still be dead." Charlotte turned her head to the side and looked away.

"What's that mark on your neck? Did you hurt yourself during the nightmare."

Charlotte looked at Lily again and touched her neck. "Um … no."

All of the weariness that had cocooned Lily throughout the day came back to her. "Is that a hickey?"

"Maybe. I cover it with makeup during the day. Dad's not gonna see it."

"That part is good, but the part about you getting it I don't like so much. Did Nico give it to you?"

"Maybe."

"Are you having sex with him?"

Charlotte pushed the covers away, pulled up her nightshirt, and tugged at her underwear to expose the fabled tattoo. "See, I wasn't lying about my ass tat. Isn't it nice? Nico likes to kiss it, and maybe he puts his finger inside me too."

Lily took the deepest breath she could and cursed silently. "Does he put anything else inside of you, Char?"

"No, but he wants to. Nico would never try to force me to do anything. Because he cares about me." She pulled her nightshirt down and settled back into her bed.

"He's twenty years old. And you're sixteen. Four years from now, that won't matter too much. But now it matters a lot … for so many reasons." Lily looked into Charlotte's eyes, trying hard to take the judgment out of her own. "Do you care about him?"

"Yes. I do. And not because he's hot. But because we talk a lot, and he gets me like nobody else. He does. We have a lot in common. I might even be starting to love him."

"What's he doing these days?" Lily asked, trying to diminish her momentary shock.

"He's going to get his certification as a mechanic. And on Saturdays he works with his uncle. The guy fixes Porsches and other fancy rides. Nico isn't sure if he wants to be a generalist or a specialist, but he thinks he prefers working on luxury cars."

"Well, that sounds like a viable career."

"Now you sound like Dad. Like totally with the word 'viable' and the kind of approval-y thing you did with your voice. Gag."

Lily flashed an uncomfortable smile. "Yeah. I think I did. I'll definitely try not to let that happen again. I only want to sound like myself, believe me."

"You're gonna leave." Charlotte stared at her. "Aren't you?"

"Why do you say that?"

She sat up in the bed and shoved a pillow behind her head. "Because you hate your life here. You hate having to take care of us. And today you cursed at Dad, and that is so not like you. I've seen you throw some epic shade at him, but nothing like this morning. That's why I know you've had enough of all of this bullshit." She paused. "No way I could do what you do in this house. And I sure as hell wouldn't dress up and play Mum at his stupid company party. That's got a creep factor of like six or seven. Not quite a ten, but I hope he won't go there next."

Stunned, Lily took a moment to catch her breath. "He *never* would. Dad isn't thinking straight, but he'd *never* go there."

"I know. But I can't help where the whole Christmas party thing made my mind go. You know, like what's next? I guess I'm freaking because I'm afraid you're gonna leave. If I were you … I would have been history by now. Sorry to say that, but it's the truth. So I guess I suck for wanting you to stay. I guess that makes me that hippo word. I can't think straight since that nightmare."

"No, you're not a hypocrite, Char. You speak your mind. You always have. I don't always like what you say, but I'm glad you're honest." She put her hand over Charlotte's. "Are you ready to go back to sleep? Or do you want me to stay longer?"

"I'm okay … I guess. Just need to use the bathroom first."

"You know where to find me." Lily stood as Charlotte got out of bed. "And I have to say this again, even if I sound like Dad: if you do have sex with Nico, which I hope you won't, please use protection."

Charlotte made a face. "Dad would never be that cool about sex … not in a million years … so no worries there."

"I'm not exactly chill with it, Char. Don't let my mellow ways fool you. I know that going full freak on you isn't going to do eff all to change anything."

"Nope. Thanks for coming in."

"Always." She started to give her sister a hug, but, anticipating the affection, Charlotte turned away. "Good night, Char." Lily walked through the bathroom into her own room, and shut the door behind her.

"Hi, Lills," Willow said, sitting cross-legged at the end of Lily's bed with Quincy on her lap. "I'm sorry to bother you. I know it's been like the worst day for you, and you're tired."

Lily walked over and hugged her. She kissed the top of Quincy's head, then sat on the bed, pulling the comforter over her legs. "This hasn't been a good day for anyone, has it? I hate that you had to see me lose it like that. I apologize. My brain exploded and I couldn't stop myself."

"I don't like to say this, but I'm surprised it took you so long."

Lily started to respond but thought better of it. "Did you hear

Char having a nightmare?"

"Yup. I opened my door and was going to come down to see if she was okay, but then I saw Dad standing at her door. I thought he was going to go in, so I closed my door before he could see me."

"I didn't know he'd done that."

"I only realized he didn't go in when I heard him close his bedroom door like a minute later. Guess he figured you would help Char better than he could." She made a face. "And probably you did."

"Yeah." Lily went limp as she felt weariness overtake her. "I hope so. I did my best. Not sure what that's worth anymore."

"Is Char right?" Willow blurted out, unable to contain the question that had been sitting on the tip of her tongue. "Are you gonna leave?"

Lily saw the panic in her eyes intensify and the lines on her young face crinkle in pain.

Willow continued talking, her agitation growing. "After you left and Dad went into his den to drink, Char said—"

"Wills … I just …."

"Oh my God! You're going to leave!" Willow's sudden hysteria sent Quincy on a quick flight from her arms to the floor. "Aren't you? Tell me the truth! Are you thinking that because I'll be thirteen in a couple months that it will be okay?"

Lily took her youngest sister's hands in hers. "I have no plans to go anywhere. I wouldn't lie to you." She looked down to see Quincy staring at Willow. "Look. Your boy is worried about you."

"He knows how scared I am." As the tears came, she reached down to pick up the compliant cat who nuzzled her face, happy to be back in her arms.

"I'll tell you the same thing I told Char: I'm not planning to go anywhere."

"You swear? You would tell me, right? It would be hard enough if you went away, and I know it's hard for you to be here, but promise you'll always tell me the truth."

"Promise, Wills." She stroked Quincy's back. "You're my witness."

Willow looked wide-eyed at Lily. "I know it's late, and I know I sound like a baby, but will you walk me into my room and tuck me in ... like Mum used to do?"

"Sure." With a smile, Lily got out of bed, and, once again, pressed the hold button on her life, content to go where the need was greatest ... to Willow's bedroom and to her heart.

※※※

Lily knocked lightly on the door to her father's den.

"Come in."

"I got your text." Lily offered a quick, awkward smile as she entered the room. "I'm here." She turned and shut the door behind her.

Dalton, sitting behind his desk, closed the newspaper he had been reading and nodded for Lily to take a seat on the couch. "As you know, I don't like using the phone to communicate within the house, but under the circumstances, I determined it the better option."

"I've never seen you reading the Sunday paper anywhere but your recliner."

"I never have. But the living room would be an awkward place to have this conversation, so I'm breaking routine. But then again, nothing has been as it once was, so there you have it."

"Right."

Dalton picked his pen off his desk and looked at it before speaking: "Sonic titanium metallic fusion resin barrel." Forlorn, he laid the pen on the desk and looked at Lily. "I sure do miss your mother."

"I know you do."

"We had some good laughs over this pen." He smiled. "Some too risqué to share with my daughter."

"Dad, maybe you want to come sit on the couch next to me. With you behind the desk like that, it feels like being called to the principal's office." She paused. "Not that I ever was, but this super-formal vibe isn't doing it for me."

His face and his body heavy with hesitation, he got up and walked over to the couch, allowing a fair distance between him and Lily. "Thought I'd leave a spot. In case your mum comes down from heaven to mediate. We won't see her, but maybe we'll know she's here."

Conscious of a nascent fragility in his voice and his words, she responded softly. "I think we can handle this. Again, Dad, I'm sorry that I spoke to you like that. I didn't like saying what I did any more than you liked hearing it. And that's the truth."

He nodded. "I'm sure it is. We'll put that behind us." He thought some more. "I just hope it won't happen again."

Disappointed by the unnecessary footnote, Lily offered no visible response.

"I saw you comforting Charlotte last night. I told you many times that she's in a precarious state, despite how she may act. I'm glad you reacted with the necessary sensitivity … not that I would ever expect you to do differently. But I know your sister can lash out."

"Yeah. She can. Things have been better lately, although we still have moments I wish we didn't."

"Well, you gave her the motherly love she needed."

"*Sisterly* love."

Dalton twisted his wedding ring. "I always prided myself on being a good father. But it's becoming clearer to me that I've been taking credit that solely belongs to your mother. She was superglue. I'm dollar-store tape."

"No, Dad, you're—"

"Funny, Lily. Dollar-store tape is a cheap product. But back in my grandparents' day, in the earlier part of the twentieth century, the place for a bargain was the 'five and dime.' Hard to believe you could once buy anything for five or ten cents, isn't it?"

"For real."

"But we're not in the twentieth century anymore," he lamented, "and my parenting might have been worth more in another era, but it has little value in this one."

"That's not true." Lily winced at the unspoken request to bolster his ego. "These have been the worst times."

"They have been. But I'm realizing that your mother made everything seem effortless. And managing this household is a far cry from that." He cleared his throat. "I was wrong to get so angry at you for wanting to keep your date with Ray. I let my own needs suffocate yours."

But do you understand that you never should have asked me to your holiday party at all? Lily looked at him, disappointed that he was not having the epiphany she wished for.

"I wish I knew how to make things better."

"Dad … uh … there's something I need to say. It's actually related to what you just said."

He tensed. "What's that?"

"Well, you're kind of drinking a lot."

Dalton lurched forward. "How else am I supposed to deal with your mother's death? Suck on a lollipop?"

Lily felt her entire body tremble but forced herself to hide any outward signs of alarm. "Char asked me last night why she should go to therapy if none of us intend to do so. I couldn't answer her."

"I don't need therapy, nor do I need a lecture from my daughter about the evils of drinking. Have you ever found me passed out drunk?"

"No."

"Have I ever fallen over in a drunken stupor?"

"No."

"Do you see me drive after I've had a few?"

"No."

"Do you think that perhaps, just perhaps, I'm entitled to numb my grief now and then so I can go on being a productive member of society and providing for this family?"

Lily gulped. "Sorry. I only—"

Dalton dismissed any response with a flick of his hand. "Wednesday will be your mother's forty-fourth birthday, and I'd like the four of us to have dinner together to celebrate her life. Will this be doable, Lily, or are you planning to spend that day with that …."

"Kady. You can say her name. I hope you remember that she's lost her best friend. And yes, I am seeing her, but only for lunch so that I'll be free to be with all of you for dinner."

He squirmed uncomfortably. "Good to hear."

"Willow's doing a digital book report for English class," Lily said, trying to get his mind off her comment about drinking. "She read *The Secret Garden*, one of Mum's favorites. She's got all of the elements for a video ready to go, but she wants my input while she puts it together. So, if there's nothing else, I'm going to her room."

He fumed silently. "That's fine."

How ironic. You're so angry that I mentioned your drinking that all you can think about right now is how you want another drink. Only it's too early, and you know you can't have one. But you want it. And you're not going to forget this. "Okay, Dad, well, see you later."

Feeling his angry eyes stuck to the back of her shirt, Lily resolved to stop in her room and change her clothes before bringing any negativity into Willow's space.

CHAPTER SIXTEEN

"Remember in the second grade, I asked you to marry me?" Raymond said, laughing, as he and Lily sat on the love seat inside the cedar gazebo with an olive-colored blanket over their laps.

"I do! I went home and told my mum that you and I were getting married when we grew up. She thinks ... I mean ... she thought ... I was adorable ... getting so excited about being married when I didn't have a clue what that meant." Lily glanced over at the large house where the Christmas party inside was winding down. "You told me we'd have a fort out on the lawn to play in. Did you mean this gazebo?"

"Well, I *was* thinking of the one my aunt and uncle used to have, which is in gazebo heaven now. It had become severely weather-beaten, so my uncle built this beauty two years ago. But yeah, to me, it was just a place to have fun, and I kept begging my parents to put a 'round fort' in their backyard too." He laughed. "My second-grade vocabulary was a logophile's nightmare. My knowledge of how things work was even worse: I thought getting married meant you'd come to live in my room with me and bring your toys."

"You didn't!" Lily giggled. "Well, at least you had a working concept in your head. I just thought the word 'marriage' was a grown-up thing to say."

He put his arm around her. "We've shared a lot, haven't we?" He paused for a moment to reminisce. "After all of these years, I finally brought you here. So I've got to ask: how do you like my fort?"

"I love it. And the party was fabulous. It exceeded all of my expectations. What a privilege to be here with you and all of these wonderful people. Especially your aunt and uncle … and the rest of your family." She glanced toward the house, through the large French windows, before returning her attention to Raymond. "I actually felt like I was living a real life tonight. I felt happy and alive. The food and wine were amazing, but not as much as the two of us being together again."

Raymond kissed her on the cheek. "You took the words …."

Lily laid her head on his chest. "I wish I didn't have to return to my regularly scheduled program." She sighed. "I wish I could change the channel more often."

"I've thought about everything you told me on the car ride here." Tenderly, he caressed her hair. "I know you promised Willow and Char you would stay, and I understand why you did, but I'm sure even they know that promise didn't mean forever, in any sense of the word."

Reluctantly, Lily sat up and looked him in the eyes. "I can handle some more sacrifice. And I completely get the fear that my sisters have. But it's my father who galls me. It will be a year on the second of April that Mum died, and never once in these past eight-plus months did he ever talk to me about going back to anything resembling what my life should be. He's said several things … some of which I've told you about … and every one of them suggests that he expects me to stay in Altrusia way down the road, even after Wills graduates from high school. *That* … freaks me completely out." She shuddered.

"I'm sorry, Lills."

"And he jumped down my throat when I mentioned his drinking, so I won't be bringing that up again. But even smelling that bourbon on him makes my skin crawl. I swear, Ray. I'm not trying to be overdramatic."

"Honestly, considering the rotten hand you've been dealt, you've actually been unbelievably restrained. Few people would be able to do what you're doing."

"Yeah. I know. Which is exactly why he thinks I'm well suited to waste away in his house forever. Only I won't."

"If you ever need to leave, you can always come stay with me in Princeton. I've told you this before, but I mean it. Maybe knowing you have a safe haven somewhere will make for fewer sleepless nights … not that I want you to have *any*. And I'm only a hop, skip, and a long jump to New York City."

"I appreciate that. Kady has a place for me in Malibu as well. It does help knowing I'd have somewhere to go if I ever had to run. But I pray the situation never becomes that dire. I hope that after a year passes, my father will think about meeting someone. He doesn't do well on his own. But he's still way too much in love with Mum and way too grief-stricken to even give it a thought."

"He may surprise you. Maybe he'll get lonely enough to consider someone new. He's what … forty-seven?"

"Yes. He'll be forty-eight in late January."

"That's way too young to be by yourself forever. Maybe if he met a woman, it would change things."

"I don't know." A glum look replaced her smile. "I'd like to think so. But I also wonder about who she might be and how a new woman in his life would affect my sisters. Could be great or it could be a nightmare." She let out a frustrated sigh. "Life is a complicated thing. You know?"

"More than I can say." He paused. "How are things with Trevor?" Raymond asked, doing his best to change the subject.

"Sounds like he's got a million places to go on his endless journey."

"Yeah, he does … too many to count. He's headed to this small town in Italy next, Garbagnate, a suburb of Milan, where I think he's going to work for four months in a photography studio while he also tries to improve his meager Italian. Then, he plans to travel the country to meet some locals and photograph them. More and more, though, he talks about his family and friends in Altrusia, Sacramento, San Francisco, and other areas. I sometimes wonder if his wanderlust isn't more of a case of 'be careful what you wish for,' you know? It's almost like he's embarrassed to say he misses anyone or wants to come home … even for a visit."

"I think you're right from what you've told me." Raymond pushed Lily's hair out of her face. "Hey, looks like we've switched roles in the hair department."

"You've cut yours. I wasn't going to mention it, but …."

"Had to. I should never have let it grow back after I cut it for graduation. It's different being at college, especially Princeton. I interact with a lot of people, and I don't want to look like a goofy high school senior. Almost as soon as I got there, I looked in the mirror, and the reality of my adulthood hit me hard. The floppy locks had to go."

"Boy, can I relate to that!" She paused. "Adulthood. Not the floppy locks."

"Oh, Lills, I didn't mean it that way."

"No worries, Ray. I know. You know you never have to explain anything to me."

He traced a heart on her cheek. "Remember I did that when I asked you to marry me?"

"I'd totally forgotten, but yes!"

"So tell me, aside from all you do for your family, are you doing anything for you? You sort of hinted at something during one of our video chats. Is it anything to do with fashion?"

"Definitely nothing in the fashion world. I've totally stopped doing any sketching or designing. I can't even think about it after Dad decimated my plans. It hurts too much."

"I get that."

"I do have a secret project, though, and so far, I haven't shared it with anyone except Kady ... because she was the catalyst to make it happen."

"How's that?"

Well, that miniature cottage she gave me on graduation day has been so inspiring. Years ago, when I was a kid, I used to write stories ... or should I say I attempted to do so ... about my family. They weren't so much about my immediate family, but my ancestors who I'd only imagined or heard bits and pieces about."

"I remember you telling me about that."

"So now, I've started to write stories again, only these are different, far more adult, not to mention that the entire process has been so cathartic. I've also been researching the Cotswolds area, looking at family photos from our trips, and trying to add some historic detail as well. I haven't had as much time as I'd like, but it's my hidden passion. I haven't told my sisters because they'd insist on reading what I've done so far ... which isn't much. Willow because she's a total bookworm and Char because she'd want to see what dirt I might have written about her or anyone else."

"That's incredible, Lills. I love hearing this. You should have told me."

"I want to keep it mostly to myself for now, because I'm just starting to take it seriously. But since you asked ...."

"I do remember that Willow loves to read."

"And I am thankful for that, because she always has a place to escape to in a good book. Unlike Char, who is escaping in ways I can't talk about right now."

"I can guess."

"I'm sure you can." Lily disappeared in thought before meeting his eyes again. "Writing stories or even thinking about them helps me to transport myself to places that my physical body can't go … at least for now. And to deal with all of the sorrows I can't handle in any other way."

"That makes me happy. Hey, how do you think your dad is doing at his Christmas event tonight?"

"I won't dare to even wager a guess. But I'm sure I'll hear about it."

Raymond looked at his watch. "We've got over a hundred miles to drive, so we probably should get on the road right after we say our good-byes."

"We should. There's so much more to catch up on; I hope we can cover it all in one hundred miles."

Lily stood outside the front door to her house, shivering as her body met the cold night air, even through her black winter coat. Though well after midnight, she couldn't escape the fear that her father would be waiting up for her. Taking her house keys out of her small rhinestone-studded evening bag, she opened the front door, quickly shutting it behind her as the cold air followed her inside.

Looking toward the wall to her right, she hung up her coat and scarf on the hook. She had only taken two steps toward the stairs when he called out to her.

"Lily!"

She felt as if her heart had left her chest and fallen into the pit of her stomach. Without saying a word, she froze in place.

From his recliner in the living room, he called out to her again. "Lily! Would you please come in here?"

After closing her eyes and saying a quick prayer, she walked into the living room. Her father, with a glass of bourbon in his hands, his tie unloosened, his dress shoes overturned on the floor, and still wearing his finest suit, sat slumped in his recliner. Pushing his round, tortoiseshell glasses up from his nose to meet his eyes, he looked at her, devoid of expression.

"Hi, Dad."

His eyes scanned her from head to toe. "Sit down, please."

Lily started to protest but thought better of it. She sat on the couch and laid her evening bag to the side. "How was the event?"

Dalton took a large swig of his drink. "In case you're wondering, I had but one glass of alcohol before driving home. Seeing that my recliner neither has wheels nor wings, thereby making it neither roadworthy nor airworthy, I'm quite content to imbibe in my living room."

"Fine," Lily choked out as the smell of bourbon wafted in her direction. "I wasn't going to say anything."

"You might as well have a thought bubble protruding from your head. Because it's quite obvious what you're thinking."

"I was only wondering how your evening went."

Dalton swirled the ice cubes in his glass. "I have never felt so utterly alone, so isolated, and so pitied in my nearly forty-eight years on this planet. I'm a vice president of a company who deals with all levels of staff and management on a daily basis, and tonight, even the simple greeting of 'hello' required a mammoth effort, much less the requisite 'Merry Christmas' and 'Happy Holidays' felicitations. Even the smallest of substantive conversation was laborious and repellent."

"I ... um ...."

"I saw them grieve for me, Lily. Hundreds of eyes taking pity on a lost soul trying to make his way through a crowd of merrymakers and pretend he was comfortable with the festive atmosphere that mocked every fiber of his cheerless being. Absolute torment. No, it was *hell.*" He punctuated his anger by chasing down his words with another swig of bourbon.

"I'm sorry the evening was so unpleasant for you."

"To put it mildly. If you'd come with me, I could have proudly introduced my beautiful daughter. I would have had reason to smile despite my heartbreak, and the pitying eyes would not have been cast upon me. I would have been able to retain the image of the strong man I have always worked so hard to project to my colleagues. I might actually have had some semblance of a nice evening. But I had nothing but ashes of my former life, clinging to me like vile, insidious leeches."

"I'm sorry." *Why do you talk so strangely when you're drunk?*

"Don't you dare say that you're sorry again." He turned up the volume. "Do you hear me?"

Lily stifled the apology that force of habit wanted her to speak.

"I suppose you had a wonderful time. You look like a vision in the dress your mother chose. She would have been the belle of the Christmas ball."

"She would have. Mum was so beautiful."

"Well," he said, his words soaked in bitter impatience. "Did you have a good time at the party?"

"I did. I met some fascinating people and loved being with Ray again. I cherished every moment and always will."

Dalton poured more of the golden-brown whiskey down his throat. "Isn't that nice?" He gave a snort of revulsion. "Just lovely."

"I thought you said you understood." Her anger fueled her courage to speak. "You said that you'd let your needs suffocate mine and you were sorry for that. Don't you remember?"

"I was delusional. I was trying to show you some kindness, but at my own expense. They're probably all snickering about the 'lonely Dalton Sheppard.' I even had someone from Human Resources ask me if I'd like to have dinner with her one night after work."

"What's she like?"

"Doreen is a lovely woman. Sadly, a widow at forty-two after her husband died suddenly from an aneurysm."

"How long has she been widowed?"

"Three years at least, I'm sure."

"And she went to the party alone?"

"She did, Lily. She has for three or four years. What of it?"

"Why didn't you spend time with her? It sounds like she might have been good company for you."

He shook his head with fury. "And have the whole of the company gossiping about the newly widowed vice president and the long-suffering human resources manager? No thank you." He took another swig.

"Dad, I don't think anyone was snickering at you or would ever snicker at you because you tragically lost your wife. It sounds like you work with some compassionate people who could have comforted you if you hadn't shut them out. Especially Doreen. Would it be so terrible to develop even a platonic relationship with her? You might be able to help one another."

"Well don't you have all of the answers, oh wise daughter. Or perhaps it's your guilty conscience that does."

"I feel sad for you. But I don't feel guilty for going to a Christmas party with my best friend who now lives in New Jersey. I deserve the happiness I had at that party and during the drive there and back. I'm not going to let you blame me for your evening. No way."

"Oh … so now I'm blaming you, am I?" His glasses slipped down his nose. "Damn these bloody things." He pushed them back up again, inadvertently smashing them into his face as he did.

Lily saw embarrassment wash over him. "I'm going to say good night, Dad." Her respect and her tolerance all but gone, she grabbed her evening bag and stood. "I hope you'll sleep well."

"I'm sure you and your clear conscience will do so. No doubt about that!"

Without giving him another look or another word to beat with his rage, Lily left the room. Ill tempered and intoxicated, he languished in the deep waters of his sorrows ... paradoxically in the comfort of his favorite chair.

CHAPTER SEVENTEEN

"How could I forget The Ides of March?" Lily asked as she sat on the Harrigans' sofa with Kady. "Mum always said that made it easy to remember your birthday … not that she would have forgotten, no matter what the day."

Kady smiled. "My mother's birthday was on December twenty-fourth and she hated it. People would forget her birthday or merge it with Christmas. She always said that when she had children, she'd pray for them to be born on notable days, but not holidays. I was born on March fifteenth and my twin brothers on December seventh, D-Day … not exactly cheery days in history. My mother always lamented that she should have been more specific in her prayers."

"Oh, interesting. Maybe your mother was right."

"An ironic coincidence and nothing more, I think." Kady smiled. "But then again … who knows." She looked at the large box on her lap with the red satin bow. "I never expected you to bring me a gift, Lily."

"Open it."

Kady slowly removed the ribbon and set it aside. "Why do I feel nervous about this?"

"Go ahead." Lily grinned. "You can do it."

As soon as she took the lid off and pushed away the layers of pink tissue paper, Kady gasped. "Lily! How in the world?" She reached into the box and pulled out a teal satin evening wrap with a beaded border. "I-I am stunned. I saw something like this when your mum and I were out shopping one day. Being insanely expensive, I told Abby that as much as I like pretty things, I couldn't justify the cost." She frowned. "That was on my birthday, come to think of it. The wrap I saw was a stunner, but this one is even prettier. This beadwork is exquisite." She looked at Lily. "How did you know? I hope you didn't buy this."

Lily smiled through her sadness. "I didn't know anything about you seeing it in a store or even wanting something like this. But after Dad asked me to go through Mum's closet, I found a box that she had tucked away with her sewing things. She had written 'For Kady' on the lid. Inside, I found this material, threads, several packages of beads, and a sketch she'd made. I think she was going to give it to you for Christmas, so she didn't make it right away." Lily wiped away a stray tear. "Because knowing Mum, if she made it immediately, she wouldn't have been able to wait from March to December. I'm not sure why she never started it, though. That's so unlike her. I know she wasn't feeling that well before Christmas. Probably that flu bug she couldn't shake. Maybe she didn't have the energy. It's so unlike her not to have had it done for your birthday."

"I think it's what you said, Lily. That flu wore her out. And she knew I'd love it whenever she got around to making it, so she didn't rush." Kady ran her fingers carefully over the fabric before touching the beaded trim. "So am I to surmise that all of this brilliant handiwork is yours?"

"It is. Nobody knew I was working on it. I didn't want Dad to think I was 'fine' doing home projects, which is exactly what he would have thought and used to justify what he's done to me. So yeah, I made this under the cover the darkness, late into the night."

Kady lifted the garment out of the box and examined it. "I can think of no greater gift than your mum designing something she knew I wanted and you sewing it for me. There's no way to adequately express how much I treasure this."

"Probably the way I treasure the cottage you made."

"Oh, Lily. That was such a labor of love. And I never imagined it would inspire you to start writing stories again that you wrote as a child."

"I told Ray all about it at the Christmas party. But no one else."

"I can keep a secret." Kady stood and put on the wrap. "I adore this, Lily."

Lily rose and gave her a hug. "Happy birthday, Kady. Wear this in good health."

As Kady took off the wrap, they both sat again. Carefully, she folded the garment and placed it in the box. "Thank you, Lily." She looked upward. "Thank you, Abby, my dearest friend."

With a nervous smile, Lily reached for her teacup on the table. "So … I have to tell you about the epiphany I had when I was making this."

"What's that?" Kady placed the box down next to her.

"Well, I wanted to fulfill Mum's wishes and make this wrap for you as well as wanting to make it for my own reasons. Let's say both were powerful motivations because I felt like I couldn't sew again without being reminded of what was taken from me."

"I wondered about that." Kady broke a tea biscuit in half.

"But when I started sewing, although I loved making this wrap for you, it suddenly dawned on me that going to fashion school wasn't my true passion. I didn't even realize it, but I think I was mostly going for Mum … since she got married and never was able to go. It's as if I wanted to make her dream come true."

Kady looked upward again. "You were right, Abby. You were

so right."

"Mum knew?" Lily put her teacup on the saucer as she looked at Kady in amazement.

"She didn't know for sure. She was thrilled you were going, but she secretly worried that you were going for her and not for yourself."

Lily rubbed her heart locket. "Mum asked me a few times if I was sure fashion school was what I truly wanted, but I always said yes. Because I thought it was. I still enjoy sewing. But I don't care about being a designer anymore. There's something else out there for me."

"Your mum was right then." Kady laid a tender hand on Lily's knee. "But she told me many times that being married and having three beautiful daughters was far better than anything she'd wished for in her youth. I'm so glad you felt comfortable telling me this."

"I almost didn't. Even admitting it to myself made me feel like I was betraying Mum."

"Oh, no, honey … the opposite, actually. Your mum would never want you to choose a career that wasn't your passion. She'd be overjoyed that you figured this out."

"I'm not sure what I want to do now. Char is hardwired to be a makeup artist, and I think Wills wants to teach English literature, but who knows; she's only twelve. Speaking of being twelve, she'll be thirteen next week, on March twenty-second. I asked her what she wanted to do and, uh … she said that a family trip for the weekend might be nice."

"And you don't think so?" Kady asked with a delicate undertone.

"Not the way things are now."

With aplomb, Kady lifted her cup and held it on her lap for a moment. "Because of your father?"

"He's angry at me, Kady. It's that whole office Christmas party thing. He's never accepted my apology for cursing at him, but he's even angrier that I never went with him. You would have thought they publicly stoned him at the event. I guess I'm naïve, but a part of me expected him to apologize after that drunken speech-kind-of-thing he laid on me after Ray dropped me off from the Sonoma party."

Kady took a couple of sips of tea and put the cup back on the coffee table. "Your father isn't a word-slurrer when he drinks. As your mother told it to me, he becomes verbose and overdramatic, like a king addressing his subjects. I think that's the way she explained it."

"That would be pretty accurate. Anyway, I think Wills hopes that this trip will help bring Dad and me together. But I'm afraid it could make things worse and ruin her birthday. I don't want to say that to her because I'm trying to shield her from as much as I can. And I never want to put Dad down to her."

"She's a smart young lady. If she didn't know what was going on, she wouldn't want to try to fix things ... whether that's subliminal or not."

"True. Thanks for that. I'll think it over some more and play it by ear. It's tough ... because ten days after her birthday, it will be the one-year anniversary of Mum's death. I wish my family could spend that day with yours."

"Me too, Lily. Me too. It breaks my heart."

"I've been thinking," Willow said, sitting at the kitchen table and snacking on a bowl of green grapes. "I don't want to go away for my birthday. Let's do something here."

Lily eyed her curiously. "Why the change of heart, Wills?"

"Well, if we all went away, then I might have to leave Quincy at Issy's house, and I don't know how that would work out with Brucie. Not to mention my boy would be confused and scared. He needs to visit Issy's house and meet Brucie a few times before I would do that.

Also because it's almost a year since Mum died, and I'd feel guilty celebrating anything so close to that day."

Charlotte, who had been sitting quietly, piped up, "And I can't go away at all, but that doesn't mean I'd be here when it's time for Quincy to eat, so there's that. Plus he would get lonely."

"Oh," Lily said, unsure whether to be relieved or upset.

Charlotte glanced at her phone as she spoke. "Also, the willow tree is worried Dad might do something weird … or drink too much. Or both."

"Don't say that, Char."

"Okay." Charlotte popped a grape into her mouth and chewed it. "I won't say it. But it's still the truth. Hello, truth calling. Is anybody home? I hear weeping inside."

Willow smirked and shot a dirty look at Charlotte.

Lily turned to Willow. "So, what would you like to do? Your birthday is on a Tuesday this year, if I've got that right."

"Yeah, it is. You know, I was thinking … funny how I'll be entering my teens and when June comes, you'll be leaving yours."

"Never thought of it that way," Lily said, "but yes."

Charlotte, not looking up from her phone, spoke again. "So Lills asked you what you want to do. Speak or weep your answer. Just tell us."

"I want to go out with my friends on the weekend before and then have dinner with all of you on my birthday. Maybe at that Greek restaurant."

"We can do that," Lily said.

A loud metal song sounded from Charlotte's phone as she jumped up. "Gotta go, freaks!" She ran out of the kitchen as she answered the call.

Willow made a face. "Nico." She looked behind her to make sure Charlotte was gone. "She said they're in love."

Lily gulped. "I was afraid of that."

"Why? Because you know they're having sex?"

Lily tried to downplay her surprise. "Do you know that for a fact?"

"Unfortunately. Yeah. She likes to tell me all about it, and I don't want to know. It's her personal business. I told her that, but I think that makes her blab even more. She likes to shock me. Like I care if the guy bought a big box of ribbed condoms."

Lily sighed. "Actually, that part I'm glad to hear. You know, that they're using protection."

"Well, I know something you won't want to hear, but I have to tell you anyway."

Lily creased her brow. "What's that?"

"Issy said that her cousin, 'Smoochy Sara,' has the big-time hots for Nico. She's nineteen and lives across the street from this garage where he works on Saturdays. Issy said she's throwing herself at him. I hope he doesn't cheat on Char."

"That wouldn't be good. At least I don't think. Does Char know about Sara?"

"Oh yeah. She said Nico told her she was actually called 'Slutty Sara.' But even I know that being a slut doesn't exactly turn most guys off. Not while they're getting something anyway. Maybe afterward when they get all high and mighty ...."

"You've really grown up in the past year. I don't—"

Willow continued talking. "I know Char is giving it up for him, but at least she's not passing out party favors to every guy in Altrusia like Sara is."

Lily's eyes scanned the kitchen for a clean escape. "Soooo, Wills, whatever day you're not with your friends, can I take you shopping for a gift? I'd love to do that. Start thinking about what you'd like."

"Sweet. And you're a champion subject-changer."

"Sorry. I guess I'm not used to having these kinds of

conversations with you. My bad. And the last thing I'd ever want to do is to give you the impression you can't talk to me about anything. Because you can."

"Okay …."

Lily could see the wheels turning in her head. "What are you thinking? I can see there's something else you want to say. Tell me."

"Um, well, Char said that after April second, since it will be a year since Mum died, you're going to leave because you'll have fulfilled your obligation."

Lily reached across the table to grasp Willow's hand. "That's not true. I'm here because I love my family. And when the day comes that I make plans to leave, you'll be the first one to know. Okay?"

"Promise?"

"Promise. And in case you're wondering, as of now, I have no plans to go anywhere. I guess I should tell Char that."

"She said even if you say you're staying, she won't believe you."

"I won't say anything then. She'll see she was wrong when I'm still around."

CHAPTER EIGHTEEN

Charlotte sat cross-legged on Lily's bed and beamed as she spoke to Trevor on her sister's laptop. "Lily is downstairs, doing laundry and boring stuff like that. Want me to call her?"

Trevor, his long dark blond hair out of his usual ponytail, smiled broadly at Charlotte as he sat on a couch with a painting of a Madonna and child, wearing a sky-blue shawl and a brick-red dress, behind him. "Not yet. Hey, I haven't spoken to you for a million years. Not since that time we first met and I was telling you about the catacombs in Paris."

"I know. Where are you now? In church?"

He laughed. "What makes you say *that?*"

"That painting behind you."

Trevor turned around. "Oh, the Madonna. Yeah, I'm in Italy … in a town called Garbagnate. I've been living on top of this photography studio on and off for almost six months … since the middle of January. The painting is a *Madononina* … a little Madonna. There's one like this painted in the niche on this wall in a nearby courtyard."

"What's a niche?"

"Like a recessed wall, ya know?"

"Oh, yeah. I guess."

"The Italians love the Madonna. There's this church nearby called il Santuario … that means Sanctuary … and it's dedicated to her. I think it was originally built in the fifteenth century. The dome looks like an onion. Totally rad."

"I guess the town doesn't look much like Altrusia."

"No way. Not even close."

"So what's different?" She laughed. "Besides everything."

"Well, there's a cool cobblestone piazza … like a town square … and it's surrounded by these large circular amphitheater-like steps. At one corner, there's a column crowned with an iron cross. So, it's called *Piazza della Croce. Croce* means cross." He picked up a glass of red wine nearby and took a few sips. "Gotta tell you something hilarious. I was eating a sandwich there the other day, and these American tourists come by … loud, obnoxious people. And the father … this dude built like an old refrigerator … tells his family they were at the 'Pizza della Croach' but he didn't see any pizza. Some young Italians, early twenties like me, heard the guy and burst out laughing. This dude gets way pissed and starts calling them 'fuckin' foreigners.' And so I stood up and said, 'Dude, you're the fuckin' foreigner. And it's *piazza,* not pizza.' And then I pronounced *croce* for him and told him what it meant."

"What did he say?"

"Told me to go fuck myself and then walked away complaining to his wife that he couldn't believe he was in fuckin' Italy and had to search for some damn pizza. What a tool. Not sure why people like him even bother to leave home, you know?"

"That is so funny."

"Yeah. I was going to tell him about the history of the place."

"Tell *me!*" Charlotte's eyes sparkled.

"Sure." Eagerly, he leaned forward. "Well, the monument, you know, with the cross, was built to thank God for having ended the plague that decimated the area back in the sixteen hundreds."

"That's cool. Not so much about the plague, though."

"No, definitely not."

"So what else is in the town?"

"Lots of cafés … many with tables outside. Little shops … Italians."

Charlotte laughed. "I guess there would be."

"Yeah, but there are people from all over the world. A lot of Chinese people own unisex hairdressing shops, bars, and tailor shops as well. You never know." He took another sip of wine. "Oh, hey, last week I was sitting outside this bar, having an espresso, when this Canadian backpacker sat at the table next to me. He had about five tattoos from the countries he'd visited. My favorite was this French bulldog on his shin. He was still debating what to do for Italy. He was heavily leaning toward a bowl of pasta. Funny, huh?"

"Totes. Do you have any tats?"

Trevor pushed up the sleeve of his tee shirt to show her a tattoo of the Earth on his upper right arm. "I got this baby in Paris because the world is my home. No one place. Just the world. Ya dig?"

"I love it!"

"Do you have any tats?"

"I've got a skull and crossbones on my ass! Wanna see it?"

Trevor's face lit up. "Hell to the yeah, girl. Damn straight! Bring it on."

Charlotte started to raise herself up and turn her body, then quickly resumed her original position. She twisted her face in discomfort. "Uh, I can't. I'm not even sure why I said that. Sorry. There's only one guy I want seeing my butt … ever. And yeah, no way would I want him showing any girls his ass tat, so there's that."

Trevor's happy face deflated like a balloon that had kissed a cactus. "Oh, okay."

"I tried to tell you about it the first time we talked … when you were telling me about the catacombs."

"I don't remember."

"Yeah, I know, because Lily whacked me on the arm before I could get the words out of my mouth."

"Bummer. And I would like to see your ass … I mean your tat." He laughed. "Hey, I'm not gonna lie. I'd like to see both."

Charlotte made a face. "I hear Lily coming upstairs. Don't tell her I mentioned it."

"No way, sweet cheeks."

Lily walked into the room with a pink laundry basket filled with freshly folded clothing. "What's going on, Char?"

"I'm talking to Trevor."

"Hey, Lily!" he called out.

Trying to hide her annoyance, Lily put the basket on the floor and smiled at her laptop screen as best as she could. She turned to Charlotte. "Why didn't you let me know he was online?"

"Um …"

"It's been forever since Char and I met that one time. Thought it would be wicked for us to chat a bit before you came on."

"I see."

Charlotte looked at Trevor and rolled her eyes. "That's my cue. Nice talking to you again."

"You too, Char! Take care. Thanks for keeping it real with me!"

Lily waited until Charlotte closed the door to the bathroom before speaking. "Hi, Trev. It's been a while."

"I know. Sorry about that. I left Garbagnate for three weeks. Went south to Venezia, Firenze, Roma, and Napoli … and to several smaller cities in between. Sorry I didn't call you on your birthday. I lost all track of time. What day was it again?"

"June sixteenth. Eight days ago."

"Oh yeah, right! So did you have a good twentieth?"

"I did. My friend Kady took me to lunch, and I had dinner with my family. Nothing too major."

"Speaking of family, you're never gonna believe this in a million years!"

"What's that?"

"So, remember I told you that my mom booked tickets to Alcatraz on their trip to San Francisco?"

"Sure. You were so shocked."

"Well, now I'm blown the fuck away. Check this out. She and my dad were in the D Block, where they kept the worst prisoners. Out of nowhere, this man starts explaining to them why ghost hunters and spirit seekers think the prison is haunted … but especially that block. Long story short, my parents end up traipsing through the whole prison with this guy because he was like a walking history book. Turns out, he's an attorney who heads up this justice program for people on death row who they believe are wrongly convicted. They'd gotten this big grant and were hiring. The guy says they needed an accountant, and who tells him he'd be interested in the job?"

"Are you serious? Your dad?"

"Sure did. And guess what? He got hired. My dad left his job and went to work full-time at this place. And if that's not enough, my mom took a part-time job there, three days a week, doing research and random administrative work. They're meeting all of these cool people, going to events, visiting prisons, and what have you. My dad was even interviewed on the news and is gonna be part of this documentary. And he's only an accountant, but I think he's doing other things now as well. He can't shut up about all of the good stuff they're doing." Trevor finished the rest of his wine in one dramatic gulp and put his empty glass down, unaware that several drops had missed his mouth and were trickling down his chin toward his neck.

"That's shocking … at least from what you told me. It sounded like your dad was going to stay at that boring job forever."

"That's what I thought." Trevor threw his hands up in the air.

"But when I asked him, he said that he just wanted to keep that office job until he paid off the mortgage and college for my sister and me. She graduated from nursing school years ago, and I decided to travel instead. So, he said he could afford to take a job with less stability now."

"Does he like it?"

"He fucking loves it. Says it's the most rewarding thing he's ever done." A look of annoyance replaced his enthusiasm. "But *now*, if I decide to go to school, I'll have to pay for it. So that's not so great."

"But you said you want to travel …."

"Yeah," Trevor said, a hint of indignation in his voice. "School doesn't take a lifetime. I might have decided to go for it. Who knows? But now, that option is probably off the table."

Lily knit her eyebrows. "But you always complained about how boring your dad was. Honestly, Trevor, now you sound jealous of him. Besides, you could always find a way to pay for school yourself if you decide to go."

"Hell no. Are you serious? I'm not working some boring-ass job to pay tuition."

Lily cocked her head to the side. "But, um, you were okay with him doing that *for* you?"

"Well, unlike some people, I didn't inherit England."

Lily's face dropped. "Whoa. I can't believe you went there. I never should have shared that with you. Stupid me. And I don't know what my property has to do with anything. And, in case you forgot, my mum is dead, and I've been taking care of my family for the past fourteen months and change. And you've got wine on your neck."

He sighed dramatically and angrily brushed the red drops away, rubbing his hands together after noticing they'd transferred. "I'm sorry. That was a totally dick thing to say."

"Maybe a little … yeah."

"Lily, you're such a special person. I think the world of you, and I would be so upset to lose your friendship. You've been my constant connection on this whole journey, and I don't think my life would be the same without you to share my adventures with. I'm sorry I came off like such a spoiled brat … and a dick."

"I appreciate you saying that. Don't worry about it."

"Oh, thanks so much. Hey, I wanted to tell you that I'm going through my photos, and I think I have more than enough for an exhibit. That's why I decided to stay in Garbagnate longer than I planned. You know, because I have this studio at my disposal when I'm not working."

"That's exciting. I wish I had news to share with you too."

"You will, beautiful. I think of you as my girlfriend, you know?"

"You do?" Lily gulped.

"No need to say anything. I know you've been waiting a long time to hear those words. I feel you. Ya dig? Don't worry, I'll be back in a couple of months to get my exhibit together … and maybe then you'll understand how fuckin' special you are to me. I can see why you were named Lily. Your parents must have known you'd be a beautiful flower."

There must be a cow pasture nearby … because you sure are shoveling the manure.

ꞅꞅꞅ

Feeling less than enthralled after her video chat with Trevor, Lily mindlessly took her clothes out of the laundry basket and put them in their respective places.

"You got a minute?" Charlotte asked, coming through the bathroom door into Lily's room.

"Just putting laundry away. A load of your stuff is in the washer now, and I've got a couple of your shirts here." Lily reached into the basket and pulled out two of Charlotte's tees.

"Oh, thanks." Charlotte took the shirts from her before sitting on the bed. "So, are you pissed off with me or what?"

Lily shut the bureau drawer she'd filled and walked over to sit next to Charlotte. "Should I be?"

"No. But that doesn't mean you're not. You sure didn't look too stoked to find me talking to Trevor."

"What if I answered a video call of yours, and if instead of letting you know, I sat there and talked with your friend? Would you be cool with that?"

"Depends on who it was, I guess. But Trevor wanted to talk to me. No lie."

"Then maybe he should have called you instead." Lily's eyes momentarily darkened.

"Whatever. Don't be pissed about Trevor because I've got something for you to be way more pissed off about."

"Great. And what might that be?"

"So you know. For the record, I'm way pissed too."

Lily sighed. "Will you tell me already?"

Charlotte frowned and held out her hand as she noticed a few chips in her black-polish manicure. "So, while you were talking to Trevor, Dad called and told me that none of us are allowed to go out tomorrow night. I told him I had plans, and he started using those stupid big words like he does when he's drunk. He goes like …." She raised her shoulders, furrowed her brow, and deepened her voice. "Charlotte, how many Saturday nights have I prohibited you from fraternizing with your friends? I'll answer that for you: zero. Just this once, I am summoning my daughters to be at home for a reason of special significance …." She relaxed her shoulders and resumed speaking in her normal voice. "I'm surprised I even remembered that much. Anyway, after he finished his speech, he asked to talk to you. I said you were on a video chat with your friend who was in Europe. He started to tell me to interrupt you, but then he said to tell you he'd talk to you when he gets home from work tonight. Guess he didn't want to make you angry before his next request."

"Do you know what he wants?"

"I think so. I didn't want to say anything, but like two months ago, I heard him outside the back door." Charlotte resumed her impersonation of her father. "'Doreen, this is Dalton Sheppard. How are you?'" Then he listened for a second and says, "'I've been contemplating the invitation you extended to me several months ago at the holiday event. I'm sorry I wasn't in any frame of mind to receive your kindness.'" Charlotte made a face. "Talking like Dad is exhausting! How does he even do it? Anyway, so then he went on to ask her if she'd have lunch that Saturday and all of a sudden he sounds super happy when she says yes, and he stops talking in that dorky way. Like magic or something. So, that Saturday, I asked him where he was going, and he said to meet an old friend. But he had the goofiest smile on his face I'd ever seen.

"I wish you'd told me then."

Charlotte stretched her arms over her head. "I know, Lills. But honestly, like a big part of me felt weird about hearing Dad ask a woman on a date. It makes it harder to pretend Mum's still here."

"She'll always be here in our hearts, and she'll always be a part of who we are. But we have to adjust to life without her. And it's not a bad thing if Dad finds a nice woman to date or have as a friend. You might have noticed … he doesn't do well on his own."

Charlotte looked incredulous. "So you're okay cooking dinner for her tomorrow night? Because you know that's what Dad expects you to do."

"I'm not in the mood to be cheerful with strangers. But I'll manage. It's important for Dad."

"Whatever." She frowned. "So if he gets married again, then you'll totally leave. Won't you?"

"Probably. But hear me out: there's a long stretch of road

between Dad having a lady friend and Dad getting remarried. I don't see that happening any time soon. We've all got enough to worry about in our todays and tomorrows. How about we don't go too far past that?"

Charlotte looked at her with pained eyes. "I'm surprised you didn't leave Altrusia already. I thought you were gonna hit the road back in April."

"I didn't though, did I? Because I know that I'm needed here. And maybe you don't believe me, Char, but I have no plans to go anywhere."

Nodding her head almost imperceptibly, Charlotte looked down.

"I won't try to convince you, Char. And by the way, that 'dorky' voice that Dad uses, and the silly big words, well … I think they're bricks in a wall he hides behind … you know?"

"Why does he need to hide?"

"Because sometimes we don't want people to see our sorrows and our pain. So we put on disguises, not realizing that instead of hiding the stuff that hurts us, we're just exposing it in a different way. Do you get me?"

"Yeah … and you think that's what I do too, don't you?"

"Am I wrong?"

"Are you talking about my bad dreams or the way I look?"

"Do you still have the nightmares? You haven't mentioned them, and I haven't wanted to pry."

"Not as much, but they haven't gone away. I don't think they ever will. They bite my tatted ass when I least expect it." Charlotte made a sad face. "And I like the way I look."

"I do too. I told you that on day one. Remember?"

"Whatever. So, um … do you need some help with dinner tomorrow night?"

Lily's face lit up. "I would be thrilled to have some help.

Thanks for asking."

"Cool!" Charlotte got up from the bed, holding her shirts in one hand. "I know the willow tree would be happy to lend a weepy branch."

ℓ℮ℓ℮ℓ℮

Lily set the assorted platter of cheeses, crackers, and grapes on the coffee table. She looked up at her father, neatly dressed in a brown-and-olive plaid shirt and green khaki pants, an extra touch of gel in his hair, watching as she arranged the napkins and cheese plates next to the main attraction.

"You've done a superb job, Lily," he said, sitting nervously in his recliner with only a glass of club soda and lemon. He glanced over at Charlotte, who was sitting on the couch next to Willow. "Thank you for not wearing a skull shirt."

"Yeah, okay."

Dalton let out a nervous laugh. "I suppose I should be happy they're only shirts. They come off. Unlike tattoos. Saw a guy yesterday who had a skull and crossbones tattooed under his neck. God only knows how many other unsightly 'artistic choices' were permanently inked on his hands and arms ... and most likely every other inch of 'blank canvas' on his body. And at that moment, I told myself that I was lucky you only wore them on tee shirts."

Willow fused her lips together and looked down to avoid making eye contact with Lily or Charlotte.

"I'm going into the kitchen to check the paella," Lily said, quickly suppressing a smile as she left the room. "And to make the salad dressing."

Dalton looked at Charlotte. "I'm sorry that I had to ask you to cancel your plans. But an evening like this wasn't possible during the week, and on Friday night, well, Doreen and I are both bushed from a long week at the office. But since it's June and you're not in school, I figured you'd have other nights to socialize."

As Charlotte was about to respond, the doorbell rang. Dalton jumped up from his recliner, shook his hands as if he were drying them, and, pushing his glasses up on his nose, he walked to the front door and opened it.

The woman with the big smile, multi-highlighted short brown hair, and deep-blue eyes, held a colorful bouquet of flowers. She drew a nervous breath and greeted Dalton. "What a beautiful home," she exclaimed as he walked her through the foyer into the living room.

Immediately, Charlotte and Willow got up from the couch as Lily entered from the dining room.

"Girls, this is my friend, Doreen Everly. She's the human resources manager at my company." He continued to speak as he gestured toward each of his daughters. "This is my youngest, Willow, this is Charlotte, and this is my oldest, Lily."

"It's lovely to meet y'all. You're all even prettier than the photos your dad showed me on his phone." She handed the bouquet to Lily. "I've heard you're the chef tonight, so these are for you."

"Thank you so much, Doreen." Lily smiled graciously and took them from her. "These are so pretty. I'm going to find a vase, and I'll put them on the dinner table."

"Have a seat, please," Dalton said to his guest, gesturing toward the nearby armchair. "What can I get you to drink?"

"Oh, gosh, I don't know. Do you have something fizzy and fruity that's nonalcoholic? I don't like to drink and drive. Otherwise, I'd be happy with a glass of wine."

As Dalton continued to speak, Willow and Charlotte resumed their seats on the couch.

"How about a club soda with lemon and lime? I can throw a maraschino cherry in there for the full fruity effect."

"That would be the literal and metaphoric cherry on top." Doreen's uneasy smile fixed on her face.

"Coming up!" Dalton left to make her a drink.

"Charlotte …," Doreen said, "I love your hair color. I've always wanted to do something like that myself, but the corporate world frowns on any real self-expression." She held the ends of her hair in her fingers. "As you can see, I've got a bit of red, a bit of brown, and a bit of blonde happening here. This is about as crazy as I get."

"It's pretty." Charlotte lifted her burgundy hair. "Check this out: I've got black lowlights underneath."

"And so you do! They're stunning, Charlotte. Your father didn't tell me about those."

"You can call me Char. Only my parents … I mean my Dad, calls me that. Well, I guess my uncle Ellis and Aunt Millie do too … but they're in England."

"Fizzy and fruity!" Full of cheer, Dalton re-entered the living room with Doreen's drink. "Please help yourself to crackers and cheese. Lily picked up a small assortment."

Doreen took the drink and put it on the coaster that sat on the small table to her side. "How nice. I'll have to indulge in a small cheese tasting then."

"May I fix a plate for you?"

"Yes, please … but not too much. I don't want to ruin my appetite." Doreen smiled at Willow as Dalton prepared a plate for her. "Your father said you read at least two books a week."

"I love to read. I probably read at least four a week during the summer."

"Tell me some of your best-loved books. Being from the South, *The Heart is a Lonely Hunter* was one of mine."

"Oh, Carson McCullers. I want to read that one. Wasn't she just twenty-three when that was published?"

"Indeed she was! Go on, tell me your favorites."

Willow thought for a moment. "Let's see: *Anne of Green Gables, Little Women,* and *A Tree Grows in Brooklyn.* It's so hard to choose because I love different things about each one. But one of my all-time faves is *A Secret Garden.* That was Mum's favorite." She looked at Doreen and then her father. "Oh, sorry."

Dalton, now back in his recliner, looking uneasy, started to speak, but Doreen stepped in for him. "I hope y'all will indulge me in this nervous little speech I'm about to give." She exhaled. "I know that this dinner is something that none of us are used to. This is unfamiliar terrain for everyone." She took a moment to breathe. "I'm not sure what your dad has told you about me, but my beloved husband, Thomas, died suddenly from an aneurysm several years ago." She smiled to acknowledge Lily, who had come back into the living room and taken a seat on the couch. "I fell into a severe depression for a long time. Things became so bad that my son, Liam, at my request, moved up north to Seattle to live with his aunt, uncle, and five cousins. It broke my heart to see him go, but his departure was far less excruciating than having him bear witness to my endless suffering. My distress was so profound that I was unable to comfort my child as a mother should. I felt selfish and inadequate, although bless his heart, Liam never saw me that way. In fact, he lamented *his* inability to comfort *me.* Poor thing! Frankly, I'm amazed I managed to keep my job, especially with the heavy load of guilt I carried on top of my sorrow." She took a sip of her drink and paused to settle her nerves. "Now that I'm okay, he isn't coming home. Not because my son doesn't love me, and not because he's angry with me, but because his life is in Seattle now."

"Oh, I'm sorry," Willow said. "How old is he?"

"Liam is seventeen. He'll be a junior when school resumes." She turned to Charlotte. "Same grade as you, right?"

"Yup."

"He was here for a two-week visit, but he's off on a camping trip with friends now. He'll be back for two days right before school starts." She glanced at Dalton, then at the girls. "I want y'all to know that even though I learned how to smile again, I was an inconsolable widow until this past Christmas. That's when I mustered the courage to approach your father at our company party. I don't think he was quite ready for that … and I certainly wasn't either … but I wanted him to know that I understood the tragedy and pain involved with a sudden loss, and that if he ever wanted a friend, well, he had one in me."

"And I didn't have a clue how good of a friend I would have in Doreen," Dalton interjected, "but I do now."

She blushed. "So, what I'm trying to say to you beautiful ladies is that we are all missing people who are deeply embedded in our hearts and who will be forever. I never want any of you to feel that you can't mention your wonderful mother. Remember, I saw her at our annual Christmas party for longer than I can remember. When I lost Thomas, Abby spent nearly an hour talking to me at the exclusion of everyone else. I wouldn't have made it through that evening if not for her kindness. Such a gentle heart she had, and mine broke into pieces when I learned what had happened to her. I am so sorry. Words can't express my sadness."

"Thank you for saying that," Lily said. "That's so nice of you."

"I hope I haven't overstepped," Doreen told her. "But I thought we all might be a bit more comfortable getting this out of the way. Grief is an awkward beast."

"It is," Lily said. "How did you get through it?"

"With time, good friends, and Pounder." She laughed. "Oh, he's my Westie-poo. Two years ago, I went to the pound with a neighbor friend of mine to help her pick out a dog. There were these two gorgeous brown pups, brother and sister, only a year old, part West Highland Terrier and part miniature poodle. The owner had died, and the bonded pair needed a home, preferably together." She smiled. "When I tell you that I had no plans to adopt a dog, I meant it. But Alice, my friend, could only take one, and I couldn't bear to leave the other one behind. I love dogs but didn't want to adopt because I work all day. But when Alice said she could keep Pounder while I was at the office, well, there was no good reason not to take him."

"I got my cat Quincy because his first human mummy died … like mine. He was about a year old."

"Like Pounder!"

"So is he called Pounder because you got him at the pound?"

"He is."

"Then he had a different name when you got him?"

"Buddy. I thought that was way too common, so I decided to call him Pounder and make Buddy his middle name." She grinned. "Pounder Buddy Everly. Has a nice ring to it, doesn't it?"

"Cool," Willow said.

"Where's your little guy?"

"Oh, somewhere. He takes a while to come near people he hasn't met before. He's shy. But he's totally a lap cat and loves for me to hold him. And so many cats hate that, so I was lucky. He's helped me a lot."

"That's lovely. Animals are special." Doreen looked at Charlotte. "Don't you think so, Char?"

Charlotte managed a half smile and muttered something pleasant but inaudible.

"I think Mum would be happy you're here," Willow said. "And that … you know, you and Dad are friends."

Doreen put her hand over her mouth as if to stop from crying. "That's absolutely the sweetest thing to say, Willow. Bless your heart, honey. Thank you so much."

Dalton picked up his glass of club soda. "I know my girls don't have a drink in their hands, but let's toast to Abby and to Thomas, who will live forever in our hearts."

"Cheers," Lily said, raising an imaginary glass. "Now, if you'll excuse me, I'd better take care of dinner. We should be ready to eat in about ten minutes."

"Thank you, honey," Dalton said with a smile.

"Here's Quincy." Willow lit up as the gray cat sauntered into the living room. "I named him after Mum. Quincy was her maiden name."

"Oh, he's gorgeous. And that's a perfect handle for this little guy."

"I love him so much." Willow picked up the accommodating cat and gave him a light squeeze.

"I don't know about y'all," Doreen said, "but I feel brave enough to repeat the very silly joke I heard today."

CHAPTER NINETEEN

"I don't like this shade at all," Willow said, sitting next to Charlotte on her bed as they leafed through a book of hair-color samples. "It's too purple. Where did you get these anyway?"

"Camille lent them to me. They're the color-swatch books that hairdressers use. I'm thinking of mixing things up. I don't get too radical because chemicals can damage your hair something fierce."

"I love the way it looks now. Why do you want to change it?"

"I don't know. Maybe because school starts after next weekend, and I thought I might tweak my look. You should tweak yours, Tree. Your hair is too mousy brown. You need some blonde highlights." Charlotte turned the page and pointed to a colored swatch of synthetic blonde hair. "Like this."

"Maybe." Willow looked at Quincy, who was sitting on the bed with them. "What do you think, boy?" She paused as if she were listening to his response. "Yeah, I agree. It might be cool."

"I'll ask Camille if she'll do it for you." Charlotte popped the bubble gum in her mouth. "So listen, did you talk to Issy about that prosty cousin of hers?

"She's not a prostitute, Char."

"Oh, right." Charlotte cracked her gum. "That's only if you

charge." She looked directly at Willow. "So did you find out anything?"

"Um, yeah. I was afraid to tell you."

Charlotte closed the swatch book to deter Willow from focusing her attention on it. "Tell me what she said. And next time, when you find out anything, don't wait until I ask. Trust me, Tree, if it was your boyfriend, you'd want to know like pronto."

Willow looked down at her lap. "Sorry."

"I'm waiting …."

"Well, Issy said that Sara wore this black leather miniskirt over to the garage this morning. I mean, like she showed up about ten minutes after Nico came in at nine."

Charlotte screwed up her face. "And what reason did she give for being there?"

"Get ready to be grossed out. She told Nico she wanted him to check her fluids, and she'd check his too. And that he should look under her hood."

"Oh my God!" Charlotte's face burned with anger. "What a freakin' slut! What happened then?"

"Nico's uncle came over and told him they had a busy day and there were several cars that had to be worked on. So Sara went back across the street to her house. Only she sat on her porch and stared at him. Then, when she saw Nico looking her way, she bent over like she was picking something up … and stayed that way for like thirty seconds. And she didn't have any underwear on so if he was looking, he could have seen … you know. But not close-up."

"What a slutty beeotch! I don't know why anyone still calls her 'Smoochy Sara.' She's 'Slutty Sara' or 'Sleazy Sara.' That smoochy thing must be a leftover from the sixth grade or something."

Willow yawned. "I'm so tired. I was up until three a.m. reading *To Kill A Mockingbird.* If I wasn't so wrecked, I would have gone to the supermarket with Lills. Shopping for food and stuff is super boring. And Saturdays are even more crowded."

"Totes."

"It worries me because Lills has looked so sad lately, but she tries to hide it."

"I know." Charlotte reached over to pet Quincy. "It's like she puts all of her pain in a bag and zips it up … then shoves it under her bed or somewhere she thinks nobody can see it. Except we can because we know her so well. Lills was explaining to me that Dad does the same kind of thing, only I don't think she realized she was talking about herself too. That's why I keep telling you she's gonna bolt. Because she's hurting so much. She's had enough of taking care of us and not having her own life. And don't tell her I said this, but I'm afraid she might fly to Europe to be with Trevor and go traveling with him. I feel it." She sniffled. "And it won't be good for us when she does."

"No. But maybe it would be good for Lills." Willow yawned again. "I'm gonna go take a nap."

Charlotte yawned. "That's contagious. Stop!"

The ringing doorbell interrupted their conversation.

"You go see who it is." Willow scooped up the cat. "I'm off to dreamland."

"Okay." Charlotte popped her gum one last time, took it out of her mouth, and wrapped it with a piece of silver foil in her trash basket, then went downstairs to answer the door.

"Holy shit!" she said, looking at the visitor.

"Man, Char! It's you in the flesh. Nice to meet you!"

"Trevor! You're back from Italy!"

"Yeah, except I went to Zermatt first, then flew home from Zurich." He walked into the foyer and looked around. "Big-ass house. Nice digs."

"You want to come into the living room? Lily's at the supermarket."

"Pfft. That's no fun."

"I don't think she went to have fun." Charlotte nodded toward the couch. "Take a seat. Do you want something to drink?"

"Got any brew?"

"Yeah, but my dad wouldn't be happy if I gave it to you because I'm underage. And also because it's not even noon yet."

"I'm twenty-two. But hey, that's cool. Don't want to get you into a jam with your old man. I'm good. Sit down and chew the fat with me."

Charlotte took a seat next to him on the couch, then turned sideways to face him. "So is Zermatt in Switzerland?"

"Yeah. You know that?"

"I guess I do if I said it." She laughed. "Yeah, of course."

"You're funny. I went to Zermatt because I wanted to see the Matterhorn and do some yodeling in the Alps. I'm kidding about that last part. But I had to stay there for three days to get a shot of the big guy without clouds in the way. I was getting pretty pissed about it."

"Oh, yeah. So like the clouds didn't move because you told them to?"

"No. They didn't. Some nerve, huh?" He laughed. "Matterhorn means 'Peak of the Meadows' if you translate it from German. That's what they speak in Zermatt too. Parts of Switzerland are French and others are German. Remember I told you about the idiot in Garbagnate looking for pizza at the piazza?"

"Sure, that was hilarious."

"I swear. I met his brother at this souvenir shop in Zermatt."

"Tell me!"

"Well, they have these little yellow phrasebooks all over Europe that people buy when they're traveling. The dude looks through all of them on this swivel rack thing, then says to the lady shopkeeper that he can't believe he's in Switzerland and they don't even have one Swiss phrasebook."

"What did she say?"

"Well, she was kind of laughing, and some other tourists were like sniggering. Then, instead of explaining to the guy that there was no Swiss language, she says in her accent, 'Oh, zarry, zir. We just zold zee last one.' Ha ha ha! Man, he was so pissed, and once he got out the door with the cowbells on it, the lot of us cracked the fuck up. She didn't even care if she lost a sale. He was such a fuckwad that he deserved to stay stupid. And, yeah, probably gave a few more shopkeepers a good laugh."

"That's funny." Char smiled. "So tell me how you get up into the mountains to see the Matterhorn?"

"By train." Trevor scanned the living room to take in his environment. "In the center of Zermatt, you catch this train to Gornergrat. That's where you get off if you want to see, well, *try* to see, the Matterhorn. Since I was there in the summer, I was able to do a lot of hiking and make the trip worthwhile. Met some cool people from all over the world. I think I took about three hundred photos. When I told people I was gonna be exhibiting in San Francisco, they all wanted to be part of it."

"Oh, I thought the gallery was in the Sacramento area."

"It is." Trevor sneered. "It's in downtown Altrusia. But saying San Fran is way cooler than Sactown or Altrusia, ya dig?"

"Sure. By the way, I hear the garage door opening. Lily must be home. She'll come through the door in the kitchen."

Trevor leaned toward her and lowered his voice. "Before she does, I need to tell you that I had a major boner when you told me about your ass tat."

Charlotte blushed. "Oh, okay."

"Even after you wouldn't show it to me, the damn thing wouldn't go down for the longest time."

"Well um … you better stop talking about it now unless you want Lily to notice you've got another one." Charlotte subconsciously moved several inches away from him.

He sat up straight. "Yeah. For sure. I know what to do." He

spoke loudly: "Blue-haired ladies, full-time jobs, tacky art, stupid tourists, uptight chicks, boring people, cheap-ass pasta in a can ...." He looked at Charlotte. "I'm saying things that turn me off. I've had to do it before. It works."

"Lily's home. She just came through the kitchen door." Charlotte stood and walked into the dining room so she could call to her sister. "Hey, Lills, you've got company in the living room."

Lily put the canvas bag of groceries down on the kitchen table and walked through the dining room and into the living room. She blinked twice when she saw Trevor. "Wow, I can't believe it!"

He got up and walked over to her, picking her up and twirling her, as if he were reuniting with a long-lost lover.

"I'll go get the rest of the stuff from the car and put it away," Charlotte said, walking by them.

"Damn, you're hot." Trevor ran both hands through her long chestnut-brown hair. "What a beauty you are." He kissed her on the lips, lingering for a couple seconds longer than he had planned. "Luscious and sweet. Like a ripe peach or plum."

Uncomfortably, Lily pulled away.

"Oh, shit, I'm sorry, Lily. I didn't mean to come on like that. It's just that for over a year I wanted to reach right through our video calls to plant one on you. I was so frustrated that I couldn't. So now, seeing you like this, I got carried away. I was a dick. Sorry."

"No worries." She looked into the kitchen and saw Charlotte placing a second bag on the table. "Thanks so much, Char."

"So, beautiful. It's almost noon. You want to go to lunch with me? My treat. I know this cool pub where they have these tall wooden booths, but with comfy cushions on the benches ... super private. We can talk, and I'll catch you up on my travels. Man, I've been waiting forever for this. What do you say?"

"Sure. That's sounds like fun. Let me grab my purse out of the kitchen and let Char know I'm going out."

Charlotte pushed open the door to her bedroom. "What are you doing here, Tree? I thought you were sleeping. You look upset … like you've been weeping. Did you hear Trevor downstairs?"

"Oh, is that who that was?" Willow lay on the bed and propped her head up with the palm of her hand. "He's back, huh? I wasn't sure because I had my white noise machine on while I was trying to sleep. The falling-rain setting is my favorite."

"Yeah. That's cool. So how come you're not in snoozyland? You said you were so tired that you had to sleep for at least an hour."

"That was my plan. My boy fell asleep right away. But I got up after only like ten minutes because Issy called."

Charlotte sat on the bed next to her. "Oh, no."

"Oh no is right." Willow sat up. "But you told me to tell you stuff right away, so here I am."

"That's right. I did. So what happened?"

"Well, Issy called to say that like fifteen minutes after Nico's uncle came into the shop, he had to leave again for the day. So Sara told Issy that Nico was so hot after seeing her flash her private area from across the street, that when he saw her come out onto the porch again … 'cause she was doing it every ten minutes, he waved her on over."

"Go on."

"Oh, boy, this is tough."

"Don't start weeping, Tree. Talk."

"Okay, but I can't use the same words Sara used."

"Whatever." Charlotte's face grew red with anger and impatience. "Tell me!"

"Well, there's this back room behind the garage where there's an office and a big blue denim couch. Sara told Issy, like in real explicit detail, how Nico told her to take her clothes off and fast. Then Sara said that he couldn't get out of his pants fast enough and they went at it hot and heavy for like a good hour or more. Oh, yeah, I forgot the part about how Nico put out the Closed sign before they went back there."

"Bullshit! That beeotch is making this up. Nico wouldn't do that! He loves me. Besides, before Issy told you that his uncle said something about having a busy day. So why would he leave if there was so much work?"

Willow made a face. "Maybe he meant it would be a busy day for Nico because he had to go out. I don't know, Char."

"Is there more?"

"Yeah. Sara told Issy that he had this hot raven tat on his butt and she was biting it."

Livid, Charlotte looked into her eyes. "Listen carefully and think hard before you answer this next question. Because it's *really* important! You can't get this answer wrong."

"Okay. I won't."

"Did you ever tell Issy that Nico has a raven tat? If you're not sure, tell me."

"No. I didn't! I swear. I'm super sure. And I don't have to even think about it. I didn't even tell Issy about your skull and crossbones. I wouldn't do that because she doesn't need to know what's on anyone's butt ... especially my sister's. I don't talk about stuff like that. You know I don't, Char. It embarrasses me too much. I think I got that from Mum, you know?"

"What else did that beeotch tell Issy?"

"Um ... that he was by far the best eff she'd ever had in her life and that his um ... thing tasted super delish. And that he kind of tasted her. And that they're gonna do it next Saturday again on his lunch break. But in her garage this time. And that's all, Char. I swear. Except for a bunch of gross detail that I can't repeat."

Charlotte pulled her phone out of her pocket.

"Are you gonna call him?" Willow looked at her in anticipation.

"No." Tears ran down Charlotte's face. "I'm blocking his number. And if Nico calls you, not that he has your number, or if he calls the house phone, I'm not here. I'm blocking his raven ass for good. No way anyone cheats on me like that with the town whore. And I wish I didn't know that the couch was blue denim, but I remember him saying how one day it matched his jeans and he was laughing about how his aunt came in when he was sitting on it and thought he was half invisible."

Willow pouted and lowered her eyelids.

"Don't look at me like that. I know you feel sad for me, and I appreciate it, but my face is an ugly streaky mess. I can't believe that someone I love this much could cheat on me."

"Issy said Sara's gotten lots of guys to cheat on their girlfriends."

"I know of two guys that did. And I thought they loved their girlfriends. She's sick, and it doesn't turn her on to go after single guys. She likes the ones who are off-limits so she can break them. Makes her feel like she's irresistible and sexier than any other girls around. But she's not … sleazy twat." She began to sob. "Go back to your room and try to sleep. But if you hear anything else, tell me, okay?"

"I will."

"And one more thing." Charlotte wept. "Don't tell Issy anything I said. I don't want it getting back to that slut. I'm sure she'd be thrilled to hear she broke us up so easily."

"I won't tell her." Getting up from the bed, Willow leaned in and hugged her sister. "Sorry, Char. I love you."

CHAPTER TWENTY

Trevor took his napkin and wiped his lips as he and Lily sat in the large wooden booth. "I was so embarrassed when you told me I had wine on my neck. Remember that?"

"I do." She laughed. "And wow, what an amazing fourteen months you've had. Thanks for sharing your stories with me. I'll bet your parents were happy to see you."

He took a sip from the beer mug in front of him. "They were. My mom said she wasn't sure if I'd ever come home."

"I wasn't either."

Trevor touched her hand. "You worried for nothing, baby."

"I didn't say I was—"

"I'll tell you, Lily. I never would've believed it, but my parents are so different. They've changed more than yours truly."

Lily smiled at the server who came by to take away their empty plates. Without saying a word, Trevor pointed to his mug to indicate his wish for a refill before the server walked away.

Lily looked oddly at him.

"Oh, sorry. Guess I should have asked if you wanted another of whatever you were drinking."

"No worries. So tell me how your parents have changed."

"Well, my dad's hair is down to his shoulders. King of the Squares, Robert Ashberry Kent, has long hair. And my mom, Suzie-freakin'-homemaker, dyed her hair red and got this hip blunt cut. Their clothes are completely different, and they changed the living room so much I barely recognize the house. She's reading all of this classic literature and shit. I thought she read tacky romance novels. No more art from yard sales, either. They go to art *shows* now. La-dee-fucking-da. Damn. They must have spent a truckload of cash."

"You must be happy to see them finally enjoying life."

"I don't know." Trevor's face turned sour. "It's like they were jealous of me seeing so much of the world so they had to do something to show me up. Pretty lame, huh?"

"From what you've told me, it doesn't sound that way at all. Didn't your dad meet his boss on a trip to Alcatraz? I got the idea that things kind of randomly happened, and your parents were ready and willing to do something different."

Trevor gave his best imitation of a smile as the server put down a fresh drink for him. "I'm glad they're happy … I guess. But I don't want to talk about them anymore. Why would I want to talk about my parents when I have such a gorgeous babe sitting across from me?" He got up, walked around the table, and sat next to Lily, his back toward the restaurant. Pulling her head toward his, he kissed her deeply, his tongue sliding around in her mouth as if he already knew the lay of the land. For two long minutes, they kissed, until Lily pulled away.

She tried her best to smile. "Okay then. You do know how to kiss, don't you?"

"You liked it?"

"It's been a long time since I was kissed like that."

"Since when?"

"I don't want to talk about my ex, okay?"

"That's good with me."

"So, listen, I was wondering if you'd like to have dinner with me and my friends tonight … Kev and Christy. They own the gallery where I'm going to have my photography exhibit. Kev and I go way back. He used to be my next-door neighbor. And I've known Christy since way before they got married. Kev's thirty-two. He and Christy worked their tails off to get that place. She paints city life in oil and he's into mixed media. They met at art school. Super cool peeps. So, how 'bout it?"

"Yes, I would love to."

"Awesome … because I've told them all about you. And tomorrow, Sunday, I was thinking we could go to William Land Park or one of the other parks in the area and have a picnic lunch. You know, the two of us, communing with nature and diggin' each other."

"Oh, that sounds nice. And tomorrow would have normally been good because Willow's spending the day with my dad and his girlfriend, Doreen. Her son, Liam, has been visiting from Seattle, and he's flying back at night. So they're going to lunch, then to the Aerospace Museum of California, and if that's not enough, to some Middle Eastern restaurant for an early dinner."

"What does all of that have to do with you?"

Lily thought. "Actually, nothing. That was totally TMI, wasn't it? I was trying to say that I wouldn't be missed at home. And that tomorrow would have worked well except that I'm booked for the whole day too. I'm going to spend the day on a yacht, believe it or not."

"How come?"

"Well, I've told you about my friend Kady Harrigan, the wonderful woman who was Mum's best friend. Anyway, tomorrow is her husband Patrick's birthday, and their friends, who have a yacht, are taking us on an all-day trip, lunch and dinner."

"Tell them you're bringing a date! That sounds rad! I can't wait! What time?"

"No, sorry. It wouldn't be appropriate to ask. Kady and Patrick's kids and their significant others will be there too. But maybe the next time I get invited onto a luxury yacht." She laughed to mask the awkwardness.

"Oh … okay." He moped for several seconds. "Well, let's pretend we're on a yacht now. It's late at night. We're out on deck. We've had an incredible meal and shared a bottle of Italian wine. There's no one around us but the moon and stars. We hear the soft sound of lapping waves in sync with the beating of our hearts. Romantic as fuck, huh?"

"Oh … yeah."

He pulled her close to him and kissed her again.

"Who's steering the boat?" Gently, Lily pulled away, struggling to do so with nonchalance as the awkward conversation ruffled her.

"Love is the only captain we need, beautiful."

And I thought you left the manure field behind in Italy.

♦ ♦ ♦

"I thoroughly enjoyed meeting Christy and Kevin," Lily said as Trevor opened the door to the room above the gallery. "They're such fascinating and kind people. And funny too."

"They're the best." He grabbed a bottle of red wine and two glasses from the top of a mini refrigerator and put them on the small coffee table. "Have a seat on the couch."

Lily smiled and sat. "I had the best time, Trevor. To be honest with you, I felt a little insecure about meeting them. When you dropped me home after lunch, I was thinking I should cancel tonight."

He sat down next to her. "Well, damn. I'm sure glad you didn't. Why did you even feel that way, beautiful?"

"My life hasn't exactly been worth sharing with strangers."

He pulled a flat corkscrew and bottle opener out of his pocket and uncorked the wine. "Christy told me you were 'positively enchanting,' so there. And I could see how much Kev liked you."

"Oh. That's flattering." She watched as he poured wine into the glass he'd put in front of her. "Only a smidge, Trevor. I had plenty at dinner, and I'm not used to drinking this much." She noticed a flicker of anger in his eyes.

"Okay then, we'll start you off with a smidge of Chianti. Whatever the hot lady wants." He sat next to Lily and flashed a smile before pouring a glass for her and a more generous one for himself.

"Thank you. You're way too complimentary." She looked at the glass. "And this is way more than a smidge."

Ignoring her polite protestation, he picked up his glass, and Lily followed suit. "To us, beautiful. To finally being together after fourteen months."

They clinked glasses and took a sip.

"My graduation night seems like another lifetime." Lily glanced around the room as if it would tame the knot in her stomach. "So long ago."

Trevor licked his lips. "I can't tell you how many times I wished you were with me while I was traveling. So often, I'd see something totally rad and awe-inspiring, and I'd say, 'hey, Lily, look at that.' It's like you were always with me." He put a hand on his upper chest and patted it dramatically. "Right here, babe, you know? And I told you before, whenever we would talk, I wanted to reach through the screen and put my lips on yours." He grinned. "Like this." He put his glass down on the coffee table, waited for her to do the same, then put both arms around her and pulled her close. Within seconds, he was deeply kissing her again, but now, in the privacy of the room, he had pushed her down on the couch and was on top of her.

Lily could feel his hardness against her thigh as he fondled her breasts. "Holy hard-on," he mumbled to himself. Looking up, he unbuttoned her blouse and pulled her right breast out of her bra. Sucking on her nipple, he thrust up and down. "You taste so good,

Lily. And I'm going to savor every inch of you like a fine wine or some bazillion-calorie, finger-licking dessert." He reached in and pulled out her other breast, raised himself up with his right arm, and stared at her. "Oh my God, you have the most beautiful fucking tits I've ever seen. So round, so fucking delicious. Shit!"

Lily, enjoying his touch more than his words, pushed her hesitation aside, moaning as his tongue circled her nipple before he took her breast in his mouth again.

"Oh, God." As she uttered her pleasure, she could feel Trevor unzipping his pants and pulling himself out. And, in that moment, reality crash-landed with a boom. She put her hands on his shoulders and pushed him up. "Trevor, please ... wait!"

"Oh, you wanna look into my eyes while you're being fucked, yeah? I dig eye contact too."

"No, no! I can't do this, Trevor. I'm sorry."

"Sure you can." He pushed her back down and stroked his hard-on only inches from her face. "Am I big enough for you?"

"Get away from me. I can't do this, Trevor! I'm saying no. I am not consenting. Let me up!"

He scoffed. "I've waited fourteen months to fuck the living daylights outta you, and now you want me to 'let you up?' Ha ha. That's bullshit! I'm gonna fuck you so hard your pussy will thump for days." He reached down and tried to unzip her jeans. "Take your pants off, you little Altrusia bitch! Stop toying with me."

With every bit of strength she had, Lily pushed his chest up and fell against the coffee table, knocking over the wineglasses. Hers fell onto the floor. His shattered on the table, splashing his genitalia like a shaken soda can.

She rolled over to the edge of the area rug. Quickly, she got up.

"You got fucking red wine all over my dick and balls, bitch! You're gonna lick every bit of it off!"

"The hell I am!" She put her bra back into place and

straightened her bag, then hurried backward toward the door. "I'm going home, Trevor."

Still stroking himself and now licking his lips, he walked toward her. "Lick it! You know you want it. Oh, maybe you just want this big bad boy inside of you right away so your pussy can get drunk. You're such a fucking tease, Lily Sheppard. But I'll play your game. It's kind of a turn-on, actually, you playing the forbidden fruit instead of the sweet and juicy kind."

Lily put her hand out to stop him. "Get the fuck away from me! I do not want to have sex with you. I'm sorry, Trevor. I hadn't been touched in a long time, and I'm not going to lie and say it didn't feel good … because for a moment or two, it did. But I absolutely do not want to have sex with you. I'm not even close to being in love with you, and honestly, I don't even know you."

Seething with rage, he continued to stimulate himself, wine staining his busy hands. "This is a game, and I know it. You're a sick bitch, and saying no turns you on like a fucking faucet. I know … because I've been with chicks before who like to feel like they're being raped. Man, do I dig that!"

"I'm *not* one of them, and I'm pretty sure they weren't either. That's vile and disgusting! I don't want you! You're not even my boyfriend. Like I said, I hardly know anything about you."

"That's a lie, bitch! I told you lots of shit about me."

"What I know the most about you was nothing you ever revealed intentionally. I know you're insecure as all get-out, and you think that traveling around the world is going to fix that for you. Only it's not. And you don't enjoy sharing travel stories; you only get off when you can play world traveler and paint your adventures like you're some kind of James Bond or some famous explorer. Only you're so not. You're a lowly tourist from northern California who is now actually pissed that his so-called boring parents have a more meaningful life than he'll ever have. So, yeah, Trevor. There's that. Not to mention you're a spoiled brat. And now that I'm in my right mind again, you're a total bore. And guess what? Your photos are as dull and unimaginative as you are, so maybe you need to find another outlet for your overflowing creativity."

He bristled. "My photos are fucking awesome, Lily!" He tucked himself back into his pants as he lost his erection.

"Uh, maybe you should ask Kev and Christy about that. When you pulled out those photos over dinner, they were giving each other looks like, 'Oh, shit, what have we gotten ourselves into.' Trust me; you won't be getting an exhibit here or anywhere else. I can read people, Trevor. I'm a deep thinker from birth. My family will tell you that. And I'm telling you that your friends weren't impressed with your little snapshots. Oh, and if you want a woman to like you, for real, try complimenting more than her looks. Just a tip for you … a useless one at that, I'm sure … considering you don't have a sincere bone in your body. And now I'm going. I'll get a Lyft … not that you care how I get home."

"No, bitch, I don't. And you know what you are, Lily? You're a cockteaser! Fourteen months of teasing my cock like some snake charmer. I've been waiting all of this time … for nothing!"

"Oh, come on, Trevor. Like how many women did you sleep with while you were gone?"

He reddened. "So what if I take a piece of ass when I can get it? I'm a hot-blooded man. I've got needs. And chicks dig the fuck outta me. I found twenty-two of them that couldn't spread their legs fast enough. Open sesame, baby. And I did several of them multiple times. I could've had more, but I don't fuck just anyone, ya know? I'm very selective about pussy." He puffed up his chest. "It's called class."

"Unreal," Lily mumbled to herself. "Twenty-two different women. Well, there you go. You were hardly waiting for me. Did I tell you that you're crude and disgusting? And that you should probably get checked for STDs?"

"Been there, done that. I'm clean. Got checked out last week."

"Well, that's good to know. And for the record, I wasn't waiting for you. I didn't care if you ever came back. And that's the truth."

Flustered, he opened his mouth but fumbled his intended comeback. He looked at her as if he were going to spit. "I bought you lunch, and my friends paid for your dinner."

Lily reached into her bag and grabbed several twenty-dollar bills, crumpled them up, and threw them at him. "This should more than cover both meals. Not that you'll *ever* return the money to them."

"Fucking bitch! Go home and play mommy to your sisters and wifey to your daddy. Shit, talk about being boring. On second thought, maybe that's why you don't want it from me. You're already getting it at home."

"That is disgusting and untrue. You're repulsive." Lily opened the door. "And good luck to you because, trust me, you're gonna need it, you fucking loser."

As the tears rolled down her cheeks, Charlotte sat in her father's recliner with Quincy on her lap. "It's you and me, boy ... together on a Sunday afternoon. Kind of feels like we're all alone in the world, though, doesn't it?" She scratched his neck. "You'll have to be the man in my life now, because Nico cheated on me with the town whore."

She looked up at the ceiling. "I miss you, Mum. Lily asked me if I was still having nightmares, and I said not as much, but sometimes they're even worse. I kind of lied because I need her and Dad to think I'm doing better so they won't try to push me into seeing some creepy therapist. I miss you so much. I wish I had died too. Then we'd be together. Or maybe it would be better if I had died instead. But then you'd feel so horrible like I do, and I wouldn't want that for you. Not ever."

Frightened by her escalating and vocal grief, Quincy jumped off her lap and left the room. "Oh, Mum ... even Quincy doesn't want to sit with me now. I'm so alone. Why did two people I love so much leave me? Why? I was the best girlfriend to Nico. I thought he cared about me. It wasn't just sex, I swear. We talked about everything. He was the best therapy for me ever because I thought he cared. And he totally listened. And now, he's—"

The sound of the doorbell startled her. "Nobody's home! Go away!" The doorbell rang again. Her strength diminished, Charlotte got up from the recliner and walked through the foyer to the door, wiping her tears on her arm before opening it. "Trevor, what are you doing here? Didn't Lily tell you she's out on a yacht today? I thought you guys had a date last night."

"Hey, sweet cheeks, why are you crying?" Ignoring her questions, he walked uninvited into the foyer and slammed the door behind him.

"My boyfriend cheated on me yesterday. With the town slut."

"Oh, man, that's horrible. I'm sorry to hear that. Gotta be a real loser to cheat on a total babe like yourself." He looked her up and down as his tongue moistened his lips. "So hey, hot stuff, I think you knew all along Lily wasn't the one I was jonesing for; it was you."

"Huh?" Disoriented, she took several seconds to put her thoughts together. "Whatever. I don't care. I'm not interested—"

"Oh, hell yeah, you are!" He grabbed her hand and placed it on his pants. "Feel this. Petrified dick!" A crude cackle escaped his lips. "Your sister couldn't make me this kinda hard if she tried, ya dig?"

Trying to outmaneuver her fear, Charlotte jerked her hand away. "You seriously need to go!"

"Not until I see your pretty ass." His face became misshapen as his rage intensified. "And of course, that tat. I've been dreaming about those cheeks of yours for many moons." He laughed raucously as some red wine dribble escaped his lips. "And after I bury my face in them, my guy Dick here wants to come inside for a visit and stay awhile, ya dig?"

"Um … I don't think so …." Fresh tears rolled down her face. "You need to go *right now.*"

"That's not friendly, Char. Where are your manners?" He grabbed her hand, placed it back on his crotch, and pressed it down harder. "All for you, baby. All for you. I never wanted anyone so bad. I'm harder than Plymouth-fucking-Rock."

"Please go," Charlotte choked out. "Please."

"Do I look like I give a rat's ass if you say 'please?'"

"G*et the fuck out of here*! Now!"

"No way. You know you want me. I knew that the minute you offered to show me your ass tat all those months ago. Then you changed your mind because you're a little cockteaser. That's okay 'cause I'm gonna see it now!" He looked around. "You're all alone today, right?"

"Um, sort of … except for my sister's cat. But my dad will be—"

"Only one pussy here I want!" He grabbed her hand and walked toward the stairs. "And your dad won't be home until later tonight. So don't bullshit me. C'mon, Char. I'm gonna take you somewhere you could never go with your cheating boyfriend. We're going to the moon and back. My spaceship is ready to blast off." He erupted into hysterics as more dribble trickled down his chin.

"You're gross and you're drunk. And I told you to get the fuck out of here. I don't want—"

"I'm gonna give you some action like you've never had before." He yanked her arm and pulled her up the stairs as fast as he could. "I'm gonna pulsate like a hard rock concert inside of you. Man, you're gonna dig it! You're gonna beg me not to stop. Which room is yours, baby?"

"First one on the right." With all of her strength, she tried to put distance between them. "But I don't want—"

With greater force, he wrenched her toward him. "Don't pull away from me again, bitch." He paused. "You're in for the biggest treat of your life." He slipped a hand up her tee shirt. "And that would be me: Trevor-I-know-how-to-fuck-a-bitch Kent. Oh, here we are. Fuck City … aka your bedroom." Opening the door with his free hand, he slammed it shut behind them.

Only Quincy, now sitting outside her door, could hear her despair … and the piercing scream that raised the hackles on his back right before the muffled cries began.

CHAPTER TWENTY-ONE

"Char!" Willow screamed, opening her sister's bedroom door. "I could hear you crying from the bottom of the stairs."

Charlotte, face down on her bed, her hair damp, wearing only an oversized Oxford shirt, all of her makeup scrubbed away, turned her head to look at her younger sister.

Alarmed, Willow sat on the bed and held her. "What's wrong? Why did you take a shower in the middle of the day?"

Turning around and sitting up, Charlotte shrugged as the tears flowed. "I-I don't know ... how come you're home so early?"

"Oh, because Doreen's son, Liam, messed up the time of his flight back to Seattle. He's leaving two-and-a-half hours later than he thought. So when we left the aerospace museum, Dad asked me if I wanted to skip dinner with them. Otherwise, I wouldn't have gotten home until after eleven. Liam was super nice and all ... smart and a quirky kind of funny, but I was worried about you and all the stuff that happened with Nico. I know you're hurting so bad."

Charlotte's face froze with panic. "Where's Dad, Doreen, and her son? Are they here?"

"No, they dropped me off and left. Liam wanted to check out this virtual reality place in the city."

"Good." Visibly relieved, Charlotte exhaled.

"I don't blame you. I wouldn't want them around if I was this upset."

As Charlotte was about to respond, the doorbell rang and she screamed, jumped up, and flailed her arms as if something under the mattress had propelled her.

Willow's jaw dropped in surprise. "Char! Are you okay?"

The doorbell rang again, and Charlotte screamed, "Go away!"

"Nobody can hear you." The doorbell continued to ring. "I'll go see who it is."

"If it's that Trevor guy, don't let him in." Charlotte trembled. "I know you never met him, but you've seen the pictures he's sent Lills. Ignore him!"

"Why?"

"Because Lills isn't here, and he knows it … and he's a fucking sicko creep."

"He is? I thought you liked him. Okay, I won't let him in. I swear."

"Promise, Wills. Look through the glass and make sure it's not him. And if it is, don't say a word. Do you hear me?"

"I won't." Willow got off the bed. "Promise."

"And I know this is a lot to remember, but you can't tell Lily what I just said or that he came looking for her." Charlotte sobbed. "You can't forget this, no matter what!"

"I won't forget. I swear I won't." Feeling the weight of her sister's angst as it escalated with every ring of the doorbell, Willow ran out of Charlotte's room and hurried down the stairs into the foyer. Looking through the beveled glass panel on the right side of the front door, she opened it.

The dark-haired man in the stonewashed, distressed jeans, wearing a black tee with a white acoustic guitar silkscreened onto it, sweat trickling down his brow, looked despairingly at Willow. "I have to see Char. Like right now."

Instinctively, Willow put out a hand to hold him back. "No, Nico, you can't. She's too freaked out, and she doesn't want to see you."

He looked into Willow's eyes and paused to show her he was in control of his emotions. "Listen, Willow, it took me all last night and half of today to get to the bottom of why Char was avoiding me, why she blocked me ... and I finally found out what lies that skank Sara told her cousin about us. You know exactly what I'm talking about because Sara lied to Issy so she'd spread her lies to you." He slowed his breathing. "I swear on everything and everyone I care about ... I didn't cheat on Char. I love her like crazy. She's my life." He paused. "So I'm going up to see her."

Before Willow could protest, Nico ran up the stairs and into Charlotte's room. Breathlessly behind him, Willow looked at her sister to gauge her reaction.

"Go away, Nico! I never want to see you again. Not ever!"

"No, baby. I'm not gonna leave till you listen to me. That skank lied. I can prove it. I didn't cheat on you, and I never would. I love you more than anything. You're the best thing that ever happened to me. I'm so glad Frannie has such good taste in friends, or we might have never met. C'mon, baby. Just listen, okay?"

Willow looked at Charlotte. After a moment, Char nodded to indicate she would hear him out, and Willow slipped out of the room. He put his arms out, longing to hold her.

"Don't touch me." Charlotte held out the palm of her hand to restrain him. "Talk."

"Okay, I won't touch you, but can I sit on the bed? I'm so messed up from this shit, I feel like I'm gonna pass out. I gotta at least sit."

"Whatever." Charlotte moved over to put distance between them.

He sighed. "Thanks, baby." He sat on the bed, one hand

squeezing the other as he tried to calm himself down.

Charlotte sniffled and stared at him.

"So, listen, last night after I finished work, I called you, and this recording came on saying that I was blocked from your number. I was kind of freaked by it, but at first, I figured it had to be a mistake. I even called the phone company, but they confirmed it was for real." He wiped his eyes as a few tears fell. "I didn't even know what to think. Everything felt so fucking surreal. I went to Francesca's room, but I didn't even tell her what had happened. I was afraid that if she knew whatever was going on, she wouldn't let me use her cell. I tried calling you for hours, but it kept going to voicemail. I guess you turned your phone off."

"Duh!"

"So then Frannie finally asks me what the hell's going on, and I told her. And she said she didn't know anything, and she's as shocked as me. But then I remembered how that skank Sara had come struttin' over to me, right after I got to the garage yesterday. She looked so nasty with her leather miniskirt and see-through top. I wasn't even friendly to her ... I asked her what the hell she wanted. Said she wanted me to check her fluids and that she'd check mine too. I wanted to say, 'Excuse me while I hurl, bitch,' but I didn't. Luckily, my uncle came over and rescued me, saying we had a long day's work, which was true. And let's not even talk about how she flashed her skank snatch from across the street. *Gracias a Dios* she was far away."

"So your uncle Raphael never left the garage?"

"Hell no! There was so much work, I even stayed an extra two hours. Things got real busy around nine thirty, right after that slut left, so my aunt came into the office to handle the accounts because Uncle Raffi had to work on this guy's Benz and finish it by one thirty. Then he had two other cars waiting for him."

"Oh ...."

"So last night, after I tried for hours to reach you, I finally figured out that Skankzilla had told some shit to Isabelle to tell to Willow to make its way to you. I drove over to her house to confront her, but there was a bunch of her family in the living room, partying it up, so no way I could go to the door. Like, 'hey, I'm here to talk to the lyin' skank and ream her ass out for spreading garbage about me.' I didn't think they'd let me in, you know? And I didn't come over here because I needed to get the whole story before I saw you. Plus it was late, and I was afraid I'd make everything worse."

"I wish you did, but I know why you didn't ...." Charlotte whimpered.

"Anyway, so all night long I'm a wreck. Even Jalapeño was worried about me. Dogs know when shit isn't right. He wouldn't leave my side. Didn't hardly get any sleep. I went back to the garage today, and even though it's closed, I watched from inside the front room and waited forever until I saw her come out of her house ... about an hour ago. I walked outside, real casual and all, and waved like I was pumped to see her. I didn't want to give away how pissed I was, or I'd never find out what happened. She comes sashaying across the street like she's on some damn fashion runway for super sluts. Big smile on her ugly face and her tongue wagging like she couldn't wait to get her nasty saliva all over me." He shook his head in disgust. "Sickening. Anyway, I asked her to come into the office and talk."

Charlotte looked at him, her mouth drooping as more tears fell from her eyes.

"She sat on the couch like 'come and get me,' and I started talking, standing by a file cabinet. I told her how I couldn't get in touch with you, and after putting the pieces together, I figured out she was behind it ... especially because I know her history for doing this kind of shit to other people. At first, she tried to lie, but she knew I would get the truth from Willow, so Skankzilla spilled. I made her tell me every gross detail too. And you know what, baby, she was getting off on telling me. I swear, she thought that instead of being pissed, me hearing those lies was gonna get me so hot I'd have it on with her right there."

"Gross! So how come she knows you have a raven tat on your ass?"

"Oh, she didn't tell me that part ... shit." He punched his forehead with the side of his fist. "No wonder you believed it." He exhaled. "I'll tell you exactly how she knows. My uncle razzes me about it all the time. He thinks it's hilarious. When she first came into the shop, making up some story about how her nonexistent boyfriend had an Aston Martin that needed fixing, my uncle had been going on about my tat to my aunt, and the skank heard him. I'm sure of it, because right then, she made some stupid comment about *her* tats, and I remember thinking how she probably had more STDs than I have fingers. But I pretended like I didn't hear her and walked away."

"So she was in the office where the denim couch is?"

"Hell yeah. She came into the back office a few times ... you know, before we got hip to her bullshit. Lots of people head back there if nobody's in the front room."

Charlotte's entire body went limp. "Oh. So go back to what happened today."

"I was raised never to hit a woman ... and it's not in my nature anyway ... but I swear, if I had it in me ... I would have beat the crap outta her. So I just stood there, told her to get the fuck away from me, never come near me again, and to never, ever talk any shit like that again or she'd be sorry." He paused. "Then I might have told her she was a fugly ho and a double bagger."

The corners of Charlotte's mouth turned up, but she wasn't able to smile.

Gently, Nico moved over and put his hands on her shoulders. "Tell me you believe me, baby. First, because you know I love you, and second, I've got all the proof in the world that it never happened."

Charlotte dropped her head onto his chest and cried. "I'm

sorry, Nico. I never should have believed that. I know she's a liar. It didn't even sound like you. I'm such a loser. I hate myself so much."

Pulling her closer to him, he kissed the top of her head as her face remained buried in his chest. "We can put this all behind us now, Char. This was torture for both of us, but nothing's changed. We're still the same two people who love each other. Nobody can touch that, right?"

Her smothered cries got louder.

Nico stroked her hair. "It's all gonna be good again. You'll see. And I'll love you forever, Char. You'll see that too."

CHAPTER TWENTY-TWO

"Two vegetable spinach wraps for us." Kady looked up at the handsome male server. "And I'll have an iced tea …."

"A lemonade for me, please." Lily handed him her menu.

"Thank you, ladies. Each wrap comes with a cup of our Monday Soup of the Day: carrot ginger. If that's good, I'll bring them out right away."

"Works for me," Lily said. "Thank you."

"Same here." Kady smiled, eager for him to leave. She turned to Lily. "I'm very pleased you agreed to have lunch with me today."

"Of course. I was surprised when you called, though, since we saw each other yesterday. Also, because I know Sabrina and Stan are staying for a couple of days before they head off to Big Sur. You had so much urgency in your voice; I figured it had to be important."

"It is. And my daughter and her husband are happy to spend more quality time with Patrick. This couldn't wait."

"Is something wrong?"

"You tell me, honey. Nobody on the yacht yesterday knows you the way I do. I know there were ten of us, and that you can be shy in a group, but I could see you were somewhere else entirely and wherever that distant place was … something was deeply troubling you. Each time you looked at me, I felt as if you wanted to say something, but clearly, that was impossible under the circumstances."

Lily slumped and looked down. "Oh, Kady."

"I hope I'm not crossing the line. But I had to see you to find out. I was afraid if I asked you over the phone, you'd tell me everything was fine, knowing I had houseguests."

"You do know me. I probably would have."

"You're a lot like your mum that way." She smiled sympathetically. "I'm glad my instincts didn't steer me wrong." Kady smiled at the server as he brought their drinks. "Do you want to talk?"

"I do. But I don't know where to start."

"Anywhere you can, honey." Kady touched her hand.

"Okay." Lily immersed herself in thought for a moment. "Well, after I did my Saturday food shopping yesterday, I came home to a shock. Trevor was in our living room with Char. He'd recently come home from Europe, but he never told me he was back. I thought he was still there."

"Go on …."

"I was a bit freaked when he literally picked me up off the floor and spun me around like I was his girlfriend. But he's kind of overenthusiastic by nature, so I didn't think much of it … not even when he kissed me and I felt a little uncomfortable." She frowned. "I'm such a jerk. Anyway, he asked me if I wanted to have lunch at this pub with him. I was happy to go, but of course, most of the conversation, like 99 percent of it, was about his time overseas. I didn't care because there was hardly anything I felt comfortable sharing with him. It was just kind of liberating to be out of the house." She sighed. "Well, after we were done eating, he came over to my side of the booth and kissed me. Like the way you kiss someone you're in love with. I hadn't been kissed since I was seeing Brian, so I let him … because it felt good. Then, he asked me to have dinner with him and his friends Kevin and Christy who own this art gallery where he stays and works."

"And you agreed?"

"I did." Lily paused to thank the server as he put down their cups of soup. She waited for him to walk away. "But I asked Trevor to take me home and pick me up later for dinner. I had a lot to do around the house, especially since I was spending my Sunday on the yacht with all of you. After Trevor dropped me off, I found Char in her room, crying her eyes out. It was awful, but I'll get to that in a bit. I need to finish telling you about Saturday night and Trevor … as much as it sickens me to do it." She paused. "This next part is the most difficult."

"I'm here, honey. Whatever it is."

"So, dinner was wonderful, but that had zero to do with Trevor. He has these friends, about ten years older than him, and they're the real reason I had such a good time. The guy, Kevin, used to be Trevor's neighbor when he was growing up. I think Kevin sort of looks out for him. I got the impression he's been like an older-brother figure." Lily picked up her spoon and tasted the soup.

"You're doing great."

"Well, after we said good night to Christy and Kevin, I mindlessly … and stupidly … agreed to go with him to the little efficiency studio he stays in on top of their gallery. It's like a converted attic." She thought for a moment. "They're nice to let him stay for free, but he helps them out so it's kind of a barter deal, though I think it's more like charity … but that aside." Despair churned in the pit of her stomach. She stopped talking and looked helplessly at Kady.

"Take your time, Lily. Go at your own pace."

Lily took another spoonful of soup. "Well, first thing in the door, after I sat on the couch, he grabs a bottle of wine and two glasses and puts them on the coffee table. Then he sits *smack* next to me. Right away, he opens the wine and starts freely pouring it. That made me uncomfortable because we'd already had wine at dinner, and I told him that. Enough is enough, you know? Plus, he was supposed to drive me home. But most of all, I'm thinking about Char, and I wanted to go home to her and see if she was all right. The dead last thing I wanted to do was have more wine." She stopped for a moment. "When I told him I didn't want more than a smidge, and even that was to be polite, I could tell he was pissed."

"You think he wanted to get you drunk, yes?"

"For sure. Right away, he started kissing me." Lily laid her spoon on the plate. "Oh, Kady, I'm so embarrassed. Not only didn't I stop him, I let him go further than kissing my lips." She swallowed the lump in her throat. "He took my breasts out and started doing things … ugh … and for a couple of minutes, it felt so good. I don't know … it's like I was hypnotized and forgot where I was and who I was with. But then, as soon as he started unzipping his pants, I freaked. I burst out of whatever trance I was in, and I didn't have a split second of doubt about not being with him. I tried nicely to ask him to stop, but he wouldn't. He thought I was playing a game and that I got off on being a tease."

"Oh my heavens. I'm afraid to ask what happened next."

"He started playing with himself and saying vulgar things. I pushed on his chest with all the strength I had, and I managed to get out from underneath him and fall onto the floor. But, um, I kind of hit the table and knocked over the wineglasses as I was doing so, and his very full glass of red wine splattered all over his … well, you know. Then it got ugly. I swear … he would've raped me if he could have. And he said something about how I was probably 'getting it at home' so that's why I didn't want him." Lily twisted her face in revulsion. "I was so angry, Kady … but even more at myself for ever having trusted him. There were so many red flags, but I was in denial. So stupid of me. I shouldn't have been surprised by anything he did or said. But I was."

"Absolutely reprehensible words … but his actions … oh my goodness. You must have been terrified."

"My heart was beating out of my chest. But I didn't leave

without telling him exactly what I thought of him. And while it felt good to tear into him … it had to be the most frightening experience of my life." She paused. "Mum dying was the worst, but—"

"I understand, honey. Go on."

"Well, then he bitched about how he bought me lunch, and his friends paid for my dinner. So I threw sixty bucks at him." She paused to catch her breath. "I *never* should have gone. I ignored *every* red flag there was. I should *never* have even been his friend. I knew he was messed up, but not that way. I thought video chatting from time to time and hearing about life outside of Altrusia was a healthy thing to do. Yeah, right! I even told you once that I thought I might be able help him because he was a lost soul like me. I'm such an idiot. I totally ignored the part where he never cared about my life at all. He's an insecure and pathetic narcissist."

"From all you'd shared, I knew he wasn't anyone who would ever be special to you. But yes, like you, I believed the casual friendship would be positive, especially with Raymond being in Princeton, and Hannah, well, being out of your life." She smiled sadly and tasted her soup.

"Thank you for saying that, Kady, but I should never have said yes to dinner Saturday night. Everything pointed to disaster, especially knowing Char was in such a terrible state of mind."

"May I ask what happened with Charlotte? More nightmares?"

"Not that I know about. But like I said before, after Trevor dropped me off from lunch, I found Char in absolute hysterics. She said Nico had cheated on her with the local slut, and she'd blocked his number and never wanted to see him again. She was a mess. I should have stayed home to be there for her, but she was so adamant that she had nothing to say and didn't need me. And Wills pleaded with me to go out and have fun … that she'd be there for Char and promised to call me if there were any problems. That's why I went. I knew Dad was at dinner with Doreen, so I didn't worry about him getting in the way."

"Oh, poor Charlotte. So much heartache for a young woman only two months shy of her seventeenth birthday."

"I know." Lily grew sullen. "So anyway, moving on to last night, when I got home from the yacht trip, Char was asleep. But Willow told me right away that Nico hadn't cheated on Char, that this horrible woman named Sara had made it all up, and that Char and Nico were back together."

"That's good then, right?"

"Yes! You'd think so. But this morning Willow said that Char was still crying after Nico left yesterday. Anyway, when I went in to see Char, just like you could tell something was wrong with me on the yacht, I could see the pain in her eyes. Even after a night's sleep, she actually seemed more unhappy after reuniting with him than she did thinking he had betrayed her."

"That's quite odd."

Lily moved her cup of soup to the side as the server placed their vegetable wraps in front of them. She looked at Kady after he walked away. "I begged Char to talk to me, but she wouldn't. Before I left to meet you, I asked Wills what she knew. All I could get from her is that Char's worried I'll go back to Europe with Trevor. I assured her that would never happen. But that's all I said. I didn't want it to sound like something horrible had gone down between us because she'd want to know the whole story."

"No. Willow certainly doesn't need that burden. And poor Charlotte … poor you! My goodness, the last thing you needed was that harrowing experience." She stopped to reflect. "It's not that easy to let go of the trauma in our lives. I know that firsthand. Keep trying, Lily, but don't overload yourself with unrealistic expectations. It only makes things worse."

"I know. I'm working on it, but it's not as easy as I'd hoped. I keep replaying the nightmare of seeing Trevor in front of me, playing with himself as he spewed such sickening words." She shuddered as if to chase away the thoughts.

"What a contemptible man!"

"He is. I'm worried sick, Kady. I can't seem to move past what that scuzzball tried to do to me, and I don't know what's got Char so upset. I know there's more than meets the eye."

"Did Charlotte see you on Saturday night after you came home from that nightmare? Maybe she picked up on your distress, and it added to hers."

"Oh, no. Definitely not. I didn't want my sisters to get an eyeful of me in my messed-up condition, so I snuck into the house. Then, I went up the stairs quietly. Luckily, they were both asleep … probably worn out from all of the emotion, you know? So it's not that. Believe me, the last thing I wanted was to burden Char or Wills with my traumatic night. I went into my room and crashed. Sunday morning, I took a shower, got dressed, went to the mall to pick up the gift I'd ordered for Patrick, then headed to your house in time for us all to drive to the marina."

"Well, it sounds like Char was well insulated from your trauma. That's good."

"It is. But why is she more miserable getting back together with Nico than she was when she thought he cheated on her? Trust me, she loves that guy with every piece of her heart. I don't get it."

"It could be many things." Kady took a small bite out of her wrap and laid it on the plate. "Remember what she's been through … what you've *all* been through."

"And you too. You lost your best friend."

"Yes, thank you." Kady started to tear up. "I did." She pulled a tissue from the side pocket of her pants and dabbed her eyes. "My guess is that all of the traumatic events have come together to put Charlotte into her former fragile and traumatized state of mind. Thinking Nico cheated on her, even though he didn't, was likely the catalyst for such a major setback."

"That makes a lot of sense."

"You're the best older sister in the world, Lily. You are. Your mum would be infinitely proud of you. And she'd be happy your father has found a friend in Doreen. It seems like she's helped to restore his humanity, and he has helped restore her soul. But I'm going to be honest. I'm concerned about *you*, honey."

"Why?"

"Because you're doing so much for your family, and I'm afraid that you're not properly facing all that you've had to give up, all of the loss you've had to bear, and all of the responsibility on your shoulders … every single day. Sometimes, when I think about you, God forgive me, I see a dam about to break. But then it doesn't. I can't stop worrying it will. Believe me, I'm not the kind of person to let unnecessary visions dwell in my head. I just don't know how much more pain and responsibility you can carry."

"Me neither." Her appetite gone, Lily pushed her plate away. "I always thought you were wonderful, Kady. But since Mum died, I understand a million times more why she loved you so much. I'm not going to lie. I do feel exactly the way you described. I don't have a clue what to do about it."

ᕦᕦᕦ

"Get away from me, you fucking creep! Don't touch me! Somebody help me! Please!"

Charlotte's screams awakened Lily at two a.m. She rushed through the bathroom into her sister's room.

"No! Don't touch me! … Mum, help me! … No! … Don't go, Mum!" She screamed again. "You have to save me!"

"Char! Please wake up. You're having another bad dream. It's okay. I'm here."

"Get away from me, you sicko! Stop!"

Lily, sorrow painted on her face, sat on the bed, taking care not to touch Charlotte while she was in a state of unconscious fear. "It's all right, Char. Nobody's going to hurt you. I'm here. And you and Nico are back together, and all's good there."

Hearing Charlotte's bedroom door open, Lily turned to see her father standing there. She put her finger to her mouth to make sure he didn't speak.

"I'm here with you," Lily repeated. "Everything's fine now."

Slowly, Charlotte awakened, still thrashing in the bed.

"You're safe, Char. You're safe."

Charlotte's eyelids fluttered as the screaming stopped. When she opened them, Lily could see the fear and confusion had stubbornly remained.

"I'm here in your bedroom with you. And Dad is here. He's coming in now."

Dalton, shaking as if the nightmare had been his own, walked over to the bed. "It's all right, honey. It's Dad. Did you have another nightmare about your mother?"

"You both need to leave me alone. Go away. I mean it!"

"Can't I do anything for you?" Lily asked as Dalton walked backward toward the door. "Anything at all?"

"Manly Bear."

Lily hurried to Charlotte's bookshelf and grabbed the overall-clad teddy bear that their uncle Ellis had given Charlotte on her third birthday. "Here he is, Char."

Her eyes again closed, Charlotte grabbed the bear and held him close, appearing to drift off to sleep again.

Lily stood and looked at her father, who nodded for her to join him in the hallway.

"Have these nightmares ever stopped?" Dalton asked once he closed Charlotte's door, and they were outside the room.

"I don't know." Lily spoke in a soft voice, moving the conversation down the hall. "This is only the second time she's screamed out. I have no way of knowing what Char dreams about or how frequently. But when I asked her recently, she said they weren't as bad. But I don't know what that means. To be honest, I did feel like she was holding back, but I wasn't going to press her. That would have only made things worse."

"I understand. That's probably hard for you to believe, but I do." He clenched his jaw as he thought. "Why did she scream out for a 'sicko' to get away from her? What does that have to do with your mother?"

Exasperated, Lily leaned against the wall for a moment and closed her eyes. "I don't know, Dad. You know how bizarre dreams can be. I don't know how the subconscious mind works. I only know that some dreams are realistic, and others are a combination of symbols that the brain uses to deal with things. I'm not an expert, and even if I were, how would I be able to explain why Char had a particular dream?"

"I understand that, Lily. Of course you can't know. Wondering aloud, I suppose. Quite upsetting to hear."

"For both of us. But even more for Char to dream it."

"Perhaps then, you might know why Charlotte didn't have dinner with us tonight. I know I was out on Saturday and Sunday, so I was hoping to see her earlier tonight. You said she was sick? Or depressed?"

"She's not feeling well. I was happy she agreed to have a bowl of soup in her room."

"I'm extraordinarily concerned about her, Lily. I worry she'll never get over the PTSD, especially as she's still refusing any help. If anything else is going on, and you find out what it is, you need to tell me, okay?"

"Sure, Dad. Now you'd better go back to sleep. Morning comes quickly, and I know you have your regular Tuesday staff meeting at eight thirty."

"Indeed I do. Good night."

As Dalton walked down the hall to his room, Lily retraced her steps to Charlotte's room and peeked in to make sure she was asleep.

"Is Char okay?"

Lily jumped. "Wills, you scared me. I had no idea you were behind me."

"I heard Char screaming, but when I saw Dad, I didn't come out of my room until he left. What was she saying?"

"She was screaming for someone to get away from her and not to touch her ... then for Mum to help her. Any idea what that first bit was about?"

"I don't know." Willow trembled as she spoke. "Maybe she dreamed that she and Nico were broken up and now other guys were trying to touch her."

"Could be. Go back to bed. You start school next Monday, so you've got to get back on an earlier sleep schedule."

Willow put her arms around Lily and squeezed her. Saying nothing, she then disengaged and walked across the hall to her room, where Quincy waited on her bed. As Lily watched, she wanted to follow her, to console her, and thereby to comfort herself. But an indistinguishable, disincarnate voice cautioned her: *Don't allow your fear to seduce you into making things worse. You'll only add to Willow's burden.*

Content in the wisdom of the transient sage, unaware it belonged to her evolving sense of reason, she wandered into her room.

CHAPTER TWENTY-THREE

Lily and Willow, sitting at the kitchen table, smiled at Charlotte as she came in for breakfast.

"Happy seventeenth birthday, Char!" Willow said.

"Happy birthday," Lily said.

"Yeah, thanks, whatever." Charlotte glanced at the cards and gifts sitting on the table. "I don't want to open anything now. I don't even feel like eating."

"You don't look real well," Willow said, her forehead creased with concern.

"I have a mirror, Tree. I know I look like shit. I figured it's fine 'cause Halloween is almost here, and if I get scarier looking, I won't even need a mask."

"You're beautiful," Willow said. "Nico thinks you're the most gorgeous girl in the world. He told me that."

"He won't for long."

"What?"

"Never mind, Tree."

"I have oatmeal on the stove," Lily said. "Ready to be served. If you don't want that, I can make you eggs and toast. Anything your heart desires, as long as I've got it here."

"Maybe a little oatmeal. It's the most bland."

"Aren't you feeling well?" Lily stood and walked over to the stove to prepare a bowl.

"Not so much. Guess I'm old."

"Totally." Lily placed a bowl and spoon in front of her. "You're positively withering." She smiled, hoping to get even the slightest smile in return, but it didn't come. "Hey, how about a candle in the oatmeal and maybe seventeen raisins?"

"No thanks." Charlotte reached for the milk on the table and poured a small amount into her bowl. She picked up the spoon and rotated it over the bowl as if she were preparing it for a crash-landing.

"You know what Dad would say if he hadn't gone off to work already," Willow said. "I mean, besides 'happy birthday.'"

"Yeah, I know." Charlotte lowered her voice. "Charlotte, that oatmeal isn't going to eat itself."

"Ha ha ha. Right. That's so funny. Like why would any food want to eat itself?"

"So," Lily began, "I know you didn't want to make any plans in advance, but now that it's your birthday, have you thought about what you want to do tonight? We could all go out to dinner. Nico and Francesca too, if you'd like."

Charlotte shrugged. "I don't think so. I'm gonna spend it alone."

"You mean with us?" Willow asked.

"No. In my room. With Manly Bear." She took a spoonful of oatmeal.

"Oh, no," Lily said. "You've got to at least spend it with your family."

"Like with Mum?" With great reluctance, Charlotte took another bite of oatmeal. As Lily was about to speak, Charlotte met her eyes. "And don't even try to tell me what Mum would have wanted, okay?"

"I won't. Promise. I wouldn't want to hear ...."

Before Lily could finish her sentence, Charlotte abruptly pushed away from the table and ran through the kitchen and dining room, toward the upstairs of the house.

Willow looked hopelessly at Lily as she stood and prepared to follow Charlotte. "I'm going up to see if she's okay."

Surprised for a moment to find Charlotte's room empty, Willow's attention was directed to sounds coming from the bathroom. "Oh, no." She ran in to find Charlotte sitting on the floor, toilet seat up, and throwing up what little had been in her stomach.

"Char! What's wrong?"

"What do you think is wrong? I'm sick to my stomach like every morning now, I didn't get my period, I'm tired, and my boobs are like all swollen."

Willow, her mouth open, could only stare.

"C'mon, Tree, you can do it. Add two and two, get four."

"Are you sure? I mean, like *really* sure?"

"Could you get my bottle of water from my night table?"

"Sure." Willow rushed into her bedroom to grab the bottle and hurried back to the bathroom. "Here you go."

"Thanks." Charlotte opened the cap and took a large swig of water. She stood, flushed the toilet, put the seat down, and sat on it. "Yeah, I'm sure. I mean, I didn't even need to take a test, but I wanted proof. So I asked my friend Olivia to go to the pharmacy for me. I couldn't ask Francesca, for obvious reasons." She burst out crying. "I don't know what I'm going to do."

Willow put her arms around her. "It'll be all right."

Charlotte sobbed. "I'm the one weeping like a willow tree now. We might have to switch names or something."

"Oh, Char," Lily said, coming into the bathroom from Charlotte's end. "I heard what you said to Wills. I know you must be freaking out. Don't worry; we'll figure this out." She stopped to pay heed to her conflicting thoughts. "I was so sure that you and Nico were using protection."

"Don't you blame him for this! It's not his fault."

"I'm sure he did his best. Things happen. Do you think a condom might have broken or something? Wouldn't be the first time."

"What would you know, Lily? Have you ever even had sex? Like with that ex-boyfriend of yours ... the one that moved away and didn't tell you until like the last minute. What was his name ... Brian Always Lyin'?"

"I'm not going to talk about him now."

"No, why should you? I'm the one that's pregnant. Not you. But you seem to know so much about everything."

"I don't know anything right now. I wish Nico had been more careful."

Charlotte stood. "It's not his baby! It's your friend Trevor's baby. That loser rapist!"

Willow and Lily rushed to either side of Charlotte to catch her as she wobbled.

"Is that why you said not to let him in?" Willow blurted out. "Did he rape you?"

"What?" Lily screamed as Willow was still talking. "Trevor r-raped you? Oh my God! I'm so sorry! When did that happen? That disgusting—"

"I wanna go into my room!"

Without saying a word, Lily, hyperventilating, and Willow walked her into her bedroom, helping her onto the bed.

Tears streaming down Lily's face, she looked at Charlotte. "When in the world did he do that? I don't understand."

"The next day after your stupid dinner date. You were whooping it up with the Harrigans on the yacht, and Wills was out with Dad and Doreen. And her son, I think. Yeah ... I was here at home ... getting raped by that drunken scum while you were living the good life." She thought for a moment. "He put his hand over my mouth the entire time. I was afraid he'd kill me afterward."

"Oh my God. I-I can't even believe it. No!" Lily screamed. "Holy shit! This is not real. No way. Please tell me this isn't true."

"It *is* true. You think I fucking like that it is ... because I hate it! You have the suckiest friends, Lily! I hate you!"

"I've never, ever ... been more sorry about anything in my entire life."

Charlotte put the palm of her hand out as Lily moved to comfort her. "Get the hell away from me. You brought that rapist into our house. He said you and me were both cockteasers and 'that shit hadda stop.' Those were his exact words before he threw me down on this bed, smothered me with his hand, and raped me. Oh, except you were getting it from ... um ... no ... I can't even say it. I don't want Wills to hear."

"I know! I know exactly what disgusting thing he said."

"You do? How do you know?" Charlotte climbed out of bed and stood. "Because he said it to you? Is that why? Tell me how you know! And when the hell did he say it, Lills? When you were on your date with him? Because Saturday night is the only time he could have said it. Did he try to rape you? Or did he actually do it?"

"He tried," Lily said, sobbing. "But I got away."

Terrified, Willow sat in Charlotte's desk chair, brought her knees up to her chin, and hugged them.

"That fucking ponytailed piece of rotting drunken scum tried to rape you, and you didn't think to warn me? Are you fucking kidding me, Lily? Because I don't have one brain cell in my head that knows how to process this shit. Not one! He could have raped Wills too. Maybe that was part of his plan, only she wasn't here!"

Willow started shaking as the tears fell.

"No, he wasn't planning to hurt Wills," Lily cried, "because he knew ... Oh God!"

Charlotte's eyes narrowed and her nostrils flared as her face turned bright red. "What? Did you tell him Wills wouldn't be home? Did you? So he knew you were out on the yacht, and I was here alone? Holy shit! Did you tell him, Lily? Did you fucking set me up to get raped by that douchebag loser? Oh my God, you so did. Why would you do such a horrible thing to me? Because I give you a little 'tude now and then? Why?"

"I didn't do it intentionally …." Lily paused to control her breathing. "Oh Char, I'm so sorry. You have no idea how much. There are no words to describe it. I've never felt worse about anything in my entire life. I swear. But listen, we have to go to the police and have him arrested. He can't get away with this."

Exhausted, Charlotte sat on her bed and stared at Lily, who was still standing. "Don't you dare call the police! Don't even think about it!"

"Why? Because you don't think they'll believe you? Because you didn't go to the hospital afterward and have a rape kit done?"

"No, genius … because they'll ask if I'm having sex with anyone. And you said it yourself, Lily. Or don't you remember all of your stupid lectures? You're the one who told me Nico was guilty of statutory rape if I'm under eighteen. Only it's not rape with him. Not rape of any kind."

"I understand now how much in love you both are. When I said that, all I wanted to do was make you aware of the law and protect you."

Charlotte took a step closer to her. "Oh, you did a great job of protecting me. You told the guy who tried to rape you on a Saturday night that I'd be home alone on Sunday. Great job! Well done, as Mum used to say. And now, not only am I pregnant, but when Nico finds out, he's probably gonna try to kill Trevor. And then he'll leave me. Because who wants his girlfriend to have a rapist's baby?"

"You're going to keep the baby?" Lily sniffled.

"Yes I am. I won't kill my baby and have it die like Mum. It's her first grandchild, even with a rapist father. The baby will be a good person … its own person. Don't even ask me again because I won't have an abortion."

"I wasn't suggesting that. I never would. I was thinking of adoption."

"I would never give my baby away!"

"I'm sorry; I'm confused and still in shock. I was only asking what you wanted to do." Lily looked at Charlotte and then at Willow, who was still shaking in the chair.

"Promise me you won't go to the police."

"I won't. I promise. But Dad will have to be told. We can't keep it from him for much longer. He's already wondering what's wrong with you."

"Hmm. What's wrong with me? Let's see: where do I even start? Maybe with my not-so-Mum-like sister setting me up to be raped." Charlotte fumed. "Keep your mouth shut. I don't want to tell Dad now. I'm afraid he'll go to the police."

"I'll make sure he doesn't."

"You can't make sure of anything because you're totally pathetic." Charlotte sat down again. "I want a new bed. I don't want to sleep on the bed I was raped on. And you know what, I don't even care about what Dad thinks. I care about my Nico. I love him so much, and I know you can't understand this, Lily, but it goes way beyond sex. We get each other. I can talk to him like nobody else in the world. He's my soul mate. But now, he's going to see me as nothing but used-up garbage. Like some kind of toxic green slime covering everything he used to love. Like worse than Skanky Sara. I don't know. I can't even think straight. But I know it won't be good."

"If he loves you the way you say, and I believe with my whole heart he does, he won't leave you."

"Get the fuck out of my room! I don't care what you think."

"Okay," Lily said, not even bothering to wipe her tears. "I'm going." She stood by the bathroom door as if she couldn't bear to leave. "I'll stay," Willow said softly.

Charlotte turned to see her sister, terrified and shaking. "No, you go to your room and hug your Quincy boy. I know crying and screaming freak him out. Make sure he's okay. And then go to school. I'll stay here alone and think about the hell my Mum-like sister made for me." She looked at Lily, who was standing like a mannequin by the bathroom door. "I said 'get out!' And I'm not going to school today. Maybe not ever!"

Lily ran through the bathroom into her room as Willow, sobbing, hurried out. Alone, Charlotte buried her head in her pillow, where the only thing she could see was the darkness that had extinguished all signs of the person she had once known herself to be.

CHAPTER TWENTY-FOUR

"Lily, hello. This is a surprise," the attractive African American woman with the knee-length graphic tunic top and black yoga pants said.

Lily scanned the gallery and looked at the large paintings on the walls. "I didn't expect to be here, Christy. I'm sorry."

"Sorry for what? I couldn't be happier to see you again." Christy glanced at the art. "This is our brand-new exhibit. These are interpretative portraits by a brilliant young artist, Zaina Solanki. She maximizes each subject's perceived flaws to show their genuine beauty. Her work is gathering incredible acclaim. Kevin and I were honored she agreed to exhibit with us." She stopped talking. "From the look on your face, you didn't come here to see the art. I'll shut up."

Lily bit her lip to stop from crying. "No, I didn't. But it's nice."

Christy waved to a woman talking to a customer, signaling she was off to speak privately with Lily. "Come on. We'll talk in the office." She led Lily into a room filled with an eclectic assortment of art on the walls. My assistant, Danielle, can handle the hordes of art lovers pouring into our little gallery." She laughed uneasily. "Bad joke." She pointed to a crescent-shaped, dark red, art-deco sofa. "Have a seat. Can I get you anything?"

"No. Uh, th-thank you. I have a bottle of water in my bag if I need it."

"Okay." The sparkle left Christy's eyes. "Something's wrong, and clearly it's about Trevor. Are you worried about him?"

"Definitely not! I've never hated anyone more in my life." Lily broke down in tears. "Is he here?" Her eyes darted nervously around the room.

"He's definitely not here. And I had no idea you two were on the outs, but it doesn't surprise me." She paused. "You'll be happy to hear he's actually long gone," Christy told her as they sat. "Kevin kicked him out the day after we all had dinner Saturday night … two months ago. The following Sunday morning, he called us at home … asked to speak to Kevin. He demanded to know if we were going to give him an exhibit." She made a face. "The question we dreaded and knew was forthcoming … had arrived. Lily, you had a look at the caliber of art we exhibit. Trevor's photos, artistically speaking, are very subpar … nice for a personal scrapbook, but not to exhibit or sell. Maybe to a stock-photo house, but not here … nor any gallery I know of in this universe, actually."

"Definitely not. Bet you'd rather hang paint-by-numbers art on your walls."

Christy grinned. "Right? Anyway, Trevor went apeshit crazy when Kevin tactfully told him there would be no exhibit. In fact, he flew into such a rage over the phone that Kevin hightailed it over here to go upstairs to calm him down. Truth be told, he was afraid Trevor might trash the gallery. He had left. I don't mean for good, but he wasn't in his room … our room. So Kevin decided to work here in the office and wait for him. Yeah, he was that shaken up by Trevor's diatribe. Anyway, around six or seven, Trevor returned. When he saw Kevin, he started cursing him all over again for lying about the exhibit, making a fool out of him, and what have you. Kevin said he was worse than he'd been in the morning … like off-the-charts, non-compos-mentis angry rambling … and reeked of alcohol."

"I'll bet you never promised him anything, did you?"

"Oh, hell no. Before he left on his trip, he went on and on about the brilliant photos he would take and how maybe he'd come back here to exhibit them in a year or so. Kevin said, 'you never know' to appease him. No more, no less."

"So you said Kevin kicked him out?"

"He sure did. And I couldn't be happier. See, Kevin grew up with Trevor and always felt sorry for him. He never fit in anywhere and was always trying to paint himself as something he wasn't and disassociate with what he was … a kid from a nice, average family. I never warmed to him because he's got a certain sleaze element to his nasty self … and I saw that from jump. But Kevin has a long history with the Kent family … his childhood neighbors … and didn't want to shut Trevor out. So I played nice and kept my feelings hidden. Trevor didn't have a clue I never liked him." She shivered. "Getting back to that Sunday night, after Trevor lost his shit again, pardon my French, the dude was actually surprised when Kevin walked him upstairs to make sure he got all of his stuff and left. He seriously thought he could still mooch off of us because he's done it for years. After he realized Kevin was done with him for good, he threw the keys at him, hurled some freshly minted insults, and left."

"He's a monster," Lily said as the tears continued to flow.

Christy jumped up and grabbed a box of tissues off the desk and put them down next to Lily as she sat again. "What happened?"

"Well, I had a wonderful time at dinner, but only because you and Kevin were such great company. When we said good night, I was in a happy state of mind, so I agreed to go upstairs to see where Trevor stayed. Stupid, I know."

"Oh …."

"I swear, Christy, we were in there for less than five minutes before things went way wrong. First, he cracked open a bottle of wine after we'd had some with dinner, and he was clearly annoyed when I said I didn't want any. Then, he started to seduce me, and when I stopped it cold after a few minutes, he wouldn't let me go and became infuriated. He would have raped me if he could have, but I got out from under him … literally … and I rolled onto the table before I hit the floor. Sorry about spilling red wine on your rug. It was kind of a life-or-death escape."

"Oh my goodness! He tried to rape you? I can't even articulate how sorry I am. And please, forget that old rug, Lily. We tossed it along with Trevor. My mama gave the room a good sage smudging too. Please, finish your story. What happened then?"

"I was so scared. I told him off before I left. And it felt good. Only that was the worst thing I could have ever done."

"I'm sure he deserved every word you said. I can only imagine what you went through. What a lowlife. Like I said, he's always been a pathetic sort, despite those edgy ways about him women seem to like … at least initially. But I never thought he was capable of rape. I'm in absolute shock … yet I feel as if I shouldn't be." She shuddered. "Please don't blame yourself for ripping him a new one. That's the least I might have done! I'm wondering … did anything you say have a connection to the exhibit?"

"Yeah. I told him his work wasn't any good … and how I could see it on your faces when he showed it to you … and no way he was going to exhibit here."

"That sure explains his crazy out-of-the-blue Sunday-morning call."

"It does." Lily made a weak attempt to brush away her tears. "Only I made him so angry, he went to my house the next day and raped my sister Char. Today's her seventeenth birthday. And I just found out what happened … *and* that she's pregnant by him."

Christy put her hands over her face and screamed, "Oh Lord Jesus, no!" She uncovered her face and returned her attention to Lily.

"How absolutely horrific. Poor girl. I don't have the words to tell you how sorry I am. If we can help you in any way, we will. But this is not your fault, Lily."

"It is! It had come up in conversation earlier that Saturday, at lunch, about how my family would all be out and about on Sunday. I only told him because he asked me to go to some park with him, and without thinking, I rattled off my plans … and everyone else's."

"Lily, you can't blame—"

"Oh my goodness. I just realized something else. I'm so ashamed."

"What's that?"

"Well, for fourteen months, I've been listening to Trevor brag about his adventures when I had absolutely nothing going on here. For the most part, he's shown zero interest in anything going on with me and has consistently put the quality of his life above mine. Way above. You know? Just now … it just hit me … and I'm so ashamed. It's so clear now; a part of me wanted to stick it to him, in a big way, that I was spending Sunday on a yacht and he wasn't. But not a conscious part of me, if that makes any sense. Still, I knew he would be jealous and pissed off that it was my adventure and not his. I had a lot of anger eating away at me, and I wanted him to feel left out." Lily bent her head in shame. "So yeah, I guess I did know what I was doing but couldn't admit that to myself at the time. But look what I did, Christy. Oh my God, look what I did! I got my sister raped! So yeah, it's totally my fault."

"It's not, sweetie." She faltered for a moment. "Did you come here looking for him?"

"Definitely not. I came to find you because I'm so confused and needed to talk to someone who knows him. I'm well aware you can't fix any of it. But I did want to find out where the bastard is because I'm afraid he'll come back. I'm petrified, actually."

Christy exhaled a sigh of relief. "Well, your trip was

worthwhile then, because Kevin spoke to Trevor's father, Bob, and found out Trevor's moved to Bali. He had met a Balinese fella while in Peru who offered him some kind of bussing job at a touristy café he owns. Apparently, after Kevin kicked him out, he messaged the guy to find out if the offer still stood, and it did. So, Trevor's parents personally escorted him to the airport. And yes, they paid for his ticket and gave him a small wad of cash. Because they don't ever want him back in their house."

"May I ask why? I can think of reasons, but I'm curious."

"He's always been critical of them … to the point of downright nastiness." Nervously, Christy fondled the colorful glass-beaded bracelets she wore. "I think he tells everyone he meets what a wet blanket his father is and how he decided to be a boring accountant in the sixth grade."

"Yeah, he told me something similar when I first met him."

"Thing is, and I'll make this short because your sister's situation is way more urgent. Trevor's grandfather walked out on the family when his dad was nine. He was sick of family life and had some floozy waiting for him. Real swell guy … not. Used another name for years to get out of paying child support … until they caught up with him. Meanwhile, Bob's mother had no money to raise her three children, Bob being the eldest. She worked three jobs to support them. Bob was such a good kid, that at his young age, he swore no matter what he ever had to do in his life, he'd never hurt his family. And yeah, that's why he got a safe job and stayed in it for years. Bob and Susannah Kent didn't even vacation farther than the California coast … so he could pay off the mortgage and have enough money to put his kids through college. He was that devoted. And now, Trevor's angry as hell his parents have a brand-spanking-new fantastic life."

"Yeah, his jealousy is as clear as glass. I kind of said so when I cursed him out."

Christy exhaled. "Um, there's something else you should know,

Lily, and, unlike the bit about his parents, I'm pretty sure Trevor has never shared this with you."

"What?"

"He has two children. Got a girl pregnant in the tenth grade. The second he found out, he turned on her immediately. Became downright scary with all kinds of threats. Her family moved back to Minnesota to get their daughter and grandson-to-be away from him."

"Oh, wow. Where's the other child?"

"In Fair Oaks, I think. Trevor got the second girl pregnant after high school. She'd been his girlfriend for three months. He broke up with her immediately, screaming 'nobody ties Trevor Kent down' and that she better damn well get an abortion. She adamantly refused. He took off for New Mexico for a while, and his parents got involved on the sly. They've been paying child support ever since … because they're good people and because the young woman's family is not one of means. The Kents will probably never see their grandson in Minnesota, but they made sure they would have a relationship with the granddaughter who lives here. Trevor doesn't have a clue. Nor is he remotely interested. So yeah, that's how he became the lucky recipient of a one-way ticket to Bali on Good Riddance Air Express." She made a face.

"I don't blame them one bit. I shouldn't be shocked, but I am. I'm glad I came here. It helps to know he's far away and won't show up at our door."

"Even if he were still in town, he's as chickenshit as they come. Hear me out on this. He'd never come back to your house."

"What a relief. But I don't know what to do. And you can't help me any more than you already have. But my other reason for coming here was I thought you and Kevin should know what a creep he is. You know, that he's capable of rape."

"You're a brave woman." She thought for a moment. "You weren't afraid he might still be here?"

"Maybe a little. But I know the car he was driving ... his father's old brown Ford Focus." She paused to think. "He actually had the balls to dis his father for having driven such a lame car. Anyway, I checked to make sure it wasn't parked in the lot or anywhere nearby on the street."

"Bob donated it to a women's shelter after he left."

"How appropriate."

Christy grinned. "You might get a kick out of knowing Bob Kent drives a Jaguar now."

"Good for him! Well, I guess I should go. I don't want to take up any more of your time, and I've got to see a friend before I head home."

"Would you like Trevor's parents' number?"

"Um, no. Not now anyway. But I would like one of your cards." Lily got up and looked at her with pleading eyes. "But please, promise you won't tell them. I don't know what's going to happen yet and it's not my place. I don't want to complicate an already impossible situation."

Christy stood to face her. "I know we don't really know each other, but I'm here if you ever need anything. And if you feel like it, down the line, please let me know how things are. I'd love that. Thank you for telling me all of this. I genuinely appreciate it. My husband has a big heart, which is why I married him, but this information will ensure he'll never have anything to do with Trevor Kent again. And I thank you for protecting my family." She put her hand on her stomach. "I'm five months pregnant. Our first."

"Oh, congratulations, Christy. I'm happy for you and Kevin. And I'll be in touch one day. I can't say when, but I will. I'm not even sure what tonight will bring. You know?"

Christy reached over and gave her a hug. "Take care, honey. And thank you. And please, no matter what, don't blame yourself for any of this ... not ever."

ᛣᛣᛣ

"I haven't stopped thinking about what you told me at lunch two months ago … when you shared what that horrid creature tried to do to you." Kady wiped her tears. "Never, in all of my tangled and twisted thoughts, did I ever imagine the agony you've just shared with me. How in the world did Charlotte ever keep this egregious crime a secret for two months?"

"I've asked myself the same question." Lily grabbed an embroidered satin pillow from the Harrigans' couch and put it on her lap for comfort. "But the answer is she didn't hide her pain. We thought the fallout from her short, but traumatic, breakup with Nico and her continued PTSD from the accident were to blame. I should have known there was more to it when she had that nightmare screaming, 'Get away from me, you sicko!' When Dad asked me why she might have said those words, I should have dug deeper. But I didn't. I genuinely believed Char's nightmare was triggered from the breakup. No wonder she was more adamant than ever about not getting therapy … she was trying to hide what happened to her for as long as she could."

"Because of what you mentioned earlier about being afraid Nico might be arrested for statutory rape? Or maybe she was afraid Nico might kill Trevor and go to prison for murder."

"You've hit the nail on the head, I think. She didn't tell anyone until she asked some friend to get her a pregnancy test. Poor thing couldn't even tell her best friend because she's Nico's sister."

"Well, I'm glad you've learned Trevor is far away. A massive relief. Have you spoken to anyone else?"

Lily nodded. "After I left the gallery, I sat in my car and called Ray. He tried to console me … he's so sweet … but his schedule is so busy and he had to get to class. Then I called Uncle Ellis. We talk a few times a month anyway, to keep in touch … and also to discuss my property. He totally broke down when I told him everything. He said he's only going to tell Aunt Millie until things are sorted here. And he's 'gobsmacked and gutted' and wants to know how to help."

"What else did he say?"

"How he is so worried about Char and said she has to get help. And he told me the same thing you, Christy, and Ray said: I shouldn't blame myself. Only I do."

"Mister filthy rapist is the *only* one who gets to claim credit for this." Kady's eyes filled with rage. "Hear me on this, Lily."

"I do, but I can't seem to forgive myself. And I don't blame Char for hating me now. I can't even try to help her because she won't talk to me anymore. She's barely spoken to me since it happened, but I chalked up her attitude to her being in a constant state of agitation." Lily paused to stabilize her breathing. "Kady, I think I might need to leave Altrusia. But it's not what I want. More than anything, I want to stay and help Char, but I think my presence will only make it worse."

"Give it a bit of time if you can. Maybe things will settle down. I know you don't want to leave, but if it comes to that, don't forget I have a place for you to go to in Malibu. In fact, I spoke to Cynthia last night, and she reiterated the space is yours if you ever need it."

"Thank you. I'm so lost and afraid."

"I know, sweetheart."

"This is the worst. And who knows what will happen when Dad finds out. Who knows what he'll do. It scares me to think about it."

"It's all coming full circle," Kady mumbled.

"What did you say?"

"Oh, I meant the sorrow, starting a year ago April, when we lost your mum … that overwhelming sorrow feels like it's returning."

"It does." Lily stood. "I'll be right back. I need to use your powder room."

Once Lily was out of the living room, Kady looked upward. She spoke in a whisper. "I hope you can hear me, Abby. I want to help your daughters, but I have no idea what to do. I don't want to make anything worse in some misguided attempt to make things better. I hope you can find a way to help them now that you have connections in such high places. I miss you, my friend. More than I could ever say. But I am forever blessed and consoled to have Lily's friendship. And I will always cherish her as you did."

CHAPTER TWENTY-FIVE

Willow sat at the kitchen table, her gaze shifting between her math workbook and Charlotte's unopened gifts and cards.

"Wills!" Lily walked into the kitchen from the garage, her face drained of color. "Were you waiting for me?"

"Yes! Because—"

" … Dad is home. I know. I saw his car. It's only three thirty. Do you know why he's here?" Lily walked to the kitchen table and sat next to her.

Willow spoke softly. "He said he's worried sick about Char … the way she's been acting, having those dreams, hiding out in her room, being angry and depressed … you know. He called her a whole bunch of times from work to wish her a happy birthday, and it all went to voicemail. She didn't answer his texts either. So he called me and asked if she was in school, and I told him she didn't go." Willow started to cry. "That's when he said he was coming home right away. We both got here at the exact same time almost. Dad said he's um, … worried Char might be suicidal and he's going to get to the bottom of everything today, because no way he'll let her birthday be her death day too."

"Oh, no." Lily hung her head. "Don't think the same fear hasn't crossed my mind as well. I'm glad Dad came home early because Char hates me now." She paused before looking up at Willow. "Where are they?"

"In her room, with the doors closed: her bedroom door and her bathroom door. Dad went upstairs as soon as he got here. I was right behind him because I was going to my room. But when I got to the top step, I got totally freaked, thinking about how you might come home and head upstairs … and how things could get ugly … you know? So I thought I'd better come back downstairs and wait for you."

"You're so sweet, Wills."

"I wasn't sure which door you'd come in or even if you'd come home at all. But I prayed you would."

"Have you heard either one of them screaming or freaking out?"

"Only Char crying. Then Dad went into her room. But since I came back downstairs, I don't know. I did kind of go to the bottom of the stairs a couple of times to see if I could hear yelling, but there wasn't any."

Lily stood. "I'm going to sneak upstairs now, while Char's doors are shut. "I'll even use your bathroom before I go into my room so she doesn't know I'm home. I don't want to upset her any more than necessary. You've been closing my bedroom door to keep Quincy out when I'm not home, right?"

"Sure, Lills."

"Good, then they won't notice if I sneak inside."

"How about your car?"

"I left it down the street when I saw Dad's car panic-parked in the driveway. I know things are bad, so I didn't want anyone to hear me come in. That's why I snuck into the garage from the side of the house … so I could enter through the kitchen. It's much quieter than when the front door opens." Her breathing became labored. "I can't believe I'm even talking about things like this, much less having to sneak into my own home like I'm some criminal." She stopped to calm herself. "Come on. Let's go."

"Okay." Willow followed Lily out of the kitchen. "I'll meet you in your room. I'll be super quiet opening and closing your door."

"We've been in here for fifteen minutes," Lily whispered to Willow as they sat on Lily's bed. "How long was Dad in Char's room before I came home?"

"We both got here around three. So I guess about a half hour, right?"

"I wonder—"

"Promise you won't make me give up my baby," Charlotte cried, her voice no longer muffled as Lily and Willow heard her speaking to her father in the hallway.

"If you are well, all will be fine." Dalton spoke with unusual calm. "I can't bring your mother back, but I can do everything in my power to help you live your best life."

"You sound like a late-night infomercial for some bogus course on everlasting peace and serenity. I hate woo-woo bullshit."

"A bad habit I need to break. One of many, I suppose. I apologize. Now, may we go?"

"No! I don't want to go to the freakin' hospital for a physical examination and a three-day psych evaluation. I've been tortured enough!"

Lily and Willow exchanged looks as they listened.

"Charlotte, I need to know you're okay and getting proper care. Nobody will torture you. And I promise you can come home after seventy-two hours. I need you to see some doctors who can help you, and I give you my solemn word on everything we discussed."

"Say it again. I want to record it on my phone so you won't say I heard you wrong if you change your mind."

"I won't change my mind. Sweetheart, you have my solemn—"

"Say it! Or I won't go anywhere. And hurry before Lily gets home from wherever the hell she is."

"I can't see your older sister right now. I'm far too upset that she brought a rapist into our lives. Of course, I know this ordeal was not intentional, but Lily exercised appalling judgment, and now you're paying the price. This entire family is paying the price."

Lily put her hand over her mouth in horror as Willow wrapped an arm around her for comfort.

"But that said, Lily is a good person, and I know she'll do right by this family. She's quite a capable young woman … as we've all seen. Although an aunt by blood, Lily will be a grandmother to this baby. If you want to leave school now, in your junior year, Lily can homeschool you. When you go back for your senior year, Lily will take care of the baby whenever you need her to. And while you won't be able to attend makeup school in Los Angeles, you *can* attend a school in Sacramento. And Lily will continue to care for the child while you're in school and after graduation when you go to work. It's up to you."

"I don't know anything now. And … I can't think too far in advance. I only know I have to call Nico before I leave and explain this bullshit to him. He doesn't even know I was raped. I wanted to tell him a million times, but how do you tell the person you love … who loves you … how some creep … you know? And I'm sure he's tried to call me a hundred times for my birthday. He must be worried. All of his calls would have gone to voicemail, like yours did. He probably wants to take me out tonight."

"I'm sorry, sweetheart. You can't call him now. It would be too long and too emotional of a conversation to have. He'd want to come over, and you'd end up not getting the help you need. I'll call him and explain you're going in for a psych eval, and he can see you in three days' time, if the doctors agree."

"No! See, you're already changing things up on me, Dad … with this if-the-doctors-agree bullshit. If you don't get them to agree now that I see him in three days, no matter what, then I'm not going … and I'll run away. I swear I will."

"Okay, honey. Before I leave the hospital, I'll speak to the doctors … with you present, and together, we'll get their word that the promise will be kept. I've been a terrible father since your mum left us, but *that* Dalton Sheppard is gone. Now, once again, may we please leave? The sooner you get there, the sooner you can come home to us."

"Okay, Daddy."

Lily made no sound as tears poured down her face. She lay on the bed and sobbed into her pillow. Willow got up and pressed her ear to the door. She listened carefully before turning to Lily. "They've left the house, but I'm gonna look out Char's window to make sure they're actually gone."

Lily sat up, unable to do anything but cry as her youngest sister left the room.

Two minutes later, Willow returned. "They're gone, Lills. And I never ever in a bazillion years thought I'd say this, because I swear I love you so much … but I think you should leave. Like in, move away. All you've done since Mum died is try hard to make life good for us. I know you only spoke to slimeball Trevor because you couldn't go out and make new friends. And there was no way you could have known he was such a bad person from hearing him talk about his stupid travels with a computer screen between you."

"Sometimes I did think he was kind of a dick …," Lily mumbled through her tears. "But no way a rapist."

"For sure. He's not the kind of friend you would have picked if your life was normal like it should be. No way! I understand, Lills. I swear, I don't blame you for anything. You could have left here a hundred times, but you stayed because you love us, and you knew we needed you." Willow wiped her tears on her sleeve.

"Thank you," Lily choked out. "Your words mean so much. But I don't know how to leave you. I know you've been so scared of this day since Mum died."

"I have been. But you have to go. If you stay, then your spirit will totally die, Lills. I know it will. I don't want to watch the life drain out of you. I don't want to see you with dead eyes and a heart so broken it can never be fixed. That would be much worse than having you go. As long as you stay in touch with me, I can handle it. You've taught me so much, and you've done everything you could to keep us all going for the past year and a half. And I know I'm only thirteen and a half, but I'm stepping up to the plate, even if the ball smacks me in the face. You know?"

"You're the best in the world, Wills. I love you so much."

"So are you going to go?" Willow sniffled, growing visibly more upset as she asked the question.

"Yes, I am. It's been on my mind … big time. I was afraid to leave you. But now I have your blessing …."

"It's an order." Willow tried to smile.

"An order then." Lily repeated her words. "I'm going to throw my things together. I've already got one emergency bag ready in my closet. But since Dad won't be back for a while, I can quickly pack some more. And don't let me leave without my precious cottage, the framed photo of Mum, or my laptop. And a couple of photo albums."

"What do you need me to do?"

Lily took her phone out of her pocket and handed it to Willow. "Call Kady … but she's under the name 'Samantha' … and tell her I need to leave Altrusia right away. She'll understand. Ask her to come pick me up and bring someone with her to drive my car. Because I'm not in any shape to get behind the wheel."

"Will she know what else you need her to do?"

"For sure. There's a place in Malibu where I can stay with Kady's friend Cynthia. It's right on the beach. It will be calm and relaxing. I'll find a job there. And you and I can talk every day. I'm going to change my number when I get settled, but you can make up a new name for me and put it in your phone. Like I did with Kady. Okay?"

"Sure, Lills. I'll hate you being gone, but it sounds like the most perfect thing for you. I'm glad Dad is remembering how to be a father again, but you're not a grandmother. And you shouldn't have to raise Char's baby. No way. Dad may think he's got his head on straight again, but he's got some major twisting to do before it sits right on his head, you know?"

"I do."

"Are you going to leave a note?"

"No. And if you don't mind … because I *hate* you being in the middle of any of this, tell him I'm gone and I promise to send him an email." She paused to mull over her words. "Actually, I'll probably shut my address down after I write to him, but you don't need to mention that part." Defeated, Lily's voice became weaker. "I have to get away from the ugliness. You're right; it will kill me. But you're also wise; I have to leave."

Willow looked down at Lily's phone and pressed the 'Samantha' button. "Hi, Kady. It's Willow Sheppard. Lily needs your help real bad."

PART II

Malibu, California

CHAPTER TWENTY-SIX

"I think this is the most tranquil space I've been in for a long time," Lily said to the tall dark-haired fifty-something woman standing next to her. "Cynthia, I can't thank you enough for letting me rent this studio apartment ... and for such an insanely low price. You're way too kind."

Cynthia nodded toward the window bench that looked out onto the Pacific Ocean. "Shall we sit and have a chat?"

Lily offered a nervous smile and took a seat next to her on the blue-gingham cushion. She glanced to her left at the gently breaking waves, then turned her attention to the gracious woman by her side.

"First," Cynthia continued, "I've been blessed in my life, and I don't need the rent money. What I do need is to be able to share my good fortune with special people ... and that's exactly why, as I told my lifelong friend, Kady Samantha, I don't rent this place to anyone ... if I rent it at all."

"But you must know a lot of people who would love to live here." Lily's eyes soaked in the calming scenery. "Kady has been telling me for a long time there would be a place for me here. But I never imagined the offer could possibly stand. I can't believe there's been nobody else—"

"Nobody has come along that I'm as happy to have here as I am you," Cynthia said with a kind firmness in her voice. "Now, moving on, I've made a phone call, and I believe I've found a job for you. I hope that wasn't a pushy or unwelcome thing to do."

"Oh, not at all! I can't thank you enough. I hope I'm qualified."

"Kady told me you worked as a server for four years at a diner in Altrusia. If I heard her right, you're more than qualified."

"You did." Lily smiled. "Is the job at a restaurant?"

"The Breezy Spirits Inn. One of Malibu's finest. It had a completely different name before the renovation some twelve years ago, but the owner, my friend Victor, was so sure his late parents were politely interfering with the construction that he changed the name to reflect their active presence."

"How fascinating. May I ask how they were 'politely interfering?'"

Cynthia laughed. "Well, whenever he had a new idea for the place, an unexpected and unexplained gust of wind would waft through whatever room he was working in. Sometimes it would mess with the new construction ... sometimes not. He was convinced the wind was his mother, showing her approval or disapproval. Of course, when I say 'mess with,' that could mean a design on paper would float away or perhaps an unattended piece of material would fall or become damaged. Those kinds of things ... or so the legend, according to Victor, goes."

"Okay ... so if the windy activity was his mother's input, what did Victor think his father was doing?"

"Making bottles fall." Cynthia laughed again. "I know. Sounds nuts, right? I'm sure there were more feasible explanations, but Vic believes his parents came from the great beyond to meddle. He has a wonderful sense of humor, so he changed the name to reflect human spirits and alcoholic ones ... and soft ocean breezes, of course. There you have it: The Breezy Spirits Inn."

"Is that common knowledge? The origin of the name?"

"Oh … definitely not. He didn't want his future clientele to think he was nuts. Only his friends are privy to such knowledge." She grinned. "I probably shouldn't have spilled the beans. Maybe we can agree a ghost knocked them over."

Lily laughed. "Will I get to meet him?"

"Not any time soon. He's gone up north to open a new place in the Big Sur area. Some of the staff went with him, so that's why there are a few openings. Jamie Tyson Scott, a jazz musician from New Orleans, is the manager. He used to own a place in the Quarter for years and more recently managed a place in Venice Beach. About two years ago, he decided to leave and come work in Malibu. Recently, after many failed attempts, Jamie was able to talk Victor into bringing music to The Breezy Spirits. Sunday, Monday, and Tuesday nights there will be jazz, and the rest of the week he's hired a young musician from Davis to play vocal standards and soft rock. So, hey, you'll have a coworker not too far from your neck of the woods … and mine."

"I'm intrigued. How cool."

"It is. Wait until you see the place. It's got a beautiful plate-glass window behind the bar that looks out onto the ocean. Most soothing. And the room has a gorgeous cobalt-blue-and-teal color scheme to die for."

"So how do I get started? Do I need to call or what?"

Cynthia glanced at the driftwood clock on the wall. "It's six-ten now, and the October sun is about to set. I know Jamie's running late today, but he should be there about seven thirty-ish. I suggest you get ready, and then go to the restaurant and wait for him. I'll text him so he knows you're coming. It's only about a mile and a half north on PCH … Pacific Coast Highway."

"Thank you so much. I'll get ready now. What does he look like?"

"He's a hunky Black man with short hair and a close-shaved

beard. About five eleven. Immaculately dressed all the time. Late fifties. He's hard to miss. And I should probably mention he's been my sister Shelley's significant other for seven years. And now they're engaged. So he's family."

"Oh, I see. How nice."

"Shell's an actor. She doesn't work at the restaurant, but she comes in now and again. They have a lovely place in Santa Monica. Anyway, Jamie is good people."

"I'll do my best to impress."

"You'll do fine." Cynthia stood. "Before I leave, I want to let you know Kady hasn't shared the details of your family situation with me. She considers your privacy a sacred trust. I only know you've lost your beautiful mother, whom I had the privilege of meeting once, and you felt you had no other choice but to leave right now. I also know Kady considers you one of the most exceptional human beings on the planet ... and her love for you is good enough for me."

"Thank you ... I hope I can live up to all the nice things she's said." Lily let out a sigh of discomfort. "I didn't know what she'd shared with you. I was wondering ...."

"I know you're a responsible adult, Lily. And you don't have to tell me anything. If you ever need a friend, I'm here. I'm a retired dancer who dabbles in watercolor and beadwork. I have one grown daughter, Emily, and she's a producer working in New York. My husband, Daniel, is a set designer, and my labradoodle, Oscar, is a digger of sand, a lover of gourmet scraps, and a neurotic but insanely lovable cuddle bug. We both give free hugs, if you ever need them. I also want you to know that when you make new friends, you're welcome to bring them here. This is your home, and I don't want you to think of it as anything less."

"I appreciate you telling me this. But I don't think I'll make any—"

"You never know." Cynthia's eyes twinkled. "I understand

your plate is full. I just thought you should know this is a safe and loving space."

Not seeing anyone who fit Jamie's description, Lily slipped quietly past the hostess and into the lounge area to the left. Even though Cynthia had told her what to expect, the large rectangular window behind the bar, offering an unimpaired vista to the sea, awed her. Although darkness had claimed most of the view, she was drawn to what she could see and welcomed the impermanent escape from visions of life in Altrusia.

Slipping away from Charlotte's cries, her father's anger, and Willow's loving release, she watched as the nine gulls and a lone pelican bobbed in the choppy gray soup of the Pacific. After only a minute or two, the rising mist reminded her of the time she nearly forgot the last of her mother's English Garden Soup on the stove, only to be made aware when the steam carried the aroma into the living room. For a split second, her mum was alive and happily cooking dinner for her family. And then she wasn't.

The waves blew and wafted … the gulls, bold and buoyant, bounced with them … fluttering. When the motion of the restless sea became too intense, they flew to still waters. Whether in chaos or calm, Lily noticed they were active and alert. She hoped she could focus as well as the birds did. She had no choice. There was nowhere else to go and nothing else to do.

"Excuse me," the voice said. "But I think …."

Lily turned to see a six-foot man in his midtwenties, with olive skin and dark brown curly locks down to his shoulders, looking soulfully into her eyes as he stood beside her. Her mouth opened, but the words stuck in her throat.

"I can't believe it. You're Lily, right? From up north? I'm Dak Falaman. I'm sure we met about three years ago … at a party in Roseville. I never forgot you, but I didn't know your last name because I didn't have the chance to ask. Your boyfriend pulled you away after we'd been talking for about a half hour or so. Do you remember?"

"I do," came Lily's stunned reply, as a bartender appeared before them. "Hello, fine people. What can I get for you both?"

"I'm waiting for Jamie Scott," Lily said, barely able to take her eyes away from Dak. "I'll have a club soda with lime."

"Good choice. Meet him sober … get tanked afterward." He laughed. "I'm only kidding." He put out his hand, "Hi, I'm Teddy Jackson. I'm sure you can tell by my smooth dark skin, beaming smile, hella good looks, and off-the-charts charisma … that I'm an actor. One of thousands working in the service industry … but one of the few who's actually going places."

Lily shook his hand. "I'm Lily Sheppard. Hope you get to where you're going."

"And I'm Dak Falaman … also here to see Jamie, and I'll have a ginger ale."

"Ah, you're the new musician," Teddy said. "Jamie said some of the female servers thought you were a chick magnet … an Italian stallion of sorts."

"I'm only here to play music. So maybe I should de-magnetize."

"No worries … I'll take the hot ones off your hands. If they don't come to me first, anyway." He grinned. "I'll be back with your drinks." He started to walk away, then turned to face them both. "By the way, Jamie called about ten minutes ago. He had an errand in Venice Beach, but he'll be here eventually."

"Well, there's a confident dude," Dak said.

"Maybe." Lily watched the swagger in Teddy's walk. "Or maybe not." As Dak sat on the barstool next to her, she soaked in his thick eyelashes, Roman nose, and slightly plump lower lip. He looked a bit tanned, not from trying, but as if his olive skin naturally turned a different shade in the sun. And with no trouble at all, she remembered the night in the tenth grade when she met him, how she'd been drawn to him, and how she'd tried to memorize his face when her then-boyfriend pulled her away.

"You definitely remember me. Not because you said so, but because you're looking at me the same way now you looked at me then." He glanced over at Teddy. "I don't want to sound cocky like our friend over there, but when Brian pulled you away, I knew you wanted to stay. And I wanted you to stay. I didn't think that dick deserved you."

"He didn't. He messed with my life big time. And he knew when we started dating that his family was moving to Virginia Beach in four months. Never said a word."

"Whoa," Teddy said, placing two drinks in front of them. "Didn't take long for you two to—"

"Thanks for the drinks," Dak said, with a solid clip to his voice to dissuade further conversation. "And there's some impatient guy in an Armani suit who's been waving at you for at least two minutes."

"Tony Baloney," Teddy said, walking away.

Dak waited for Teddy to leave and refocused his attention on Lily. "Brian and I had a mutual friend, Sam. He's the one who told me Brian had this gorgeous girlfriend he was lying to ... and it made me angry. And when I met you, and saw your appeal went way beyond your beautiful face, I was pissed. If I'd had even ten more minutes with you, I probably would have let it slip he was leaving town soon. Which is exactly why I think he pulled you away when he saw us talking. He knew I knew. Good thing he was off flirting with someone else's girlfriend or I would have never gotten any time with you at all."

"Yeah, he was a total player." A self-conscious smile formed on her lips. "I never forgot you, and I always wanted to see you again." Lily surprised herself with the ease of her revelation. "But I didn't live in Roseville and had no idea where you were from. I thought we were ships that passed in the night." She glanced out the window long enough to see that several more gulls had joined the raucous party. "This sounds insane to say, but even though you didn't get to tell me about Brian, you saved me from him anyway."

Dak's eyes met hers with intensity. "Will you tell me how?"

Now self-aware, Lily looked down at her club soda and took a sip. "I shouldn't have said anything. It will come off totally inappropriate and, um ..."

"Sometimes I love 'inappropriate.'" The light danced in his dark brown eyes. "But you know, somehow I don't think anything you tell me would be remotely inappropriate." He tasted his ginger ale. "I always hoped I'd see you again. Everywhere I went in northern Cal, I looked for you. And here you are ... in Malibu, of all places. Waiting, I presume, to interview for a job at the same place where I'll be working too. That's about as serendipitous as it gets. Sometimes fate doesn't mess around."

Lily smiled. "My uncle Ellis always told me it's a small world. He and my aunt Millie live in the Cotswolds ... in England, but when they were on vacation in Spain many years ago, they ran into my aunt's best friend from high school who she'd lost contact with. And now they're besties again. My aunt always says true life is stranger than fiction. Now I think I believe her."

"It's true. Life *is* stranger than fiction ... in good ways and bad ways both. There's that six-degrees-of-separation thing ... you know, how all people are fewer than six social connections away from one another. I think it's easily true. I'm from Davis, and I've run into many people who know people I know ... all over the country. And it's probably even more common than we know ... but human beings don't stop to give strangers a list of all the people they're acquainted with, you know?"

"I do." Lily giggled. "I mean I *don't*. But I *do* understand; I *don't* give out lists to strangers." She rolled her eyes. "Sheesh! Leave it to me to bungle a two-word sentence with all of three letters in it."

He laughed. "I knew what you meant. And you didn't bungle a thing." A slight smile played on his lips. "So … I'd love to know how I saved you from Brian."

"I'll be so embarrassed."

"If it has anything to do with you being attracted to me, I'll say it first: I was totally wrapped up in you. Everything about you …no BS."

His words carried her tension away, and she spoke with ease. "I felt the same way. Two days later, when I found out Brian was moving, I was so angry that I'd been played … and used. But then I thought about you and remembered our conversation … and the chemistry we had. Like magic, those thoughts kind of erased Brian in my mind and freed me from any lingering feelings I might have felt for him."

"That's actually wonderful, Lily."

She looked around the lounge as the bar filled to capacity. "I never told anyone because I didn't want to be lectured about some guy I never thought I'd see again … whose last name I didn't know."

"But you must have moved on to someone else …"

"No. I never did. I only let one other guy into my life … as a friend … someone I met at a graduation party … the biggest, most unforgivable mistake of my life."

"I hate hearing that. And I'm not asking you to tell me any part of it, but if you ever want to … I'm here. By the way, meeting you raised the bar for me with women. Again … no BS … I never met anyone who I felt as drawn to as I did … as I *do* … to you."

Lily blushed. "There's one more thing. And I should be way too embarrassed to tell you, but I will."

"I'm intrigued."

"Well, it's about that pendant you're wearing …of um …."

Dak touched the blue copper-enameled pendant hanging around his neck on a black cord. "This is Kokopelli. A Native American friend of mine from Arizona gave this to me. His grandmother made them. This hunchbacked flute player is very prominent in Hopi legends. He was known as a symbol of fertility ... but also as the spirit of music."

"Fertility?"

Dak laughed. "Yes, but it also applied to planting, abundance, and much more. My friend gave it to me because of the musical connection. Long story. But right now, I'm much more interested in what you were going to tell me."

"I heard you lovely folks were waiting for me," the voice interrupted.

Lily turned to see Jamie Scott, exactly as Cynthia had described him, beaming at her. "Hi, I'm Lily Sheppard." She put her hand out to shake his and felt comforted by his firm grasp.

He looked at Dak. "If you're good with starting tomorrow night, I only need to go over a couple last-minute things." He turned to Lily. "If you'll meet me in about two minutes by the hostess stand, which is right as you come in the door, we can go to my office and talk privately. Sound good?"

"Perfect."

"And, Dak, when I'm done chatting with Lily, I'll only need a few minutes of your time."

"I'll wait here."

Jamie motioned to Teddy not to charge Lily and Dak for their drinks. "Excellent," he said as he ran off to speak to an employee eager to get his attention.

Dak smiled at Lily. "So ... it looks like we both will have some free time tonight. I was thinking maybe you'd like to get a bite to eat with me at Sal's Crab Shack, up the road a bit, and afterward, we could take a walk on the beach ... or whatever you're good with and wherever you're good with it. And if you'd prefer to take separate cars, I'm cool. I'm eager to get to know you and pick up where we left off."

"I am too. After what I've been through, I'd normally be running for the hills outside if that invitation came from any other man. But you're not 'any man.' And I know we've met again for a reason. I do."

CHAPTER TWENTY-SEVEN

"Well, it looks like The Breezy Spirits Inn has a new server." Jamie leaned back in his leather swivel chair. "You'll work in the lounge Wednesday through Saturdays. The hours will vary, depending on how busy we are, but consider it a night job. According to California law, if you're under twenty-one, you can't serve drinks after ten. And the drinks you serve prior will only be considered secondary to the food. That's why you'll always be working with another one of our servers. If you're still here when you turn twenty-one … we'll adjust accordingly."

"Thank you," Lily said. "I was aware of the law, and I worried it would be an issue that I'm only twenty."

"It works out fine. A large number of our clientele eat in the lounge to look out our 'window to the sea' behind the bar, especially when they can't get a window seat in the main dining room. And lucky you … Dak Falaman will be gigging on nearly the same schedule. He comes in a bit later and leaves later. The good news—you'll have musical accompaniment as you serve our crazy guests." He chuckled. "Hope I didn't scare you, Lily. For the most part, the Malibu crowd is a hip one … and we get some tourists as well. Most are good tippers and polite people. You'll get your share of the less-friendly types … and unfortunately, there are some too-friendly types who tend to hit on our more attractive servers … male and female. I hope that won't throw you. A solid 'no thank you' is all you need. If there's ever a problem, you come find me. If I'm not here, Big Mike will gladly step in. He's our dishwasher slash bouncer. We don't tolerate any kind of sexual harassment from customers. Or staff."

Lily let out a sigh of relief. "Good to know. I had my share of creeps at the diner. But Mr. McCauley was a family man, and he treated the staff like his children. If anyone messed with us, we never saw them again."

"Exactly as it should be. Now … there's one more thing I need to discuss with you."

Lily noticed the uneasy look that had settled on his face. "Which is …?

"Well, it's our server, Bonnie. She's been here for seven years, and *many* of the customers love her to pieces. Several of them come in specifically to have her wait on their table … and some want nothing to do with her. She rambles on like a stand-up comedian … because she'd like to be one full time … but she usually knows when to cut the chatter for folks less inclined to appreciate her ofttimes free-flowing verbosity. She works in the main dining room, but you'll certainly cross paths. Sometimes you'll need to help her out … get drinks for her and such. Bonnie is … well … a bit eccentric."

"I see …." Lily felt her nerves again.

"I think Cynthia told you we had a couple of openings because Vic took two staff members up to Big Sur with him. What she didn't know was those positions were filled immediately. The reason your job in the lounge was open is because two nights ago, my most recent hire ran out of here in tears. She was totally intimidated by our longtime and most-popular server as, sadly, a weak person in Bonnie's midst is often akin to a shiny object dangling in a cat's face. She can't resist batting it around and beating the crap out of it."

Lily, without realizing she was doing so, clutched her locket for comfort. "I hope she'll like me, but I'm glad you warned me. In the past year and a half, I learned I'm way stronger than I ever thought, but some of the skills I've discovered aren't ones I like to use. Unless absolutely necessary."

"Cynthia told me about your mother. That's absolutely tragic, and you have my deepest sympathy. I know you need a new start. I'll do all I can to help you." Jamie picked up a pencil twirled it.

"Thank you. I'm extremely grateful." Lily let go of the locket as she realized what she was doing.

"The reason I'm talking to you about Bonnie is because you'll be shadowing her for a day or so before you begin. And I need you to be prepared. She has a big personality. Big hair, too … bright red with blonde highlights … you can see her coming at you in the fog and hear her whispering in a thunderstorm."

"What a description."

"An *under*description; trust me." Jamie laughed as the pencil he'd been twirling flew out of his hands, across his desk, and landed on the floor by Lily's chair. "That was to prove that I'm not perfect."

Lily picked up the pencil, stood, and handed it back to him before sitting down again. "Good to know."

Jamie continued speaking. "I should tell you Bonnie's full name … wait for it … is Bonstance Constance Universe."

Lily giggled. "No way."

"It is. Her mother named her Constance, but the nurse filling out the birth certificate heard Bonstance. When Bonnie's mother repeated the name Constance, the nurse made a face as she scribbled down what she thought was a rhyming middle name. I have no idea what her original surname is, but at eighteen, because she hated her father, she legally changed it to Universe … so she could be associated with the stars and planets, instead of him. So, Lily, there you have it: Bonstance Constance Universe. And she'll be training you."

A blanket flung over his shoulder, Dak took Lily's hand as the two of them walked toward the beach, the glow of the moonlight welcoming them in the late, solitary hour.

"You pick the spot," Dak said. "Anywhere you'd like to sit."

"Hmm. How about over there … to the left of the lifeguard station." She looked up at him and smiled. "How did you know I have a beachy feng-shui thing going on?"

"Easy. It's right there … in the right corner of your left eye."

"Interesting. 'Cause I was transmitting it from the left corner of my right eye."

They both laughed as they walked over to the spot Lily had designated. Dak opened the small plaid throw blanket onto the sand, and they sat. He turned to Lily. "I wish I always felt as peaceful as I do right now."

"Me too."

"Thanks for opening up to me at dinner, Lily. I know from experience, when you've been traumatized, hurt, and all of that stuff … it's hard to trust … hard to confide in other people … especially in someone you don't know. I've had trust issues my entire life."

Lily noticed he looked at her as if to detect any hesitation after hearing his revelation, but she had none. "If someone told me I'd be sitting in Sal's Crab Shack in Malibu, telling someone the story of the last year and a half of my life in Altrusia, I wouldn't have believed them. Seriously, I'd have been much more likely to believe I'd come to the beach alone, dug a hole in the sand, and buried myself in it. But you're not anybody, Dak. I don't know you … but when we met three years ago, I felt like I'd *always* known you. And that feeling was even stronger tonight."

He gently squeezed her hand. "I'm one to talk, but I need to work hard to prove your trust in me isn't misplaced. How about a few dozen cartwheels in the sand while I sing the song of your choice in Donald Duck's voice?" He laughed. "And I'm serious! I'd do it."

"You'd better watch it. I might surprise you and tell you to go for it." Lily gave him a lopsided smile. "But you don't have to work that hard. I know my trust isn't misplaced. I only wish our first dinner together wasn't all about me."

Dak searched her eyes. "I wanted to hear every last thing you were comfortable sharing. When I first saw you again, earlier tonight at the bar, even before I got over the shock and elation, I felt the same attraction to you I did that night in Roseville. Only I could see a light had gone out. There was something different … and the fact that you confided in me … well … that's major. Seriously humbling. And trust me, I know how someone's past can fuck them up. I'm not the poster boy for the repercussions of an abusive childhood, but I could've been. I came way closer than I like to admit."

Lily put her hand on his. "I monopolized dinner … even if you asked me to. So it's only fair that this time on the beach belongs to you." She hesitated as she looked to the moon for inspiration. "This isn't a quid pro quo. You don't have to tell me about yourself. But I'd be lying if I said I didn't want you to. Because I don't think we'll ever get to know one another if you don't." She looked down, then into his eyes. "But now doesn't have to be the time."

Dak looked far away into the underlit waters. Lily could see he had transported himself to another place … an unhappy one … not dissimilar to where she often dwelled … to where she was. She studied him … conscious of his pain that was so eerily familiar to her own. She didn't dare interrupt the silence, understanding that quiet on the outside often denotes screaming on the inside. She could only wait.

He turned to her a couple of minutes later, breaking his self-imposed silence. "I want to tell you. I have a lot of fears … but my greatest fear right now is not recognizing that something much greater than ourselves brought us together again. I don't know what that something is, but I'm bowing to its power." He reached into the sand, grabbed a handful, and let it slip through his fingers. "This … is what I won't let happen."

Lily responded with a bashful smile, then waited for him to speak.

"I want to tell you my story, but I should probably explain something. I've lived my life in what feels like pieces … as opposed to one continuous stretch of time … and so when I talk … well … it's likely I'll do so as it comes … in those same pieces. Also, because I've never told anyone this story before, I have nothing memorized in any real chronological order."

"I want to hear anything you have to say … any way you want to say it." She touched his hand again to reassure him.

Dak glanced into the night sky before fixing his gaze on Lily. "I hope it won't sound horrible to say this … when you've lost the incredible woman, Abby, who was your mother … but the female who gave birth to me, Marsha, is the most evil, manipulative human being I've ever had the displeasure of knowing."

"Who did your father think she was when he married her?"

"From what my metaphor-loving aunt Zoey explained, he saw this tempting candy in brightly colored shiny wrapping … never stopping to read the fine print: Lethal if consumed in large doses. He was dazzled by the facade and hungry for sweets. Apparently, not much time passed before Marsha's colorful disguise began to unravel … because she never fools anyone for too long. I'll never forget the way Zoey phrased it …." Choked up, he paused. "Damn, I miss my aunt." He took a deep breath and exhaled. " She said Marsha knew her true colors were showing … like an old lady's slip that has no more elasticity around the waist and is on its way down to her ankles."

"An excellent description." Lily offered a tender smile. "What happened next? In your parents' marriage?"

Dak smashed the small mound of sand he had been building. "Sorry, didn't even realize I was doing this. Nerves." He laughed uncomfortably as he made full eye contact again. "Marsha ... scared to death of losing the husband she'd snared, panicked. She stopped taking the pill, calculated the best time to get pregnant, and did everything she could to reapply the faux wrapping. And *not* because she wanted children ... but to keep her claws in a man who was rapidly falling out of love with her ... and who didn't want kids either."

"And this is when you were born?"

"No. My brother was: Jonah Paul Falaman, Jr. He's about three years older than me, minus a month or two. My father was always called JP."

"So your father stayed?"

"He stayed because of Jonah ... but not too long after ... he strayed. Marsha never missed an opportunity to harangue him ... gossiping about people, complaining about what he hadn't bought for her, bitching about how having a kid changed her body, and giving him a laundry list of what he needed to do to make her happy. Nothing he did ever satisfied her."

"That doesn't seem like the best way to hold onto a man who's losing interest. Or even one who's not."

"You know it. But like I said, Marsha has little ability to maintain a facade. Zoey said her true colors ... her *manipulative* colors ... ooze out of her." He paused to reach back into his memory." 'With every smile, there is guile; behind the eyes, there is disguise. That playful wink ... is not what you think ... this demon shatters ... all that matters.'" Dak, hearing himself, shivered. "What I recited to you ... was the first draft of a poem she was working on. At twelve, well after we'd moved in with her, I found those words scribbled on the back of a supermarket receipt at her house. I easily memorized them, and when she found out I'd done so, she tore it up. She said it was inappropriate for her to have written it. And despite what she thought of my mother, her brother was a grown-assed man who was every bit as responsible … or irresponsible … as Marsha."

"So how did their marriage finally end?"

His eyes followed some quickly moving clouds overhead, then focused on Lily again. "Well, Marsha had accused JP of cheating so often, he figured he might as well find someone who would make him happy."

"I take it he was successful. Who was she?"

"A woman named Deborah … a private investigator in Davis. As far as I know, they're still together."

"Oh … interesting."

"But here's a funny twist to a pathetic story I was telling before I digressed." Dak twirled his index finger in the sand. "Once Marsha was sure he had another woman, she actually went to Deborah's PI office to hire her: to tail JP and find his lover."

"No way."

"Yup."

"What did Deborah do?"

"She smiled, took Marsha's money, waited a couple weeks … reported to her every other day with bogus updates … then gave her a virtual soap opera about JP's activities. To make it look real, she and JP would go to clubs and take staged photos to prove she genuinely tailed him. Bottom line: Deborah told Marsha he was out and about in bars and clubs … alone … sometimes flirting and always drinking. When Marsha looked somewhat relieved, Deborah told her JP was alone *only* because the woman he was reportedly madly in love with …was pregnant and had moved home to a major city in Texas to have his baby." He smirked. "She purposely chose a big-ass state like Texas and gave the fake woman a super common name … like Mary Smith … to send her on a wild-goose chase."

"What a story!"

"Isn't it? So then Marsha spent a fortune tracking down this nonexistent woman, often at the expense of our basic needs, and eventually gave up on PIs ... at least back then. I got all of this from Zoey, of course."

"Wait. I don't understand. Why wasn't your father making sure your basic needs were met if he knew Marsha was spending the money he gave her on a private eye?"

Dak made a fist and twisted it into the sand but stopped. "Because, as Zoey told me when I found her poem, he was no prize either. JP was thrilled to learn the money he gave Marsha was coming full circle back to him. He was never home long enough to see the crap she served us for dinner ... like macaroni and powdered cheese from a box. Our chosen fare most nights. If we were lucky enough to get something different, she'd boil up some hotdogs or ramen-noodle soup. If she didn't feel like turning on the stove, we'd get peanut-butter-and-jelly sandwiches or cornflakes. To this day, I can't look at any of that stuff. I'm hard pressed to even refer to it as food. But none of Marsha's transgressions ever excused our father's absence in our lives or his apathy regarding his kids. Not for Zoey, not for us. Never."

"You and Jonah didn't deserve any of that."

Dak continued. "All of our clothes were secondhand. She bought some of them at thrift stores, but most of the time she waited for the neighbors' kids to outgrow their stuff and have a yard sale ... or better yet ... give everything to her ... the poor woman struggling to support her kids on no money ... or so they believed."

"How awful ... and sad. But I can't get over how random it was your ... um ... Marsha ... happened to hire Deborah."

"Not entirely coincidental. A close friend of Deb's, Harold, was one of the better-known PIs in the area. Potential customers would often swing by his place first; he came up at the top of most Internet searches, and he was well known. Anyway, as soon as Harold realized who Marsha was, he told her he was way too busy to take her case and said Deb was the best PI he knew." He paused. "My father, Deb, and their small circle of friends were always a step ahead of her."

"Was that a good thing?"

"For my existence, maybe. Because Marsha became even more obsessed with holding onto a man who didn't love her, and one night, she got JP drunk enough to sleep with her again. Angry, I-hate-your-fucking-guts kind of sex … as per what he told Zoey. And yeah, that's how I came into the picture. Welcome to the world."

Lily inched closer to him on the small blanket. "I hope it doesn't hurt you to have come into the world as a result of their sickness and drunken sex. You were meant to be here, no matter what the circumstances were."

Dak shrugged. "I don't know. But I do know I was named after Deborah."

"I'm not quite following."

"My father told Marsha he wanted to name me Dak because he had a childhood friend by that name who was the strongest person he ever knew. He said his old friend Dak's real name was Zach, but became Dak when his baby brother consistently mispronounced it. Complete and total bullshit. Dak stood for Deborah Annalise Kennedy … and to this day … I don't think Marsha has a clue. Again, I only learned this from my aunt."

"What's your middle name?"

"Michael. JP's father's name."

"May I ask where your father is now?"

"No idea. But probably out of the country. He almost lost Deborah after he got drunk and slept with his estranged wife again, so after begging for her forgiveness, he gave Marsha a wad of cash to divorce him in exchange for making her sign a document allowing Zoey to manage the child support payments."

"And that was important because …."

"He knew we'd never survive our childhood with Marsha … not that the SOB cared … but he figured if Zoey ever had to take us in, which she eventually did, there wouldn't be any fight over transferring payments. And he'd never have to be in contact with any of us again. So Zoey doled out money to Marsha ... until she didn't. But I'll get there in a bit."

"So that was the end of your father ... as far as you and Jonah were concerned."

"Yup. He and Deb took off to parts unknown. My aunt knew where he was, and after something like seventeen years of listening to his promises about reuniting with us 'tomorrow' ... she gave him an ultimatum. Either he got in touch, or she'd tell us where he was. But then she died. For a brief moment, we were curious as to whether the SOB would contact us, knowing we were all alone in the world, but nope. I'm sure he felt sheer relief." He bit his bottom lip as anger burned in his eyes.

"You okay?"

"Yeah." Dak flinched as if he were evicting a large bug from his body. "It's all for the best; we were long past giving a damn about him. And yeah, Zoey could have told us where he was before she died, but I think she realized nothing good could possibly come from a reunion at that late date. She always wanted to spare us any more pain, especially when she wouldn't be around to comfort us."

"How sad for you and your brother."

"I loved her. She was the mother I never had. She died so young. I grieve for her the way you grieve for your mother. She saved our lives and loved us unconditionally. I think she sacrificed getting married and having her own kids to make sure Jonah and I had all of her love."

As he hunched his shoulders, Lily saw that the darkness had cloaked him and pulled him away from her. "You can stop now, Dak. I know this is hard."

He put up a hand as if to ask for a moment to regain his presence of mind. Understanding him perfectly, Lily waited.

Dak looked at her as the corners of his mouth drooped. "I did love my father once. Even as a little boy, I was cool with the choices he made … until he disappeared. He took the easy way out … he left us like we were two bags of trash at the end of the driveway … waiting for pickup. So, while he wasn't an abusive monster … I don't have anything nice to say about a guy who abandoned his kids. I guess he tried to absolve his guilt by never missing a payment to Zoey. He even paid for my college … but in absentia and in hiding. So yeah … fuck him for not trusting us, not caring about us, not being a father to us, and for leaving us with that sadistic monster, Marsha, who abused us until we could escape."

"Appalling. How old were you when he disappeared for good?"

"Six. Jonah was nine."

"Couldn't he have found a better way to leave her and still love his sons?"

"Tell me about it." Anger crept back into his voice. "When Jonah was ten, Marsha began sexually abusing him and calling him JP. My big brother was afraid if he fought back too much, she'd come after me. He saw how she slapped me around and called me horrible names. She said I was a worthless hunk of flesh and not worth the damage I did to her body. She said she'd teach me how to be a real man. Jonah saw me cowering in a corner … crying my six-year-old eyes out. He was afraid I wouldn't survive the sexual abuse … so he took it all." Dak bit his lip. "He was only nine."

"When did you eventually get away from her?"

"About two years later … when I was eight and Jonah was eleven. Zoey got hip to what was going on. She gave Marsha an ultimatum: sign over custody or she'd go to the school where Marsha worked as a substitute teacher and get her license revoked … and *then* report her to the authorities for child abuse. Marsha caved right away. Plus, she knew Zoey wasn't going to hand over another dime … so, except for having two kids to abuse … there was nothing in it for her."

Lily touched his leg gently. "Was that the end of her for you?"

"Yes and no. I don't have solid proof, but I think she's still out there … her anger simmering in a cauldron somewhere as she stirs it. Thinking about everything both experience and Zoey have taught me, she's likely hell-bent on revenge because we loved our aunt and not her."

"Even if she didn't love you or Jonah?"

"Facts don't matter to sociopaths with addictive and obsessive personalities. You know?"

"I hope that's not the case. Do you think she's out to get Jonah as well?

"Probably. But he got a scholarship to Oxford years ago, and he lives and works in London now. I'm betting she knows … and probably that I used JP's money to get my music degree." He paused. "For the record, I hated touching even a dime of his money, but Zoey told me not to cut off my nose to spite my face."

"So the last time you saw Marsha was when you moved in with your aunt?"

"Not exactly. When I was thirteen, she showed up once at my school. I was playing piano and singing in a concert one night. My entire class and their families were there. Guess who stood up in the audience and cursed at me until she was physically escorted out."

"Oh, please tell me she didn't."

"Humiliating as fuck." Dak's face tensed. "Some kids were cool about it, but others never let me forget … all the way through until high school graduation. And I'm sure imagining my torment gave her great pleasure."

"I'm surprised she wasn't at least arrested for disturbing the peace."

"The school didn't press charges because they thought it would traumatize me. I wish they had."

"I'm getting why it's been hard for you to trust people."

He rubbed the wide leather bracelet on his left arm as if he were making a wish. "It has been. When so-called friends taunt you because your mother is a twisted psycho … well, yeah … there are consequences. Not to mention when the two people who should love you most in the whole world … don't. A minor detail."

Lily frowned. "Am I correct that you haven't seen her since that awful time?"

"No, I haven't. I turned twenty-five in late August, so it's been about thirteen years." He twisted his finger in the sand again. "I know I might sound like a paranoid lunatic … thinking she's still out there plotting … but some weird shit has gone down over the years … too many times to be a fluke. I won't go into all of it now because it doesn't matter … and yeah … because I'm happier when my flesh doesn't crawl … so there's that."

"How have you dealt with your pain for so long?"

"Music, humor … compartmentalizing … denial … and keeping my distance from most people." He swallowed the lump in his throat. "Lying to avoid certain truths … kind of habitually. Not proud. Just telling you." He dropped his head in shame. "But I fight the dark side of myself when it comes around. I'm much better, but I can't entirely shake her presence or the wreckage that takes refuge inside of me." He reddened with embarrassment. "Sorry, didn't mean to get too heady there."

"You didn't. Not at all. Please go on. I'm listening."

He gulped. "I always feel like she's keeping tabs on me, and I've never stopped looking over my shoulder. Literally and figuratively." He looked out to sea for a moment, then back at her. "I have friends, Lily, and I can pretend to be the most social person you've ever met … but I'm usually more comfortable around five hundred people … or even five thousand … than I am with one. Except for you. As for what I've shared with you … while a couple of old friends know little scraps … I've never laid it all out like I just did. And every word was the truth. So now you understand how much I trust you. I trusted Zoey, but she died two years ago, and I've never been the same."

Lily put her hand on top of his and squeezed it. "Those words hurt my heart. I wish I could tell you the pain would stop. I know what an effort it took for you to share."

"There's more, but there you have the story in a nutshell. I feel a bit freaked even having said what I have. This is totally out of my comfort zone." He looked out to the ocean again. "You know why I came to Malibu? Besides one friend introducing me to Jamie Scott and another friend having an RV I could sublet?"

"Tell me."

"First, for me, going to the ocean is going home, because that's where we all began." He took a difficult breath. "When I say *home,* I don't mean my childhood home ..." He choked up. "I mean ..."

"I know," Lily said. "I understand you ... in both a scientific and a metaphorical way. I do. Not trying to get too deep, but you wanted to return to what you believe to be square one of your existence ... of all of our existence, right?"

He looked at her in awe. "Part of me is dumbstruck you understand me so well while another part is saying, 'Of course she does.'" He gave the moon a quick study, then returned to Lily. "So many people would say I'm crazy for even *thinking* the way I do."

"Not me." Lily smiled. "My mum had this sea globe with the ocean floor inside ... sand and seashells. It was handblown glass. When you looked at it from the front, it was blown in such a way that the swirly blue-colored glass on the back made it look like there was water inside. Hard to describe, but I loved it. Anyway, my sister Wills wanted it something fierce, so of course, I let her have it. On the base, it has a plaque with the most beautiful quote from Rumi: 'You are not a drop in the ocean; you are the entire ocean in a drop.'"

"Seriously, Lily?"

"Of course. Why do you ask?"

"Unreal." Dak exhaled. "Zoey taught me that quote the first time she took us to the ocean because she wanted us to know we were anything but insignificant, even if it seemed so, looking out over the vast expanse of the sea."

"Whoa. My mind is a little blown here. My mum said she saw it in a shop in San Francisco and bought it for herself because it reminded her how not going to fashion school, and choosing to have a family instead, was the greatest and most important thing she could do, and to never feel insignificant because of her choices."

"Mind blown here too. We really are connected," Dak said. "And in ways we've yet to learn. I'm sure of it."

"Tell me more. About why you came to Malibu, of all places, to play music."

Dak fanned himself. "I'm still getting over the magnitude of the Rumi quote." He stroked her hair, then pulled his hand away. "I could have been doing a lot of things right now ... bigger and better than working in a restaurant lounge. But I had to reset my life. Something was missing, and I didn't know what that something was. I was in a constant state of flux, and I didn't like it. Nothing that came my way felt right. Most days, I wanted to jump out of my skin. Miraculously, when the opportunity to live and work in Malibu came to me, from two people within two days, I knew this was where I needed to be. I just *knew*. I was guided here ... to a place that had never been home but *was* home ... and would be a physical home ... until the same voice told me otherwise." Overwhelmed with emotion, he pointed out to sea. "And then I thought about the waves ... they drew me here too. Look at how they break ... but see how they gather their strength and form again ... only to keep breaking ... over and over again? This is exactly what life makes us do if we want to keep going. We have to learn how to break. Isn't it ironic? I needed the water to feel grounded. But most of all, I wanted this peace, Lily. I was so drawn to come here." He stopped to reflect. "Maybe I knew you were on your way here and we'd both reset our lives. Together."

"I'd like to think that was true."

"Me too." He looked at her wistfully. "Could be. In fact, I feel certain it is. You know how? There are truths you feel with all the cells in your body but you can't prove with words. You know, beyond all reason and beyond anything written in any book or spoken by any scholar, things are how you imagine them to be."

Lily took a long moment to replay his words. "I want to ask you something. But if it's too personal, don't answer."

"It's okay. Ask me."

"Do you ever cry now?"

"Only when the sky cries, and it looks like rain on my face. Or when nobody is listening but the wind. But my heart cries all the time."

"Mine too." Lily snuggled up to him. "All the time." Before she knew it, they were kissing ... deeply and passionately. She couldn't even remember who initiated it. She only knew she had never felt so alive ... and despite her inexperience in love ... there was nobody out there who could ever make her feel exactly like she did in that moment. And there never would be.

CHAPTER TWENTY-EIGHT

"Hey, Wills, I hope I didn't wake you. I wanted to catch you alone."

As she lay on the bed and looked out at the waves that welcomed the rays of light from the east, Lily could hear her sister suppressing tears on the other end of the call.

"I got up five minutes ago. I've been so worried about you. Kady called to tell me you made it to Malibu okay, but then I didn't hear from you."

"Sorry! Yesterday I was with people the entire day until well after midnight. I didn't want to call or text you so late … and earlier, I was scared to get in touch because I thought Dad might be around. And I don't even know if Char's still in the hospital."

"She is, but she's coming home tonight. I'm here alone now with Quincy. Dad left for work at his usual time."

"Okay, good. Listen, I'm calling you from my new number. Can you save it on your phone under someone else's name?"

"Yeah." Willow's voice brightened. "You know how I have two sort-of friends at school named Fallon?"

"Sure. You often tell us about all of the mix-ups with their names."

"Right. Not that Dad or Char ever see my phone, but if they did, the name wouldn't look out of place or anything."

"Okay, put me under 'Fallon' and grab one of their photos to go with it. As soon as we get off this call, I'm going to open a new email account. It won't have my name in it. But be careful in case someone decides to search your computer."

"I will. But I think calling is safer because my phone is always on me, and it's easier to remember to delete the call record."

Lily stifled the tears aching to fall. "I'm so sorry, Wills. I hate how I've made you complicit in all of this. It's so wrong, and I feel like some hardened criminal on the run. If you'd rather not be involved … I'll totally understand."

"No!" Willow sniffled. "I told you to leave because it was the right and *only* thing for you to do. But I want to be in touch. I *need* to be. It's the only way I can survive."

"What's been going on there? I hate to even ask how Dad responded to my good-bye email. Especially since I shut the account down right after I sent it."

"He read it after he got back from leaving Char at the hospital. I was downstairs and could hear him cursing in his den. Especially when he read the part where you told him Trevor was in Bali. I know because he was screaming about going to Bali and getting that um … you know, a word starting with mother … so he could rot in prison. Then, he came out into the dining room and made himself a drink. I swear, he swallowed half of it in about three seconds because when he yelled up the stairs for me to come down, there wasn't much left in the glass. And I know it wasn't because he only poured a little."

"Oh, Wills. I feel so horrible. I've left you to deal with my problems."

"No, you didn't."

"What did Dad say?" Lily got out of bed and walked to the window bench for a better look at the ocean.

"He wanted to know if I told you what he and Char were talking about before they left for the hospital."

"And you said?"

"I said I didn't tell you anything. Then he called me a liar."

"Oh, no!"

"Then I said I didn't have to tell you because you heard it for yourself."

"That couldn't have gone over well." Lily groaned.

"No. He apologized for calling me a liar, but he got all pissed off and said I should have told him right away and not played word games with him and …."

Feeling guilty for having such a peaceful panorama before her eyes, Lily walked away from the window and slowly padded around the room. "What, Wills … what did he say?"

"It's so hard to repeat."

"Please tell me."

"He said we had some nerve not making our presence known, and you're a bad influence on me like you are on Char."

"Oh …."

"I told him that wasn't true and you're the best sister ever. I said you could have left a long time ago, but you gave up your own happiness to keep us all together. And how I love you with all my heart." Willow stopped to blow her nose. "Sorry. Then I told him bad things happen to people all the time, and it's not always someone's fault. They just happen."

"And what did he say?" Depleted, Lily collapsed onto the bed.

"He told me to go upstairs and leave him alone because he had to find a tutor or a teacher for Char and do some heavy thinking about a whole lot. He was kind of mumbling, so I'm not sure what else he said."

"Was that the end of it?"

"He said he knows you're going to call me from your new

number and I'd better give it to him straight away."

"I should've known he'd—"

"I told him how before you left, you already said you wouldn't be calling for a long time. I know that's a lie, but I don't care. I had to do it and don't worry, I'll delete every call and text we have."

"You should have asked me before you told him …."

"I purposely didn't wait to ask you." Willow spoke emphatically. "Because I didn't want you to be upset about asking me to lie. I knew you'd feel even worse about this whole mess. So I made something up all by myself. And I'm cool with it, so you need to be too."

"You're the sweetest person ever … wanting to protect me like that."

"You've always protected me, Lills. Because I'm younger doesn't mean I'm not looking out for you. And also, I have an idea. So you don't have to worry about Dad being around if you call; you can text me something and pretend you're Fallon. That way, I'll tell you if I can talk, and if anyone tries to grab my phone from me, they won't know it's you."

"Thank you. You're slightly brilliant, Wills. Now tell me: is there anything else?"

"Just that Dad had dinner with Doreen the last two nights. Also he said never to order in because he doesn't want any strange men coming to the door."

"I would agree. Is there anything I can do?"

"I'm okay, Lills. Issy and her mom have been great, and I had dinner with them the last two nights. That's why Dad was okay leaving me alone. They're always here for me, and Kady told me I can call her night or day." She paused. "I will call her, and I'll delete her calls from my phone as well."

"This is all so awful." Lily fought the urge to cry. "I can't believe this is where our family is now. Will you text me and let me know how

Char is doing after she gets home from the hospital? And tell me how she reacts to my being gone. No matter what she says, I need to know." She hesitated. "I hope I'm not asking too much. I'm very concerned about her … and Dad. But at the moment, leaving you to fend for yourself is front and center. On second thought, maybe I shouldn't have asked—"

"No. It's fine. I'll do it, and I'll be okay. As long as I can reach you, I'll manage. I'm so glad you helped me to get Quincy. I think I'd be so lost without my snuggle boy."

"A love meant to be … you and Quincy." She paused. "You'd better get ready for school. I love you, Wills."

"Bye, Lills. Love you more."

Sorrow enveloped Lily and hugged her tight. As she went to put her phone down on the night table, she saw a text had come in.

Last night was the best night of my life. I wish I knew the name of the angel who brought us together. See you tonight. xo Dak

"So, you're our new lounge server," the woman with the red hair and blonde highlights said as she stood at the wait station between the lounge and main dining area and gave Lily the once over. "Lily Sheppard, huh? I see you remembered to wear black pants, a white shirt, and the teal tie you were given. That's a good start. I take it Dara schooled you to our routine here and where to find what you'll need."

"I am and she did. Nice to meet you, Bonnie."

"Yeah, yeah. Sure it is. Did she tell you to pay attention? She should have … because I can talk at the speed of light. Did she tell you

Bonstance Constance Universe don't play when it comes to servers not restocking the station ... or keeping it clean? Don't even *think* of telling me someone else was supposed to do whatever. 'Cause pass-the-buckery is downright fuckery in my bookie, rookie. You hear me, cookie? Now lookie ... just like Santa, you read the list, then be checkin' it twice ... or thrice. 'Cause Bonnie knows who's naughty, and she knows who's nice. Look at everything ... from stocking all six kinds of tea to extra salt-and-pepper shakers to the thin dinner mints wrapped in shiny blue paper with our logo. Get it right. And we'll all be happier."

Are you for real? "I hear you." Lily forced a smile.

Bonnie made a face and scratched her chin. "So you don't feel like having a good sob yet? Or shrinking in horror?"

"I'm good. I have four years of experience. I think I'll pick the routine up quickly."

"No doubt Jamie warned you about me, yeah?"

"He said you were his most popular server."

"He didn't stop there, sweetie." Bonnie counted the inventory with her eyes as she spoke. "He never does."

"Um ...."

"He told you about the chick who ran out of here in tears, didn't he?"

"Oh, yeah, now that you mention it. I think he did."

Bonnie puffed out an angry gust of air, cocked her head to one side, and put her hands on her hips. "Now ... see here how you're already bullshitting me, Lily Sheppard? By the way, do you herd sheep or what? If so, do you herd them through the grapevine? If there was any takeaway from what Jamie told you, sending a babe blubbering into the dark, salty ocean breeze had to be it. Don't give me this now-that-you-mention-it crap. Because then you're branded as a liar right away ... and Bonnie don't be diggin' liars. Only their graves."

"I'm not a liar." Lily spoke quietly to tamp down the rising tension. "I'm only trying to be professional and diplomatic."

"Are you saying you find me difficult and you're trying to be non-con-fron-ta-tion-al?" Bonnie slowly broke down the long polysyllabic word as she said it.

"That would be accurate."

"Score one for Lily." Bonnie licked an index finger and marked an invisible chalkboard. "At least you told the truth there."

Lily let out an all-too-obvious sigh of relief.

"You probably think I want you to make tracks outta here bawling like that wimpy chick, don't you?"

"I think you want effective people working with you. And maybe you're trying to weed out the ones who don't fit the bill."

"Oh, you're good. Quick with answers." Bonnie snapped her fingers three times. "But you're right, Lily. As much as I love my customers, I'm not here for my health. Especially since my former matrimonial partner left his wife … yours truly … and three kids to wallow in shit while he snorts coke and chases carpet that never matches the drapes. And, yeah, I call him my former matrimonial partner because his name is Ray, and every time I say, 'my ex, Ray,' people think I've broken bones and shit and ask me why I had to get X-rays, and hearing dumb shit makes me wanna punch out whatever wattage is left in their dim lights and force-feed the wrong end of a broom up their nether region. You may have noticed two things about me. I don't always come up for air, and I don't suffer fools gladly. Dumbasses make me wanna give *them* some broken bones to scan, and the worst of them, like I 'splained to ya, turn me into an interior re-designer. So yeah. And fuck my ex, Ray."

"My best friend's name is Ray." Lily cringed, immediately wishing she could take back her words.

"No shit!" Bonnie spoke loudly. "You have a friend with the same name as my ex-husband?" With an exaggerated gesture, she raised her arms into the air and cupped her hands. "Hold the Earth right there. Let the world stop spinning so we can all let this wild coincidence and fascinating tidbit burn into our brains." She huffed and fixed her stare on Lily. "Ask me if I give a flying fuck." Her eyes looked up, then down, then scanned the area nearby. "Nope. Don't see any winged fucks here, do you? Guess I didn't have any to give." She refocused her stare. "Got any more front-page news to share, rookie? If there was a story somewhere, baby, you buried the lede. Tell me, are you always this fucking riveting?"

"I hope not." Lily's voice quavered. "I admit … that was stupid."

"Yeah, yeah. Okay. Yesterday's news. Listen, I'm not as bad as you think. I'm like the restaurant version of the hooker with a heart of gold … or at least gold-plated. You don't fuck with my income, which is paramount to my survival … and I won't have any reason to make your life a scene out of *Les Mis.* If you need to say something … say it. Don't be sheepish, Sheppard. You have a working mouth, yeah? I had five years of having to take care of my hellcat-of-a-whoring progenitor. Bitch got progressively worse and turned mute. Trust me; that was a blessing. I gave her my dog's filthy old chew toy, Roger the raccoon, and she'd squeeze it once for yes and twice for no. I think the germy old thing finally did her raggedy ass in … hey, kidding … but you know what … maybe I'm not." She winked.

Lily smiled pleasantly as she watched Bonnie turn around and scan the lounge.

"You know the musician who's starting tonight, Daiquiri in back o' me?"

"I do."

"Yeah, I'll bet. I can see he's got a hard-on for you … like the way he looked over here … lust in his eyes and shit. I'd ask you how you know him, but that's none of my business. I'll just tell you this. If you're fucking him or planning on it, don't make it too obvious to the chicks who frequent this place. I don't care if you wait at the bar for him after your shift is over … just avoid leaving big puddles of drool anywhere or engaging in PDAs during his break. If those chicks think the well is dry, they'll leave. Let them have their fantasies while he's on the clock. Afterward, I don't care. You hear me? This is serious shit 'cause he is hot, and you're beautiful ... and bitches can get some serious hate on. And hate ain't good for business."

"I hear you. And thanks for the compliment."

"You're welcome. And one more thing: Teddy Jackson ... our regular bartender. The guy is so full of himself he'll polish a glass to see his own reflection in it. The only thing he loves more than the ladies is a full-length mirror. You can bet if he pulls out his phone, he's gonna show some chick the commercial he did two years ago. The fool is dressed up in a red-and-white striped uniform with a big ole smile saying, 'Did someone order a pepperoni pizza?' Oh, and he had two words on a soap once, but thankfully there's no digital footage to awe the world with." She twisted her face in disgust. He's a user and a heartbreaker ... and a suck-up to studio executives. Pay his scrawny black ass no mind."

"Okay."

"So, yeah, if you're gonna be fuckin' anyone, stick with the Daiquiri. Out of sight makes it all right."

"Thanks for the advice."

"Be the epitome of professionalism, like you see before you in the form of Bonstance Constance Universe, and we'll get on fine. Now, my shift starts in ten minutes and so does yours. I'll be back to find you, and we'll see how well you play shadow. I'm warning you; I've got eyes in the back of my head and maybe even a Cyclops in my ass. Don't underestimate me."

Lily smiled politely and nearly missed the grin on Bonnie's face as she hurried away.

CHAPTER TWENTY-NINE

"So, you survived your first night." Teddy placed a glass of sparkling water and lime in front of Lily as she sat at the bar listening to Dak finish his last set.

"I did. I actually ended up waiting on a couple of tables in the main room … with Bonnie watching my every move … and yeah, my nerves were a bit wracked."

"Only a bit? You want me to top off your water with something stronger?"

"No thanks." Lily picked up her glass. "I'm good."

"You're allowed to go home now, you know?" Teddy smiled as he eyed her with prurient pleasure. "I guess you know because you changed your clothes."

"I want to chill. Is that okay with you, Sir Teddy of Jackson?"

"You're waiting on Dak, aren't you?"

Lily took a sip of her drink.

"I know you are. I heard him ask you to wait before he even started the first set."

"Good thing your ears work so well. Must make it easier to get your drink orders right."

"He's not the only fish in the sea, you know." Teddy grumbled.

"FYI, the guy's living in a sublet IV."

"He is?" Lily laughed. "Tell me, how does someone live inside intravenous therapy? Or did you mean RV, as in recreational vehicle?"

"Duh. I can't believe that came out of my mouth. You're just so hot you've burned my brain cells."

"Jamie is staring at you."

Teddy turned around and nodded at Jamie, who didn't want anything except to wave and let Teddy know he was watching him.

"Guess where I'm living for a couple months?" Teddy went on. "In a director's crib here in the Bu … while he's shooting a movie in Georgia. I'd love to take you there and give you a taste of the good life."

"It sounds like you and I have different ideas of 'the good life.'"

"I have full access to his private bar and can order in any food I want. I'm getting to stay there because I worked some parties for him, and he likes my style." He made a wavy hand gesture. "Smooth, baby. Like a lazy wave. I promised to work for free at his next two parties. I don't mind because he hangs with A-listers, and you can't buy that kind of opportunity."

"Sounds like maybe you shouldn't get too attached to this lifestyle, unless you can also impress him with your acting skills. In the meantime, there's a customer trying to get your attention."

"I'll impress him, all right. And you're so hot, you're gonna burn my eyeballs too." Teddy swung around to see who wanted his attention, then refocused on Lily. "I'll have to show you my pizza commercial. And then I'll tell you how to get a slice or two of Teddy J. for yourself. With the works!"

Lily grimaced the second he turned his back. When she glanced over at Jamie, she saw him laughing and realized she'd been more expressive than she intended. Turning away from the bar, she fully focused on Dak, watching him sing "Moondance" while playing the piano. Listening to every word, she knew without a doubt he was singing it for her.

When the song was over, she gasped to see Jamie standing by her side. "There's an old one. Came out in early 1970. I played it on many a gig. I don't remember seeing it on Dak's set list, but he's a wild card, so I'm not surprised. His musicianship is brilliant." He stopped to listen. "Love this one too. Another oldie but goodie. Foreigner. 'Waiting For A Girl Like You.' Nineteen eighty-one. Don't remember this one on his list either." He winked. "Someone must have inspired Dak to sing these." He paused to allow her to speak, but she gulped and said nothing. "Anyway, Lily, I'm impressed with you both tonight. And you survived Bonnie's mini-hazing ... so I think you're going to work out well."

"Your approval means a lot to me. I have four years of experience, but working here is a big step up, and I'll try my hardest not to let you down."

"The glowing reports about you were not exaggerated. Oh, and if Teddy gets out of hand, feel free to tell him off and let him know I encouraged you to. See you tomorrow night."

Lily watched as a blonde woman slipped Dak a piece of paper, then put a bill in his tip jar. The moment she turned to go, he ripped up the paper, scooped it up inside a used cocktail napkin, and put it on the tray of a server who had come to collect the empty glasses and paper trash at a nearby table.

Within seconds, Dak was at her side. "I'm so glad you waited for me."

"There was no place else I'd rather be, and you are so incredibly talented. I watched the crowd, and some of the biggest blabbermouths went silent when you sang. Jamie said you were brilliant."

Dak smiled. "He told me something like that on my break. I'm glad he's happy. So listen, I want to be with you. Anywhere, any place you choose. I don't want you to feel pressured in any way. I'll say good night right here if you'd be more comfortable."

"Don't you dare. From the moment you walked me back to my car last night, I couldn't wait to see you again. I'm not even going to pretend to be nonchalant about it."

"Good. Because I felt exactly the same way … still do." He looked over his shoulder. "I have to pack up some equipment."

"I'll leave you to that while I go home. There's a private beach behind my studio, believe it or not. I'll text you the address right now, and when you get there, you can park behind my car in the driveway. It's right off PCH, like a mile and a half south of here. Text me, and I'll come out."

"I'll bring a large blanket this time."

"Perfect. See you in a bit."

It took every ounce of willpower she had not to kiss him right there, and the light dancing in his eyes clearly told her he was resisting the same urge. She walked out of the restaurant, trying not to smile as she thought about what the night would bring. Once outside, Lily pulled out her phone. Immediately, she saw the text she'd requested from Willow had come through.

Char got home safe & she agreed to get regular therapy now & Dad is happy about that. Glad U R where U R Lills b/c Char blames U for everything. Not fair. Dad is hiring home teachers 4 Char. Nico sticking by her. Knew he wd. Don't txt me now b/c I G2G 2 bed. Will delete this 1st. <3 U so much. W.

"Love you, too, Wills," Lily whispered as a tear trickled down her face. She took a breath of the cool night air, then texted her address to Dak.

"Cheers!" Lily said, clinking imaginary glasses with Dak as they sat on the full-size blanket under the Malibu stars.

"Is it colder tonight than last night? It *is* October, right? But I have no idea what the date is."

"It's the twentieth. Does it matter?" She looked curiously at him.

"It does ... because that makes yesterday, the nineteenth of October, our anniversary. If you knew me better, you'd know how completely out of character it is for me to even think of things like this, much less say them. This is a first for me." She saw the vulnerability in his eyes as he smiled at her. "But I've never felt so drawn to any human being in my life." He picked up the throw blanket they had sat on the night before and put it over her lap.

"Thank you. Your touching confession warmed my heart even more than it did the rest of me. So how was your first night?"

"Let's see. Well, some woman slipped me her phone number."

"I know. I saw her. And I saw you get rid of it."

"And I could see Teddy was hitting on you."

Lily laughed. "His come-on lines are straight out of a B movie. And I doubt he even gets cast in those. He told me he was as smooth as a lazy wave."

"Wanna bet he's the lazy wave ... too lazy to come up with new material? The first time I came in to talk to Jamie, I heard him use the same line on some woman. Only, unlike you, she agreed to meet him when his shift was over."

"Oh, and I thought that spark of creativity was custom made for *moi.*" Lily mock frowned. "Not."

"Did you happen to see the stiletto-wearing blonde who put a small snifter of cognac on the piano for me?"

"I missed it."

"Awkward. I didn't ask for it. I wasn't sure what else was in it, and I don't like to drink on the job. So I nodded thanks and left it there. About fifteen minutes later, another woman came over to make a request and thinking my drink was my tip jar, stuck a ten into the Remy Martin."

"Darn. I missed that too." She laughed. "Actually, I did see someone come up to the piano, but her body must have blocked the action."

"Well, she gave me an excuse not to touch the drink … not that I needed one."

"I guess you get hit on a lot."

"Yeah. I do. But I play music … not women … so it's a job hazard for me. A perk for Teddy."

"He wishes women would fall all over him like they do you. His jealousy is obvious."

"When I see dudes like Teddy … so cocky and all … I see someone overcompensating for whatever is missing or twisted outta shape inside them, you know? And I wonder what it is. But I don't have time to take on the baggage of everyone I meet. I'm doing the best I can to get a handle on my own … and to not self-destruct." He shifted his gaze to the waves, rolling in the moonlight. "Or self-sabotage."

"I hear you."

He looked at her again. "Hey, before we talk about anything else, last night you were going to say something regarding my Kokopelli pendant … then Jamie interrupted us, and we never got back to it. Do you still want to share? I hope so, because I'd be lying if I said I wasn't really curious."

Lily blushed. "I do. But even though we've talked so much since the last night, which definitely makes this easier … it's still a bit embarrassing."

"I'll bet it's not. In fact, I'm thinking it's something that will bring us closer … or already has. Want to give it a go?"

"Sure." She traced the blanket's oak-leaf pattern with her index finger as she mustered her courage. "So, like I said, I never knew your last name. All I remembered was your face, our conversation, and the pendant you're wearing. In fact, I was just about to ask you about it when Brian pulled me away." Her face tightened as she remembered. "After I got over him, which didn't take long, thanks to you, I became obsessed with identifying the man on your pendant. I wanted to find one as close to it as I could. In the not-so-back of my mind, I hoped it would lead me to you. Like maybe a stranger would see my pendant and say, 'Oh, my friend Dak wears something like that.' Honestly, I'm not sure what I expected to happen; I just felt compelled to follow through."

"I'm riveted. Go on, Lily."

"Well, one afternoon, I was hanging out with Ray, and we ran into his friend Jeremy who's a folk artist. Out of nowhere, something told me to ask him about your pendant. As soon as I described it, he said it was Kokopelli and that he was very common in Native American art and folklore." She laughed. "But he didn't mention the fertility part ... probably because he was running late to pick up his girlfriend. Anyway, that weekend, I went to this boutique in Altrusia that sells Native American jewelry, that Jeremy recommended, and I found a pendant similar to yours. It was on a black cord, and it was made of rusted metal. I bought it, and I wore it for a long time, thinking it would draw you back to me. My friends and family asked me about it, but I just said the little guy made me smile. Anyway, when it didn't bring us together, I told myself I was being silly and put it in my jewelry box. Then my mum gave me this locket for my eighteenth birthday, and I've worn it ever since."

Dak put a hand over his mouth and swallowed the lump in his throat. "That's so incredible. And you know what; I think that what you were asking the spirit of Kokopelli to do ... he did. Only in his time ... when it was right."

"I never knew who I was asking. I didn't think of it that way. I just sort of put it out there in the universe. It's kind of miraculous, don't you think?"

"I do … intense and beautiful too. When I said the other night that I knew something much greater than ourselves had brought us together … I started thinking maybe it could have been my aunt or your mother. Maybe all three of them worked together." He paused. "I have no idea, but I like to dwell in possibilities. There's so much we don't understand. I'm open to miracles … probably because my aunt always told me to never close my mind to them. She said that where there is life, there is hope. Where we plant seeds, wondrous things can grow. It was one of the last things she told me before she died."

"I'm getting choked up thinking about it." Lily brushed a wisp of hair from her eyes.

"Me too." Dak exhaled. "And a bit overwhelmed. So, while we both process all of this, please, tell me … did you hear from your sister … Willow?"

Lily could only reply with tears.

"Oh, Lily." He moved closer to comfort her. "What happened?"

"Don't mind me. My eyes leak. I should call a face plumber."

"You've got me instead." Dak wiped away her tears with his index finger. "Did you speak to her?"

"No. When I went to text you my address, I saw she'd texted me earlier. My sister Char is home from the seventy-two hour psych hold, and she's agreed to get regular therapy. Finally … after a year and a half … so I'm happy. But she thinks everything is my fault and hates me. And I won't lie and say I'm not crushed."

Dak put his arm around her and kissed the top of the head. "Time will heal her pain. Not-so-wise words from someone who wishes *he* could heal your pain right now." He paused. "But all is good with you and Willow, right?"

"Definitely. One-third of my family in Altrusia loves me, and

100 percent of my family in England. So I guess I'm doing better than most people."

"You are … only I'm sure it's 100 percent in Altrusia too. You haven't said much about friends." He brushed some sand off the blanket. "I know it sounds kind of silly … like I should already be privy to that kind of information … this only being our second date and third time together … but I feel like I've known you forever."

"Me too." Lily hesitated before continuing. "Well, I had a best girlfriend, Hannah, for four years. I met her at the diner where I worked. She graduated a year ahead of me from a different school. I thought we'd be friends for life, but she got pregnant, then moved to Massachusetts and got married because her now-husband is attending Harvard Medical. I tried to keep up the friendship, but she wasn't interested. I got a generic thank-you after I sent her a baby gift, and, well, 'the end.'"

"I guess people drift apart."

"They do. But with Hannah, this was an intentional drift. She looked down on me for staying in Altrusia; I know that. In her own way, she cares about me … but the way you have affection for a childhood memory that is no part of your present whatsoever."

"I can't say I have any good childhood memories at all." He thought for a second. "I should clarify … from my *early* childhood."

"Oh, I'm sorry. How stupid of me. I shouldn't have said anything."

He cupped his hands around her upper arms. "Not stupid in any way, shape, or form, Lily. No apologies. Or I'll apologize for letting that slip at the wrong time. And then we'll end up editing our thoughts before they ever become words. I don't want us to be that way."

"I don't either." Lily smiled and kissed him on the lips. "Thank you. Really. Thank you."

Dak ran his fingers through her long chestnut-brown hair. "So tell me … aside from Hannah … any other close friends? You just mentioned your friend Ray. I think you told me at dinner last night that he's your best friend."

"Yes. I love and cherish him. And he loves me. But he's so busy at Princeton, and now, he's even more unavailable because he's met someone. Only he doesn't know I've figured that out. He won't dare tell me."

"Why not?"

"Because after all of these years, he still doesn't think I know he's gay. I've always known. I know it sounds insane he hasn't told me, because he knows it would change nothing between us, but his father is a bit rigid, and I think Ray is still afraid to come out to the world at large. So, instead of hiding from some people, I think he hides from all of us. Probably easier for him."

"What a shame. Can't you lovingly tell him you know … and that it doesn't matter to you and never has?"

"I've played a similar scenario in my head so many times." She picked up a shell poking out of the sand and examined it. "But in the end, I don't want to force Ray or anyone to share something so personal when they're not ready to. Besides, he'd be embarrassed that he went to such lengths to keep up the charade for so many years. I know him well enough to understand that much."

"I can see why you wouldn't want to go there."

"No. More than anything, though … my life has been like one big domino effect … how do you think my sister got raped. So I'm not forcing anything. I don't want to be the catalyst or the reason any more bad things happen to anyone … much less the people I love." She threw the shell back onto the beach.

"I respect that completely."

"Anyway, the only people I'm close to are Willow and Kady … and my uncle Ellis in England.

"I hope I'll be on your special list soon."

"I think you're gaining ground by the minute. Would you tell me about your brother, Jonah? Are the two of you close?"

"You know what you said about Hannah ... seeing you the way a person sees a childhood memory? Well, I think Jonah sees me the same way ... only as the worst possible kind of memory. I know it's not intentional, and I don't even know if he's aware of it ... but he keeps his distance. And I don't mean because he lives overseas. I think he feels like being close to me brings him closer to Marsha and in some way to the abuse. And, of course, that's crazy because we both left her house the same day, and neither of us has had anything to do with her since."

"So she doesn't know where he is?"

"She does, unfortunately. When he got promoted to VP at the telecommunications firm in London he works for, it made the trade news. Marsha found out about it because she clearly does routine searches for us online. So, now she knows his place of employment. Jonah said she called his office several times, but he wouldn't take her call. Eventually, she gave up trying. Both of us avoid social media to make it more difficult for her to keep tabs on us ... greatly helped by the fact that it doesn't interest us. But Jonah has a couple of profiles out there for business reasons."

"I don't have any accounts. Char has several. I hope one day, you and Jonah can come together. I'm glad there's no bad blood between you."

"No. He was only a child when he took the brunt of Marsha's abuse so I wouldn't have to. I hope one day he'll let me in. But a genuine relationship will have to come naturally."

"I'll keep good thoughts."

"Speaking of those ...." Dak took her hands in his. "We both have three days off starting Sunday. I was wondering if you'd like to take an RV trip up the coast ... maybe to Morro Bay. My friend's RV sleeps six ... in case you're—"

"What?" Lily laughed seductively. "Wanting to invite four

other people?"

Dak smiled self-consciously. "In case … you know …."

"Um, there won't be a problem. I can pretty much guarantee it. And yes, I would love to go."

Dak responded only with his eyes.

"So listen, the last song you sang tonight … 'Moondance' … well, it made me want one. What do you say?"

Dak stood and put out a hand to help her up. "We are indeed under the cover of October skies, aren't we?"

"We are." They both kicked off their shoes. Lily held his hand tightly as they walked closer to the water. "So if we have an anniversary, does this mean we now have a song?"

"We do." They let the gentle swash roll over their feet. "And here's your own private a capella version."

CHAPTER THIRTY

"Well, don't you look all anti-platonic and ready for your first three days off," Bonnie said to Lily, who had emerged from a bathroom stall after changing into street clothes.

Lily walked into the front room of the ladies' lounge, laid her garment bag down on a teal velour love seat, pulled a makeup bag out of her purse, then stepped in front of the mirror for a touch-up. "Thanks. I guess."

Bonnie followed and stood next to her. "You aced your first three nights here. I thought for sure you'd fuck up ... seeing how you and the Daiquiri are stuffed to the gills with matching lust and have the potential to spontaneously fornicate in plain sight with all the subtlety of a bomb exploding in a nunnery ... but hey ... you're down with the routine, and they love the hell out of his music."

Lily finished applying the cream-colored eye shadow under her brows and turned to Bonnie. "Well, I guess I can say with absolute certainty nobody has ever said anything remotely like that to me in my life." She put her shadow compact back in her makeup case and pulled out a black eye pencil.

"Accentuate."

"I wouldn't think of doing more." Lily gently applied the

pencil under each eye.

"I haven't seen you overdo the mascara, or even wear any, for that matter, so I hope it's not your bag ... or *in* your bag. Most women dumb enough to clunk that crap on end up wearing it everywhere but their lashes. By the time the night's done, they look like a dump truck turned right at Nasty Face Street, spilled a load of cow shit, and kept on rollin'. I hope you don't ever do false eyelashes ... because let me tell you ... they look like el garbagio and end up in the wrong place-io. When I was in my early twenties, before I married the SOB who ditched me, I was pash for the lash. So, one night, I'm in the back of my then-van, giving some oral pleasure to a biker I was boinking, and when I'd finished, he looked down at his schlong and screamed bloody fuckin' murder. It's like he thought a centipede had slapped on a bib and was fixing to chow down on his worn-out willy. Only my damn eyelash was the culprit, having fallen off in the heat of my arduous activity. And because he'd recently produced Mother Nature's natural lotion, the damn thing stuck to him like Velcro. Not stopping to figure out jack, he karate chopped the hell out of his own schlong. Then, after seeing my lashless eye, realized his tomfoolery, knew he'd been conned at dumb-fuck schoolery, and left the van quicker than he'd come. Literally. So yeah ...."

Lily suppressed a smile. "Who hasn't had *that* happen a million times?" She pulled out a reddish-brown lipstick, applied it lightly, then put it back into her makeup case, picked up her garment bag, and headed out the door.

Bonnie trailed her into the restaurant toward the bar. "Only trying to aid the young-and-hopefully-not afraid."

Just as Lily was about to respond, she noticed an older man, counting his change, had dropped a couple of fifty-dollar bills on the floor and failed to notice what he'd done. Before the words, "Excuse me, sir" could fully escape her lips, Bonnie had picked up the bills and shoved them into her pocket.

Surprised, Lily said nothing, headed into the bar, and took a seat. Within seconds, Bonnie was at her side.

"Hope you're not judging me, calla lily." She stared at Lily with an odd look on her face, then spoke in a strange voice. "'The calla lilies are in bloom again.'" She huffed. "Hello? I just did a superb impersonation of Katharine Hepburn … not that you were able to appreciate it. You're too damn young to know who she was … much less how she was famous for the calla lillies' line … said in a disaster of a play called 'The Lake.' I'm way too young to know it myself, but my cultured upbringing reveals itself every time I speak. You do notice my more refined ways, yes?"

"Clearly." Lily, having already mentally dismissed Bonnie, was focused on Dak who appeared preoccupied with thought.

Bonnie rambled on. "I've got three mouths to feed. My son is two, and my daughters are four and six. I have to pay a neighbor to watch them when I come to work. Paying her cuts into my salary. I need all the help I can get. So hear me out: the fat old geezer who left, Gouda the Buddha, is a rich fuck who don't want for shit. Therefore, Bonstance Constance Universe ain't no thief for picking up any chump change falling outta his greasy, chubby fingers. Finders keepers and all that jazz … you got me?"

Lily fixed her gaze on Dak. "We're good, Bonnie. No judgment from me."

"Oh, you're wondering what's up with the Daiquiri, aren't you?"

Stunned, Lily turned to look at her.

"I don't have a clue what ruffled his feathers, but during his break, he checked his phone and saw a text that made his eyes bug out. Two minutes later, he walked outside and made a call. And he hasn't looked right since."

"You're hurting," Lily said to Dak the second he appeared by her side at the bar.

"Is it that obvious ... or are you permanently tuned to my station?" He laughed. "Wait, I'm taking those words back. They sounded a bit too Teddy Jackon-ish."

Lily laughed. "No they didn't. But to answer the question, your eyes are sad and distant, your music is melancholy ... though every bit as brilliant ... and I want to hold you so much."

"And I want to hold you too. As soon as we get out of here."

"If something has happened ... we can put off our trip."

He started to touch her face, but stopped, noticing the audience surrounding them. "No way. Our trip is more important than ever."

"Why don't you stay with me tonight?" Lily spoke softly. "At my place. Then in the morning, we can go pick up your RV and be on our way."

"Are you sure?"

"I am."

"Won't the lady you rent from, Cynthia, mind if a stranger's car is parked in her driveway all night long ... especially knowing said stranger is also on her property?"

"I had lunch with her today. And she told me you were always welcome. I didn't even say much about you ... but she understood. She said we reminded her of when she and her husband met. And of how they have been for all of these years. She said we have something rare and special."

"How does she know?"

"Because the first thing I told her was how we both care about the other's lives ... and feel one another's pain. We were only chatting.

I didn't want to say too much, but what little I shared resonated with her. She said she likes to ask people who are gushing over someone they've met … what attracts them. She said it's usually the person's physical attributes, maybe their job, who they know, what kind of car they drive, their money, and all of the social opportunities they expect to open up by being a couple. I said none of those things … except maybe you're the most beautiful man I've ever seen."

"Did you tell her I think you're the most beautiful woman *I've* ever seen?"

Lily gave an embarrassed smile. "No. But I told her how drawn to one another we felt after only thirty minutes together at a party … three years ago."

"And what did she say?"

"That we should hold on tightly to one another … because we have something many people never find."

"We do." Dak smiled. "Let me pack up here. I'll meet you at your place. But before we go inside … because I've been so comfortable with our nights at the beach, I think it will be easier for me to tell you all of this there. And this is what blows my mind. What I'm dealing with at the moment, well, it's something I wouldn't normally have spoken to anyone about. I would have shoved it under a floorboard in an abandoned room in my mind and let it rot and fester."

"How does our fourth night on the beach feel like we've been doing this forever?" Dak looked out over the dark expanse of sea.

"Maybe we have … in a previous life."

"I think so … because there aren't a lot of people in this life I'm comfortable with."

Lily put her arms around his neck and kissed him. "Same for me. Do you want to tell me what happened?"

Dak returned the kiss, lingering even longer, then drew back to look into her eyes. After letting silence find comfort between them, he shifted his position on the blanket and looked down for a moment. "So, there's what happened … which means nothing to me … and there's what it's stirred up. They're completely different things, and I thought I should make that clear from the beginning."

"Okay. I'm following you so far."

"Jonah texted me during my first set. On my break, I went outside and called him. Seems he got a call from Janis Clayton, this woman who was Marsha's best friend a *long* time ago." He paused. "I guess they were still friends … though it's hard to imagine, if not impossible … but it doesn't matter. The thing is, Janis told Jonah that Marsha died. Apparently, she got a cancer diagnosis a while back. Supposedly, she was trying to get in touch with him at work … to let him know. Janis said Marsha gave up trying and told Janis to call Jonah when she was gone."

"I see."

"Thank you for not offering condolences."

Lily put her hand on his. "I know you don't want them. It never entered my mind. I only care how her death is affecting you … and Jonah."

"I'm thinking I should feel some surge of huge relief … only I don't. She cast a long shadow … and I still feel haunted. But monsters routinely cast long shadows, don't they?" Dak picked up a shell, dug it into the sand, and watched the grains spill out like a waterfall. "Jonah tried to find out what Marsha had been doing in the years since we last saw her, but all Janis would say is she still worked her old job … with the school district … and that she was a good friend. When my brother tried to get more details, Janis hemmed and hawed and spoke in vagaries: Jonah's words, not mine. He said he thinks Janis called him out of obligation, not because she gives a damn Marsha's dead. He said there was zero remorse in her voice ... and a tinge of anger, actually."

"Interesting. Was that the entirety of their conversation?"

Dak picked up the shell and repeated his previous actions. "I didn't tell you this before, because I wanted to see if anything came of it, but after our conversation the other night ... about the emotional distance between Jonah and me ... I sent him a short email. Told him where I was working and how I'd met, for the second time, a beautiful woman named Lily Sheppard from Altrusia. The only reason I even said what I did was because I remembered how right after the Roseville party, I'd written to Jonah to tell him I'd met the girl of my dreams and some dick pulled her away from me ... and I was angry at myself for not stopping him ... even though I knew the girl I fell for was the guy's girlfriend. And Jonah wrote back saying grabbing you away would have been Neanderthal, lame, and uncool ... and that if we were meant to be, we would happen. I told him I didn't need any clichéd bullshit from a stale fortune cookie, and I was pissed with him for even saying it ... only he was right. So I had to tell him I'd found you here in Malibu ... and apologize." Dak smiled uneasily. "Then, I asked how his wife and daughter were doing ... and said I hoped all was good."

"I'm amazed you told him about me the first time ... and so touched you want him to know we're together now."

"Finding you again has been the first good news worth sharing. I've done some gigs on big stages and opened for some superstars. They were jobs. Nothing I'd put in the good-news category."

"But that is so impressive."

"Not for me. I want to write and record my own music ... and to learn more instruments ... like the pan flute and the ehru. The latter is the Chinese equivalent of the violin, but with only two strings. They both produce hauntingly beautiful sounds, and I plan to learn them in the coming years so I can take my music to places where traditional instruments can't go." He smiled. "So, you can see why doing covers, even in front of large audiences, doesn't mean much to me. But you do."

Lily blushed. "Thank you for explaining that … about your musical aspirations. I'm fascinated."

"I can show you clips online … and maybe one day, you'll hear me play them live. Anyway, what were we saying?"

"Well, I was going to ask you if there was any more conversation between Jonah and Janis?"

"The usual chitchat. She asked how he was doing … how I was doing … and said there wouldn't be any services for Marsha because all of her friends, except Janis apparently, had long moved out of the Davis area. Jonah said that part was awkward because they both knew she didn't have any friends by way of being a flaming, manipulative, and cunning bitch. But neither of them said it."

"And all of this has left you feeling …?"

"Kind of sick, actually. So many memories are flooding back I'd repressed. Like the time she pulled out one of my father's belts he'd left behind. I was scared to death she was going to whip me with it, but she never did. No, Marsha had an even better idea: she knocked me over, put the fucking thing around my neck, and started pulling me, saying, 'Let's go for a walk, bad doggie. You're gonna do your business outside with all of the neighbors watching.' Jonah pushed her away, and then I started kicking her legs. And that's when she got even more vicious, saying we both had one hell of a nerve disrespecting her authority … and we'd pay. Then she started with the 'bad doggie' shit again. She was so enraged, I don't think she even considered the neighbors would have called the police on her in a heartbeat … had she managed to drag me outside."

"How horrifying."

"Know why she was choking me?"

"I can't begin to imagine."

"Because she lost a ten-dollar bill and thought I'd stolen it. Of course, I hadn't, and I was a little kid who not only didn't steal, but who wouldn't have even known how to spend ten dollars. So that's why she decided to 'choke the truth' outta me." With only the moonlight on his face, Lily could see his olive skin redden. "Because what good parent doesn't try to strangle their kid to death if they think they've lied."

Lily put her hands on either arm and rubbed them. "I just got the chills, and it's not because we're sitting on the beach at night in October."

"I remember," Dak continued, "about an hour after she tried to choke me, I saw her reach into her pocket for a Kleenex and pull out the bill instead. In that second, she realized I hadn't taken it. But when she saw I'd been watching her, she blamed me for stealing the money. Said that I planted it in her pocket to make her look forgetful." He paused to exhale. "I didn't even know what 'planted' meant. Then she said to me, 'Only I don't forget shit, little boy.' She's said so many reprehensible things, but those words stuck in my head. Before that moment, I didn't understand that you could be good and people would still treat you like you're bad. I was way too young to know she was punishing us by proxy because JP had left her."

"So wrong."

"And it's so wrong you lost your mother, Lily. I know it doesn't sound like much of a blessing, but to be able to remember her with love as you do ... well, that's special. Not only do I not have one good memory of Marsha, but now I think of her as a ghost, stuck in purgatory, who's gonna haunt the fuck out of me with traumatic memories."

"You only found out about her tonight, right?"

"Yeah." Dak appeared distracted, as if he were gearing up for an anxiety attack.

"Just because she was a monster, it doesn't mean her death still hasn't shocked you. I'm here for you ... every day you want me to be. And she will start to fade, especially as you and I make beautiful memories. When I left Altrusia, I made sure to take a couple of my favorite photo albums. I'll show them to you. They're comforting. But it doesn't sound like you have any albums, real or imagined, with any happiness at all. At least from her."

Tears ran down Dak's face, but he didn't wipe them away. "I told you I only cry when it rains, but I guess I lied ... unless it's raining now. And no, I don't have any happy memories with her ... only with my aunt Zoey. Still love her to pieces."

Lily took her index finger and wiped away his tears as he had done with hers.

"Thanks. Sorry ... didn't mean to be a wuss."

"I love men who can cry. If you cry, you can emote. If you emote, it's because you can feel. C'mon, let's go back to my little place. It's warmer in there." She stood and reached for his hand.

He got up and grabbed the corner of the blanket and folded it. "I've only seen the photos of your mother you have on your phone. I can't wait to see the albums. It will be like meeting her."

"She would love you so much." Lily pressed her head against his chest.

Dak let the blanket fall back onto the sand and wrapped his arms around her. "When I was dealing with fallout from the abuse ... in a different way than I am now, I thought the weight of the world was too much to carry. Some days I didn't even want to be here. My aunt would always tell me our burden is never greater than the sum of our sorrows. She said after we add everything up, if we're still able to go on, it means we're stronger than they are. There's more, but you get the gist."

"She was right. Here we both are. Still standing. And if we create happiness, it might not diminish what we've lost, but it will give us purpose and reason to go on in a world that seems upside down and inside out a lot of the time."

"I never thought I'd be able to even begin to think any differently. But in four days, you've changed so much for me."

"Same here. When I left Altrusia, I was destroyed after hearing the ugly things Char and my dad said about me."

The light in his eyes shone on hers. "I want you so much, Lily. But I don't want tonight to be our first night together … not that way. I don't want my first night making love to you to be forever entwined with the day I learned the monster died. So let's be close tonight … and wait till the time is right." He attempted to laugh. "Which I predict could be less than twenty-four hours away."

Lily gave him a knowing smile.

Without saying another word, Dak picked up the blanket and threw it over his shoulder. Hand in hand, they walked toward the light Lily had left on for them.

CHAPTER THIRTY-ONE

"Hey, Wills ... it sounds like I woke you."

"It's okay. You said in your text yesterday you would be calling early. Sorry if I sound groggified."

"Did you make that word up?"

"Yeah," Willow said, still sounding half asleep. "I'm super clever when I'm tired."

"You're silly too. And adorable."

"I'm awake now, Lills. Tell me what news you had ... that you didn't want to text."

Lily sat on her bed and looked out at the ocean. "Do you remember a couple of years ago, after you finished reading *The Diary of Anne Frank*, you asked me if I kept a diary?"

"Yeah. And you said no."

"Right. But then you asked me if I *did*, what secret would I put in it."

"I remember." Willow giggled. "Boy, I was being nosy."

"I didn't mind. I actually had a secret I hadn't shared with anyone, so I was happy you asked."

"Oh, I remember now! But tell me again."

"Well, I told you I'd met my soul mate at a party in Roseville a year before ... but then Brian yanked me away from him ... even though he was about to tell me he was moving out of town."

"What a crummy thing to do. Even being a kid, I knew a jerk when I heard about one."

"I also told you how I wished I'd stayed at the party and gotten to know the other guy ... the one who I knew was my soul mate. I never even told Hannah about him then ... only you."

"I totally remember now. Because I asked you what a soul mate was ... and after you explained, I ended up reading all about them online ... and in books. I even wrote a paper about soul mates in literature, and my teacher, Ms. Delacroix, was shocked. But she loved it and gave me an A."

"I'd forgotten about your paper. So cool you were inspired to write it. Anyway, it's a long story, but by some miracle, the beautiful man I met in Roseville that night ... happened to end up at the same restaurant in Malibu where I'm working ... only he's a musician. We recognized each other right away, and we've been together ever since. And if you hadn't pushed me to leave, and if Kady hadn't introduced me to her friend Cynthia, I never would have found him. I'm eternally grateful to both of you."

"Oh, wow! Is he with you right now?"

"No. He left my place to switch out his car for his friend's RV. Then he's going to come back and pick me up. He suggested that so I'd have time to call you and talk privately. We have three days off so we're going to drive to Morro Bay. It's about three hours north of here."

"When I get out of bed, I'll look it up. I'm so happy. You've been so good to all of us, and only bad things have happened to you. Mum always said the Lord works in mysterious ways ... maybe this is what she meant."

"It is, sweetheart. I'm sure of it. Please don't tell anyone, okay? Kady knows because we had a long talk yesterday before I went into work. But absolutely nobody else knows except the nice lady who owns the studio I live in."

"I promise. You can totally trust me."

"I know. That's why I wanted to share."

"What's his name?"

"Dak Falaman."

"Super sexy name."

"You think?"

"For sure."

"Tell me what's going on in Altrusia, Wills. I never stop thinking about all of you. Is Char any better?" Lily stood and walked to the dresser, pulling out clothes to take with her.

"Well, it's kind of a bummer because Char really likes this lady, Lisa, who is homeschooling her, but Lisa's daughter in Tacoma is going to have twins, and her husband is in the service, so Lisa's leaving in four days to help her out until her son-in-law's tour is up. The person her daughter hired had to bail at the last minute. That's why Lisa thought she could be Char's regular teacher when Dad hired her. Total bummer of a situation: it was a miracle to find someone Char likes, so now Dad's all stressed out about finding a replacement before Lisa has to leave. And of course, it puts Char in an even worse mood. But the day after she got home from the hospital, Nico told her something that made her happy. She didn't tell me, and I didn't ask. You know, Char—the best way to get cursed out is to ask her something personal. And if you *don't* want to know something, then she'll be sure to tell you."

"That's Char." Lily gulped as she suppressed a swell of emotion. "So—um—who's making dinner these days?" She grabbed an overnight bag from the closet.

"Starting tonight, Dad said that Doreen will be cooking for us. I think she's going to make stuff for the freezer too."

"Yeah. That freezer has one heck of an appetite."

Willow giggled. "That's funny. I'm going to help Doreen when

I can, because I don't want her doing everything, even though she swears she's looking forward to it. Last night, Char made spaghetti and garlic bread, but only because Nico was here."

"Well, good." Lily put her phone on speaker as she laid it on the bed and began neatly packing the clothes into her bag. "I was so worried the burden would fall on you."

"No, it's cool. Besides, I kind of like cooking, and I'll learn how to make new things. It's only been like six days since you left, but things will work out, so you don't have to worry ... especially where dinner is concerned. Oh, and I'm going to have lunch with Kady today. Dad knows and didn't even try to stop me. He doesn't want her to come here, though, but he stopped freaking out about us talking to her ... for whatever reason."

Lily took the phone into the bathroom, where she took down her pink toiletry bag hanging on the back of the door. "That's good." She walked toward the bed with her bag. "Kady is one of my favorite people on this planet ... and so are you. Knowing you're there for each other makes me feel infinitely better. I'm surprised Kady didn't mention your lunch to me."

"Because I didn't get Dad's permission until last night at dinner. Kady probably didn't want to stress you out anymore."

"Has Dad asked you if we've been in touch?" Lily sat on the bed again.

"Yeah. I said I already told him you said you weren't gonna call for a while. Because hey ... I already did tell him. I hate to lie, but this way, technically, I only had to do it once."

"I hate for you to do *anything* that goes against your character, Wills."

"Then it's all cool because protecting my sister is totally in my character. And I've been deleting all of our phone communication." Willow's voice became softer. "I better go. I hear Dad. Don't worry about calling me on your trip. Have a fabulous time."

"Okay. But I'll check my voicemail often in case you need me. I never want you to feel cut off."

"Thanks, Lills. I love you. And I'm happy for you. Tell Dak I said that, okay? Bye. Gotta go."

Lily looked down at the phone on the bed. "Love you too, Wills. Bye."

"I've never felt happier in my life than I did being here with you today," Lily said as she and Dak walked back into the RV park under the soft moonlight. "And I love how we have such a great view of Morro Rock. I took some great shots at sunset. Before today, I'd never even heard of a volcanic plug. To me, it looks like a big dome sitting in the ocean."

Dak smiled as he unlocked the door to the RV and helped Lily inside. "You know what they don't tell you about it?"

"No, what?"

"It's the forehead of a petrified sea monster."

"Oh. Is that so?" Lily grinned as she sat on the taupe-colored corduroy bench behind the small table. "Poor thing. I was going to ask you exactly what a volcanic plug was, but now I guess that's a moot point."

"Would you like a glass of Pinot Grigio?"

"I would." Lily's mind flashed back to the night at the gallery when Trevor uncorked a bottle of red wine.

"You went somewhere just then." Dak put down the corkscrew. "Only for a second, but I saw you leave. And wherever you went, you weren't happy."

"You're right. But it was a quick trip and I'm happy to be back. I didn't buy a return ticket. Promise."

"Good." He picked up the corkscrew and opened the bottle.

"And a volcanic plug is actually the neck of an extinct volcano."

Lily smiled. "Volcanoes have necks? Who knew?"

"You've heard of the 'eye of the storm?'" Dak laughed as he pulled the cork out.

"How about the Finger Lakes in New York?"

"Well …." Dak poured some wine into each glass. "Technically, those lakes don't have fingers … they *are* fingers. Like corn doesn't have ears, they *are* ears." He turned his head for a second to hide his smile. "So, sorry to say, but I don't think that counts."

Lily reached out to take the glass from him. "That was quick. So now we have rules for this game?"

"We do." Dak edged in next to her.

"Okay then; rivers have mouths."

"Good one."

"And mountains have feet."

"How do you figure?" Dak's eyes radiated joy as he waited for her response.

"Well, you've heard people talk about the foot of a mountain, right?"

"Yeah, but 'the foot.' You're stretching it to turn that into feet."

"Then I'll turn the mountains into yardsticks. They have feet … three, as a matter of fact. And security gates have arms."

"You're going downhill fast with this." He laughed.

"Oh, let's see you do better then."

"Roads have shoulders. And tables have legs."

"Not all of them." Lily peered under the table. "This one has an aluminum pole with a suction cup at the bottom." She gave him a side-eye glance with a smile. "And you're too quick."

"Well, that is *one* leg. I might have to name him Long John Silver."

Lily grinned. "If you must. But while you're at it, you need to concede that not all tables have legs. *Plural.*"

"The lady is getting technical." Dak laughed. "I'll stop, if you will."

"Deal." Lily picked up her glass. "And may I point out the gentleman was getting technical on me."

The corner of Dak's mouth turned up as he raised his glass to hers. "Clocks have hands!"

"You are such a cheater!" Lily put her glass down, finding it impossible to hide her smile. "You *had* to get that in, didn't you?"

"Guilty. I'm done now. Promise."

"You'd better be!" She raised her glass again, chuckling. "To us … and to a moratorium on body-parts games."

Dak winked. "You sure?"

"If you are talking about *my* body parts, then I give you permission to play all night long."

He took her hand and helped her out of the tight space they were sitting in. As they stood there together, he looked down at himself before meeting her gaze. "Words have power, Lily. I'm standing proof."

She took a sip of her drink and following his lead, put her glass on the small table they'd vacated. Lowering her gaze, she smiled. "You so are. Impressive proof."

He started to speak but stopped, kissing her deeply instead. As he pulled her away, he finally spoke: "I want you more than I've ever wanted anything or anyone … but only if you're 100 percent ready. I want to show you how much you mean to me. I want us to carry each other away to a place we both need and want to be."

"I'm so ready." Her breathing was labored as she put her hand on him. "And if you touch me, too, which you're welcome to do, I think you'll know how much I want you. I have from the moment I saw you."

"Me too. Actually, from the *first* moment I saw you … in Roseville."

"I kind of wanted you then, too, but not with the hunger I have for you now. Not even close."

"No, not for me either." He walked her over to the bunk beds in the right corner of the RV and nodded toward the lower mattress. "But I did know you were someone I *could* want with this kind of intensity … and love completely."

"Do you love me?" She looked into his eyes as he undressed her.

"I do love you, Lily. In ways I never thought I could love a living soul."

"I love you too, Dak. So much." She ran her fingers down the side of his face as she glanced over at the wineglasses they'd left behind on the table. "Think they'll wait for intermission?"

"They will." He watched as Lily began to undress him. "Hope they know it's going to be a long first act."

CHAPTER THIRTY-TWO

Half asleep, Lily reached over in her bed to see who was texting her. She picked up the phone and, to her shock, saw a text from Charlotte.

Don't ever come home again bitch. We are all happier without your stupid ugly face. You are the scourge of the earth.

"Oh my God."

Dak walked out of the bathroom with a towel around his waist. "What's the matter, baby?"

Lily looked at him and lowered her eyes. After a moment, she sat up, grabbed the water bottle on the nightstand, and took a few swigs.

"Come on. You've got to tell me." Dak sat on the bed next to her. "No more hiding whatever it is. I remember … like four weeks ago, not long after we got back from Morro Bay, you had this same expression on your face. That was the *first* time I saw it. Then again, on our long weekend in Dana Point, on Friday morning, I saw your entire face fall like a broken window shade. You said you were upset by a conversation your father had with Willow, but that reasoning didn't add up for me."

Lily handed her phone to Dak. He read the message. "This blows. I know your sister has a grudge against you, but why would she send you random garbage like this?"

"I don't know. But the real question is: how did she get my new number? Only Wills and Kady have it, and Wills would have told me immediately if something had happened … if she knew."

"Oh, right. I completely forgot the part about Char not having your number. Maybe you need to ask Willow."

"No way. I didn't respond to the other texts, and I'm not responding to this one either. And I'm definitely not telling my little sister. She's got enough on her plate without having to worry about this. If somehow Char got my new number from her phone, Wills will feel like she's let me down in a big way. I won't put a burden on anyone, not even you or Kady."

"Nothing about you is a burden." He lifted her chin to look into her eyes. "By the way, is 'the scourge of the earth' an expression your sister routinely uses?"

"No. I never heard her say those words before. But then again, she never had reason to hate me the way she does now. She's a creative person, so I guess she's having fun thinking of new ways to insult me. This is the second or third time she's called me that."

"Come here, honey." He put his arm around her.

Lily noticed his focus had momentarily left her, but she went on. "It's bad enough to get these texts, but they always come around the same time in the morning … and they stick to me the whole day. Like moldy molasses covering my body or something. And no matter how hard I mentally try to scrub them off … I can't."

"How many texts have you received?"

"You can look at the phone if you want. I can't bear to read them again. They're all so cruel. But I think there's about five of them from when they started a month ago."

Dak scrolled through the messages. "Damn, honey. These are some kind of ugly."

Lily sniffled. "I know how angry Char is, but I've dealt with it because I always believed in my heart, she loved me. Now I don't. And that makes me think my father doesn't either."

"No, don't go there. I know you've had your problems, but trust me when I say you're wrong about this. In these four-plus weeks that we've spent days and nights together, we've gotten to know one another better than some people ever do in a lifetime. And take it from someone who's had pure evil for a mother and not much better for a father … your family loves you." He kissed her cheek. "And so do I. With everything I have."

"I know that was hard for you to say …."

"It used to be. But maybe because I never loved anyone the way I love you."

She blushed; then her face turned serious. "Next week is Thanksgiving. The first time we had it without my mum was gut-wrenching. But this will be the first time ever without my family."

"I know how much this is hurting you. Did you say we've been invited to have dinner with Cynthia and Daniel in the main house?"

Lily nodded. "If you're okay with it. I know she's invited some friends as well."

"I think it will be good for you. Good for us." He paused. "But I know it won't begin to replace not being with your family. Not even a little. I know the warmth of home must be a special thing." Dak got off the bed and walked to Lily's miniature cottage sitting on a nearby dresser. "I haven't told you this, but I think I've grown to love this little cottage as much as you do. It represents the home I always dreamed about … and had … if only in the blink of an eye. At night, when you turn on the tea lights, it feels so comforting. I wish we could shrink ourselves and go inside. Do you think high heat in the dryer would do the trick?"

Lily laughed. "First, we'd have to fit in the dryer in order to be shrunk, you know? And neither one of us is 100 percent cotton, so the probability of that happening is pretty small."

"You're so logical." Dak looked at her with an uneven smile. "But seriously, this is the coolest little thing."

"It's my second-most treasured possession … especially because Kady made it for Mum. My most-treasured possession is this rose-gold bracelet my mum had crafted for me before she died." Lily took a moment to look at her wrist. "I know I told you the story behind this."

"You did. And of course, I know about the locket you wear."

"Yes. This was the last gift she ever gave me while she was alive. Except for the gift of herself." She brushed a tear away. "I have to change the subject. I'm getting too emotional."

"We can talk about anything you want."

Lily looked at him and raised her eyebrows. "How about how great you look in that towel. Have I ever mentioned it before?"

"I think you have."

"So … what are you going to do today before work?"

"I'm going to spend the day in the RV, working on a couple of songs begging to be written. And looking at my muse, as I am right now, I'm thinking they're going to pour out of me."

"Your towel is rising. It's levitating itself from your body."

"Oh yeah. Are you sure?"

"Yup. It's rising. Like magic."

"I think, before I leave, you and I better check it out … together."

"For sure." Lily scooted over on the bed to make room for him. "Something's giving rise to the occasion. And I think a little magic is just what I need right now."

"How come you never let Teddy J. get closer?"

Lily turned around on her barstool and looked at Teddy, who was smiling broadly at her. "This is how I like it. You on that side of the bar and me on this side."

"I can give you a taste of something much sweeter than sparkling water. I can pour it out of a bottle or I can—"

"You can put a lid on it, Teddy. Aren't you bored hitting on me four nights a week when I have zero interest in you and am clearly madly in love with another man? Like what's even the point of this? To keep yourself feeling virile or what?"

"I get lots of chicks." Teddy wiped down the bar nearby where a customer had left.

"'Lots of chicks.' That alone shows how much respect you don't have for women. Both the word 'lots' and the word 'chicks' easily clue me in. But I guess there's nothing offensive in the word 'of.'"

"You're such a spitfire." Teddy glanced around the bar to see if anyone needed a refill. "Such a turn-on. We'll be together. You'll see."

"This is getting old, looking more like sexual harassment by the second, and I'm bored … not to mention pissed off with it. So stop. And like I've told you several times, I have Jamie's permission to tell you off. Maybe you should stop this nonsense before he fires you."

"He knows this bar wouldn't run well without me. He started here about two weeks after I did. If I hadn't been kicking bar ass for the last two years, he would have axed me long ago. I'm that damn good."

"Nah. There are plenty of ace bartenders in LA. Maybe he feels sorry for you."

Teddy licked his lips. "How 'bout you let me take you to the director's crib where I've been crashing and let Dak spend some time on his own? Or maybe find another chick … if he doesn't already have one. In fact, I've heard a rumor he does."

Lily's eyes narrowed. "Again: you're pissing me off, Teddy. How about this: Malibu is a small community. And guess what little tidbit I've learned? The director who's letting you stay at his 'crib'? He found his last three so-called boyfriends by letting them house-sit while he was away shooting a film. So I'm guessing he's lined you up to be his next."

Teddy reeled back, horror stinging his eyes. "I'm not gay. That's not why I'm there. I have great bartending and organizational skills."

"Have you organized a check for cameras in the bedroom when you bring a 'chick' home? Did you ever think maybe you're being filmed for blackmail purposes? You know, so you might stay on and express your gratitude for a taste of the 'good life.' Or maybe the guy wants to make you an unwitting porn star?"

Trying to swallow his shock, Teddy, looking as if he were about to be sick, walked away.

Lily turned around to watch Dak and found Bonnie staring at her.

"What kind of shit are you spewing to Teddy?"

"You're suddenly his protector?"

"If I need to be."

"I'm tired of him hitting on me every night. It's lame, and I'm not interested."

Bonnie sat on the barstool next to her. "You know, just because you and the Daiquiri look fucking radioactive with your just-laid matching glows or because you know you're the envy of the cob-webbed va-jay-jays who cream themselves when your man plays, doesn't mean you're the queen bee who can tell Teddy … or yours truly … to buzz off."

"Okay, well, that's a bit gross. Mega gross actually. And we don't have matching glows."

"The fuck you don't. If this joint ever has a power outage, you two could light the place up, and we'd have business as usual. As it is now, having the both of you around, we've been able to save money on electricity by lowering the lights."

"Bullshit."

"I can go on."

"You definitely can. But I'm not going to have this conversation, Bonnie, because it has no point to it. I've finished my shift and I want to listen to Dak's last set. In peace."

"This convo has a point to it, all right, and it's about to stick you in the eye, in your gut, or up your butt ... wherever you usually receive your shocks."

"I thought you liked me okay. I thought we got along well."

Bonnie looked through the window at the ocean for a moment, appearing lost in thought, then looked at Lily. "I guess we're not getting along as well as you thought."

"Apparently not." Lily redirected her attention to Dak.

"Did he tell you he's still seeing his old girlfriend?"

Lily stared.

"He does her every chance he gets." Bonnie made a crude gesture using both of her hands to illustrate her statement.

"You're disgusting, and I don't believe a word you're saying. I know he loves me. Also, I'm not sure when he'd be seeing anyone, considering the amount of time we spend together."

"He likes you okay, like maybe on alternate days ... or even weeks ... but you're making him feel strangled ... suffocated is the word I think his real girlfriend quoted to me. See, the Daiquiri doesn't want to mess up the good juju at work, so he stays with you. Also out of pity, I think. But she's his true love. Always has been."

"Liar!" Tears pooled in her eyes.

Bonnie laughed. "If you didn't believe me, you wouldn't be fighting back the weepies."

"Wrong. I'm fighting back tears because I can't believe how malicious you're being. It's like you and Teddy have joined forces to hurt me … only in your own unique ways." She sighed in exasperation. "I'm tired of being the object of cruelty."

Bonnie sang: "Oh, Mali-bu-hoo hoo. He's doing you-know-who. Oh, weepity weep weep weep. She's had way more than a peepity peep of his bobbity boo hoo hoo. Oh, sobbity sob sob sob. She's doing your old job. Oh blubbery blub blub blub, you've lost your lub and future hub … in Mali-bu-hoo hoo." Bonnie took a moment to smile at her own improvisational skills. "Who else is cruel to you, Lily?"

"Leave me alone, Bonnie. And get away from me with that verbal sludge and your vile lies. I'm less than impressed. And I can rhyme too."

"She was in here today." Bonnie's look changed from one of amusement to one of deadly seriousness. "And I happened to be covering Henry Dayton's lunch shift. The lady wanted to know when you're working because she wants to meet you and to personally let you know you're being taken for a complete and total fool."

"Like I said: liar."

Bonnie swiped her phone and went straight to her photo gallery. "Okay, then, take a gander at this: a photo of her and the Daiquiri taken a year ago. She told me to take a photo of it with my phone to prove they're together. Your competition is one hot blonde. Take a look."

Lily looked at Bonnie's phone to see a photo of Dak, smiling, with his arm around a pretty blonde woman with a large red rose in her hair. "This means nothing. And it proves nothing."

"You're being played, sweetie. I know it hurts, but if I were you, I'd leave right now and never come back."

Dak, now appearing fully aware of the disturbance going on,

stared at the two of them as he continued to play.

"The Daiquiri looks worried. But then again, he had to know the dam was gonna burst eventually. How long can you boink two hot babes and not get found out? Have STDs will travel and all of that!"

"Stop!" Lily said, more loudly than she had planned.

"Oh, and she said to tell you, if by any chance you don't believe her, the Daiquiri has a little birthmark on his left thigh … up high and next door to his junk. You know, they're like friendly neighbors."

Lily felt her body go limp. Before she could respond, Dak was standing at her side, holding onto her, while Jamie, who had been chatting with customers, noticed the disturbance and was hurrying over.

"Look who's panting breathlessly by your side." Bonnie smirked as she looked at Dak, then Lily. "I guess he's gonna come clean with you, sweetie. Tell you what he really thinks of you."

Dak, his eyes black with rage, stared at her. "And what the fuck would that be, Bonnie?"

Lily noticed for the first time that the restaurant's most popular server appeared nervous, but within seconds, she regained her composure. "Only that you think Lily is the scourge of the earth."

"Say what?" Dak's eyes widened.

"You think Lily is the scourge of the earth. You say it all the time; I don't think you need me to repeat it. Not that I mind. It does have a nice ring to it."

Lily and Dak exchanged looks.

"What the hell is going on here?" Jamie asked. He turned to Bonnie. "If you've done something less than professional to mess with Dak and Lily, I don't care how many years you've worked here—I'll fire you on the spot. Try me."

Bonnie shrugged. "Don't think so, Jamie. I have a little insurance policy. So maybe you want to reconsider."

Jamie looked oddly at her. "I'll deal with you later." He turned to Dak and Lily. "Do you know what the hell is going on?"

"I think I might," Dak said, his angst escalating. "But Lily and I have to leave right now. Listen, Jamie, I'm gonna grab my guitar, but do you think you could lock the rest of my equipment up for me?"

"I will. Right away. But I need to know: are you two coming back tomorrow? It's the last Saturday before Thanksgiving, and we have a huge crowd coming."

"We'll let you know as soon as possible. Right now, no disrespect intended, but the status of our employment is the dead last thing on my mind. And I would imagine Lily's." He helped her off the barstool. "Come on, baby. I think I know what's happening ... and it's not pretty."

"He's gonna take you somewhere and lie his ass off," Bonnie screamed at her as they walked away. "I gave you proof, Lily Sheppard. Don't you forget it! He loves someone else! Boinkety-boinkety boo and all that rot!"

CHAPTER THIRTY-THREE

Lily's breathing was fast and shallow as she opened the door to her studio, with Dak behind her, and fell onto the bed.

"Thank God you drove home safely." Dak sat by her side and cradled her in his arms. "I know it's only a mile and a half from the restaurant to here, but I should never have let you drive. Never."

"You had no choice. I wasn't going to leave my car there."

"I would've walked back there and driven it home for you. I could've made it easily within a half hour."

"We're here now." Lily tried to slow her breathing. "Besides, there's no sidewalk on PCH, and people drive like maniacs. Not to mention it's night." She paused. "You have to tell me what's going on."

"I will, honey. I promise." His arms slipped to his side. "But before it gets any later, I have to ask you to do something for me. It's urgent and then some."

"What? You're kind of freaking me out."

"Can you get your sister Willow on the phone. I need to talk to her."

"Seriously? You want to talk to Wills?"

Dak answered her with a steady gaze.

"Okay." Lily dug nervously into her purse. "I'll call her."

"Sorry, I know it's late."

"She doesn't go to bed until after midnight or so. My little bookworm reads into the wee hours." She paused. "Give me a minute to catch my breath, Dak. I'm freaking out."

"Take your time, baby. Only hurry."

Lily pulled her phone from her purse and pressed Willow's name.

"Lills?"

"Hi, sweetie. Yeah, it's me. I know I don't usually call you this late. Only this is urgent. Please tell me you're alone and nobody can hear you."

"Dad's downstairs with Doreen, and Nico took Char to a special late-night showing of *The Little Shop of Horrors* at that little retro theater in downtown Altrusia."

"Good. But make sure your door is shut and talk quietly, okay?"

"All right … but what's wrong, Lills? I mean besides all the stuff I already know is wrong. You sound super upset."

"I am upset. You know my boyfriend, Dak, right?"

"Yeah, of course. Is he okay?"

"Yes. He's fine. He's here with me. But he needs to talk to you. Right now. I don't even know what he wants to say, only that it's important. Is it all right if I put him on the phone?"

"Sure!"

"Okay, sweetie. Hold on." Lily handed the phone to Dak.

He smiled nervously and put the phone to his ear. "Hi, Willow. This is Dak Falaman. Sorry to meet you so late at night—in a crisis—but I need to talk to you."

"Sure. And you have a nice voice. I'm happy you and Lily are together, or I would worry about her way more than I do."

"I'll always take care of your sister. You have my promise. Now, do you mind if I put you on speaker so Lily can hear you too?"

"Sure. Okay."

Dak pressed the speaker button. "Can you hear me all right?" he asked as he held the phone in the palm of his hand.

"Yup."

"So, about four or five weeks ago, Lily told me your dad had hired this lady to homeschool your sister Char, only she had to quit suddenly because her daughter was having twins and needed her."

"Yeah, Lisa. Char loved her. So did I. She was cool."

Dak drew a long breath and exhaled. "Then I heard your dad went to the school district to find another teacher to take Lisa's place."

"Yeah … her." Willow's response landed with a thud.

He shivered. "And Lily said you thought she sucked up to Char and to your dad … and you even felt she wanted to make a move on him … but you didn't say anything."

"Um, yeah. I totally thought that … I *think* that … because for one thing, I saw her take in the mail one day, and even from halfway up the stairs, I could see there was a card from my dad's girlfriend, Doreen. I recognized the envelope because she sends him cards like once a week, and they're always bright-colored envelopes with pretty stickers on them."

"Go on," Lily said.

"Well, she didn't know I saw her, so she took the card, looked at the return address, ripped it in half, and shoved it down her blouse. Then, later that night, she announced she was staying for dinner, not that anyone wanted her. Dad looked too embarrassed to tell her to leave. Anyway, she was making eyes at him and trying to get him to drink a lot … only he didn't pay much attention to her because he drinks way less since he's with Doreen. So he didn't pick up on her games, but Char did. And I did too. We're not stupid."

"No, definitely not. So how does your sister like her as a teacher?"

"Not even close to how she liked Lisa. Actually, I don't think too much at all, but if she complains, then Dad won't let her be with

Nico. They made this deal, and Char had to promise to get her education and regular therapy ... or else. So she has to behave. And Char doesn't always like to behave ... like Lily can tell you."

"What's the teacher's name?" Dak asked, turning pale as the question came out of his mouth.

"Um ... Joan Hennessey. But she likes us to call her Joanie."

Dak closed his eyes and dropped his head. After a moment, he spoke again."

"What does Joan look like?"

"Um, she said she's forty-two, but I saw the contract Dad signed. Her name is M. Joan Hennessey, and she's fifty-one. She's got hideous dyed black hair, and my friend Issy said she has 'resting bitch face.' Because she totally does. If you want me to tell the super-honest truth, I hate her. But I can't say that in front of Dad or Char. Oh, and my cat, Quincy, hisses at her every time he sees her. And he's a super friendly boy."

Lily looked at Dak as she saw him develop the panic symptoms she was still fighting off.

"Excellent description." He bit his lip as he thought. "Now I need you to think hard about my next question, okay?"

"Yeah, sure."

"Has Joanie ever gotten a hold of your phone? Even in the most innocent of situations? Has she ever held it in her hands or looked through your contacts? And I'm sorry to sound like a lawyer. I hope I'm not making you feel like you're in the witness chair or anything."

"No, you're cool. So, um, let me think. I'm not sure."

"Take your time. The important thing is to reach back into your memory. I'm most interested in when she first came to work at your house. About a month ago or whenever that was."

"Oh, yeah!" Willow said. "She did! But that was only on the first day. She said she was so nervous about getting here, she left her phone at home. And she asked to use mine so she could call her daughter to let her know she made it."

"And how long did she talk on your phone?"

"About ten minutes. She said her daughter, Janis, was having some personal problems, and she needed to talk to her privately. So she went out on the back porch."

"Right. Good job, Willow. So tell me, did Joanie have her phone the next day?"

"Yeah … only she had it later that day! I heard it ring in her purse."

"Did you say anything to her?"

"I looked at her like to say, 'I know you have your phone,' and she snapped at me, real ugly and all, and said she and Char had work to do."

"Can you tell me the routine when she arrives at your house in the morning? You know, what time she gets there, when they get started?"

"She comes at nine in the morning."

"And she and your sister get right to work?"

"Most of the time. But if Char had a bad night—because she still has nightmares—then she might be running a bit late, so Joanie waits in her room while she takes her shower."

"Any reason why Joanie wouldn't wait in the living room and give Char her privacy."

"Because she's evil," Willow said. "Nosy … *really* nosy. She asks questions all the time that have nothing to do with teaching … mostly about Lills, actually. Sorry, Lills, I should have told you before, but I didn't wanna freak you out. Also, Char did ask her to wait downstairs, and that was the day I found her snooping in your bedroom."

"What the …. what did she say when you caught her?" Lily asked, her face tensing.

"Oh, how she thought the room was *so* pretty and she was admiring the art on the walls. Yeah, right!"

"And then what happened?" Lily asked.

"I gave her a death stare, and she went back into Char's room. Anyway, yeah, she acts like she cares about our family."

"Ugh." Lily felt her entire body convulse.

"You've been so wonderful, Willow," Dak said. "So listen. Tomorrow is Saturday. Am I correct she isn't due back at your house until Monday?"

"No, not exactly."

Panic filled his eyes. "What do you mean?"

"She won't be back until a week from Monday. Because it's Thanksgiving week, and Dad promised Char no school."

"Oh," Dak said, visibly relieved. "Was Joanie okay with the revised schedule?"

"Actually ... um ... no. She invited herself to Thanksgiving."

"Holy shit! Seriously? What did Dad say?"

"He said no and said it real firm and all. He said it was family time. Joanie said he was lucky to have family because she didn't have any at all. And I said, 'How about your daughter, Janis, who you borrowed my phone to call on the first day?'"

"What did she say?" Lily asked.

"She gave me a dirty look and told me I heard her wrong. Then she put on this fake smile ... but still tried to show Dad how miserable and alone she was. Then, with this droopy face, she said good-bye, and she hopes we all have a warm family holiday together while she eats by herself. Then she faked like she was gonna cry."

Dak put his hand over his mouth and looked at Lily.

"You guys still there?"

"We are, Wills. Sorry."

"Listen, Willow," Dak said. "I don't want to upset you or anything, but if she shows up, don't let her in the house. Don't worry, though. Lily will call you back tomorrow and explain the whole deal to you as soon as I explain it to her. I'm sorry to be so mysterious now, but you'll know everything soon, okay? Promise."

"Sure. I don't know what this is all about, but I knew she was some kind of psycho. Quincy and me both."

"I wish it were that simple," Dak said. "Thank you so much for being so honest with us. I owe you big time, and I'll meet you soon."

"For real?"

"Definitely. Good night, Willow."

"Good night, Wills. I love you. Take care. And give Quincy a big kiss for me."

"Bye, Dak. Love you more, Lills."

Dak and Lily sat and looked at each other. After a minute, Dak spoke, "Please tell me there's wine here."

"There is." Lily got up from the bed. "I'll go get it."

Dak walked to the couch while Lily grabbed a bottle of white wine from the refrigerator and put it on the coffee table. "I'll be right back with two glasses and a corkscrew."

Once Lily had returned, Dak opened the wine in silence and poured two glasses. Lily gulped, noticing a look of despair on his face unlike anything she'd seen before.

"So," he finally said. "Have you figured out that my mother isn't dead, and she's currently homeschooling your sister?"

"Let me pick my jaw off the ground." Lily sat next to him. "Yeah, so that's exactly what it sounded like, but I couldn't figure out how in the world it could be possible. How did you even put it all together and know to ask Wills all of those questions? And where did Marsha get the name Joan Hennessey and how did you know it was her?"

"Easy. She's using her maiden name. And her middle name is Joan. Did you hear Willow say the name on her contract was M. Joan Hennessey? The M being for Marsha, of course."

"Oh, wow. I actually missed that. So how did you figure it all out?"

"The text you supposedly got from Char this morning. Remember when I thought Marsha had died, and I told you I'd forgotten so much of what happened in my childhood?"

"Of course."

He picked up his wineglass and took a sip. "Well, over the weeks, I've realized I'd repressed way more than I thought … in the interest of staying sane. But when you told me your sister had texted that you were 'the scourge of the earth,' something twigged in me big time. Only I didn't know what. After our wonderful morning distraction, I decided against going back to my RV to work on songs. I was way too upset, and I needed to be alone to think. I took a long walk on the beach. I didn't want to stick around here any longer … because you would have known something was way off-kilter."

Lily nodded in affirmation as she picked up her glass.

"Anyway, I could barely function today, and when I got to work, I sang only songs that pretty much can play and sing themselves, if that makes any sense. You might have noticed I was playing like some kind of music bot. Toward the end of my last set, when I saw something going on at the bar, first between you and Teddy and then between you and Bonnie … I finished the song and came over. And when Bonnie said I should tell you I think you're the scourge of the earth, it all hit me like a ton of fucking bricks. Marsha used to tell me that all the time when I was a little kid. But it wasn't a phrase I knew or ever heard another person say … so I let it fade away. Remember how I told you I've had a lot of practice putting things under floorboards in the abandoned rooms in my mind … and letting them rot?"

"I do. You actually said 'rot and fester.'" Lily took a sip of her drink and put the glass down.

"Right. It's pretty clear now that when Jonah wouldn't take

Marsha's calls, she decided to fake her death … because hey, what sane person doesn't go that route, you know?" He took a few sips of wine. "And she knew Jonah would open up to Janis … if she was dead … and she was right. And none of this is because she misses us. It's about revenge for things she perceives others to have done to her. It's *never* her fault. Ever. She's not a person you can reason with. It's almost like she's a villain out of some comic book who is totally evil with no redeeming qualities. No gray areas. She moves from one vengeful act to another … always against people who have done nothing to her except fail to comply with whatever she thinks they should do or say."

"So why would Janis make that kind of call for her?"

"Marsha must be threatening her with something, because Janis is a good person and wouldn't lie without a helluva good reason. I might give her a call and find out. But that's beside the point. Anyway, it suddenly became crystal clear your sister's new teacher had to be Marsha, and she'd probably gotten your number from Willow's phone and then texted you from Char's phone when she wasn't looking. Then, of course, she deleted the texts. She took a calculated risk you wouldn't text back or call." He drank some more wine.

"Yeah, because she probably knew I left and didn't want to talk to Dad or Char right now … and vice versa. So how would she have known which number on Willow's phone was mine?"

"How many numbers with Los Angeles area codes do you think Willow has on her phone?" Dak asked, swirling the remaining wine in his glass.

"One. Mine. Oh my God." She pressed the palm of her hand into her forehead. "I should have figured this out … I feel so stupid. I've only been mulling it over for a month, but I figured Willow forgot to delete a text, that Char found it, deleted it for her, and Willow was none the wiser."

"Yeah, it didn't take Marsha long to go through your sister's contacts."

"How did she even know about my family or to show up in Altrusia as a substitute teacher?"

"I guess that's my fault, honey."

"How do you figure?"

"Like I told you … I happened to email Jonah about you. So he knew your name, where you were from, and that we worked together at The Breezy Spirits. He paused to catch his breath. "I shouldn't have told Jonah what I did."

"This is so not your fault. You wanted to let him know we'd found each other again. That's beautiful, especially when you've had such a distant relationship with your brother. There's no way you could have foreseen your mother doing any of this."

"True. But she's so manipulative; it shouldn't surprise me. Maybe I should have called Janis and pressed her for details. Only the thing is, I didn't want to know them. I didn't want to remember anything that wasn't necessary." A solemn look washed over his face. "She's made me sick, Lily. More than I want to admit." He finished his wine and poured a bit more in his glass. "Anyway, it wouldn't have taken much for Marsha to poke around about your family and find out your sister needed a home teacher. Marsha could have even paid someone off from Davis. She's a licensed teacher, after all, so it's not like she doesn't know people who could do some digging online and who have access to school files … or even people who know how to hack them … especially within the same state. When she wants something … she's relentless. Too bad she's never used her skills for any good in this world. Ever."

"How awful. Even thinking of her prying into my family's business makes me sick. … much less being in my family's house."

"Me too. I don't know exactly how she did it, but I don't think my guesstimate is too far off. And yeah, she would probably love to move in on your father if she could."

Lily creased her brow as she picked up her glass again. "So how do Teddy and Bonnie fit into all of this? I'm confused." She took a few sips and put the glass down.

"I'm not. Marsha's always been into hiring private investigators or paying random people to do her dirty work … unless she can blackmail them … like she probably did with Janis." She found out where we work, and she did what evil monsters do … sabotage other people's happiness. Do you think Bonnie and Teddy can't be bought?"

Lily made a face. "I'm more than sure they can. They're both opportunists. And remember I told you how Bonnie picked up that man's money when he dropped it? She had zero guilt. She can justify anything."

"She can." Dak touched her hand. "Honey, I hope you didn't think for a millisecond I was cheating on you. I didn't even have time to ask you: what bogus garbage did she say to try to convince you?"

"Oh, yeah. I almost forgot her 'evidence.' She showed me a photo with your arm around some pretty blonde woman."

Dak wrinkled his face in confusion. "I had my arm around a pretty blonde in a photo. Can you tell me anything else?"

"Oh yeah … she had a big red rose in her hair."

"Unbelievable! That's my cousin, Rose. She's been wearing roses in her hair for years. I went to see her two years ago when she had her first baby, Noah. She probably put the photo of us on social media, and Marsha snagged it from there. Anything else?"

"Just about the birthmark on your upper thigh."

"Yeah, I guess Marsha would know, wouldn't she? Leave it to a twisted mess of a woman like her to go there. Was that it?"

"If there was anything else, Bonnie didn't get to tell me, but honestly, I don't think she had any more. I think she wanted to plant the seed of doubt in my mind. And if that didn't work, well, who knows what they might have come up with next."

Dak looked forlorn and put his glass on the table. "I hate to repeat myself, but I'm sorry I wrote to Jonah when I did. I feel so responsible for all of this."

Lily rested her hands on his shoulders. "Listen to me; I already told you how I feel. I'm flattered you did. If you want the truth … it's my fault. Once again, I put my family in danger. I'm like a walking curse. I shouldn't be allowed out in daylight without a warning sign flashing on my forehead." She lowered her head in shame.

Dak pulled her close and kissed her. "How can you even say that, baby? What in the world did you do?"

"I wanted to spare you more ugliness, because you've had so much in your life … so when the first text came in … looking like Char was calling me the scourge of the earth, I let it go. And the next one … and the two after that. When the text came in this morning, I was shocked because it had been two weeks, and I thought I'd seen the end of it. If you hadn't come out of the shower and heard me freaking out, I might not have even told you then."

"Oh, Lily, you can't blame yourself."

"Yes I can! I knew Char didn't speak that way. But I figured she picked it up somewhere. And I assumed Char had somehow gotten my number off Willow's phone. It wouldn't have been hard for her to do if she wanted. So even though it didn't sound like her, and it wasn't something she would probably do, I kept it to myself. And by being so stupid, I let crazy Marsha infiltrate my family for a month."

Dak stroked her hair as he looked lovingly at her. "You know me now. I'm much stronger than I used to be all of those years ago. When you're hurting, when someone hurts you … tell me. And I promise … I'll tell *you*. That's the only way we're going to get through this life. And we're so lucky to have each other. But right now, we have the task of getting Marsha away from your family. The way I see it, there's only one way to accomplish that."

Lily looked at him. "Go to Altrusia and tell my dad."

"Yup."

"What about work?"

"We'll talk to Jamie … if he's good with us taking a few days off, then maybe. But the even bigger question is: do we want to work with Bonnie and Teddy … people who would sell us out and put us in danger? Also, I'm not sure how comfortable I am being where Marsha can get to us … especially to you. So, I'll call Jamie now and tell him we can't work. We can go in tomorrow night, around six, when he comes in. I'll pick up the rest of my equipment, and we can hash this thing out with Bonnie and Teddy. Then, on Sunday morning, I guess we go to Altrusia."

CHAPTER THIRTY-FOUR

Bonnie, her arms folded and her eyes narrowed, sat in the armchair in Jamie's office, while Teddy, devoid of expression, sat stoically in the stiff-backed chair next to her. Across from them, having been offered seats on the couch, Lily and Dak traded looks with their coworkers while Jamie settled in the black leather office chair behind his desk.

Jamie held a large stapler in his hands. "Should I bang this baby and say 'court is in order,' or does someone want to begin?"

Moving her tongue around awkwardly in her mouth, Bonnie finally spoke, directing her words to Jamie. "I don't know why I need to answer any questions these two ask. If I'm under arrest, then let's see the warrant. Give me my phone call, and maybe I won't lawyer up."

"Let's cut the dramatics for once, shall we? How about a civil chat? Can we do that?" He looked at Dak. "You wanted to ask Bonnie a question?"

Ignoring the dirty look she was giving him, Dak hesitated before leaning forward to speak. "I did. I was wondering, Bonnie, who paid you to get nasty with Lily ... and to spew those lies?"

"I don't know. And I know you don't believe fuck all I say, but I don't know."

"Sure you do. Someone paid you to say all of that. Someone

had to give you that digital photo you have on your phone."

"Yeah. Maybe."

Dak sighed. "Please, Bonnie. Can you tell us the whole story so I don't have to drag every little piece of information out of you like it's an iron weight?"

"We'd appreciate it," Lily added.

"Bullshit, Sheppard. You hate me now. You think I'm a lowly sellout. Well, try having a husband walk out on you with three kids to take care of. See how *your* morals hold up, sweetie cakes."

Jamie squeezed a multicolored ball of rubber bands he'd pulled from his side desk drawer. "Talk, Bonnie. If you want to have even a chance of keeping this job … talk." He snapped a red band to punctuate his point.

Bonnie rearranged herself in the chair and snickered at him. She continued speaking. "Okay, so this nameless, fat, balding dude in a look-what-I-found-at-Goodwill suit comes in one night and sits at the bar. Didn't talk to anyone. Parked his portly posterior there for hours, slowly drinking, ogling the staff, and sweating a bit. You know, a slow drip from the forehead like a leaky tap or something. Kept taking his cocktail napkin to wipe his forehead. Then, he'd grab a fresh one from the holder, stick it under his drink, and leave the dirty one on the bar. Teddy here had to wash his hands each time he threw one out."

Teddy's cheeks bloated as he remembered.

"The guy looked nervous and out of place," Bonnie continued. "After he eavesdrops on a convo I had with some customers, he calls me over and asks which server is Lily. After I point her out, he asks me if I'd like to make a quick five hundred bucks … and a thousand more if I continue the job for a week."

Disgust swept over Dak's face as he listened.

"So I ask him what I'd have to do. He says I need to convince Lily how Dak is cheating on her, is back with an old girlfriend, that he said she is the scourge of the earth … and so on, and so on." She looked directly at Lily. "Sorry, but fifteen-hundred bucks is a big deal to me, and it's not like you're my bestie. I don't exactly have one."

"Right," Jamie said. "Because there's nobody you won't sell out if the price is right."

Bonnie sneered. "Do you want me to finish, Jamie? Because if you do, then don't interrupt me with your holier-than-thou cheap shots at my character." She refocused her attention on Dak and Lily. "The guy slipped me five Benjamins right there. Then, he asked if there were any good-looking men around who would take a chunk of cash to hit on Lily. I told him Teddy does it every night for free, but for money, he'd be more than happy to dial it up a few notches … that he's an actor and a gig is a gig. The guy sized Teddy up, said he'd do fine, then slipped me another three hundred for him."

Teddy turned sharply in his chair and looked at her. "You only gave me two hundred."

"Agents get a percentage, honey. If you'd ever had one, you'd know a thing or two."

"Fucking bitch," Teddy mumbled under his breath. He looked at Lily. "Sorry. I suck."

Jamie looked blankly at Bonnie. "Do you have any remorse? Any at all?"

"Damn straight I do!"

"Well, that's something," he said, fiddling with a glass saxophone paperweight.

"Yeah!" Bonnie said loudly. "Of course I do. Because now I'm not gonna get my grand. And I've already spent it."

Jamie leaned back in his chair and rolled his eyes.

"Unbelievable," Dak said, shaking his head. Seeing the upset on Lily's face, he put a comforting hand on her leg.

"You know," Jamie said to Bonnie, putting the weight down with a larger clunk than intended. "Over these past two years as your boss, I've looked the other way more times than I care to acknowledge. But this time, well, I'm finding I don't have the same generosity of spirit. Especially since I happen to be fond of the people you've hurt. So, that said—"

Bonnie put the palm of her hand out in a dramatic stop motion. "Before you say one more fucking word, Jamie, have a think about Luke Skywalker …."

"What in the hell are you talking about?"

"And Darth Vader … and—"

Jamie's eyes widened as his expression changed from confusion to clarity.

"Don't even ask me how I know, sweetie," Bonnie went on, "because it's always been in my best interest to have insurance policies."

"I won't be blackmailed. If the truth comes out, then I guess the time is right."

Bonnie squeezed her eyes defiantly. "Bullshit!"

"I'm not playing," Jamie said. "This is too significant to be made into any kind of game."

After quietly spewing a string of expletives, she scowled at Jamie. "Well, if you're firing me, then I'm gonna deny you the luxury of telling things your way." She turned to Teddy. "Jamie here is your father, you dipshit loser. All those years ago, your mama, his then-girlfriend, lied to him. Said she was on birth control because she wanted a baby and needed a sperm donor. After getting preggers, she dumped Daddio here and found another dude—a rich one—and ended up marrying him. Step-daddio adopted you, and real Daddio, this yellow-bellied fucker behind the desk, agreed to vanish into the ether if she would keep him up on your life. He didn't even put up his metaphoric dukes when he found out she referred to him as 'James Orleans,' a long-distance trucker who had died years ago. Can you think of anything more pathetic!

"So, when guilt-ridden Daddio found out you got hired here,

he left his music-slash-managing gig and weaseled his way into this gig so he could get to know his precious wittle boy. Why do you think he watches you all the time and lets you get away with shit other dudes would have been sacked for?"

Stunned, Teddy looked at Jamie for confirmation.

"It's true, Teddy, ... outrageous embellishments aside. And I'm sorry as hell you had to find out this way and that Bonnie can be so cruel. Not a mystery how she knows. Your mother asked me to hire a friend of hers at the joint in Venice. Brenda is loose-lipped, but I didn't think she'd share this."

Bonnie shrugged. "I'm not the only one who can be bought. Only I didn't have to pay the bitch shit 'cause I had the goods on her ass too."

Jamie stood and walked around his desk to face her. "Gee, Bonnie, so much to be proud of ... what a stellar human being you are ... not. Clear your stuff out, and when you're done, pick up your last check at the hostess stand. I'll give you an extra week's pay, on top of the severance, because you have kids. Now scram. I'll work your shift if I have to. Do me a favor and disappear."

Bonnie stood. "Fuck you all to the bowels of hell." She made a big sweeping arm gesture. "May you live your lives up the devil's ass." She stared down Lily. "And hey, even though I was making shit up, don't mean the Daiquiri ain't cheatin' on you. Ya know? He's got roving eyes and a wagging tongue." She looked at Teddy, who was staring in awe at Jamie. "Put your eyes back in your head before they fall out and roll away. And close your mouth before you get lockjaw. You look stupid." She paused. "More than usual."

Before anyone could respond, she left and slammed the door behind her.

Teddy mouthed a few expletives as he looked at the door. He turned toward Jamie. "My head is still spinning. This is incredible. I wish you'd been the one to tell me, but damn ... you're the coolest dude I know. I'm glad you're not dead like Mom told me you were … and I'm jazzed you're my bio-dad. But this *is* some serious Luke-Skywalker-Darth-Vader shit. For real."

"It is, Teddy." Jamie let a few tears escape as he walked around his desk to speak to Dak and Lily. "I don't suppose you two can work tonight. To say I'm shorthanded and in a bit of a crisis is an understatement. Not to mention after only five weeks, we've got a regular crowd coming for the music. But y'all know that."

Dak and Lily exchanged looks.

"I've got my guitar in the trunk of my car," Dak told her.

"Okay," Lily said. "We'll work tonight. But we have to leave town tomorrow, for at least a week, and beyond tonight, we can't promise anything because we have no clue where our life is going."

Relief washed over Jamie. "More than fair. Thank you both so much." He looked at Teddy. "How about a little talk before your shift … and a long one after it? Sound good?"

"Yeah, thanks," Teddy said. "And, Lily—and Dak—I'm sorry for every asshole thing I've done. Also, Lily, you were right about the director. I don't know how you found out, but yeah, he's a sleazebag, and I never should have agreed to house-sit. I appreciate you telling me. I know you did it to show me what a naïve asshole I've been, but you saved me from digging in any deeper. And now I'm thinking it's way past time I learn to grow up. For the record, I didn't even stay there last night. Took every last thing I own out of his place and slept in my car along PCH."

Jamie looked at Teddy. "How the hell didn't I know anything about this mess … especially the way you talk a blue streak?"

Teddy looked sheepish. "I can keep things under wraps sometimes. I know it doesn't seem like it. You've been so much like a father to me, so I thought you would tell me I was being stupid. Especially the part where I gave up my apartment."

"Hello!"

Lily looked at Jamie, then at Teddy. "Thanks for the kind words. And I wouldn't worry about sleeping in your car again. I think someone here will make sure you're okay from now on." She smiled.

"Come on, baby," Dak said, taking Lily's hand. "We owe this man a great night."

ᏃᏃᏃ

Lily inspected the RV with her eyes. "I don't see any more personal stuff here, honey. Are you good locking this place up now?"

"I am. How about you? Almost ready to go?" Dak stood by the door.

Lily shook off the melancholy that had embraced her. "I think so. All of the things from my place are in my car. If we come back to Malibu, then it won't be any big deal to put it all back. But for now, everything comes with me. And you're good leaving your car keys with the neighbors?"

"I trust them. They're a nice couple, and they've been here for years. Not to mention it's an old car." He smiled. "You've got some important calls to make before we leave. Are you sure you don't need me to stay with you while you call your dad?"

"I'm good. I'm going to tell him we'll be there in about seven hours. And to never let 'Joan Hennessey' in the house again. The rest can wait. But I'm going to make a quick call to Wills first, to let her know our plans. Then, after I talk to my dad, I'm going to try and get Kady on the phone. I'll make it as quick as possible. We need to get on the road."

He nodded. "While you're making the calls, I'm going to walk down to the beach for a private good-bye. If you need me, call." Dak kicked off his shoes. "I think I'll leave these here. Don't want to get sand in your car. Sure you're okay?"

"I'll be fine, baby." Lily took a seat at the small table. Enjoy your farewell."

Dak slipped quietly out of the RV. Deep in thought, he made his way through the park, waving to people who he knew wanted to chat, but moving with a purposeful and steady stride west to send a clear message that he had no time. He looked upward at the tall palm trees bending left toward the sun. To Dak, they were merely a row of gossips, waiting to hear whatever secrets were blowing in the wind.

Once on the beach, he looked north up the Malibu coast, wondering how many miles he could actually see. For Dak, the vast expanse of the horizon paralleled the uncharted waters in his own life.

With great respect, he watched the large gray-and-white gulls with the dark yellow beaks sporting a seemingly stray orange dot on the bottom of their lower beaks. He was mesmerized by the way they preened in a nibbling fashion, under their wings, then at the front of their breasts. They all appeared to do exactly the same thing. How interesting DNA was, he thought, hoping he had managed to escape the evil of biology that had brought him into existence.

In the light-blue house on stilts, with the stenciled number on the side and an American flag waving on top, he imagined a lifeguard on duty, scanning the busy summer beach. He wondered if ghosts of lifeguards past stood in for them on cold November mornings. His thoughts shifted for a moment to the Getty Museum. He had always meant to visit … maybe next time.

Across Pacific Coast Highway, he marveled at the exquisite view the owners of the precariously placed homes on the hills must have but had no envy as he imagined how one act of God could send them tumbling, plundering downward, and out to sea … just as his life had once taken him. Only by the grace of unknown forces had he been washed ashore and found the love of his life.

He watched the gulls scouring the sand, each one stopping to check the contents of a discarded bag, taking a nibble, then fluttering to find a rock on which to perch. The gull standing closest to him wore a bead of water dripping from its beak ... a perfect drop, he thought, a beautiful pearl. How gorgeous it would look on a gold or silver chain around Lily's neck.

He ambled down to the water's edge and let his foot touch the foamy white of the breakers, to see how adventurous the couple wading in the ocean were. An almost-smile formed on his lips as he heard them scream loud, indecipherable words to one another before hurrying out of the water.

As he was about to walk away, he felt a presence leave his body and stand next to him. He didn't look. He only listened: *Stop fooling yourself. Lily may be everything you've ever wanted, but you don't need to tie yourself to her for life. Or worse ... let her be tied to you. Remember, you don't do commitment. You're a loner. Meeting her family is a step farther than you're used to walking. You need to cut ties now ... before this shit gets even more real. You'll break her heart and your own along with it ... but better now than down the road. Ya think? Can't fuck up as much by your lonesome. You're damaged goods ... the spawn of a monster. Don't pretend you're not.*

Dak stood for several minutes as he replayed the words, wincing in pain as emotions overwhelmed him. He let the tears fall. He didn't care if the presence saw them, but he was glad the couple had left him alone on the beach. He dug his foot into the wet sand, ground his teeth, and clenched his fists, unable to liberate his rage.

See. You're a fucking wuss. Like I said: damaged goods. You don't have it in you to be worthy of anyone. Go back to the RV and say good-bye to Lily. That'll give you some fine muck to mire in ... yeah, you'll have a sack of memories to mope about for years. Misery is your thing, dude. Go on; tell her what a fake fuck you are. Let her cry and beg you to stay. Soak in the drama so you'll have enough sentimental slop to haunt your dreams forever. Then move on. Tell her you're too impaired to burden another soul. Watch her cry. Let the tears flow from your eyes too. Then haul ass outta there. Go on. It's what you do best. Run, coward, run!

He remembered the last words Marsha had shrieked at him before she was escorted out of his school auditorium: *You'll never be half the man your father is!*

"Really, Marsha?" He surprised himself with the amplification of his own voice. "I'll never be half the man JP Falaman is? The man who abandoned his sons and never had anything to do with them again? That man?"

Dak looked around to make sure he wasn't scaring anyone who might have happened onto the beach. Seeing no one, he continued. "I was so fucking ashamed of having you for a mother that as soon as I went to college, where people didn't know who the fuck you and JP were, I started lying. About my childhood … my family … everything … because I thought maybe I had done something to deserve the abuse … even though I knew Jonah hadn't. I told people you and JP were off helping people in developing countries … rich, huh? … because I was sick of people asking me why my parents never visited or why I never went to see them. I had a photo of Zoey in my dorm room, and I told everyone she was my mother. Because she was.

"I told so many lies. And I could justify doing so—most of the time—because I was only trying to survive … and that meant never talking about the horrors in my young life. Never explaining to people why my personal history was so aberrant. Easy, I thought. I'll just rewrite it. I'll lie. How could that hurt anyone?" He paused. "Liars lie to themselves … all the time … but you know that. I had no clue that a part of me was taking revenge on you for all of the times you called me a liar when I told the truth. Naïve to the core, I perpetrated your crimes in the name of condemning them." His eyes followed a gull overhead. "That was bad enough. But then … it all escalated. I graduated from college and had a nervous breakdown from all of the pent-up anger inside of me. One day I almost jumped off a bridge, and then, when I was too fucked up to work for eight months, well, I got creative. I started making up gigs I'd played, trips I'd taken, and anything I could to hide the truth. Two of my friends found out and ghosted me ... because they no longer believed a word I said. And they were hurt. And then I lied to cover up *their* absence to the few friends I had left. One day I realized I was making up shit that didn't even matter. Like what I had for lunch, what concerts I'd been to, or where I bought my clothes. I didn't understand why I did it. I felt like the truth ... any truth ...was too scary and lies were better. This is how I lived my life, Marsha," Dak screamed into the ocean. "Because of you! I was getting worse every fucking day!" His voice softened: "Until Zoey called me out on it ... and once again, saved my life. And even though she was fighting terminal cancer, she got me into therapy and made damn sure I didn't bail. She never shamed me either. Never. Not Zoey, because she understood what was happening and only wanted me to get better. Trying to renew any semblance of mental health I had was the hardest thing I've ever done. I sat there for the first two months digging my fingernails into my thighs every time I told my therapist the truth. Because yeah ... it had gotten *that* bad ... because I lied so much ...and because I was *that* broken ... more broken than I ever thought ... for having had you and JP as parents ... especially you, Marsha Joan Hennessey. You are malevolence ... you skulk among the dregs of society ... you are the lowest form of life that swims in scum ... nothing or nobody is safe from your destruction.

"And you know what ... when I stopped lying ... I felt nobody would ever believe me when I started booking these incredible opening gigs for rock stars, not to mention working as a studio musician for some of the biggest names in the business. Talk about irony. But I felt as if I didn't deserve any accolades. So I went about my business quietly, with no fucking fanfare ever. And I'm good with living that way ... I learned I don't need fanfare to be whole; I don't even like it. I'm a much better person now ... I'm not the man I want to be … not yet … but I'm getting there. Yet … look at me … despite everything I've said and everything I've learned, I'm letting your evil voice speak to the insecure child in my head that can't quite dissolve the memories of you … or unlearn and unleash the depraved lessons you taught him. But guess what …? I'm banishing you to a place where your iniquities can feed off one another while you still pollute the air around you on planet Earth … where *you're* the scourge …because you're through hurting me. We're done here, Marsha! We're *so* fucking done!"

Taking several calming breaths, he closed his eyes. For the first time, in his mind's eye, the reruns of his early childhood were fading, as if he were seeing them through opaque cloth … getting denser as he watched. What he *could* see, ever so more clearly, was Lily's face, her eyes shining as she looked at him, her face emanating happiness. She was the one for him … and he was the one for her … they'd both known so immediately. And she wasn't looking for flawless any more than he was.

He opened his eyes and gazed out at the water. He could hear his aunt's voice, saying what she had said many times: *Never let that monster win … nor the man who abandoned you. Their crosses are not yours to bear. Do you hear me, Dak?*

As the breakers came to shore, he watched as they separated and made shapes … especially hearts. As kids, he, Jonah, and Zoey loved to watch nature's ephemeral art appear and disappear before their eyes. And in those times his aunt reminded them that Mother Nature was far more powerful than any "mother" named Marsha could ever be. *She is weak, Dak. She is evil. She can only have power over you and Jonah if you allow it. You are greater than the sum of your sorrows.* Zoey was right. Jonah had heeded her words years ago. Now he had to do the same.

The memory of his aunt's wisdom allowed him to unclench his fists, relax his jaw, and feel the wet sand beneath him as the sound of crashing waves simultaneously became louder, reminding him that as the ocean had a voice, so did he. As the gray-blue water crashed on the rock formation to his right, he remembered what he had told Lily: waves break, only to gain strength, form again, and break. He was allowed to make waves too.

This thing called life had a lot of moving parts. People were allowed to break and grow strong again. Joy is so much greater when we have known pain. Victory is so much sweeter when we've met defeat. Why had he spent so much time rejecting such simple truths? No more.

Dak wiped the tears from his face that hadn't already dried. "This is where I take the road less traveled ... time to write a new script, new songs, and move ahead. This is the moment I will *not* look back on forever and regret a thousand times over. Not letting it happen. Any residual evil still hoping to bring me down ... listen to me ... I'll drown you out every time until you're gone forever. And that's a promise. Try me."

Turning to his side, the presence ... his shadowy alter ego ... was gone. All he could see was a small rock in the wet sand ... a stand-in for the darkness that always pulled him out of the light. He picked it up and tossed it as far as he could. He felt his body and his mind soar with it. To his right, in the distance, he saw a young couple, not dissimilar to him and Lily, stop walking and fall into a passionate kiss ... one too impatient to wait ... precisely what he needed to see to solidify his resolve.

He took one final glimpse at the ocean. As if he were returning its gaze, he waved. After a moment, a smile broke through. "Hey, you must be able to see me ... you're waving back." His face became solemn again. "Until we meet again, old friend. Whether it be next week or years from now, I'll never forget you." He nodded in the direction of the RV park. "I've got to be going. My life, in whatever form it takes, awaits me."

PART 3
Altrusia, California

CHAPTER THIRTY-FIVE

Lily and Dak sat in her car, two doors down from the Sheppard home, and looked at the house as if it were a great historical monument they'd driven over six hours to see, only to be frozen in awe by its mere existence.

"This is insane," Lily said, squeezing Dak's hand. "I'm absolutely petrified to go into my own home and see my family."

"I get it. But it's going to be fine. Your father said he was thrilled you were coming home and that Char would be too."

"He did. And I made him promise to call me back if he learned otherwise."

"And he hasn't called."

"No." She twisted her lips. "But so much has happened, and even though I know they want to see me—and to meet you—I don't feel any less responsible for what happened."

"Unless you want me to take blame for Marsha insinuating herself into your family as Char's teacher, then you need to stop blaming yourself for what some piece of garbage did to your sister. You can feel bad … but you'd feel bad if *anyone* had hurt her. So go with that."

"What if my dad and Char *think* they want to see me, but then when they do, they realize they don't?"

Dak unbuckled her seat belt and then his own. "*Andiamo!* Come on. Let's go in. It's not going to get any easier staring at the house and mulling over what-ifs … the polar opposite, actually. And I'm lecturing myself as well." He smiled. "Do you want to pop the trunk so we can grab our bags? I'll bring my guitar in too, but I can get the rest of my equipment later."

"Lills!" Willow screamed as she ran down the stairs, then threw her arms around her sister. "I missed you so much!"

"I missed you too," Lily said, holding her as tightly as she could. "Let me look at you!"

As they pulled apart, Willow turned to Dak and hugged him. "Thank you for being there for Lills. You're even more handsome than she said. If you were a pop star, I'd rip your photo out of a magazine and hang it on my wall."

"You don't put up celebrity photos," Lily said to Willow. "So not your thing."

"I know. But I could start with Dak." She laughed. "I'd like to have a photo of the two of you I can put in a frame, though." She eyed the luggage and guitar case they'd brought in from the car. "Leave your stuff here for now, but play music for me later. I'm dying to hear you sing too. Come on. Let's all go sit down."

"Sure." Lily took Dak's hand and walked through the foyer into the living room.

His eyes blurry with tears, Dalton rushed in from the dining room. "Oh, sweetheart, I've never been so happy to see anyone in my life. I honestly didn't know if this reunion would ever take place." He wrapped his arms around her tightly as she joyously returned the embrace.

"This is Dak Falaman, Dad," Lily said as they separated.

Dalton vigorously shook Dak's hand. "I couldn't be more pleased to meet you. Please, make yourself comfortable. And call me Dalt."

Lily guided Dak to the two dining room chairs placed at a right angle to the couch.

"Thanks." Dak took a seat. "And my deepest apologies for that woman who gave birth to me worming her way into your home."

"She's not your fault," Willow blurted out. "Anyone want a drink? We've got some great apple cider Doreen made."

"Exactly what I've been craving," Dak said. Lily and Dalton nodded in agreement.

"Coming up!" Willow dashed into the kitchen.

"First," Dalton said, "Doreen is out with Charlotte and Nico. I expect them home soon." He looked at Dak, then at Lily. "If I've learned any lesson, it's that bad things can happen as a result of simply living our lives … when we make mistakes and even when we don't. We never know what event will cause another one. I'll get into that in a bit, when everyone is gathered … in more detail than you can imagine. But right now, I want to let you both know I've called the woman who goes by Joan Hennessey and told her we won't be requiring her services anymore."

Dak looked nervously at Lily before addressing Dalton. "I can't imagine she took it well."

"No. She didn't. She cursed me out and then said her youngest son and my oldest daughter probably filled my head with lies."

"I feel sick," Lily said. "How did you respond?"

"He said exactly what I would have said to her," Willow exclaimed as she re-entered the living room with four drinks on a small tray. "'I thought you said you didn't have any children.'"

Dak stood and took the drinks from Willow's tray. With a big smile, he thanked her, then handed a glass to Lily before sitting down with his own.

"Exactly what I said to her." Dalton graciously took the cider from Willow's tray. "And then she told me I could do something not anatomically possible."

"Sorry," Dak said. "For the record, I haven't seen her since I was a little boy. Except when I was thirteen and she showed up uninvited at my school concert. That's a memory I'd like to bury forever."

"How old are you now?" Willow asked.

"Twenty-five."

"Oh, wow, yeah, so it's been a long time. You don't look anything like her … just sayin'."

"Glad to hear it."

"Willow is right," Dalton told him. "You don't. Anyway, I told her if she came anywhere near this house again, I would call the police. And then I let her know our neighbor across the street is also the Chief of Police."

"They're all back from the store," Willow announced as the garage door into the kitchen was heard opening.

Dak turned quickly to Lily. "I'm worried. Marsha isn't of the mindset to slam on the brakes because the jig is up. Somewhere out there, I fear she's stepping on the gas."

"Let's pray this time is different," Lily said, standing to greet Charlotte as she came into the living room. "Hey, Char! I'm so happy to see you. I missed you more than you'll ever know!"

"Me too," Charlotte said, brushing the tears out of her eyes. "I'm so glad you came back. There's so much I need to tell you." She hugged Lily as Nico and Doreen walked into the room.

"Me and you both, Char. This is my boyfriend, Dak Falaman."

"Hey," Charlotte said, giving him a quick hug. "Great to meet you. I'm so glad I don't have to pretend to like that woman who used to be your mother anymore. She was a major snoop, and you could tell she didn't give a damn about teaching. And also … a major bitch and other things I won't say in front of Dad."

"An articulate description," Dak said.

Nico, dressed in jeans, a black shirt, and an olive bomber jacket, put out his hand to shake Dak's. "Nico Vargas. Nice to meet you." He put his arms out to hug Lily. "Char isn't lying when she says she's glad you're home. We all missed you, girl."

As Charlotte and Nico took a seat on the couch, Doreen walked in from the kitchen, a huge smile on her face. "Oh, Lily, I'm ecstatic to see you again. And this must be Dak. Hi, I'm Doreen Everly, Dalton's friend."

"You can say 'girlfriend,'" Willow told her. "We know you and Dad do more than have meals together."

Doreen turned scarlet. "Am I red?"

"A wee bit," Dalton said, laughing, "but it goes nicely with the highlights in your hair. Have a seat, honey."

After greeting Lily and Dak, she took a seat in the armchair next to Dalton's. "Lily, I hope you don't mind; I've been using the chair that once was your mother's. If it upsets you …."

"Not at all. Mum would like you. I know she'd be happy you're in our lives … especially Dad's. I said that the first time we met, remember?"

"I do. Thank you, Lily."

As she sat, Dalton spoke to Lily and Dak. "Instead of having a formal dinner tonight, Doreen, Charlotte, and Nico have returned from a caterer friend of Doreen's, who has prepared several trays of food for us to eat casually, perhaps here in the living room. Later tonight, we can set up a buffet and some tray tables. For the present, I'm waiting for one more guest who should be here any minute … being one of the most punctual people I know." He glanced at his watch. "It's four o'clock. I expect the doorbell to—"

"I can't even imagine who it is!" Lily said, getting up to answer the door as the bell rang as if on cue. "But I guess I'll find out." She rushed into the foyer to open the front door.

"Oh, honey, you are a sight for sore eyes!"

"Kady … I'm absolutely stunned and thrilled to see you here."

"I was certainly surprised to be invited, especially when your father was so insistent and spoke to me with such sincerity. Just like the Dalt I've known all of these years. That was all I needed to hear." Her eyes swept the area.

"You were looking for Mum just then, weren't you?" Kady wiped a lone tear from her eye. "Silly, huh? You know me too well, Lily." She paused. "It's been a long time since I've been in this house … and for a split second … well, I suppose I was." She shook off her melancholy and smiled. "I'm excited to see Charlotte again … and to meet Dak, Doreen, and Nico. But not until I get a hug." She looked up the stairs. "Oh, and look who's coming down to meet me … this must be Quincy."

Dalton waited until Lily had stopped speaking. "Thank you, honey, for telling me about your life in Malibu, your love story with Dak, and the colorful characters you met. I look forward to hearing even more about it." He looked at Kady. "I'm grateful to you for taking care of my daughter when I was handling things so horribly. Believe it or not, the only solace I got was in thinking you must have had some part in Lily's relocation. If you hadn't, I figured I might have gotten a panicked call from you."

"You would have." Kady smiled. "But I probably would have shown up at the front door … *without* an invitation."

Dalton turned his attention to Willow. "And you, young lady, were far too calm under the circumstances, so that assured me even more your oldest sister was okay. I didn't believe for a moment that Lily wasn't going to call you for a long time, but I didn't have an issue with you saying it. You were in a tough spot ... not to mention an emotionally charged one, as were we all."

"Sorry about lying," Willow told him, petting Quincy, who sat quietly on her lap.

"You handled it like a champ. I wasn't in my right mind. In terms of getting help for Charlotte, maybe ... but in every other way, I was a complete failure. I have been." He turned to Doreen. "Even you have no idea what I'm about to reveal. I couldn't tell you first because I was scared to death I'd chicken out if I had to do it twice."

Doreen, her face steeped in concern, said nothing.

"And Kady," he said to everyone, "has been treated egregiously by yours truly, because I was afraid. Of what ... you're all wondering. Well, Kady is the only one of you who I'm quite sure already knows the truth. I was stupidly afraid she'd divulge it, even though doing so goes completely against the character of this wonderful woman I've known all of these many years."

Lily glanced at Kady to gauge her reaction, but she was focused on Dalton.

"And that's the pathetic reason I didn't want her near any of you. Though, after a while, it became clear she wasn't going to say anything, but by then, I'd already damaged our relationship ... the way tires are shredded when you drive the wrong way over a spike barrier." He looked at Kady. "Yet, I hope our friendship is not beyond repair."

Encouraging him to continue, Kady offered a slight smile.

He turned to Doreen. "I'm not so sure you'll want to carry on our relationship when you hear my confession."

She nodded as if to tell him that wasn't going to happen.

Lily, feeling a sudden chill in the air, rubbed her arms as she tried to imagine what her father might say. Noticing, Dak put an arm around her.

"I've gone over this speech in my head so many times," Dalton went on, "yet, I still stumble on where to begin." He sighed." Let me go back to about a year after Willow was born."

Lily, Charlotte, and Willow looked curiously at each other, while Kady's gaze remained fixed on Dalton.

"Willow, you were only a toddler, but we never told Charlotte, then about five, or Lily, who was eight, that your mother was pregnant again. Your mother kept saying this pregnancy felt different than with the three of you, but she didn't know if it was because she might be having a boy or because something was wrong. Of course, she had excellent pre-natal care, but only her intuition prepared us in any way for losing the baby. She was well into her second trimester, so we believed all would be fine."

Kady nodded slowly, a clear sign to Lily she was reliving what her father was saying.

"Oh my God," Lily said softly, feeling another chill.

Char and Willow, with stunned faces, paid rapt attention to their father as Nico put a comforting arm around Charlotte.

"We were devastated," Dalton went on." Kady no doubt remembers that time well."

Katy nodded.

"And indeed, the baby had been a boy. We were so heartbroken, we decided it would be best not to try again."

Lily watched her father scan the room in an attempt to measure everyone's response. Content the road was clear to continue, he went on.

"As heartbreaking as the loss was, it pales in comparison to what I'm about to tell you." Noticing the increasing expressions of alarm on the faces of his audience, he paused. "You see, we had put our loss behind us. Well, I thought we had. Ten years later, your mother got pregnant again. And yes, she did so intentionally because the loss of our first son still haunted her. Also, though I didn't know it, she'd consulted her doctor, who gave her the green light to try again. When she finally got pregnant, she saw the doctor regularly. She was told everything looked good, and chances were extremely probable she'd have a healthy baby. But she still didn't want to tell me."

Kady pulled a tissue from her pocket, put her hand to her forehead, and delicately dabbed the light perspiration.

Dalton paused. "This is the hardest part."

"Go on, Dad," Lily said. "You can do it. We're all here to support you."

"I hope you all can," he said, looking around. "Well, eventually, your mother learned she was pregnant with another boy. She even had a name picked out this time: Kenneth Ellis. She was so excited, but she continued to keep it from me. I'm quite sure the only person she told was her best friend."

Kady nodded again.

"Eventually … after the doctor assured her again and again all looked well, and she knew it would be impossible to excuse any more of a weight gain, she gave me the news. And this is where I made the worst mistake of my entire life. Instead of being thrilled and understanding that Abby had wanted to protect me, I got angry with her. Not only was I deeply upset she'd kept me out of the loop, but a decade had passed, and I didn't see how a newborn would fit into the family. Instead of being joyful … guess what I did?"

"You got drunk," Charlotte said. "I didn't know why, but I remember you being drunk the night before the accident."

Dalton chewed his mouth, as if the words he wanted to say were stuck inside. "I did. I got disgustingly drunk. And the next day, when your mother was gracious enough to expect an apology, and willing to accept one, I was still angry. Sober, but angry. And that's why she couldn't stand the sight of me and said she was going out."

"And I asked her where she was going," Charlotte said. "And she said, 'I don't know, maybe the mall,' and I begged her to let me come because I wanted to do some stupid shopping."

Lily, feeling another chill, fell back onto the chair as Dak tenderly comforted her. Kady, on the right end of the couch next to Willow, hugged her tight with one arm.

"So … if I had been a noble man and not shut out my pregnant wife, I never would have lost her along with another son … nor would we all have come way too close to losing Charlotte. This entire tragedy rests squarely on my shoulders. It's my fault your mother is gone."

"No, it's not!" Charlotte screamed. "It's my fault. She got killed because of me!"

"No!" Dalton said. "No, no, no. It is not your fault."

"It is," Charlotte persisted. "You know how Mum loved classical music, especially when she was stressed or needed to calm down? Well, she put on an all-classical-music satellite radio station and turned it up. I couldn't stand it, and I said, 'C'mon, Mum, do we have to listen to this?' And then I slightly raised my left hand, because I felt a sneeze coming on. Mum thought I was going to turn the station off, and she was so upset she slapped my hand away. And in that second, the guy's pickup truck slammed into our car. He was slightly over the line, but if Mum hadn't been distracted, she could have avoided him; I know she could have. But she was too upset because I was bitching about music that made her feel better." Exploding into tears, Charlotte, sitting on the right end of the couch, buried her head in Nico's chest and sobbed.

"Oh, Char," Lily said, "it's not your fault! This is the real reason why you freaked out at Ray and me when he said he liked classical music, and you liked metal."

Still sobbing, Charlotte raised her head. "Yeah. And that's why I said classical music was dead people's music. Because it killed Mum and because people play it when they're sad. But the music didn't kill her ... I did! And that means I killed our baby brother too."

Dalton, tears running down his face, jumped out of his chair and hurried to the couch where Nico and Charlotte were sitting. With a nod, he let Nico know that he wanted to hold his daughter. Nico let go, then stood as Dalton sat by her side. Seamlessly transitioning from one man to another, Charlotte continued sobbing.

"Losing Abby was a terrible tragedy," Kady said, turning to them. "We are not perfect human beings, but nobody here did anything remotely close to bringing on this accident." She wrapped her scarf around her arms. "And, yes, I knew what had happened the night before, and I knew why Abby wanted to get out of the house. But I know something else none of you do, and I was unable to share before without revealing a story not mine to tell."

Dalton and Charlotte, now next to her on the couch, stopped crying and looked at her.

Kady waited a moment before speaking. "Dalton, as you know ... Lily, as you know, and maybe Charlotte and Willow do, Abby briefly woke up the day after the accident and the day before we lost her. And I was in the room." She turned to Lily. "You asked me once what your mum said, and I didn't give you a clear answer. I'm sorry, honey. I didn't feel I could."

"I remember."

"When Abby woke up, she told me if there came a time when everyone learned what happened, to let Charlotte know she was sorry for almost getting her killed and that *she* was reckless, not Charlotte. And Dalt, she wanted me to tell you she knew you would've come around, that her pregnancy was a shock and a worry, and her death was not your fault either. And then she said she loved us all so much, hoped Dalton would find love again, and that I would always love her children as I did her. And then she closed her eyes. I believe those were her last words." Kady turned to her left and put one hand on Charlotte and the other on Dalton. "I believe she willed herself awake, knowing

I was there, so she could tell me this. There's no way to prove anything, but even at the time, I could see she was using extraordinary strength. Because that was Abby … a strong woman who loved her family with all she had."

Doreen, tears in her eyes, dropped her head in despair.

Kady smiled at Doreen. "She would be so happy you two are together. And now, I hope you know—you all know—that's fact and not any kind of supposition on my part."

Dalton, still sitting with Charlotte on the couch, turned to Lily. "How do I begin to apologize for the destruction I caused in your life? I was a one-man demolition team. I tore your world apart until nothing but rubble lay in your midst. I asked you for things I had no business even wanting or expecting. Looking back, I'm absolutely horrified, and I am grievously sorry. And I know you heard what I said to Charlotte on her birthday: I virtually promised her you would give up your life to do whatever she needed … as if I had the right to do that. Reprehensible doesn't begin to describe my behavior. The only reason I have … which by no means I consider an excuse … is because my reaction to your mother's pregnancy brought forth her death … and when I learned Charlotte was pregnant, and how it happened, well, I was determined to do things very differently. No matter what, I told myself: remain calm. Oh, I remained calm all right, but sent you fleeing for your life. I don't know how you can forgive me."

Lily got off the chair, leaned down, and put her arms around him. After a long moment, she sat again. "I won't lie now. I hated how you wrecked my life. I barely recognized you as being the same man I'd known all of my life and loved as my father. I was hurt in ways I didn't know I could feel pain. Some days, I felt like I would be happier just staying bed. I always got up, though, shoved my pain away, and took care of things as usual, because I love you all so much. But when I thought I had done way more harm than I could ever do good, when I heard you both talking outside of Char's bedroom, I had to leave."

"I told her to go," Willow said. "I begged her because nothing else would have worked. Lills was falling apart. It's like I could already see pieces of her floating away … so I thought it would be better for her to leave as a whole person."

Lily gasped. "Oh, Wills! You never told me that."

"I know. I was afraid to say it out loud."

"Well," Dalton said, brushing away the tears. "Good for you, Willow. You had far more sense than your old man. I'm glad someone was there to look after Lily as she's looked after us." He turned to Lily. "Can you ever forgive me?"

"Because you're my father and because my love for you is deeper than my pain … yes. But it's not quite that simple. It's complex, layered, and it may be difficult for us to talk about. It's something we have to do, for both of our sakes. We won't work it out in an hour or a day. I do think, though, when we get to where we need to be, we'll have a stronger relationship than ever before. But, yes, I do forgive you." She smiled at Dak. "And remember, because of everything that happened, I went to Malibu and found this incredible man again … three years after meeting him at a party in Roseville and thinking we'd never see each other again." She looked into Dak's eyes. "I know you are my destiny. Not fashion school." She kissed him before turning to Dalton. "Yeah, I know I can have both now, but I no longer want both. The career part I'm still figuring out. But I found my soul mate."

"And I found mine," Dak said. "Like finding a needle in a haystack, but we did it."

Dalton looked at Dak. "I am so happy something so wonderful came out of this for both of you. Earlier, when I told you one event causes another, I wasn't even considering the good things that can happen too. This game we're all in, it's called life and it can be difficult … it can be traumatic … and it can be wonderful." He winked at Doreen.

"It can," Dak said. "And I hope all of us, no matter what we're blaming ourselves for, big or small, can let go. I know that's easier said than done … but I don't know any other way forward."

"Thank you," Dalton said. "I'll take those words to heart." He turned to Kady. "Please accept my profound apologies for the way I've treated you."

"Of course."

Dalton smiled. "From the bottom of my heart, thank you." He paused to take a breath. "I heard Willow say the other day that neither of your kids can make it to Altrusia for Thanksgiving this year. Will you and Patrick join us? Please."

Kady smiled. "We will. We all have so much to be thankful for."

CHAPTER THIRTY-SIX

Lily and Dak sat on her bed as she went through the large photo album on her lap. "And because we had a mum who knew how to sew, we always had the best Halloween costumes in the neighborhood." She turned the page. "But this Anne of Green Gables costume for Wills is my all-time favorite. Didn't she look adorable? Mum took about a hundred photos before Wills was allowed to wiggle out of it."

"Anne must be one of Willow's favorite fictional characters."

"Aren't you smart?" Lily said, laughing. "Absolutely. But she might have changed her mind after being held prisoner in the costume."

"Funny. The only costume I remember is the bumblebee my aunt picked up one Halloween. She told me it was 'all the buzz' and I had to have it." He laughed. "It had these enormous wings, and they kept smacking my friends when I was out trick-or-treating. The girl next door complained that my wing hit her. I said, 'You love it,' and her mother, who was escorting us from house to house, told me I was 'fresh.' I thought she was complimenting me at first. Anyway, the next year, I told my aunt I was too old for Halloween, and she readily agreed."

Dalton knocked lightly on the open door. "Don't mean to

startle anyone."

Lily noticed he had a large expandable folder in his arms. "Come in, Dad. What do you have there? Should I be worried?"

He walked over to her desk chair. "May I have a seat?"

"Of course."

Dalton sat on the wheeled desk chair and turned it to face Lily and Dak. "I found all of this two weeks ago when I was going through more of your mother's things … a slow and painful process. But the most painful part of it all was that I knew you would want these treasures, and I wasn't sure if I'd ever have the chance to give them to you."

Lily tried to downplay the gravity of his words with a bright smile. "So, what do you have there, Dad?"

Dalton got up and handed it to her. "I wouldn't look inside now, as it will be time-consuming, but it seems that in your mother's youth, up until the time she moved to California, and maybe even afterward when possible, your mum collected a voluminous amount of historical information on her family. There are several letters in there, written by your ancestors, local publications dating back centuries, sketches, watercolors, blueprints of family cottages, and several diaries written by your great-great grandmother from Bibury … where your property and your mother's family home stands. You also had family in several towns not too far away: Burford, Barnsley, and Cirencester are the only ones I can recall from memory.

"How special." Lily held the folder to her heart. "This is all so precious. You couldn't give me anything that would mean more."

Dak's eyes radiated euphoria as he took in her happiness, then Dalton's. "Lily told me all about the stories she wrote as a child." He turned to her. "How great you inherited your mother's passion."

"I did. Only it's not the passion I originally thought I'd inherited."

"I'll dig out the rest for you tomorrow," Dalton offered, "but I know for a fact that your mum kept a diary for years. She told me that she started doing it as a child because it rained so often there, and she couldn't go out and play. That's when she discovered and fell in love with journaling. I haven't read any of her writing, but I did take a gander at a page or two of one of your great-great grandmother's diaries. She was a hilarious woman. Far from dull and proper, despite her traditional upbringing."

Lily put the folder on the bed and went over to hug her father as he stood. "Thank you for this, Dad. Thank you so much."

"You're welcome, honey. And believe it or not, I'm going to the kitchen to help Doreen and Willow with Thanksgiving dinner. I'll probably get kicked out before too long, but you'll be happy to know I'm evolving into a different man." He whispered. "Don't tell any of my friends, but I do laundry now too."

Lily and Dak laughed.

"I'll have to see that to believe it," Lily said. "I hope you don't mind, but we're going over to the Bostwicks' for an hour or so. Ray is home from Princeton, and I want to introduce him to Dak … and to see him, of course. And there's someone he wants to introduce me to as well."

"You've done more than enough for this family. Enjoy your Thanksgiving morning with Dak and the Bostwicks, and we'll see you later on. And please, send my best regards to Ray."

"Thanks, Dad. I will."

Dalton walked to the door. "Oh, one more thing. And while I say this in partial jest, I don't underestimate the pain I caused you."

"What's that?"

"I've learned to iron. I do my own shirts now. Not as well as you or your mum did, but I do them."

"Thanks, Dad." Lily pushed away the emotion as she smiled. "Now you're starting to scare me, so you'd better go."

Dalton chuckled to himself as he walked away. "See you later!"

Lily looked at Dak. "I haven't seen him this happy in a long time."

"What a superb feast," Kady said to Doreen as everyone headed from the dining room into the living room. "I heard a rumor Dalt might be responsible for those delicious green beans with the caramelized onions and almonds."

"I cannot confirm or deny." Doreen winked. "But I'm glad you enjoyed them. It's been such a pleasure getting to know you and Patrick … but even more so … being accepted in Dalt's life. I never envisioned my life would turn around like this."

"Kady," Lily said, walking over. "Would you mind if I had a word with you in private?" She looked apologetically at Doreen. "I don't mean to be rude. This is kind of important."

"Don't think twice about it. I was on my way to do a few laps around the dining-room table to work off the pie." She laughed. "I'm thinking it should burn off at least three of Dalt's green beans. Whoops!" She laughed and put her hand over her mouth.

"We'll see you in a few minutes." Kady smiled. "And I heard nothing!"

As Doreen walked away, Lily quietly pulled Kady out into the foyer. "So, listen … this is going to maybe sound crazy, but here goes. On Sunday, when Dad was apologizing and telling us what happened leading up to the accident, I could feel Mum's presence. It felt like she was there to give him courage, or maybe to see him do the right thing … you know, before she moved on." She sighed. "I wouldn't even have the nerve to tell you this if we both didn't hear her speak to us not too long after she died. Remember?"

"How could I forget?" Kady looked from left to right before

saying more. "You must tell me; what happened on Sunday to bring you to this conclusion?"

"Well, a couple of times, I got chills out of nowhere and had to rub my arms. Then, I can't explain it, but I got the strongest feeling Mum was there … overpowering, actually. But I needed to tell you before I share this with Dak."

Kady stood silent for a moment. "You know, now that I think about it, I felt a chill too. I remember taking my scarf from my neck and wrapping it around my arms. I had a brief thought about your mum, but I dismissed it as wishful thinking. I thought the sentiment stirring in me was working overtime … draining my energy … and hence the chill."

"I believe Mum was here. I do. And that means she saw us all reunite … and she kind of met Dak and Doreen. I hope we all made her proud."

"I am quite sure we did, honey. And those aren't empty words. I know how intuitive you are, and I do believe she was here. As I said on Sunday, your mum was … is … a woman of extraordinary strength."

"Oh, here you are," Dak said, walking over to Lily. "Hi, Kady."

"I'll disappear and leave you two alone," Kady said.

"Not necessary," Dak told her. "I have some news I want to share. It's not the kind of thing I wanted to bring up before or during dinner." He chuckled awkwardly. "Call it an after-dinner treat."

Lily eyed him curiously. "Okay, well, everyone is reassembling in the living room now. And I think Char and Nico have some news as well."

"In that case, by all means, let them go first."

Within a few minutes, Dalton and Doreen were in their chairs, Willow, Char, and Nico on the couch, and Dak, Lily, Kady, and Patrick were sitting comfortably on dining-room chairs that had been brought back in after the meal.

Dalton smiled as he watched Willow lovingly scratch Quincy's neck. "So, Willow, how did your boy enjoy all of those fancy scraps you fed him under the table?"

Willow's eyes darted from side to side as she stammered, "Um, uh …."

"He must have found them tasty, because he looks as full as the rest of us do." He winked at the cat. "I see you're still licking your chops. We'll have to make this a tradition, won't we, boy?"

Willow exhaled in relief as laughter surrounded her.

Dalton addressed Charlotte and Nico. "You two have some news, I believe?"

They shared a look and whispered to one another.

"Nico is gonna do the talking," Charlotte said.

Smiling, Nico stood. "I don't know why, but I don't think I should say all of this sitting down. And, um, if I look nervous, it's because I am. We wanted to say something sooner, but Char said we should wait as long as we could … because … um … maybe Lily would come home, and we would be able to tell everyone at once. And we'd all be happier then. And, hey, that's how it worked out … because my girl is so smart, and she knew what she was talking about. So, yeah, Lily. Glad you're home and real glad you brought Dak with you."

Touched, Lily put her hand on her heart and smiled as she took Dak's hand.

"Anyway, in order to tell you this news, I've got to embarrass myself. That's usually not something I do knowingly and all … but, um, … sometimes there's not a lot of different ways to say certain things."

"You're doing great." Charlotte glanced adoringly at him.

"When Char and I got serious … when we went from being friends to, um … better friends …."

Laughter rumbled through the room.

"Um … Lily told Char we should take certain precautions, and we did. What happened is about three weeks before that bastard ...."

Charlotte tugged at his shirt. "Don't get upset, baby. You know my dad and I filed the police report. It's all we can do now."

"We took in the evidence that Charlotte had saved, and they're building a DNA profile on the son of a bitch," Dalton said. "One of these days, he'll come back to California, and when he does, he's going to be in for a big ... and well-deserved surprise. I can't say any more, but know this, everyone: Charlotte's complaint was not the only one they received. Not even close. That thrill-seeking predator will pay for his crimes with adventures I'm quite certain he's never imagined." He mumbled a few expletives under his breath.

Lily whispered to Dak. "The Chief of Police is our neighbor and a friend of Dad's. Bet he told him something. This makes me feel so much better."

"Me too," Dak whispered back.

"Sorry to interrupt your important moment, Nico," Dalton said. "I want everyone here to know Mr. Kent will reap what he has sown. And he alone is to blame for this. Nobody else." He looked at Lily. "I hope you hear me."

Lily, too choked up to respond, only nodded. She looked at Nico, who was visibly shaken.

"Please, Nico," Dalton said. "Continue."

Nico took a moment to calm his nerves. "Sure. That kind of knocked the wind out of me. Kinda can't help myself." He paused to steady his breathing. "Anyway, about three weeks before *that* happened, my, um, 'precaution,' sprang a leak. I didn't say anything to Char because I thought I'd freak her out for nothing. And I swear, I forgot about it. But, um, the night she got home from the hospital, she told me the whole story. You know ... that she was pregnant and what that effing bastard did to her. As I was trying to go to sleep later on, I suddenly remembered what had happened with my, uh, 'precaution.' Never prayed as hard as I did right then and there that things might be different from what we thought they were.

"The next day, I told Char and my sisters. Camille, my older sister, has a close friend who works for an OB/GYN. She managed to get Char an ultrasound test the next day. So yeah, to our great happiness ... and I think to all of yours ... we found out Char got pregnant three weeks before that SOB ... um ... you know."

"I'm carrying Nico's baby!" Char cried out. "Nico's baby!"

A swell of relief swept the room.

"Oh, honey, I'm so happy," Dalton said. "We would have loved the baby no matter who the father was, but for reasons I don't need to articulate, this is the most fantastic news."

Nico surveyed all of the happy faces. "So, um, Mr. Sheppard ..."

"Dalt ...."

"Right, Dalt." Nico fiddled nervously with his jacket pocket. "I know Char is only seventeen, but since we're having a baby in April, I'd like your permission to marry her. Like maybe in the middle of December. I love her with all my heart ... and I would be asking to marry her even if the baby wasn't mine ... because that's how much I love your daughter. I never met another girl ... um, woman ... who understands me so much and who I get in the same way. We're meant to be. I know it. She's got my heart forever, and I promise to be the best father and husband I can."

Lily, tears running down her face, squeezed Dak's hand as she continued to hold it.

"That was so beautiful, baby," Charlotte said.

Dalton immediately got out of his chair and walked over to Nico. Without saying a word, he hugged him close to his chest before pulling apart to shake his hand. "I'll be proud to have you as a son-in-law, Nico. I've come to fully recognize how much you and Charlotte love one another ... and I couldn't be happier."

"Thanks, man. Oh, sorry, I mean ...."

"Hey, I'm cool," Dalton said. "I haven't given anyone that impression in the last year or so, but I am." Dalton patted him on the back. "Congratulations … man!"

Another rumble of laughter circulated through the room.

Nico turned to Char and got down on one knee as he pulled a ring box from his pocket.

"Oh wow," Charlotte said. "I was totally not expecting this!"

As he opened the box, Nico drew a nervous breath. "You are the love of my life. I could look around the freakin' world and never find someone like you. You see my soul and my heart. And I see yours. You feel my pain before I know I'm hurting. And I feel yours. We're meant to be; I'm more sure of this than anything in my whole life. I wanna love you till the end of time, and you know I mean it. Will you marry me, Char?"

"Of course I will!" Charlotte cried as she hugged his neck. "I'm so happy."

"This beautiful ring was my grandmother's." Nico put it on her ring finger. "Remember when your skull-and-crossbones ring went missing. I used it to get this one sized."

"Well, I've got another skull and crossbones that isn't going anywhere."

Charlotte, Nico, Willow, and Lily laughed.

"What so funny?" Dalton asked.

"Ah, nothing. One of those you-had-to-be-there stories," Nico said as he sat down and put Charlotte on his lap. "Not sure how much longer I'll be able to do this."

"I'm wondering," Dalton said, "if the two of you will accept my offer to live in this house for a while … unless you have other plans, of course. Nico, I know you're a stand-up guy and a hard worker, but this is a big house with room for everyone. I'm thinking that living here might help you save for the future. I promise to respect your privacy. This house would be as much your home as it is ours. And my bedroom is way far away from yours. What do you say?"

Nico peered at Charlotte, who was eagerly shaking her head yes.

"Yeah, sure. Sounds great. My uncle Raffi was going to rent me a small apartment, but this will be much nicer for all of us … and I'll be able to save some serious money for the day when we can buy our own house. Thank you."

Fifteen minutes later, when the congratulations had all been said and Char and Nico's happiness had lifted everyone into joy, Lily turned to Dak. "Did you have some news you wanted to share?"

"Cool," Willow said too loudly, startling Quincy as he jumped off her lap and ran for dear life. "Are you going to stand too?"

"Whoa!" Lily said. "Slow down, kiddo. It's not that kind of news … not now."

Dak laughed. "Lily's right, Willow, but one day it will be."

Willow giggled. "I didn't think so, but I kind of hoped."

"What's on your mind, Dak?" Dalton said.

"Well, since Nico stood for *his* news, I think I'll stay seated for mine. It's good … in a different kind of way. As all of you remember from Sunday, except you, Patrick, as you weren't here, when Dalt called Marsha … aka Joan Hennessey … the monster who gave birth to me … he told her never to come back here again. That's when she cursed him out and said her younger son and Dalt's oldest daughter must have filled his head with lies. This, of course, after saying her former friend Janis was her daughter, denying she said it, then crying because she was childless. Well, for all intents and purposes, I suppose she is. But that's entirely her doing. Anyway, when Dalt said he told her to stay away, I turned to Lily and said something to the effect that Marsha doesn't respond well to being told no. And there was no more to say … until today."

"So, there's a new chapter in this story," Patrick said.

"Yes," Dak said. "And I sure as hell hope it's the last one."

"I hope everything is okay," Kady added.

"It will be." He paused. "Late this morning, Lily and I went to meet her friend Ray and visit for a while. When we got back, my brother, Jonah, called from London, and I went outside to talk to him. It seems after Marsha spoke with Dalt and was given the old heave-ho … in typical monster fashion, she vowed to take revenge … on Lily and me. She didn't have any idea we weren't still in Malibu. So, she leaves Altrusia and goes down to Mexico. She has some charming associates here who told her where to go to buy drugs. Her intention was to come back to California, head into The Breezy Spirits during the day when Lily and I don't work, and plant drugs in the piano and other places that would point straight to us. Oh yeah, and she was going to personally, but anonymously, tip off the cops. Rich, huh?"

Willow looked at Lily. "Did I tell you she was evil or what?"

"Total tacky dye-jobbed, cheap-perfume-wearing, pancakey-faced, coffin-nail-smoking, nasty-assed bitch," Charlotte said. "But damn, an effin' criminal one."

"What my girl said and wow." Nico eyeballed Lily and Dak. "I knew something was off. People joke about shifty eyes and all, but hers were everywhere but in the schoolbooks. Always looked like she was casing the place, ya know? Because she probably was. Didn't trust anything she did or said."

"Yeah," Willow blurted out. "And she was trying to seduce you, Dad, but you didn't notice."

"Oh yes I did." He looked at Doreen. "But I played dumb, much to her chagrin. Go on, Dak. Finish your story."

"Well, guess who gets her felonious butt nabbed at the U.S. border coming back into California."

"Oh, my!" Kady said.

"Sounds like a karmic boomerang," Patrick chimed in.

"But that's not all. When they arrested her for drug possession, they found out she has several aliases and has a crap ton of warrants out on her for things like blackmail, theft, conspiracy, and several other similar and notable achievements." He turned to Lily. "No wonder she had cash for her 'associate' to bribe Bonnie and Teddy with. Blackmail is a cash business."

"Holy shit!" Lily laughed and looked at Kady. "I mean, holy shiitake mushrooms."

Kady dissolved into laughter. "Beautiful! I love it. Please, go on, Dak."

"Anyway, they let her make a phone call, but instead of calling a defense attorney, she rings up her old friend Janis, whose uncle is a well-known *corporate* lawyer … but that didn't matter because she wanted Janis to talk the guy into representing her … pro bono. Specialty be damned if the price is right. Unreal, huh?" He paused to make eye contact with his audience. "Janis is the same lady Marsha blackmailed into calling Jonah with the greatly exaggerated reports of her death." He twisted his face in disgust. "Marsha's such a sweet lady. She threatened give Janis's abusive ex the lowdown on her whereabouts if she wouldn't do her dirty work. Didn't give a damn if Janis or her kids got hurt in the process. Luckily, Janis found out the bastard is terminally ill … and rotting in prison … so all's good there. Marsha didn't know that when she called to browbeat her old friend a second time, thereby wasting her phone call. Janis calmly told her to fuck off, hung up, and changed her number."

"So what happens now?" Patrick asked.

"Not entirely sure. But there's a dude my brother works with who's brilliant at getting information. From what he's uncovered, Marsha has enough crimes on her record to put her away for life."

"What else?" Willow asked, her eyes practically bulging.

Dak laughed. "Isn't that enough?"

"Yeah, it's awesome," Willow said. "But I could easily listen to more."

"I think the good news is we're unlikely to ever hear from her again, but my brother's colleague will continue to monitor her legal situation, for our collective peace of mind. As much as I'd like to wrap all of this up with a pretty bow, I'm fully aware of what Marsha is capable of doing, especially via surrogates, so I'm not entirely celebrating, even if she goes to prison. She's got a long enemies' list, so I hope she'll leave all of us alone, not that I want to see her hurt anyone. The woman is a piece of work, and she won't let a little thing like being incarcerated get in her way, if she's so inclined. I think all will be good, but I speak with cautious optimism. She kept tabs on *us* for years; now we're returning the favor."

"Damn, what a story," Nico said. "And I'm glad to hear it. Don't want any nutjobs messing with my soon-to-be wife and baby. I'm always gonna have the eyes in the back of my head peeled … for the rest of my life."

"That sounds so weird to hear you say," Charlotte told him. "The part about me being your wife. But I love it."

Willow giggled. "I thought you were going to say how weird it is picturing Nico with eyes in the back of his head."

"We have a lot to be thankful for," Dalton said.

"We do," Doreen said. "I also have some news to share."

Willow looked at Dalton. "Are you gonna stand, Dad?"

All eyes fell on Dalton as the room broke out in nervous laughter.

"Um, not quite yet. But be cool. You never know."

"Oh, my goodness," Doreen said. "I wasn't even thinking y'all would take it that way." She laughed. "No, my good news is my son, Liam, called me this morning to say he's moving back to California after high school. He's been living in Seattle for several years. I was so sad he couldn't be with us tonight, but I'm tickled by this news. It won't be for a while yet, but I'm so excited."

As good wishes were offered to Doreen, Dalton smiled warmly at Lily and Dak. "How about the two of you? What are your plans? Or don't you know?"

"Well," Lily said. "We haven't figured that out yet. What we do know, and want to share with you all, is we'd like to stay here through the holidays. I want to spend as much time with my family as I can, and, Dad, I especially want us to be able to work through everything that happened … so we can truly move on."

"I'm so thrilled," Kady said.

Willow jumped up and ran over to hug Lily and then Dak. "That's like the best news ever … almost." She looked at Charlotte and Nico.

"We're gonna have a full house," Charlotte said.

Willow beamed. "Yeah, I feel like pouring awesome sauce over everyone. We'll be like one giant ice cream sundae."

Charlotte gave her a pseudo stink eye. "Tree, I don't know where you picked that up, but put it back where you found it … and leave it there."

Everyone laughed.

"I'm overwhelmed," Dalton said. "I was afraid you might leave after the weekend, and I wasn't sure when we'd get to truly repair our relationship. And I hated the idea, but far be it from me to have asked for more. I know you've forgiven me, Lily. But that's not enough. You're right; we do need to talk about so much. There's been far too much pain and sorrow."

After listening intently to her father, Lily whispered in Dak's ear, and he whispered back.

"You're so right, Dad. We've all been through so much. I just asked Dak if I could share something with you. When we were in Malibu, we talked a lot about our respective sorrows. Dak told me what his aunt had said to help him through some tough times. I asked him if I could share her words with you, and he told me his aunt had also written them in a poem." She paused. "I had no idea. Anyway, I'll let him tell you the rest."

"That's so lovely," Kady said. "I'm sure we'd all love to hear it."

"Absolutely!" Dalton agreed.

Dak stood. "Don't get any ideas, Willow." He winked. "But I am standing because I want to honor my aunt's poem. It's special to me because she put her philosophy of life into words when she knew she was dying. I'm sure she hoped to immortalize her wisdom for my brother and me ... so we wouldn't forget what she most wanted us to remember. If everyone would like, I'd be happy to recite it."

"Oh, please," Doreen said amidst the cacophony of voices.

Dak drew a long breath, then turned to see the loving faces in the room, riveted, waiting for him to speak.

"The Sum of our Sorrows. By Zoey Ophelia Falaman. We have no way to know, if we can count tomorrows, but we should never count, the sum of all our sorrows. In doing so, we take the risk, that they will pile high, and thus obscure the blessings, that then may pass us by.

"For when we clutch to sorrows, we're encompassed by defeat, and miss the joyous faces ... of friends we've yet to meet. Sorrows are a part of life ... they're part of you and me ... and no soul is without ... pain that others cannot see.

"But when we push on forward, ... despite our grief inside ... we stand to reign victorious, from all the tears we've cried. For even with our sorrows that can multiply and grow ... the fact that we are here ... means we're stronger than we know." Dak, stirred by sentiment, looked upward. "I love you, Aunt Zoey. Thank you for all of the gifts you gave me. Without your wisdom and the gift of your guidance, I wouldn't be standing here. You've given me so much more than you'll ever know ... but somehow, I believe you do."

EIGHT MONTHS LATER

EPILOGUE

"You've checked this mantelpiece about seven times," Dak said as he and Lily inspected the row of frames. "Everyone's photo is proudly displayed. I promise. You're not missing a single person."

"I know!" Lily gave him a lopsided grin. "I'm being totally OCD, aren't I?"

"Obsessive Cotswolds Disorder?"

She laughed. "Oh, I like that. Now, what should I obsess on next? Hmm." Her eyes lit up. "I know; I could count the chairs Uncle Ellis and Aunt Millie brought over and make sure there's room for everyone to sit."

"Let's see. We've got a couch to seat three or four people. Two upholstered chairs, four chairs from your aunt and uncle, and two cribs for the baby ... one upstairs and one downstairs. Not to mention, we have several chairs in the dining room and kitchen we can bring out if your cousins or other relatives come over. And there's absolutely nothing I've said you don't know a hundred times over." He smiled. "S'okay, honey. I'm a bit nervous too. I'm still living in a world I've never known before."

"I hope my entire family isn't here at once. I can't count that high. Especially if Caroline brings her new boyfriend." She laughed.

"Kidding … I think." Lily walked to the old built-in bookshelves. "I picked up some classics at the town bookshop …*A Woman in White* and *Tess of the D'Ubervilles,* and a few others. In case Wills gets the urge to read while she's here. I found some real treasures … well over a hundred years old."

"I can't imagine she won't be spending every spare moment soaking in the scenery or enjoying her time with you."

"True, but she does like to sneak a read at night. And I would amend that statement to 'her time with us.'" She glanced at the vintage-style replica of a Victoria Station clock that hung on the old stone wall behind the fireplace. "They should have been here at least a half hour ago."

Dak took a seat on the couch. "Come on, honey. Sit with me. Chill time." He glanced to the right of the clock, smiling at the large rusted wall ornament of Kokopelli playing the flute on a crescent moon. "His spirit is making sure everyone has a safe passage; I'm sure of it. I still believe he helped bring us together."

"Me too." Lily smiled and sat by him, resting her head on his shoulder. "They better get here soon, because if I keep worrying, I'm going to look older than those books I found for Wills."

"Yeah, I can see the crow's feet around your eyes starting to do their thing. They're spreading even as I talk." He burst out laughing.

Lily picked up a pillow and smacked him. "Where's the loving reassurance I need?"

"Always here." Dak smiled as he turned his head to look at the bookshelves and the miniature cottage that sat on the middle shelf. "Remember in Malibu, when I said I wished we could shrink ourselves and be inside your little cottage?"

"I do. Who knew you had such extraordinary wishing powers?" She smiled. "Never, in a million years, did I imagine we'd actually be living here … at my family's home in Bibury. Our home now."

"I never saw myself living in a picturesque English village

...not ever. Especially a civil parish ... because I didn't even know what it meant until we moved in." He managed a nervous laugh. "I still have so much to learn. I was reading the history of some of these cottages, what they were like a couple of centuries ago. They looked nothing like this inside. They were dank and gloomy." He looked up. "No finished ceiling and beautiful wooden beams like we have now ...only the dark underside of the roof. Families and equipment were all crowded into a small space. No room for anything that wasn't functional in some way." He laughed. "I hope I'm functional."

Lily licked her lips as she sized him up. "Have I told you lately how *very* functional you are?"

"I think you have. Hey, uh, someone's looking at the clock again."

"You don't miss anything." Lily offered a twisted smile. "I'm sorry. I worry too much, and I think it's wreaking havoc on what's left of my common sense. By the way, I forgot to thank you for finding the perfect place for the little oil painting of San Francisco that Christy did for us. The wall space by the sliding glass door is perfect. I'm glad I went back to the gallery again ... and took you with me. Christy and Kevin have turned into such great friends. Who would have thought, seeing how we met? I hope they can come visit when their baby boy is a bit older." She glanced at the clock again.

Dak smiled. "If there was any meaningful delay, Ellis would have called. We're quite a distance from Heathrow ... not to mention it's anyone's guess how long it took them to go through customs."

"Exactly. And, yeah, it *is* a long drive. Uncle Ellis and Aunt Millie were so nice to pick everyone up so I could get things ready here. Dad offered to take the train into Bibury, but that schedule can be less than accommodating. And they would have been exhausted. Remember the major jet lag when we first arrived?"

"Hey," a voice said. "I've got some dodgy-looking folks out here who claim they're family. Shall I let them in?"

Lily smiled at her uncle Ellis as he stood in the doorway, with his Cheshire-cat smile. "Yes!"

"Are you sure? The bloke with the round specs looks especially suss."

Tears filled Lily's eyes as Willow, followed by Charlotte holding her baby, entered the cottage, with Nico, Doreen, and Dalton not far behind.

Willow rushed over and threw her arms around Lily while Dak greeted everyone else. "I can't believe we're here. This village is like a fairytale or something ... so beautiful. Uncle Ellis showed us Arlington Row on the way here. We have to go back again and take a gazillion pics."

"My turn," Charlotte said. "Let go of Lills now."

Willow moved aside and showered her affection on Dak.

Lily beamed. "Char, it's surreal you're here ... and I finally get to meet my niece."

She smiled as Charlotte delicately pulled aside the pink blanket over the baby wrap to reveal her sleeping daughter's face. "Look, Abby. It's your aunt Lily. Show her how beautiful you are."

"You are the most gorgeous baby ... and such a head of hair. Your photos and videos don't do you justice, little one."

Nico strode over and gave Lily a hug. "Hey, girl! You look great! And this place feels like a dream." He looked at his daughter. "Like this princess. Don't we have the prettiest little baby you ever saw? She's got the thick Vargas hair, my nose, and Char's eyes and lips. You'll see her eyes when she wakes up. They're starting to turn brown. But right now, she needs to keep snoozing."

Before Lily could answer, Dalton was at her side, hugging her, as Doreen waited for her turn.

Millie Quincy, a freckle-faced woman with short auburn hair, walked into the room, a broad smile on her face, and touched Lily's shoulder. "As soon as you get these weary travelers settled, I'll bring out the eats you've prepared. Okay, love? Ellis and I are going to leave you, and tomorrow we'll see how our visitors are doing and make the sightseeing plans from there."

"Thank you, Aunt Millie ... for everything!" Lily addressed her family. "Everyone, please, have a seat. Char, you and Nico would probably be most comfortable on the couch, so you can sit together with little Abby Elizabeth."

"I'm going to plunk down here by the bookshelves," Willow said, sitting in the dusty-rose upholstered chair. "Even though I kind of already feel like I'm a character in a book who's been transported to fantasyland. Or maybe I'm this teen girl who grew up here, and she likes a boy who's like royalty or something, only the family is snobby and won't let their son even speak to me. So we have to sneak off to be together ... in like a stable or something."

"You've been reading overtime," Lily said. "Does this boy have a name? Like Heathcliff or Harry?"

"Try Sebastian," Charlotte said as she and the baby snuggled up next to Nico. "That's the guy the willow tree weeps for."

"You need to zip it." Willow gave Charlotte an embarrassed look before turning to check out the books.

"Don't worry, Wills. We'll change the subject." Lily laughed. "But is he cute?"

She noticed Willow's face had warmed to an undeniable shade of crimson.

"Okay, Wills. I'll stop. By the way, while you're checking the bookcase out, I did pick up some classics for you. They're on the bottom shelf. You might find something else you like better, though." Lily took the food and drinks from Millie and put them on some tray tables within everyone's reach.

As Millie and Ellis bid everyone a good day, Doreen and Dalton settled on the additional chairs, while Dak took the lone upholstered chair that was left, leaving the sofa free for Lily.

"Sit down, honey," Dak said. "I knew you'd want the spot next to little Abby."

"I certainly do. I guess we can show everyone the rest of the house and the guest rooms later."

"Totally," Willow said. "I'm dying to see everything, but we want to talk to you and Dak first. We've all missed you so much. Tell us what's going on."

"We will. But first, I'm more curious to know what's happening with all of you. Who wants to start?"

Dalton stood. "I think I should."

"Dad is standing!" Willow exclaimed. "Not like in 'Dad stood up,' but in like 'Dad is standing' because he's got some news. Like *that* kind of news!"

Everyone looked at Dalton.

"Do you have *that* kind of news, Dad?"

"I do," Dalton said as he took Doreen's hand and helped her up. "I hope you will all forgive the secrecy, but Doreen and I got married two days ago. We decided to do an elopement of sorts because we didn't want Lily and Dak to be excluded from the ceremony, not to mention tiring everyone out before our big trip." He paused for a moment to take in all of the smiles.

"And," Doreen said, "while it would have been absolutely lovely to get married here, I couldn't bring myself to have an official wedding in your mum's hometown. I hope y'all are okay with this."

"I'm elated." Lily jumped up to congratulate them. "This is the best news. Where are your wedding rings?"

"We're going to exchange them again now," Dalton said, pushing his glasses up on his nose, "in front of all of you."

While enthusiasm overwhelmed the room, Lily took her seat. Only minutes later, all eyes were on Dalton and Doreen as they repeated their vows and exchanged rings. When they finished, after ten minutes and a celebratory toast of tea, the conversation resumed.

"Goodness gracious, I forgot!" Doreen said. "Willow, I hope it's okay with you, honey, but Quincy is about to get a canine brother: Pounder. He's great with my neighbor Alice's cats, so I'm pretty darn sure all will be good. But what I don't know is if Quincy likes dogs. The few times I brought him to the house, I'm afraid your boy has hidden. Might take a bit of adjustment." She smiled awkwardly. "Maybe in getting used to both of us, for that matter."

"Quincy already knows you, so don't worry. I'm sure he'll love Pounder. He's never stayed long enough for Quincy to figure that out. I'm so excited we'll have a dog in the house."

"I love hearing that," Lily said. "Dak and I are planning to get a dog too. We didn't think right now was the best time to train a puppy."

"Fantastic, Lills! I know how much you miss my Quincy boy. You definitely need a pet."

"Coolio!" Nico said. "A dog will fit in perfectly here. Oh, and I'm gonna bring my dog, Jalapeño, to live with us too. Our visits aren't enough. He's missing me something awful. And vice versa."

"Oh, please!" Willow said. "That's so exciting! Wow! Two dogs and a cat!"

"Segueing from the topic of our home zoo," Dalton said, laughing, "I've booked a room at the beautiful hotel here in town, idyllically set on the River Coln, for my bride and myself … so everyone will have their privacy."

"The hotel probably has better soundproofing too," Willow blurted out. "You'll need it because this is technically your honeymoon, right?"

"I think my husband and I may have just blushed in synchronicity," Doreen said. "Bless your heart, Willow. You do make me laugh more every day."

"Anyway, we do have more news to share," Dalton said, "which is most relevant to Charlotte and Nico."

"For real? Like what?" Charlotte asked, her admiring gaze going from her baby to her father.

"Well, Doreen has quit her full-time job at our mutual place of employment, but she'll now be working from home as a part-time consultant for the company." He turned to her. "Why don't you take it from here?"

"One of the reasons I wanted to do this is so our new mother can go back to school and enjoy her senior year." She spoke directly to Charlotte. "I also want you to be able to go to makeup school when you're ready. So, sweetie, you no longer have to worry about anyone to look after little Abby. I'll be able to do that for as long as you need … if you and Nico are okay with these arrangements, of course. You're the parents, and the decision is yours."

"For real?" Charlotte said, elated. "Oh, that will be such a help to us. We weren't totally sure what we were going to do. You are the best grandmother, Doreen. And we can return the favor by taking care of Pounder when you need us to."

Lily watched as tears pooled in Doreen's eyes.

"This is freakin' fabulous, Doreen. Thank you so much," Nico said. "My mom was going to see what she could do, and she still will, but she works two or three days a week. So yeah … this is perfect. You two can work it out, and she'll be there when you need time off and vice versa. Make like tag-team grandmas and all that."

Laughter bounced throughout the room.

"That's quite a visual. But I love it." Doreen picked up a tea sandwich from the tray in front of her. "These are delightful, Lily. And the china is beautiful."

"Thanks. The china was my grandmother's. She had several sets, so Aunt Millie was more than happy to give me this one. And the sandwich recipes were hers as well."

"Are you like triple sure you want to do this," Charlotte asked Doreen. "I mean, Abby is a good baby, but I hope she won't be too much for you. You might wish you were back in the office or maybe a padded cell. This girl has a set of lungs on her."

"It's all good," Doreen said. "Liam is much quieter as a teenage boy than he was as a baby. I'm well trained." She paused to finish her miniature sandwich. "I've been wanting to get away from the nine-to-five life for years. But I didn't have anything to replace it with, and part-time work doesn't come with health insurance, so there was that as well. But now that we're married, I can hop on over to Dalt's plan. It's all so perfect for me. Promise. I'm very content." She reached over and grabbed Dalton's hand. "More than I ever dreamed possible. Now then … enough about all of us. Tell us about your lives here in this enchanting village and environs."

"Yeah. For sure," Willow said. "Like who does the back garden? They don't grow 'em like that in California. Looks like you have a bazillion plants."

"We have a wonderful gardener, Peter, who's teaching Dak and I how to tend to it. But there's so much to know: things to do and things not to do."

"What's something that's good to do?"

"Oh, like using hedges to create little rooms within the garden itself. It's also important to choose plants that change as the seasons do. I couldn't possibly explain it all, but there are books on the shelves you're welcome to look at."

"Tell me one thing not to do," Willow said.

"Flap your gums incessantly," Charlotte told her. "How's that, Tree?"

Lily laughed. "I'll explain a bit more, Willow. For one, you don't want to use too many hardscape materials … like brick or cobble …limestone … things like that. And you don't want to have too many focal points."

"It's gorgeous," Charlotte said. "And how nice to sit here on the couch and look through the sliding glass doors. The patio is sweet!

Do you eat out there a lot?"

"We do," Dak said. "We've found the same kind of peace in the garden … and here in the village … that we had in Malibu. Granted, very different settings … but all good for the soul. Still, because the ocean is special to us, we take trips to Bournemouth or Brighton when we can. A bit of a drive, but each one offers us something different."

"Are they like Malibu?" Willow asked.

"Not too much," Dak said. "We usually go to Bournemouth, but when we want to have fun and be more social, we choose Brighton. It all depends on our mood, you know?"

"We're moody people," Lily said with an inconspicuous smile.

"Cool," Charlotte said. "The best of both worlds."

"Exactly," Dak confirmed. "The perfect balance for us."

"I guess without balance, you'd fall over," Willow said.

Dak laughed. "We definitely would." His tone became more serious. "And we have. But we always remember to get back up again." He swallowed a lump in his throat as he fought off his momentary unease.

Willow jumped up and ran to the door where the luggage was sitting. She reached into her backpack and carefully removed a box. As she walked toward Lily, everyone watched her.

"What do you have there, Wills?" Lily asked.

"Something that should be yours," Willow said. "I have more presents in my suitcase, but this is for you and Dak." She handed Lily the box and resumed her seat.

Lily looked inside the unwrapped cardboard box and gasped. "Oh, Wills, it's Mum's sea globe … your sea globe."

"No, it's yours and Dak's now. I wanted to give it to you before you left for England, but things were so crazy that I forgot."

"But it was the first thing of Mum's that you said you wanted."

"I did. And it helped me a lot. First, it reminded me of Mum and the times we went to the beach as a family. Then, after you left for Malibu, I'd look inside and picture you and Dak there. I could almost see you, and it made me feel you were safe and happy. Over the holidays, when you came home, twice when you were in my room, I saw the way you stared all dreamy-eyed at it, and then you'd turn away when you realized I was watching you."

"Oh, Wills … I'm sorry. I should have been more careful."

"No. I'm glad you let your emotions show. I knew you wanted it before you went to Malibu. But you let me have it. Because that's you, Lills, putting your family first. So now I'm putting you first. It comforted me for a long time. And it's time for you and Dak to have it now. You'll be able to look inside and remember your time in Malibu. The globe will help you keep your memories. I don't mean like you're old and forgetting them, but you know."

Charlotte laughed. "You're funny, Tree. But that's so nice of you. How come I didn't know you were doing this?"

"I didn't want you to blab it by mistake."

Charlotte checked to make sure the baby was sleeping. "I only blab on purpose. I wouldn't have said a word."

Dak took the globe from Lily and looked admiringly at it. "I've heard so much about this, but I never actually saw it." He choked up as he silently read the Rumi quote engraved on the brass plate on the base: 'You are not a drop in the ocean. You are the entire ocean in a drop.' "Willow, are you really sure you want to part with this?"

"What Dak said."

"You guys need to stop." She giggled. "I hope Mum didn't hear that. She hated 'you guys.' And yeah, I'm positive."

"Thank you so much," Lily said. "We will cherish this."

"More than you know," Dak said. "Thank you, Willow."

"I'm really happy for the globe to live here now. Besides, Kady is making me a miniature of this cottage, almost like the one you have, only a little bigger. When I told her how I used to look for you in the globe when you were gone, she asked me if a cottage would comfort me in the same way. And I told her it would even more. Especially since Mum's aunt and uncle lived here when she was a child. And Mum grew up in Uncle Ellis's house across the street, right?"

"She did. And that's so lovely of Kady," Lily said.

"She's the best. It's gonna take her a while to finish it, but she said she's an old hand at it now, so it won't take as long as yours did."

"Why do you have that silly grin on your face, Wills?"

Willow giggled. "Because of the part I didn't tell you. I'm gonna take photos of everyone standing up ... except Abby of course ... and then I'll cut them out like paper dolls ... then we can always be together inside this house."

Doreen looked tearfully at Willow, then at Dalton. "How sweet this child is!"

Lily hurried over to Willow. "Stand up and let me hug the stuffing out of you." She squeezed her youngest sister as hard as she could as Willow joyously hugged her back. Finally, Lily disengaged, smiled at Willow, then walked back to the couch.

"So what kind of work are you both doing?" Nico asked, breaking the unexpected silence. He looked at Lily. "Beautiful ladies first."

"Well, I'm getting into property management. Right now, I'm working with the company that has been managing my cottages, and I'm leasing guest cottages for tourists. I'm definitely learning the business faster than I'm learning to tend to an English garden, though. And I'm *very* slowly acclimating myself to driving on the left side of the road.

"But what is most special to me ... is my ongoing rummage through all of Mum's historical materials Dad gave me. I'm developing fictional characters based on our ancestors and learning the history of the area. It's been fascinating, draining, and uplifting. I started writing stories in Altrusia, but that was before I got this material. So I'm starting from scratch again, but I am using a few of the ideas I came up with earlier. When I get through everything, including the online writing classes I've signed up for, I want to write a series of novels. I know how hugely aspirational it is … but it's my new dream. I'll probably go to college as well, but down the line a bit."

Dalton gulped. "There are no words that could make me happier than those right now. Your mother would be over the moon. We miss the heck out of you, but this life suits you. I'm so proud of you. And I had no idea you had all of these plans."

"I didn't want to tell you on our video chats," Lily said. "It's kind of special, so I wanted to save it for when you were here."

"It's all so wonderful," Doreen exclaimed.

"By the time I'm an English literature professor," Willow said, "you'll have written a whole series or something. I'll make my students read all of your books, and I'll flunk them if they don't say good things."

"You're a trip, Tree," Charlotte said. "And that's seriously awesome, Lily."

"Thanks, everyone. I'm pretty excited."

"How 'bout you, Dak," Nico asked. He laughed. "Damn. Did you hear what I said? I'm startin' to sound like someone's father already. 'How about you, son?' Poor Abby when she gets older. I'll be a pain in her butt."

"Maybe you already are." Willow giggled.

"A bit of advice, Nico," Dalton said with a grin. "As long as you don't sound too much like I did the past couple of years, you'll be fine."

"Don't be hard on yourself anymore, Dad," Charlotte said. "You did the best you could. We all did." She turned to Dak. "So, what keeps you busy?"

"As I hinted on our last video call, I have a job at a premier recording studio in Gloucestershire. I usually work a few days a week, but they're long days, and I often put in forty or fifty hours. When I'm not slaving over a hot console, I'm writing and recording my music. Oh, and I'm super excited because our friend, Jamie Tyson Scott, who was managing The Breezy Spirits in Malibu when Lily and I worked there, is coming over here in September to hook up with some jazz musicians he used to tour with … and they're going to record an album in the studio where I work. Jamie is back to being a full-time musician."

"How amazing," Charlotte said. "Was that a coincidence? Like you and Lily meeting again?"

"Definitely not. Lily and I keep in touch with Jamie. When I told him where I was working … he couldn't book fast enough. And they were about to go with another studio outside of London. I can't tell you how much I'm looking forward to working with Jamie and his friends. Not to mention spending time with him and his wife, Shelley. They recently got married after many years together."

"Very special," Dalton said.

"Oh, and I'm starting to play local gigs," Dak added. "But only the occasional one when time permits, because I'm also learning new instruments."

"And he's learning how to be a gardener too," Lily said. "Tell them the rest. You know … about your family."

Dak paused to find his courage before he spoke. "Since we moved here and Marsha is out of our lives and enjoying her days and nights in a women's prison … my brother, Jonah, and I are becoming close again … like we were as small boys when he protected me and I *tried* to protect him. Lily and I have been getting to know his wife, Bethany, and their daughter, Avery. You'll meet them in a few days." He paused to let the emotion settle. "It's been a very long time since I had anything resembling family. Only when Zoey was alive … and Jonah still lived with us … that was it. And I don't mean to diminish how special those times were, but they passed way too quickly. After Jonah graduated from high school, he was only around for a year before he left for Oxford … and then, about four years later, Zoey died. And I was so alone." He gulped. "Sorry … my demons are trying to silence me here." He looked at everyone. "These are the kinds of emotions that used to make me act like a magician and disappear. You know, when you think your life has taken a better turn than you deserve, so you need to leave *it* before it can leave you." He took a sip of spring water. "The memories of being that damaged person are becoming more distant by the day … fewer and far between. I look at the world quite differently now. And I have the most wonderful life and this huge family."

Lily turned to him. "I know it wasn't easy for you to share with everyone."

Dak lowered his eyes. "Just keepin' it real," he said softly. "All part of my evolution."

"Are you going to stand now?" Willow said, lightening the mood.

"No, not standing time yet," Dak said with a wink. "But I'll give you the lowdown. Lily and I plan to get engaged in October on the anniversary of the day we found one another again. And somewhere in the neighborhood of a year from now, we'd like you all to come back for our wedding. We'll be inviting Kady and Patrick too … along with some other friends from California and thereabouts."

As congratulations swirled around the room, Charlotte spoke softly to Lily. "I'm sorry I was such a bitch about this property. Mum knew exactly what she was doing even though she didn't know she would die. It makes me sick to think I wanted to sell this place. You have the perfect life for yourself now. I'll be eighteen in four months, and I already have a college fund for my daughter and security for my family. I'll tell you, Lills, having a child makes you stop being one." She stopped to admire her baby. "Like taking over for Mum changed you." She lowered her voice to a whisper: "But I'm still me …still love metal and I still love to rock the ass tat I have … only for my husband

… of course." She glanced through the sliding glass doors. "Wow, it's coming down in buckets."

"That's England for you," Dak said. "There's a reason the scenery stays so green."

"This seems like a good time for a house tour …to show Char and Nico all of the baby things Aunt Millie brought over … and then we can all congregate back here. It's not exactly sightseeing weather …and I know you're all pretty exhausted as it is, so we'll take it easy."

Dalton rose from his chair. "If you've got a brolly … or whatever you call an umbrella here … Doreen and I will run across the street to Ellis and Millie's place."

Lily laughed. "People here call them umbrellas. I'll get you two."

Dalton tried again. "Ellis is going to take us to the hotel to check in, and he'll bring us back afterward. He has our bags in his trunk …boot …as you call it here."

"They do call it a boot here," Lily said, chuckling, as she opened a closet door and pulled out two umbrellas. "Here you go."

Willow walked up to Dak and playfully batted her eyelids at him. "Will you play your guitar for us and sing later? Pretty please."

Lily turned to him and smiled. "I can't think of a better way to top off this wonderful day, can you?"

THE END

ABOUT THE AUTHOR

LISETTE BRODEY was born and raised in the Philadelphia area. She lived in New York City for ten years and now resides in Los Angeles.

She is the multi-genre author of nine novels and one short story collection. Her books include: *Crooked Moon; Squalor, New Mexico; Molly Hacker Is Too Picky!;* The Desert Series (*Mystical High, Desert Star, Drawn Apart*); *Hotel Obscure: A Collection of Short Stories; Love, Look Away;* and *The Sum of our Sorrows.*

She has also published two short stories in an anthology called *Triptych's (Mind's Eye Series, Book 3)*.

All of her books are available in both Kindle and paperback.

Website & contact: lisettebrodey.com
Amazon author page: Author.to/lisettebrodey
Twitter: twitter.com/lisettebrodey
Facebook: facebook.com/BrodeyAuthor
Instagram: @ca_lisette
Pinterest: pinterest.com/lisetteca/